THE

CLOISONNÉ

BROOCH

A Serpent's Coil Time-Travel Romance

by

KAT DRENNAN

ISBN 978-1-7342584-0-0 (ePub)

ISBN 978-1-7342584-1-7 (Trade Paperback)

KC Publications
Ojai, California

Dedication

I dedicate this book to my aunt, Dorothy Spearman, who took me in as an unruly teenager along with all headaches and angst that comes with it. I treasure the moments we shared together, for showing up for all my high school musicals, and for sticking up for me in the principal's office. Her home on Balboa Island was truly magical in my eyes and provided the indelible spark for this story. Auntie Dot, your unconditional love and support are forever in my heart.

The house was one of the oldest on the island, a Spanish Revival bungalow standing like a sentinel near the east end of the Grand Canal. My Grandfather built the main floor in 1921; by himself, one room at a time, on a sandy lot facing the seawall.

After the stock market crash of 1929, he held on to his property while many of his neighbors lost theirs. He was one of the few undertakers practicing in Orange County at the time. Business was good.

According to my mother, the house was a dark, damp monstrosity, built without second thought to comfort or convenience. The fragrance of forgotten funeral sprays her father brought home from services only made it worse. She blamed the drafty house for the eventual death of her mother from pneumonia.

It wouldn't take a lot of imagination to think that my mother's sour disposition was an outgrowth of being raised by an undertaker and his sickly wife. It would be a good excuse if she hadn't been spoiled beyond repair. She was once a great beauty, inheriting her mother's sable hair and deep blue eyes. I, on the other hand, took after my grandfather, most definitely the brighter side of the family, both in coloring and disposition. Indeed, I looked more

1

like my blond-haired, ice-eyed uncle Theo than either of my parents.

When her father died in 1961, my mother wanted to sell the house immediately, settle the estate, and be done with it. Theo, who had continued to live in the house after my mother married and moved to a ticky-tacky suburb of Los Angeles, insisted they wait for the predicted real estate boom that would quadruple the property value. Mother refused. Forward thinking had never been one of her strong suits. Which was why, after my father was killed in an unfortunate auto accident when I was seven, she came at Theo again.

"How do you expect me to raise this child the way she deserves unless you sell this sow's ear of a dump?"

Being a city girl raised in a housing tract of cookie-cutter homes separated by driveways and neat patches of lawn, I had no idea what a sow's ear was. I would soon learn that Uncle Theo had a special place in his heart for them. He made my mother a generous offer of cash in exchange for a quitclaim, which she willingly accepted and set off in search of husband number two.

More than once after his prediction of the house's increasing value came true, my mother tried to get him to sell and give her a "rightful" share. Each new man in her life ultimately beget a new pilgrimage to Theo's, which predictably ended in a door-slamming, window-rattling exit.

At first, I dreaded these visits and my mother's inevitable sulk for days afterward. But as I grew older, I was happy to visit Uncle Theo under any circumstances. He was the most interesting and caring person I had ever met.

He made his living uncovering old things. While my mother whined and sniveled in his wood-paneled living room, I was invited to pour over his collection of archeology books and journals. Images of Roman baths, ancient gold jewelry, and carefully documented digs fed my fertile imagination.

But it was the front yard that captured my attention the last time my mother took me to his house. I was ten years old. Her most recent boyfriend had left without notice, leaving her once again in need of support. In the past (and I would later learn, mostly for my sake), Theo would write her a check and make her promise to put the needs of her daughter first for a change.

This day, however, was different. Theo poured me a glass of lemonade and set me up in his little living room with an antique stereopticon and a box of heavy slides. I'd never seen anything like it and was quickly absorbed in 3D pictures of Cleopatra in her fabulous long boat until the discussion in the kitchen became so heated, I longed to run outside.

Sensing my discomfort, Uncle Theo came to my rescue, inviting me to go downstairs while my mother and he carried on with whatever argument dominated their visit.

Like the stereopticon, his yard was designed to capture the imagination. Unlike his neighbors who had covered their lots with rental property, Theo had created an intricate mosaic of broken tile and buried bottles, abalone shell planters and criss-cross walkways. At the center, a shiny red ball sat atop an ornate pedestal. I was drawn to it like a bee to a flower.

"It's a gazing globe," Uncle Theo told me, pulling the sides of his mouth down with his fingers.

"Theo," mother called from the top of the stairway, an impatient edge to her voice. Her face was all pinched and red and she gripped the stair railing like she would rip it right off the balcony.

"What's wrong with her?" I was used to her ill temper, but there was something different in her expression that day that made me cringe.

"Don't worry, my love. I just gave her something to think about and I expect she'll have to stew on it a bit before she settles down." He leaned in, bending me with him. We could see our faces reflected in the shiny red globe. "If you look closely, you can see the beginning of the universe."

"You can?"

"It's magic. Give it a try."

With his hand at the small of my back, I pressed my face closer, peered at the distorted world reflected in the ball. All I could see was my own face. But Theo had, as always, triggered my imagination, and I soon forgot all about my mother's discomfort.

Time stretched as I played in the yard that morning — running the paths, dipping below a trellis of tea roses, and standing on the picket fence rails to watch the incoming tide.

By the time my mother's hand finally clamped around my arm, the water had risen almost to the top of the seawall. My mind was still focused on fantasies of hidden, magical things as she dragged me across the yard, through Theo's cluttered garage, and out to her car. She didn't speak to me all the way home.

Two months later I awoke to find a pile of boxes and bags packed by our front door. Uncle Theo picked me up and drove me to a little valley town up the coast where I was enrolled in boarding school. It was a magical place of oak trees, bright orange sunsets, and barn owls hooting to each other in the misty dawn.

I would never see my mother again, though I didn't know that at the time. That might seem to some a scary thing, but except for the shock of having my life yanked up by the roots and planted somewhere completely foreign, I can't say as I missed her that much. To say that our relationship was never warm is the kindest way to describe it.

I was given a horse to care for and a room to share with three other girls who, like me, rarely saw their parents. One of the girls would become my very best friend.

Theo would come and get me for Christmas and Thanksgiving, and for two weeks in the summer. The rest of the time, I spent at the school and he sent me postcards from wherever he was in the world. Our arrangement was simple: if I kept my grades up, he would support me through college as long as I chose a science major. This was a shoo-in, considering how he'd groomed me to love his research.

My two weeks of summer were filled with adventures. We poked spikes down bubbled holes in the sand and came up with clams, studied small octopuses and starfish from under the island bridges, fished for halibut off the pier, and by night I studied his books on archeology and the history of the ancient world.

Over the years, he built on to his house, eventually adding a third-floor bedroom on half of the roof and a sun porch on the other. This room became my favorite. From the sun porch you could see out over the island rooftops toward Little Corona and a beach where feral cats lived among the rocks.

By the time I finished college and entered graduate school, Theo's health had declined. He spent less time traveling Europe and Asia and more time at home, shutting down slowly as people do. My studies at UC Irvine consumed most of my time and resources, but I stayed close to home and made sure he was comfortable.

By the time I got my engineering degree focused on metallurgy and secured my first job in the field, he was a bent and tired shell of the man he'd once been. Lexi, my roommate from school, who had completed her doctorate in psychology tended to his needs during the day and I took over in the evening.

He told me the house would be mine when he was gone. I didn't want to hear it. He was the only person in my life who ever gave me an ounce of love or encouragement and I wasn't anxious to see him go. We were in his yard smiling into the ruby gazing globe the day he gave me his last blue-sky smile.

When he passed, I thought all the magic had gone out of the world.

I was wrong.

CHAPTER ONE

Balboa Island, Republic of California, 2019 CE

Libra: As if through walls, voices from the past
echo in your ears.
Travel is in your future.

"Tessa!" Phillip's voice echoed inside the house they now lovingly called *The Old Girl*. After working all day, Tess had taken a much-needed break. Now, she sat on the landing overlooking Theo's garden. A chill worked prickly fingers up the back of her neck. She put down the astrology section of the newspaper and sipped the last of her iced coffee, then drew herself in, shoulders hunched, arms wrapped around her knees.

The damp ocean air had weakened The Old Girl's bones, the Southern California sun had parched her skin, and her walls leaked a musty odor of dry rot. But it didn't matter. Tess felt a tug of longing every time she looked down on the patchwork yard. The red globe in the center glinted in the late afternoon sun. She could almost hear Uncle Theo's voice at her shoulder. *If you look closely, you can see the beginning...*

She shook off another set of chills. "Coming," she called to Phillip. She wasn't that enthusiastic to return to the mess she knew was waiting for her inside.

When Lawyer Phinney suggested Tess sell the old wreck and net a couple of million despite her disrepair, Tess had answered without hesitation: "Absolutely not." Theo had entrusted his beloved house to her, and she wasn't about to sell it. She had no dreams of restoring it to its original grandeur. Truth be told, she had to agree with her mother, the house had never been grand. But it had been special. The fact that Uncle Theo had entrusted it to her made it all the more precious. She might never be able to make it grand, but she would definitely make it her own.

Now, she was having second thoughts. After two solid months of renovations, and a huge chunk out of the trust account, the place was still a disaster. They hadn't even touched the hoarder's paradise in the garage that had her parking her Volkswagen on the street. While she'd realized her childhood dream of taking over the third story bedroom, she still had to climb a ladder to get to it.

The stairs would take another bite out of her renovation budget, which meant she wouldn't be quitting her day job any time soon. Clearly, that upstairs room should be the master suite, and that meant a bath, and replacing the casement windows facing the sun deck with a set of French doors.

Lucky for her and her repair budget, her boyfriend, Phillip, was good with his hands in more ways than one. He actually enjoyed helping her out in his spare time. Together they were working their way through the tasks they could do without hiring a professional builder. This method had its advantages. Phil spent most of his spare time at her house, something she was beginning to like. A lot. His tall, lanky frame was good to look at and even better to wrap her arms around when the mood struck.

But it also had its pitfalls.

Every time they pulled off a piece of paneling, they uncovered another disaster. If it weren't for Phillip's sunny disposition and sense of humor in the face of adversity, she might consider taking a long vacation while somebody else did the work.

She rested her hand on the railing; a hollowed-out emptiness persisted in the corners of her soul. She should be happy, dammit. After all, what twenty-five-year-old started life with a house on Balboa Island and money in the bank to keep it going? All it needed was a little TLC and a lot of elbow grease.

Tessa had never been afraid of hard work. But as she gazed out over the Grand Canal, she knew that empty feeling had nothing to do with the house. Sure, Phillip was a bright spot in her life, but it wasn't his job to make her happy. It was her own. That was the trick, right? Only, if suddenly getting the home of her dreams didn't do it, then what would?

With one last look at the yard, she rose and stepped inside.

Phillip grinned at her from in front of the dark wood paneling he'd been stripping from where they'd planned to install the new stairway. He held something behind his back, his bright grin lit with mischief.

She sauntered across the room, circled her arms around his neck, and pressed her body against his. She kissed his jaw, then his chin, then his lips, drawing him in. Then she zipped her hands down his back and tried to grab what he was hiding.

Phillip spun away, laughing. "You think you can ply me with kisses?"

"I know I can." She stalked him again. He stepped back, taunting her.

That grin. Those eyes. Seeing him standing in her living room amid the chaos of demolition — paint on his clothes and sawdust in his hair — made her pulse notch up to a dangerous level. To hell with the damned house. To hell with what he was hiding. That grin and those shoulders were enough to make her forget it all.

She wanted *him*. Now. "Put that down and put those hands on me."

His eyes shone with the same little boy innocence that had caught her attention on the day they'd met. She had wanted him then, too, she recalled with a hit of heat. He'd followed her out to her car on the first day of her job at Cauldron Industries, leaned against the passenger door of a silver Porsche SUV in the reserved spot next to hers. He'd noticed the Balboa Island sticker on her windshield and boldly asked if she'd give him a ride home because his car was in the shop. They'd shared small talk on the way, and she'd agreed to pick him up for breakfast the next morning on the way back to work.

It wasn't until the next day she'd learned the Porsche belonged to him and he hadn't really needed a ride home. When she asked him why, he just smiled and told her he wanted his children to have dimples just like hers.

Yeah. He liked to plan ahead. He'd asked her to marry him nearly every day since, a sort of running joke that was easy to dismiss. More than once she'd broken out the old Magic 8-Ball she'd found among Theo's things in the garage, and so far, the answers had been nebulous. Not that she put stock in such things. But it was a game she played mostly to let him know, she wasn't ready to be serious about her future.

Now, he held her off with one hand like a boxer with a long reach. "You might want to take a look at these before you drag me up to your lair, miss horny pants." And with that, he brought two crystal goblets from behind his back, short stemmed glasses dulled with dust and time, but lovely just the same.

"Found 'em on a cross beam between the studs," he announced proudly. "That uncle of yours was a real nut job sealing this stuff up in the walls."

Her mother had always said Theo was a little off. Tessa had never believed her. Now she wasn't so sure. She took one of the goblets, plinked the delicate rim with her fingernail, and was rewarded with a bright "ting".

"Can't wait to tear down the rest of the paneling," Phillip went on with renewed interest in what had been a difficult, dirty job. "No telling what he's got stashed in there."

Tess plucked the other glass from his hand and took them to the kitchen, then ran soapy water in the sink. When she held a clean glass up to the light, colors swirled on the shining surface like a sunlit soap bubble.

She filled each one with a shot of whisky and settled on the sofa to watch the muscles ripple and play across Phillip's broad back. After a quick shot, he had attacked the paneling with new vigor, each removed piece revealing another treasure.

The next hour's work produced four more goblets; several jars full of clamshells, bottled by size; most of a set of silver flatware, a jet-beaded drawstring bag full of gaudy, costume jewelry, and on a separate stud, a coiled serpent bracelet.

Tess snagged the bracelet, fascinated with its red rhinestone eyes. A frisson of excitement tickled her shoulders as she entertained the thought the bangle might actually be gold, or at least gold plated. The piece reminded her of the pictures in her Uncle Theo's books. She and her long-time roommate, Lexi, had hauled most of his books down to the garage when they'd moved into the house. She mused momentarily about digging them out again as she slipped the serpent coil over her wrist.

She dumped the beaded bag's contents out on the coffee table and was picking through the pile when she heard Lexi's familiar footsteps coming up the back stairs and into the kitchen.

"Lexi." She squealed with delight. "Get in here right now."

Her BFF from boarding school appeared in the dining room, swiped her beanie off her head, her wild hair springing back to its usual mass of tight, dark curls. She looked tired; her volunteer sessions at the suicide crisis center often left her drained. But the moment she saw the junk pile on the table, she pounced on it like a kid at Christmas.

Tess told her where it had come from and Lexi's mouth dropped open.

"No way." She clipped a gaudy lion's head brooch to the front of her Boho sweater, then tested the weight of a bejeweled earring. "Girl, these are too heavy for costume."

Phillip snorted. "I wouldn't clean it with anything too strong. Stuff'll probably dissolve." He slipped one of the rings up to the first knuckle of his little finger, examined it more closely, then tossed it lightly at Tess. "You're the expert."

Tess slid the ring on her pointer finger. "I don't know. Most costume jewelry in the fifties was made of non-precious metal — nickel, zinc, a little copper, sometimes lead."

She turned the ring over, looked inside the band for a 14K or European 583. All she saw was a faint delta mark. Who knew what that meant? "You see lots of this stuff at garage sales. Grandma's old rhinestones are pretty popular these days."

Lexi scrunched her forehead. "Why on earth would your uncle seal costume jewelry up in the walls?"

"Yeah, right next to the clam shells," Phillip added.

"No telling," Tessa said. Uncle Theo had spun some pretty wild stories about finding treasure in the most unusual places. Her fingers went to the bangle on her arm. A sudden chill made her shiver.

"Cold?" Phillip strode to the doorway. "I saw some firewood underneath the front stairs. We could try out the fireplace."

Tess nodded and hugged her waist against another chill, and as he headed out the door, she felt suddenly separated from the scene, like a thick, translucent veil had dropped around her. It closed her in its clammy grip, until the only light left in her vision flickered, then went out. Out of the blackness, a voice filtered through her consciousness, modulated, lyrical, cloaked in icy cold.

Tessa. Where are you?

She ran her hands up her arms, rubbing her biceps against the chill. A band of heat circled her right biceps. She raised her fingers to find the serpent bangle had settled there like a long-worn wedding band finding its groove.

Tessssaaaah. Louder now, the voice tugged at her, sent its melodic tendrils around her heart. "Who are you," she whispered.

"Babe? You okay?"

Like a warm knife through butter, the sound of Phillip's voice melted the veil's grip. She opened her eyes to see him kneeling in front of her, a bundle of wood under his arm.

He let the wood clunk to the floor and took both her hands in his. "Tessa? Hell-o?"

She traced a finger over the bracelet's serpent scales, then shivered again under the distinct sensation it was a living thing. As though her touch were a command, it loosened its grip and slid to her wrist.

Phillips eyes narrowed on hers. He brushed a hair off her forehead. "Welcome back."

Tess caught the shared look of relief between her boyfriend and her bestie. "What?"

"You kind of checked out there for a minute, girl." Lexi tilted her head like a robin eyeballing a worm.

Lexi was right. She *had* checked out. Something had called her from a swirling void.

No.

Not something.

Someone.

"I don't know, I ... maybe the whisky?" It was plausible. They'd worked through the day without lunch, and she rarely drank whisky, let alone in the middle of the day. Of course, she'd feel a little woozy.

Phillip gathered the wood and carried it to the fireplace. "You sure? We can call it a day if you don't feel well."

Tess shook her head. The last time she'd felt anything near what she'd just experienced she'd passed out cold in the line at the grocery store and learned she was pregnant. Two weeks later she'd miscarried and the man she'd expected to soothe her through the loss was visibly relieved instead. Water under a rickety bridge.

"I'm fine. I'll just get us something to eat."

She went to the kitchen and made up a tray of cheese and cold cuts to hold them over until dinner while Phil worked on getting the fire started.

With a few bites of food in her tummy, and a smile from the man she had dared to think of as *hers*, Tess felt like herself again. Phillip Koenig could pull her out of a funk with a look, and she was grateful. A funk from who-*effing*-knows where, but she was okay now, and that was all that mattered.

They stood together on the balcony for a moment, watching clouds wheel deeper pink across the sky. Tess slid to his side and gazed up at her man. "Thank you for all the work you put in around here. You are good to me."

"Not as good as I'll be tonight," he murmured into her neck and ran his hands down her backside.

Lexi burst outside, coughing and flapping her arms.

Tess pulled away to see smoke pouring out the door.

"Oh, shit!" Phillip dashed inside, covering his mouth with his t-shirt. Gray smoke grew denser by the second. "Open the doors, you guys."

Lexi jumped at his command, throwing the veranda's French doors wide.

Phil yanked his T-shirt all the way off and used it to grab the flue handle over the smoking fire.

"I know I opened this damned thing." He stuck his arm as far into the opening as he dared, eyes squeezed shut, holding his breath, clanging and banging metal against metal. The smoke thinned as it trailed out through the doors.

Phil straightened. "Do we have a flashlight? The flue is open, but I think there's something stuck in there."

Tess brought Phil the flashlight from the kitchen. He shone the light up the chimney, coughing and sputtering obscenities. After a moment, he sat back on his heels and wiped his forehead in the crook of his arm, then reached up into the chimney again. With a heavy grunt, he brought out a large, partially blackened platter. Under the soot, it appeared to be a piece of fine, translucent porcelain. A proud turkey was painted on the surface and the words "Happy Thanksgiving" repeated around the fluted edge in flowing, gold script.

Lexi took it gingerly and turned it over. "Wow. That's pretty special."

Tess ran her fingertips over the plate's fluted edge. A fresh set of chills prickled up her neck. The whole house had been a gift, and now it seemed more were forthcoming. What would it ask of her in return? Strange thoughts for a supposedly down-to-earth girl. Old Theo must be giggling somewhere, watching them discover his little presents. She shook off the chill and raised her eyes to find Phil smiling at her.

He leaned against the red brick hearth. "Kind of makes you wonder what's in those tile mounds down there in the yard, right? They look like graves."

"Nobody touches that yard," Tess said, channeling Theo. "It's a work of art."

Phil laughed softly. "More like the work of an old eccentric."

Tess gathered the odd junk they'd collected from the house, piled it on the blackened plate, and carted it to the dining room table.

"That eccentric was a sweet old man and I wouldn't have a place to live if it weren't for his generosity."

And I loved him.

Phil came inside and cupped her face in his hands. "Okay. Front yard is off limits." He burrowed his face into her neck. She guided his lips up to hers and kissed him long and deep until they were interrupted by a frenzied knock on the back door.

CHAPTER TWO

Lexi rose from the leather sofa and rolled her eyes at them. "I'll get it." She carried her whisky dramatically aloft as she sailed into the kitchen. "Coming," she sang out, scrunching her nose at remnants of smoky odor lingering in the air. "Audrey!"

The self-appointed watch woman who doubled as their next-door neighbor strutted in as if she owned the place. Her huge ginger tabby cat wound through her legs with an equal air of entitlement. In her late seventies, her female energy — straight out of Gloria Steinem's playbook — could still own any room she occupied. In the few months since they'd moved into Theo's house, Tess and Lexi had learned to give her that space.

Audrey's husband, twenty years her senior, had been a prominent citizen in the beach community, and along with Tess's grandfather had been one of the few people who had retained his property through the Great Depression.

"I saw smoke; is everything all right?"

Tess joined Lexi and Audrey in the dining room and gave her a hug. "We just had a little problem with the fireplace."

19

Audrey's glance landed on the pile of goodies on the table and her mouth dropped open on a gasp. "My *plate!*"

She swiped the jewelry out of the way and seized the half-blackened platter, clutching it to her bosom like it was a newborn.

Tess held out her hands. "It's covered with soot. Let's give it a real washing before you blacken your clothes." Audrey gave it over reluctantly.

They stood together at the sink as Tess dipped it into sudsy water.

"My husband bought me that platter the year before he passed away. He was so sweet to indulge my love of antique stores. I remember hoping that day as I watched him pulling crisp bills out of his wallet — he never used credit cards — I remember hoping he would live to see the next Thanksgiving."

She gazed into space beyond the kitchen window, her eyes a little misty. Tess allowed her a moment of silence. She dried the clean dish, which now sparkled and shone, its background a translucent, creamy white. Audrey took it absently at first, then, as if touching the plate recharged her battery, she started into her story again.

"The next Thanksgiving when I went to get it from the china cabinet, it wasn't there."

"We found it up the chimney. And these." Tess held up one of the goblets. "Ever seen these before?"

"Why, no." Audrey took the stem and held it up to the light. "They're beautiful." She set it on the windowsill. "It looks like Cambridge crystal to me, probably from the late twenties or early thirties."

20

Phillip strolled into the kitchen, refreshed his whisky. Audrey sent him a curious grin. "And where did you find these?"

"On the wall studs when I tore down a piece of paneling for the new stairs."

Lexi rearranged a few of the flatware pieces on the table. "Look at all the other junk he found. Seen any of these things before?"

Audrey lifted one of the forks and inspected it closely. "No. Well, maybe …"

Lexi's eyes narrowed. Tess had known Alexis Hill since they were roommates in boarding school. She was a born psychologist with the Ph.D. to match. Tess had never known her to be completely separated from her *shrink* self. She could almost see the wheels turning inside her head.

"Audrey?" Lexi's voice assumed her smooth, clinical tone. "Did you know Tessa's uncle well?"

The older woman drew back and gave her a quizzical look, fidgeting with a little pearl broach at her collar. "Well of course. We were, uh … neighbors."

Lexi guided her through the pile of junk. They nodded their heads, oohing and ahhing as they picked through the pieces. Audrey picked up a silver dinner knife and harrumphed. "This is from my set."

Lexi's head popped up. "Oh my gosh! What if *all* this stuff was stolen from the locals?"

Phil leaned against the door jam and sipped his whisky. "Are you saying that Tessa's sweet old uncle was a *klepto*?"

"Phil, that's crazy--" Tessa scoffed.

"I wasn't going to put it that bluntly," Lexi said. "I'm only suggesting—"

"I don't understand." Audrey lifted one of the silver forks. "I lived next door to Theo for fifty years. Why, his wife and I were best of friends, and when she died; well, we were all like — *he* was like — one of the family. He wouldn't steal from me."

Tessa rested her hand on Audrey's arm. "A kleptomaniac can't really be blamed for what he does," she said. "He can't help it. He —" She stopped. Audrey was clearly upset. She put her arms around the older woman's shoulders and softened her tone. "Audrey, I'm sorry. Lexi was only speculating. You knew him and – we didn't." She glanced up at Lex for support.

"Oh, it's not that." Audrey sighed softly, waving away her concern. "I'm just a silly fool."

She pulled a handkerchief from the inside of her dress sleeve and dabbed at the corners of her eyes. "You kids are probably right, anyway. Theo was a goofy old coot." She shifted her gaze to Tessa. "I was really happy when you came home from school to live here. I wasn't sure if he had Alzheimer's or was just plain crazy. I tried to help him, but he'd changed, you know? Like parts of him were stolen, too."

Lexi raised an eyebrow at Tess. She was right; Audrey *had* known him well.

"It doesn't really matter how these things got in this house." She got up and stood with Audrey. "There's a whole lot more stuff just like this in those boxes down in the garage. If Lexi's right, we could have some neighbors' family heirlooms down there."

Phil huffed out a laugh. "More junk."

Audrey shrugged. "Maybe." Her eyes took on an about-to-cry shine. "I — I wish he was still here. I miss him." There was more than a neighborly longing in her deep sigh.

"Me too," Tess admitted. More than she'd realized.

Audrey straightened her back, pulled out a smile. "But, I'm glad you're here, all of you." She glanced at Tess, Lexi, and Phillip in turn. "It's time The Old Girl had some life in her again." She sent Phillip a wink, leaned into Tess's ear and stage whispered, "That one's a keeper if you ask me."

Tessa's ears heated. Phillip definitely tickled all her sensitive spots. But it was too soon to think of anything permanent. Her forays into love had so far led only to disaster and scars she feared would never heal. She covered her discomfort with a laugh more lighthearted than she felt.

"I'm sure Theo didn't mean any harm," Lexi said, bringing the conversation back to the point.

Audrey let go a little laugh, at last a tear worked its way down her cheek, and her chin puckered like Tess had never seen before. "He just might have been the love of my life."

Tessa sucked in a breath.

Audrey laughed. "Oh, don't look so shocked. I might be all fat and shriveled now, but my heart thinks I'm still twenty-one."

"Good news," Lexi said, nodding. "Only I hope my heart feels more like thirty when I'm your age. I was a major fuck up at twenty-one."

Audrey smiled at her. "Yes. We had some fun, Theo and me. I'm not ashamed to admit it, some of the best times of my life; did I mention Theo and I had known one another since we were kids?"

She hadn't, but it made perfect sense. Their families had been on the island since 1921.

Audrey pursed her lips. "Once, when we were supposed to be in school, we got on the electric car and rode all the way to Long Beach. We roamed the downtown streets happily together, as if it had been our right. It was shameful and exciting and we --"

She closed her eyes tight a moment, then shook her head, and kept whatever she was thinking to herself. "— he— bought me a bag of saltwater taffy."

So, they were lots more than neighbors. Who was Tess to judge?

Audrey pointed the knife at her. "You know, most people around here lease these houses from season to season. You won't find many who live on the island full time anymore." She pointed at the pile on the table. "I doubt anyone besides me would recognize that stuff."

Lexi stood suddenly, an idea filling her eyes with excitement. "Maybe we could do, like, a yard sale. We can clear out the garage, and if somebody recognizes something, we'll hand it over. If not, we'll sell it to 'em."

CHAPTER THREE

They all agreed a garage sale would be a great idea, and that they should put the plan into action sooner than later. Lexi volunteered to escort Audrey home and wouldn't take no for an answer. Tess watched Phillip bank the fire, then led him up the ladder through the hole in the dining room ceiling to her room.

The first time she'd invited Phil up that ladder, she'd known there'd be no going back. She'd dated a few men, some of them while still in high school. She'd been serious about one. A narrow escape, looking back. But he had never lit the fire in her the way Phillip Koenig did. The man had moves.

Still, they had agreed — well, she suggested, and he agreed — to take things slow. He'd asked her to marry him five minutes later. She told him to ask her again later.

If she'd learned anything about relationships, it was, *if it was too good to be true, it was too good to be true*. Tess's last relationship ended with a trip to the ER and a couple of black eyes, only one of them hers. Turns out that expensive self-defense class Lexi had insisted they take had been worth the money.

At six months and counting, Tess wasn't ready to let Phil stash shaving gear in her bathroom, though she did allow sleepovers now and then. She was no fool. Phillip was indeed good to look at, and even better to touch.

Now, he reclined on the chaise lounge on the rooftop deck. Tess poured each of them a last shot of the golden liquor and held her goblet aloft for a toast. "To junk."

"To junk," Phillip echoed, lightly tapping her glass with the rim of his. Then he drained it in one noisy swallow.

Tess sipped hers thoughtfully, admiring the goblet in the moonlight. What parties had it graced over the years? Family Thanksgivings and Christmases, New Year's Eves, moonlit trysts on the seawall.

Life was full of surprises.

A year ago, she'd never have believed she'd be standing on the rooftop of her own home on the island with a man who cared enough about her to take things slow. She worried sometimes that things were going too well. That she didn't deserve all this and love, too.

Lexi lectured her not to worry when things went well. "Good times are for savoring," she always said. "You've got to save quality worrying for when things go to shit."

Good advice.

Tess drained her glass, grabbed a quilt off the end of the chaise, and pulled it over her shoulders, then propped herself up on the low rooftop wall.

"Careful, baby," Phillip warned.

She smiled at him over her shoulder. "I'm fine. I'll be careful."

The moon had worked its way around to nearly full; there would be an eight-foot tide tonight, about as high as it gets. Uncle Theo's mosaic of tiles in the yard below gleamed in the soft light reminding her of the day she'd played there so long ago. It was odd how the yard looked different from up here.

From ground level, and even from the main floor veranda, the converging lines and arches, intersecting and circling, seemed chaotic and random, as though he had added each section at his whim and fancy. But from up here on the rooftop, the pattern took on a different dimension.

Tess sipped her whisky and cocked her head. Maybe it was the light, or the whisky, or maybe it was the full moon, but when she studied the design as a unified piece, it hit her. The tiled outlines formed a cohesive whole; an array of colors and shapes converging at the center; a pattern she'd swear she'd seen before. She leaned over to get a better look, steadied herself against a sudden wave of dizziness.

"Tessa?" Phil shot to her side and had his arm around her waist before she could take her next breath. "You probably shouldn't hang out by this wall until I add a railing."

She blinked at him a moment, realizing he had likely just saved her from what might have been a disaster. "I — You're right. I just--" She peered over the wall to the garden again. "I thought I saw —"

Phillip took a look, shook his head, and shrugged.

Tess shivered in the resonance of the vision. "Guess I better take it easy on the booze."

But it *had* looked like something. A pattern she'd seen before.

Phillip pulled the quilt snug about her shoulders, turned her in his arms, and kissed her lips gently. "Let's go inside."

His eyes darkened to match the whisky as he drew her into their warm, calm, center and she let herself go there, giving up everything else. "Okay."

She raised her arms to circle his neck. He carried her to the bed and ceremoniously unwrapped the quilt.

He slid down between her legs, and ran his hands down her sides, sending a delicious shiver up her spine, before he dropped his face between her legs and huffed a long, hot breath through her jeans.

Now that is real.

"Promise me you won't go out there anymore until we put up a proper railing," he murmured into her belly.

"I promise." Tess breathed the words like a prayer. "Do that again."

He obliged, working her zipper down to expose her panties. *Oh, yes. That is even more real.* The random patterns she had seen in her front yard fled before the flush of heat between her legs. Everything she needed was right here in her arms. "Again," she whispered, pumping her hips.

He raised his head and caught her eyes with a heated challenge. "What do you say?"

"Bastard."

He ran his hands up her sides and arms, then clamped down on her wrists and stretched her arms over her head. "Um, pretty sure that's not the magic word."

Tess caught her breath as the pulse of desire ran through her. God, this man. She dug her fingers into his hair and let go a moan. "Please."

His gaze lingered another moment before he dragged in a ragged breath, then shifted her wrists to one hand and unfastened his jeans with the other. In a movement so swift it took her breath away, he peeled off her jeans, pushed up her T-shirt and lowered his hips between her legs, an exquisite blend of sweet and savage that left her breathless. Where had this guy been all her life?

But as the heat built between them, something shifted inside her. A new sensation, primal and seductive, superimposed itself over her reality.

She stood before a crowd, stripped naked, men's eyes wandering over her flesh, their hands running up her legs. Someone grabbed her hair from behind and forced her to the front of a raised wood platform. Men crowded forward, pinching and prodding.

No!

She went rigid. Her eyes flew open.

She was safe in her room with Phillip.

The fantasy was terrifying and — okay, a little erotic --

"You with me, babe?" Phillip murmured against her neck and stopped moving.

Reassured she was safe in her lover's arms, she gave into the heat. "Yes. I'm with you," she said; but the moment she closed her eyes, Phillip morphed into a stranger. Dark and powerful.

Her mind followed the dark thread, deeper into a world she didn't recognize.

She was consumed by the heat of him, answering his thrusts without restraint. He moaned under the fierceness of it; she felt him empty himself into her, and then their passion exploded out of the safe zone and into something darker. The deeper she went, the more difficult it was to breathe, until she felt she would suffocate.

She bucked hard, tried to get away.

"Stop!"

"Tessa? Honey? Did I hurt you?"

It was Phillip, but she couldn't see his face. A thick membrane persisted between them.

"Phillip!" She clawed desperately in the direction of his voice, but she couldn't reach him.

Hands grabbed for her and she scrabbled away, her chest heaving. "Don't. Touch. Me!"

Her upper arm burned, and she clawed at her skin. A sharp band of heat clenched tight at her biceps. Digging her fingers under it until she felt her skin would tear, she finally loosened its grip and pulled it off.

"Okay, baby. Just — chill. It's okay." She still couldn't see him, but she could feel his lips against her ear. "God, I'm sorry."

She lay on her back covered in a fine sheen of sweat and gulping air like she'd just run a marathon. She opened her eyes; the serpent bracelet dangled in her fingers. Warm hands cupped her cheeks, holding her still.

"Tessa. Look at me."

CHAPTER FOUR

Her eyes shifted to his, blinked, teared. She gasped for air, tears streaked down her cheeks. Rose-patterned wallpaper covered one wall of the room. Dark wood paneling surrounded a row of casement windows leading to the deck. She could hear the faint moan of fog horns out on the jetty, smell the familiar musty odor of old wood.

She was safe.

In her room.

Phillip by her side.

"What the hell just happened?" His whiskey eyes focused on hers. "Other than we just had unsheathed sex."

She blinked at him; the memory of the fantasy tattooed on her brain. No way was she telling him where she'd gone. "The whisky?" she offered, for the second time that night. And then his words hit her. "Unsheathed?"

He rubbed the back of his neck. "Sorry. You were on me like Gorilla Glue, sweet cheeks." He got up and shoved his legs in his jeans.

"Wait. Where are you going?"

A heavy sigh escaped through his *everything's okay* facade. "I think it would be best if I slept at home tonight. Give you a chance to get some rest."

Read: This is too creepy for me.

31

She didn't blame him. It was too creepy for her, too. She gathered her hair at the back of her neck, tied it in a loose knot, missing him already. But he was right. With a hefty proposal load on her desk at Cauldron and non-stop work on the old house, she was exhausted. Maybe more than she realized.

He drew his t-shirt on over his head and down over his hips, hesitated a moment, then pulled her into his arms. "I've been putting off doing some work at my folks' house. Maybe tomorrow, while you girls are doing your yard sale thing, would be a good time to get that done."

Tonight, and tomorrow. Okay. He was really spooked. Hell so was she. She braced her hands on his forearms, gave them a squeeze.

"I agree. I could use a good night's rest."

"I'll stop by after the yard sale, okay?" He nipped a kiss on her forehead. "Promise me you'll take it easy tomorrow. Sleep in?"

Wait. Forehead kiss? Not sending him home with a forehead kiss. She lifted up on her toes and gave him a lingering kiss on the lips, savoring the familiar taste of him. She wanted him to stay now, more than ever.

She laughed. "It's a garage sale. People will be here like vultures by seven a.m."

"Right," he said on a laugh, and headed for the hole in the floor.

A little stab of regret shot thorough her. "I promise," she murmured, letting her hands fall to her sides.

"I'll let myself out."

She tried to brush aside the fact that they'd had sex without a condom. They'd done it before. Carefully.

Tonight had not been careful.

At all.

She wondered now if that had spooked him more than the rest. She hadn't dated for so long before Phil, she'd gone off the pill and was loath to go back. The timing was right at least. If she had her days right, there was little chance of getting pregnant this week. She made a mental note to schedule that doctor's appointment.

Soon.

She should go downstairs and take a bath, but she felt too exhausted to move. Instead, she switched off her bedside lamp, lay back, and listened to Phil's footsteps clumping down the back stairs. Her body was exhausted, but that didn't stop her mind churning too fast for sleep.

Her gaze fell on the serpent bangle tipped up against the lamp base on the nightstand. The soft light of the moon through her uncovered windows shown on its blood-red eyes.

I see you.

"No way," she said aloud.

She turned on her side and propped her head up on her elbow. The eyes stared back at her, testing her resolve.

It's a stupid bracelet, Tess. A hunk of metal.

If she wore it again, would it take her back where she'd been? Should she put it on and see? Or should she take it out to the seawall and pitch it into the canal?

She picked at a loose thread on her duvet and listened to the wall clock tick the seconds away.

Oh, for chrissakes. She sat up and snapped on the bedside light, dropped the bracelet flat on her palm, and tested its weight. It was heavy enough to be solid gold. She polished it on the surface of her duvet. She'd worked with gold enough in her college jewelry class to know the color, and the difference between commercial grade fourteen carat and the purer eighteen found in older pieces. Twenty-four was so golden it looked fake. This piece was leaning toward the fake. There were no markings on the inside to indicate its purity. She rubbed her fingertip over the scales. They were worn down, the way a wedding band lost its pattern rubbing up against the years.

Her pulse kicked up a notch. The longer she held the bracelet, the stronger the urge to slip it on.

She let go a little laugh. "Oh, no. You have no power over me." She held the bangle between her fingers once more. "*Whadaya* think of that, my friend?"

Her cell phone jangled *Your Body is a Wonderland.*

Could Phillip be home already? She looked out across the bay to the houses perched on the cliffs where he lived on top of the garage of his parent's home. Where had the last ten minutes gone? Without the binoculars, she couldn't tell which of the glowing lights might be his, but she imagined him there, looking across to her.

She dropped the bracelet on the nightstand and picked up her phone. "Hi there." Tess rolled up to sitting in front of her windows Yoga style. "Did you miss me?"

"Yeah. That was strange, earlier. We should talk about it — not now," he said. "I just — I shouldn't have left."

"No worries." Hopefully. "Looking forward to the yard sale tomorrow."

"Okay, babe. You'll call if you have any problems, right?"

Like a golden snake stealing me away to some erotic dream? "I'm fine. See you tomorrow."

"Okay. G'night."

"G'night. Wait! Hey—"

"What?"

"Flick your light on and off a couple times."

"What?"

"Just do it."

She scanned the cliff, watching for the signal; and there it was. Oh my gosh. "I see it! I can see your light from my window."

"Do yours."

She flicked her bedside light on and off.

"I don't know."

She did it again. Three times, on, off, on, off, on, off.

"Wait, yeah. Yeah, babe. That's cool."

"Yeah. G'night Phil."

"Night sweet cheeks."

Tess clicked off her cell phone and glanced up at the cliffs again. Without the flash, she couldn't really see his place, but she knew he was there, and it calmed her.

The bracelet was a beautiful piece of junk, or by some providence, real. Either way, it was going back in the pouch it rode in on.

She grabbed the darned thing off the nightstand, strode to her dressing room, and buried it deep in the back of her lingerie drawer.

CHAPTER FIVE
Circa 324 CE - A Village Outside Chalcedon

A cool breeze blew off the Bosporus, stirring the curtains next to Haldor's bed. There was a heaviness in the air, foretelling a long, hot day. He could feel the humidity deep in his bones. The air would be sultry with it by the time he arrived at market square.

As a younger man, he'd have welcomed such a day. Now that his young man's body had given way to a bent back and twisted limbs, it made little difference whether it was warm or cool, dry or humid; his bones ached, and his joints were stiff and swollen. It was torture just to get out of bed, let alone carry on the business of the day. But carry on he would. The alternative was to lay down and die.

Haldor sighed deeply. Bent as he was his mind was keen; he wasn't ready to die this morning. He willed himself forward, calling on all of his strength to do what he had to do.

A party of younger men, most likely from Constantinopolis, jostled him as he joined the flow of citizens in the main street, a swelling river of humanity, pushing its way toward the square.

Haldor struggled to keep pace. There was no respect for an old man in the street anymore. Tired as he was, he smiled to himself. An old man has his ways. They would arrive at the square before him;

37

but Beggan, the auctioneer, would see that Haldor got his chance. Haldor had paid him well.

As he passed the last slow-moving cart entering the square, he could hear men shouting. Rich aromas of spiced meats and breads cooking in vendor stalls lining the square had already begun to rise in the still air. Haldor's stomach rumbled in reply, reminding him that in his haste he'd set out without having even a drink of wine or a crust of bread. Now, food would have to wait. The auction had already begun.

Haldor hurried as fast as his tortured bones would take him. "Be quiet, old man," he told his stomach. "Today we have more important business than to cater to your constant rumblings."

He pushed his way through to the front of a large wooden platform, elbowing past two Praetorian guards who'd passed him on the street. He glared defiantly at their efforts to block his view. He was old and bent, but he was still able to hold his place in a crowd. Ignoring the guards, he turned his attention to the auctioneer.

The first woman had been brought out; she wrenched and squirmed under the keeper's grip on her arm. Slipping a coin on the platform, one of the guards bought his right to handle the goods. And handle he did.

Older than the others on the block, the woman flaunted large breasts, wide hips, and a sullen expression that begged a conquering. Once he would have paid his gold to have more than a look at the likes of her. Alas, today it took more than large breasts and a thick thatch of hair below to wake the sleeping dragon between his loins.

Ha. It was questionable whether anything could. Let the younger men vie for the flesh. He was looking for something more. He waited in silence as the man paid the auctioneer several more gold pieces and led the woman away. Haldor suspected the man was fooled by her ample womanly delights; he didn't think they would get much cooperation from her. She'd be back on the block in a week.

Haldor stretched his hands before him, working at the painful knots in his joints. He had no need of a woman in his bed; he needed a pair of hands to replace his own.

The next girl, although appearing meek and sound, was young; too young for his purposes. He needed a woman who possessed hands with passion, young enough to train, but old enough to develop a feel for his work — a love for it. One who wouldn't pine her days away waiting for a man and then run away with him straightaway. He was searching for a woman with a special pair of hands that would be faithful to the work.

He had spent a lifetime wedded to his true love: Gold. Not the gold itself as a value, but the working of it, the warmth of it, the timeless beauty of it. He braced himself against the platform and stretched his neck to see the other slaves who waited their turn on the block. Some affected a sultry look, some were obviously terrified. Animals, the lot.

However, fifth from the end of the line, a young woman stared out into the crowd, not with fear, but with expectancy, as if anything that could happen to her now would be better than where she had been.

Even compared to the slave population, she was covered in the most meager of garments. From its size, Haldor surmised she had grown several inches since this garment was new, if it ever had been. She was angular, gaunt, raven hair falling over what could be a stunning facial structure. When the auctioneer stripped her bare in preparation for her turn on the block, some of the men in the crowd scoffed.

Fools.

Haldor asserted his position in front of the platform, never taking his eyes from the girl as she moved forward until, just as the keeper pushed her out onto the block, he reached into his purse and fingered his coins, double checking his buying power.

The bidding started low. She was not a "desirable" he overheard some of the men around him saying.

"She has the chest of a boy," one said.

"Skin and bones, that one," complained another.

Haldor no longer had an interest in female endowments. He bid only for her hands. He fingered the smooth black stone fastened to a thong about his waist. The touchstone was the measure by which he learned the value of gold. He wished he had such an exacting measure to consult in this transaction. Alas, his only tools were his own two eyes. He must examine the hands more closely before his final offer.

Beggan made no move to give him access. Haldor was expecting this. He placed another coin on the platform. Beggan scooped up the offering and gave Haldor a hand up in one fluid movement.

The young woman was wide-eyed, but compliant. His heart thumped hard in his chest as he held her hands in his. They were slender, but strong, sinewy. He turned them over and back; they were calloused, but undamaged by hard labor, her fingers long and tapering. They had been worked hard, and they could work harder still, and hopefully take some joy in the process.

With no other bidders speaking up, Haldor handed two more coins to the auctioneer, and the man made no argument. He passed the girl into Haldor's custody, and returned to the next woman in line, a satisfied grin stretched across his face.

Haldor led his prize toward the side of the platform and pushed his way through the crowd again, pulling the girl along with him by her arm without looking back. He had work to do, much to teach, and no time to waste.

He stopped in front of a stall where bolts of dyed cloth were displayed, shoved aside some of the more expensive silks. He selected a sturdy linen and tossed a coin at the merchant, enough to purchase the entire bolt. She could use it to outfit her chamber and herself.

CHAPTER SIX

Kindra lovingly buffed the enameled surface of the brooch, bringing the blue, green, and red colors to a liquid shine. In the two years she had worked for Haldor, she had crafted hundreds of bracelets, fibulae, neck rings, brooches and other adornments intended for women of the upper classes; each piece a little more accomplished than the last.

Haldor supplied smelters, crucibles, and tools needed to melt, cut, cast, and polish. Kindra supplied nimble fingers to replace his gnarled ones.

The pieces she created brought prices far exceeding anything he had made even before his hands shriveled into useless claws. The more her pieces were coveted in the empire, the more vigorously he guarded the identity of the true artist.

Kindra had mixed feelings about her mentor. In one sense, he had given her an invaluable gift. What woman wouldn't love to hold gold in her hands the way she had done? Certainly not her if she'd stayed in her parent's household. Her father could barely afford candles and meat, let alone a solid gold bangle for his wife to wear on her arm.

Kindra had grown to love the feel of gold in her hands, loved to watch scraps of yellow form a shining bead in the bottom of the crucible when she smelted them down. In her whole life, she had never been so satisfied as when a piece she dreamed of in her head, then designed in charcoal on slate, and

43

finally cast and cut and set, turned out exactly the way she had first imagined it.

Haldor had bought her as a slave, but he had molded her into an artist.

He was, however, a relentless taskmaster who refused to accept less than perfection. He worked her late into the night by lamplight until her vision blurred. He demanded finishes that kept her polishing until her fingers bled and throbbed with pain. His lectures droned on and on, reaching far beyond what was needed to cast a gold ring, or create a colorful mosaic of glass. He drilled her on the properties of all the precious metals, how they responded to heat, how the colors varied on the touchstone to determine their purity, and therefore, their value.

He poured into her everything he'd learned in all his sixty years of working the gold without pausing to let her take a breath.

She recognized the gift, the privilege, the training he had given her; yet a part of her longed to be free of the labor that left her fingers raw and her back aching. How long could she go on slaving under his roof before it sapped every ounce of her strength and left her bent and tired just like him?

Bent and tired and lonely.

She had known little love in her life, and what she recalled lived in the far reaches of her memory, lost under a mountain of isolation and despair. She missed her mother and sister and had little opportunity to talk with other women.

Haldor had given her a chance to do something besides carry slops and other peoples burdens, but she was a prisoner just the same.

Now, she held the finished brooch to the lamplight, her heart swelling with pride. She put it back on the bench in a nest of soft kid skin, centered the brass rod over the back of the brooch, and gave the rod a delicate tap to stamp her delta mark. In an act of satisfying defiance, she put her brass rods away, leaving off Haldor's signature 'H'. At least for now, the brooch was hers and hers alone.

She turned it over again. She had created a beautiful medallion of enamel, pearls, and precious stones in a design so intricate and advanced even Haldor would catch his breath when he saw it.

The piece had been commissioned by Emperor Constantine for his mother, Helena after her momentous discovery of a pagan temple built over what was believed to be the burial site of Jesus. Kindra had conceived, designed, and created the basic framework for the piece all on her own.

When he saw what she'd done, Haldor's eyes would take on a glow she planned to manipulate. He was going to become very rich on this piece and she was going to make him pay.

Unlike the fragile, frightened girl she had been when he dragged her away from the market two years before, Kindra had come to understand her value and reminded him often. She may be his slave, but his future, and his habit of gambling on the ponies, would be over if not for her. What had she to lose, after all? She was a slave. He couldn't debase her further.

Knowing her skill was the sole reason he prospered, she had demanded and eventually received better food, more oil lamps, comfortable furnishings for her chamber in the villa, and thread and fabric with which to fashion a palla that pleased her to wear over her working tunic.

She had even negotiated a few hours of free time now and then, to go to the public baths and befriend other women of her stature in the village.

These things he had grudgingly given, once he realized that beating her into submission was useless and only slowed her productivity. As long as she didn't reveal her role in Haldor's household she could hold onto that small bit of freedom.

It was a good trade. With his ruined hands, Haldor could no longer work the gold. As a woman, Kindra could never legitimately join a trade guild, nor could she legally own property. As much as she longed for freedom, without Haldor's protection — his enterprise -- Kindra would have no way to make a living other than cleaning and cooking for some wealthy family, or selling her body, which was, despite its ubiquitous presence in the empire, against the law.

So, they had come to an agreement: Kindra would continue to produce high quality works of art he could sell for premium prices as long as he passed some of the proceeds down to her in the form of better living conditions and a degree of freedom.

As Haldor's slave, she had a better life than most single women in the city, and some degree of security.

Until recently.

Haldor had begun to spend more time gambling than procuring commissions, and the more he gambled, the more he lost; the more he lost, the more he drank; and the more he drank, the more he returned to the villa with nothing to show for his time away.

Trips to Constantinopolis that should have taken a few days — it was only a short barge ride across the Bosphorus — stretched into a couple of weeks and resulted in fewer and fewer commissions. She had overheard him boasting of his winnings at the local racetracks and gaming casinos. He had, on one occasion, told of a trip to Rome and the Circus Maximus to bet on the chariot races. Even a trip to the nearby port city of Chalcedon would see him gone several days. Lately she had heard him bargaining with suppliers to advance credit against future sales. If he wasn't careful, they would both end up on the street.

While his frequent absences were a worry, they also afforded her more freedom. She had learned his pattern and wasted no time taking advantage. When the morning dawned without his arrival in the villa, Kindra would wrap herself in the palla she'd made and venture into the village. Visiting the public baths during the women's early hours reminded her of her life at home with her mother and sister, before she had been sold and she went there whenever she could.

It was on one of these occasions she befriended a young woman who reminded her of her older sister. In truth, anyone who saw them together might think they were related. Alba had dark, naturally wavy hair like her own. And although Kindra had gained some womanly curves over the past year, she was still angular and lean like her friend, with eyes the color of bright amber.

After several meetings, steeped in the steaming water of the small caldarium, Kindra confided her worry about her master.

Alba's musical laughter came easily. She straightened, let the water sluice off her shoulders. "You have nothing to fear, my friend." She looked Kindra up and down. "You are every bit as lovely as any of the rest of us. You could draw the attention of the handsomest of the Praetorian Guard. A young courtesan can make a decent living in this village, and in Chalcedon, well ..." She raised her hand to indicate the entire sky.

Kindra blanched at the thought. "But, are you not afraid the guards will arrest you?"

Alba smoothed a stray tendril of hair behind Kindra's ear. "Oh, my dear, you are naïve."

Not so naïve. She had never been with a man but that didn't stop her from dreaming about it. She had seen her parents and her older brother in acts of sex and knew in general what was involved. She sank deeper in the water, closing her eyes. What would it be like to be held in the arms of such a man? To feel his hard shoulders against hers, his hands on her hips? The sudden twinge between her legs took her by surprise. She had a lot to learn.

Alba grinned at her as if she could see right into her soul. "Well?"

Kindra's cheeks burned with a sense of excitement as they rose from the water and dressed. "Do you … like it?"

Alba coiled a piece of her hair around her finger. "Most of the time."

"And when you don't?"

Alba's eyes came back to hers. "I defend myself."

Kindra doubted Alba could put up much defense against a man who wanted to take more than she offered. She looked at her own hands, nails worn to the nubs, but strong.

Alba touched the hem of Kindra's embroidered palla draped over the bench, her fingers tracing the swirled stitch pattern. "You wear this one evening to the high bath up near the prefecture and those men will give you a good bit of coin for your trouble, and who knows? One of them just might show you why you were born."

It was hard to believe the smile on Alba's face came from one so young. She didn't appear to be any worse for the wear.

Kindra's heart knocked excitedly against the leather braiding at her ribs. With enough coin, and the little freedom she'd already managed to squeeze out of Haldor, it might be possible to escape altogether.

She lifted her chin. "When do you do this again, my friend?"

Alba cocked her head. "You want to come with me?"

Her mother wouldn't be happy about it, but then her mother had let her father sell her into slavery. Their apartment had been perfect for a family of four. But when she came along, their family unit was disrupted. Her father had no particular fondness for any of them. The closer Kindra drew to puberty, the more fretful her mother became. Being the youngest and a second girl, it had been only a matter of time before her father exercised his right to sell the extra mouth he had to feed.

"When?" Kindra asked.

"Anytime you like." Alba rose from the bath, selected a strigil from a clay pot on the bench and scraped droplets of water and oil from her skin, turning her leg this way and that. "I have to admit, I'm rather addicted to the practice."

Kindra considered a moment. Haldor had been gone for two days to the emperor's palace which, if he followed his pattern, would give her two more days of freedom. Her fingers tingled at the thought. Helena's brooch was completed. She had the time. She needed a plan for the day Haldor lost his last penny; this one was as good as any. Consequences be damned.

"How about tonight?"

Alba sent Kindra a sly grin. "My friend is eager to give herself up?"

Kindra shrugged. "Any animal could do it, right?"

Alba burst out in a laugh. "Brave words for someone who has never done the deed. Let me know what you think when you end up with a babe in your belly."

Kindra blanched. She hadn't thought of that possibility.

"Oh, don't look so worried." Alba turned Kindra around and scraped water off her back with the curved strigil. "We women take care of each other."

Kindra's mind raced with her new plan all the way back to Haldor's villa. She had already begun to save tiny stubs of gold and pieces of gemstone against the day he returned broke, or so drunk and angry, she feared for her life and would have no choice but to flee. Following Alba's lead, she could leave when she was ready.

The night couldn't come soon enough. She needed to prepare herself. She donned her cleanest tunic and wrapped her palla around her chest and over her shoulder, thinking all the while of her mother. Kindra missed her warm green eyes, her tender touch, the way she'd oiled and combed Kindra's hair. All she had of her now was the tattered tunic she'd worn leaving home, and a gold serpent bracelet her mother had given her.

She slipped her hands under her cot, found the leather pouch she'd hidden there, and took out the gleaming gold. Ruby-red serpent eyes glinted at her. As far as she knew, the serpent's coil cuff was the only thing of value her mother had ever owned. "Keep it safe," she had whispered, slipping it into a slit in the hem of her tunic she'd created for that purpose. "It may someday bring you back to me."

Kindra hoped that was true. She had hidden it away these past two years. Now, she slipped it on, feeling the gold warm to her skin. It was the first time she'd dared wear it anywhere except in her own chamber when Haldor was away.

She was looking for a fibulae to pin her palla to her shoulder when her gaze lifted and caught on the brooch.

She ran her fingertips over the polished stones, her heart racing. She'd made the brooch with her own hands. Once she handed it over to Haldor, she would never see it again. Why shouldn't she wear it now? She huffed out a laugh. If Haldor caught her, he would choke her with his bare hands, that's why. But, she reasoned, it was her work, after all, that put food in their stores and financed his gambling. It is a wise dog who learns not to bite the hand that feeds him.

She rubbed her thumb over the red stone at the brooch's center, drawing courage from its color. To hades with Haldor. He wasn't here, and when he returned, he'd head straight for his chamber nursing his aching head like he always did.

She fastened the brooch at her shoulder, drew in a deep breath, and straightened her spine, then tried on the sultry pose Alba had demonstrated, hand on hip, relaxed and turned slightly to the side. Draped in linen of a soft, mossy green, the serpent bracelet warm against her skin, Kindra felt more like the woman she was than she ever had before. What would her mother think of that?

She'd probably done something similar to secure her place in the home of a man who worked in the emperor's stable.

She cherished her mother's memory, though she had to admit, her life was much better here at Haldor's than it would have been if her father had not sold her when he did.

Considering the stories Kindra had heard told at the fountain among some of the younger slave girls, she knew she had been lucky when Haldor picked her out of the crowd. He'd been too old to take advantage of her sex, and because of his position as a tradesman to the Emperor, his villa, though modest, contained all of the amenities for a healthy, comfortable life.

There was an atrium at the center open to the sky, and Kindra had a private chamber off the workshop — something she'd never have had in the city with her family. And the fresh stream at the back of the property was better than running water inside the villa.

While she'd heard her brother had been conscripted to the Roman Army, outfitted no doubt with the money her father had received for her sale, she had not seen nor heard anything of her mother and sister since she'd been sold two years before.

She supposed she should count her blessings. There was always a mountain of work to do at Haldor's villa. In addition to creating fine works of gold to his standard, she was responsible for laundry and cleaning and cooking. However, she had a comfortable place to sleep, and Haldor was often gifted with fruits and meats the average person never saw in their lifetime.

It would be foolish to trade a life with Haldor for the life of a street courtesan. At best that road led to another kind of slavery; or worse, an early grave. But with enough coin, and the right circumstances, she just might get far enough away from Haldor to escape both.

53

She hesitated a moment longer, touching the brooch at her shoulder. She was taking a great risk. She clenched her hands into fists at the thought. He'd be gone at least another day, maybe two. She'd have the brooch back on the workbench by morning.

"Haldor be damned," she said aloud, and slipped out the door and closed it firmly behind her.

CHAPTER SEVEN

Alba was waiting for her at their designated spot, about a stadium length from the exit to the hot bath at the gymnasium.

"So, there are the regular guards who live here in the village and support the Praetorian Prefects." Alba grabbed her hand and they hurried along the narrow corridor leading to the baths where men of higher rank took their entertainment. "Sometimes, there are guards ordered here from Constantine's Palace — you can tell them by the gold circlet they wear around their necks."

Kindra was well aware of the neck rings. She had made enough of them to outfit an army of men. Some of the neck rings were as thick as her thumb.

"But, won't they arrest us? Or take us into custody for being out at night without an escort?"

Alba laughed and shook back her hair. "What? And miss their opportunity to bury themselves in pleasure with one of us?"

"But, if we're caught, we could be—"

"Shhhhhhh," Alba hissed, a finger at her lips. "They'll be coming out soon. It's quite amazing," she went on excitedly. She lowered her voice as they drew within a few paces of the caldarium exit. "On cool nights, their bodies steam with heat."

As if conjured by Alba's words, a man emerged from the portal carrying his bundled clothing. A leather strap was draped over his shoulder, and there was a sword and scabbard at his hip. He wore naught but a loin cloth below. His hair was still wet from the bath, his body gleamed in the light of the third-quarter moon, his legs were as strong and sinewy as tree trunks. He headed toward the colonnade leading to the Prefect's quarters.

Kindra gasped. Living behind the locked doors of Haldor's villa, she hadn't seen a man so virile since she was too young to notice.

Alba pressed her hand at Kindra's back. "Watch me, then do as I do when the next one comes out."

Kindra clamped a shaking hand over her mouth. Maybe she should have thought this through a bit more. Alba turned a stern look at her as if she could read her mind.

"It will be all right, my friend. You were bound to be taken someday, and most likely, you would not have been paid for it. Just remember, we are there for the coin, not to fall in love."

Kindra sucked in a sustaining breath, gave her a quick nod, and shrank back against the corridor wall. By the gods, this was really happening.

Alba strolled to the man, leading with her breasts, her hands clasped coyly behind her back. She called out to him; he glanced up, and his expression softened from one of challenge to a wide grin of pleasure. Alba glanced over her shoulder at Kindra and gave her a wink as the man led her away through the shadows.

Well, that part appeared easy enough. Kindra eased down the corridor and crossed the colonnade to where the couple had met. She pressed her hands against a column and tried to see where they had gone. Were they just there, in the shadows of the courtyard? She couldn't see them, but she thought she heard murmurs and the rustle of clothing.

"What are you doing there, woman?"

Kindra jumped nearly out of her skin at the sound of the gruff voice behind her. She turned to see a wall of a man standing before her. Indeed, there was steam rising from his body in the cool night air. Her eyes scanned slowly up, taking in his wool tunic, a lightweight breast plate, and — it was difficult hold back a gasp — a thick circlet of gold around his neck. There was no doubt in her mind if she saw inside the gold coil it would bear her own mark.

The man swept her body with his own gaze, his eyes resting on the brooch at her shoulder. Kindra drew in a breath, speechless.

"Are you unable to speak, then?"

"I — no. I mean, yes. I —"

Get yourself under control, Kindra. Her freedom depended on carrying through with her plan. If Alba could do it, so could she. "I was told the men from the palace seek … entertainment here." She hoped he could not detect the shaking in her voice.

The man's gaze went to the garden where her friend had gone, then returned to rest on the brooch. Now she regretted her boldness. He would probably accuse her of stealing it, then haul her off to prison, or worse. He didn't smile like Alba's man had done, only stared at her like she had offered him bad meat.

Coins. You're here for coins. It's only sex, girl. The words came as if spoken from afar, reminding her of what she wanted to do. *Needed* to do. Now wasn't the time to give in to fear. It was too late for that.

She dragged in a ragged breath, worked a smile towards her lips, and leaned against the column, her arms crossed under her breasts, pressing them against the fabric of her palla as Alba had showed her. "Don't wait too long. Plenty of men will be willing to pay for what I offer."

"Is that right?" He took a step closer, tipped her chin up with his finger. "Some would have you taken to the magistrate and thrown in prison."

Kindra forced herself to breathe. This was going all wrong. Alba had made it look so easy.

Are you kidding me? Look at this guy. You are about to lose your virginity, better to a handsome hunk than some dolt. He's baiting you. Don't let him run the conversation.

Kindra balked at the thoughts blooming in her head. It was as though a stranger spoke to her in a language she barely understood. The words were foreign, but the tone stoked a growing fire in her belly, propelled her forward. She straightened her shoulders.

"I hear the emperor's prefects make the best lovers," she said, mimicking her private messenger's tone. She'd heard nothing of the kind but played to the only thing she knew about men via Haldor and her own father: they loved themselves ahead of everything else.

This one, however, didn't seem to respond. Instead, he gripped her forearm and dragged her up the steps of the colonnade, his forward motion so swift and strong, she had trouble keeping pace.

They turned away from the garden. He pushed her ahead of him down another corridor lit with oil lamps. Slowing their pace, they turned into an alcove with a heavy wooden door. She swallowed a scream, suddenly seeing herself in chains.

He pushed open the door and thrust her inside. It was a large room with a row of tall windows opening out on the interior courtyard where Alba and her man had disappeared. A fall of fine linen curtains had been drawn aside to let in the cooling night breeze.

A pair of oil lamps provided enough light to see the room had comfortable furnishings: a low bench and table set with a large bowl of fruits and nuts, and in the corner, there was a wood-framed bed with clean woolen blankets and head rests of colorful woven material. There was a marble basin at one end of the room; a pair of white lilies scenting the water.

Did the Emperor treat all his guards this well? Or was there something special about this one?

Her heart slowed its racing and she took a full breath for the first time since his voice had startled her in the colonnade. She was still taking in the room's finery when she heard the heavy door close behind her.

Her hand went to her throat when she turned to see the man had removed his outer clothing and now stood in nothing but a loin cloth strung low about his hips, a swirl of dark hair dove down the center of his taught belly.

Her mouth went dry. His bared chest and heavily muscled legs made him look even more powerful than the man Alba had taken to the garden. He straightened, hands on hips; his eyes devoured her with unmistakable interest. Her nipples drew instantly taut.

She fought the urge to cover herself. Alba's words repeated in her head. *Coins. Think only of the coins.*

With a deep inhalation, she matched his stance. "I expect payment for your entertainment, in advance, as is the custom."

The man cleared his throat. "The custom is that women without escort are detained in the court."

Kindra bit her lip. *He's bluffing,* came the voice inside her head. *He's already hard beneath that cloth. Already yours.* She couldn't stop herself from confirming the fact with a glance and the verity send a spike of heat between her thighs. She had nothing to lose but a bit of skin.

She dipped her shoulder, letting her palla slip to reveal more flesh. "Really? And miss the opportunity to partake of unspoiled goods?" She fisted her hands to stop their shaking.

He stared at her, his chest expanding with each breath. She could almost see the battle going on behind those dark eyes. At last he shifted his weight to a more relaxed stance.

"Remove your palla so I can see what I am offered."

Coin, Kindra. Not before getting your coin.

She edged away from the windows to place herself between the man and the door. She would ask for the highest price possible. If he denied her, she would simply run.

She lifted her chin and stood her ground. "I have never been with a man before. That is worth two of your precious gold coins."

"Yes, and what is that brooch on your shoulder worth?"

Kindra froze, her feet rooted to the floor. The weight of the brooch grew suddenly heavy. It was too late to go halfway. It was too late to turn back from her purpose. If she was risking her life, she'd better make it worth her while. One coin certainly wasn't enough to get her away from this village, let alone far enough to have a chance at freedom. Two would be better. This might be the only chance she would get.

She could not count on Haldor being away again before his fortune failed and she'd have no place to go. It was now or never. *Own it, girl,* came the voice in her head. The bold words boosted her confidence. It was too late to turn back.

She shot up her chin and took a step forward. "That is none of your concern. We are here for a purpose, am I right?"

His eyebrows raised, and his eyes glinted in the lamplight, dark and provocative. The first hint of a smile played at the corners of his mouth. "One gold coin is a month's pay to someone in my position. I could get what you offer at one tenth the price."

Kindra waved her hand at the empty bed. "I do not see anyone else here."

He laughed. "You flatter yourself. If I go outside right now, there will be ten women waiting in the shadows whom I already know are well worth the price."

Heat spread from her face to her shoulders. It seemed she had successfully changed the direction of the conversation. Now everything was on the table. She preferred losing her maiden status to losing her life.

She straightened her shoulders and fixed her eyes on his. "You are offered a rare bargain then," she challenged. "I could not earn back what I tender here in a lifetime. What is a month of your pay compared to that? *Two solidus*. In advance."

She took a step closer to the door, and extended her hand for the payment, half expecting him to throw her out instead.

His eyes swept her body again and his grin widened. He went to his table, turned his back on her. There was a heavy thump, and the sound of coins, then he turned back to her, stepped close, and dropped one gold coin into her hand.

She hefted the weight of it, turned it over and back in her palm. She had handled larger pieces of gold, worked them into things of beauty, but never in her life had she held the official tender of the empire. The *solidus* appeared newly minted, the picture of Constantine raised in sharp relief.

"One now," he said, leveling his gaze at her, "and the other when it is proved you are in possession of what you offer."

She rubbed her fingers over the surface of the coin. It would truly be worth her effort even if he failed to pay her full price in the end.

Without taking her eyes from his, she reached beneath her palla and tunic, removed a soft leather pouch from a thong around her waist, and pressed the coin inside, then draped it over the bolt on the door. With his eyes burning her skin, she slowly unfastened the brooch.

CHAPTER EIGHT

Marcus sucked in a breath as the young woman let the soft green fabric fall to the floor.

Dark hair spilled over her shoulders covering one of her breasts, the dark areola and heavy curve of the other fully exposed. She stood like a statue before him. Would she come alive under his touch?

Never had he beheld such magnificence, and as one of Constantine's chief aides, he'd been offered the most beautiful courtesans anywhere in the empire. This girl might present herself as a street walker, but her bearing told a different story.

She belonged in one of the palaces, immortalized in marble, not on the street selling herself for gold. The fact that he had just bought her for one coin hadn't quite sunk in. The women he was used to demanded much more and were more aggressive taking his measure.

Something about this one gave him pause — the way she stopped breathing when his gaze touched her flesh, the way her hands clenched at her sides, the way she kept one eye on the door. She was a cornered animal ready to bolt. He stood still now, giving her that option.

Much as he thought of plunging himself deep inside her, the last thing Marcus had wanted when he left the gymnasium was the continued attention of servants and slaves making over him like he was some kind of god. He preferred keeping his whereabouts secret, as did his Emperor.

Constantine boasted much of his good deeds in leniency toward the Christians, but he was no different than any before him when it came to protecting and fattening the palace treasury. Christianity may be good for controlling the masses, but it had little bearing on the affairs of state where the treasury was concerned. Anyone who jeopardized that effort was soon met with harsh punishment.

The fact that Marcus had been sent here to investigate reported thievery meant the transgression was grave, indeed. His very presence in the village would send any potential suspects into hiding.

Word traveled fast. It was nearly impossible to travel in secret when he visited the smaller prefectures. If he could have removed the golden circlet about his neck, he would have. Many thought him privileged to be at the emperor's back. Few were trusted to be in the that position. In reality, Marcus was nothing but a very expensive and well-tended slave.

The woman was a puzzle. Perhaps his first impression had been correct; she worked for the emperor, too. Deep inside, his most animal urges — fear and lust — rose to the surface. He was spellbound by the sight of her. He wanted — needed — to be inside her. The way she stood with her head erect, nostrils flaring like a wild filly, the way the moonlight ran its silver fingers through her hair — her profile, her bare shoulder, and the serpent of gold coiled around her bicep. There stirred in him an edginess that went beyond the possibility of a sexual encounter. It fed his latent fear someone had sent her to spy on him.

"Well. What are you waiting for? I don't have the entire evening to wait on you," she prodded.

He drew in a long breath. "Bold words for one who is unspoiled." Words that cut through his hesitancy.

He closed the distance between them with one swift move, took hold of her arm and drew her close. There was a fine sheen of perspiration on her lip. How he wanted to wipe that away with his thumb, feel the curl of her lip against his. He ran a hand over her shoulder and down her arm, his thumb grazing the roundness of her breast.

Her lips parted, and her breasts rose with her sharp intake of breath; her eyes darkened with something deeper than fear now — more visceral, expectant. He circled a hand behind the small of her back and pulled her against him, dipping his mouth to taste the skin on her shoulder, over her clavicle, and that darkened areola.

She trembled but didn't pull away. He shifted his hips, fitting himself in the cleft between her legs where their thighs met. She stiffened holding her breath and the heat between them rose until his erection was painfully thick and urgent. Still she began none of the moves one would expect of an experienced consort.

Instead, she shuddered in his arms like a half-drowned puppy. He wanted her, but not like this. Not under force and fear.

He lowered his arms and stepped toward the door, put his hand on the bolt and the purse she'd laid there. He'd give her one last chance.

"Shall I take back my coin?" He lifted the latch and pushed open the door enough to show her she was free to leave, then stepped out of her way.

She stared a moment longer, her fingers tracing the gold serpent around her arm. As if drawing strength from the gold, she dragged in a full breath, then slowly straightened her back, her fine cheeks blooming crimson, her eyes flashing defiance.

"We struck a bargain and I intend to keep it." She crossed to the bed and sat, then lifted her hair over her shoulders, leaving her lovely breasts in full view.

Marcus's heart thumped hard against his breastbone as he pulled the door closed. There had never been such a beauty in his bed. Where there had been fear in her amber eyes, there was now determination, and something else — something akin to the hunger he felt from the moment he first saw her outside the garden.

His father's deathbed words rose in his memory as if he were speaking into his ear: *There are moments in this life on which everything else turns.*

There was no doubt in his mind, this was one of those moments. By the gods, he should take her into custody on the sheer evidence she had pinned to her clothes and clenched at her arm. The pieces were indeed of the quality described by the palace treasurer as subject to thievery. He doubted one so young and innocent could be the mastermind behind such an enterprise. It was possible she could lead him to that person. But his desire to bury himself inside her went far beyond catching a thief.

This was the moment his father had foretold, a moment with the potential to change his life: but for good or ill? Was he trading his loyalty to the Emperor to satisfy his carnal desire? Or was there something else at work? Something that would mark his soul?

If he took this slow, perhaps he could satisfy himself and his emperor.

Resolved, he forced his heartbeat to settle, went to the marble basin, selected a tall urn, and returned to sit on the bedside.

"Come here and lay on your back." He kept his voice low, without threat or urgency, and waited for her to comply, though it took every ounce of his own will. He gathered her wrists in his hands and lifted them to rest above her head, then let go gently until she relaxed them there.

He tipped the urn high over her body and guided a silky golden thread of oil from the center of her breasts, down across her stomach, and over the fine curls of hair at her delta. Her eyes grew wide and followed his every move.

Setting the urn aside, he spread the oil over her velvet skin with his fingertips, working around her areolas, down over her ribs, her sunken belly, her inner thighs.

Her hands clenched tight above her head; she quivered under his touch, her breath coming in short, surprised gasps. Her hips lifted almost imperceptibly each time his fingers dipped closer to her sex.

She did not shrink from his touch or run away. Instead, her eyes widened, and her teeth sank hard into her bottom lip when he ripped off his loin cloth and straddled her, hard and thick and painfully ready for release.

CHAPTER NINE

Kindra couldn't take her eyes away from the pure maleness of him. His muscled chest, the way his shoulders bunched and flexed when he moved, the heat of his sex where it rested hard and heavy between her legs.

She gasped for air, then bit her lip. By the gods she hadn't really thought this through. She had only thought of the gold and her eventual escape. Which is why, when he'd given her the chance to flee, she'd gathered every ounce of courage and gone to his bed.

She had of course known what people do. Her family had lived in close quarters and it was no secret when her mother and father had been intimate. But she had never actually seen a man ready for sex and the sight was alarming in ways she hadn't anticipated, particularly the slow coil of heat that grew between her legs.

Their mouths were almost touching, breathing the same air. The smooth tip of him rested against her most intimate place. He lowered his face to hers, his dark eyes smoldered with desire. A rush of heat awakened a sleeping hunger inside her; so raw, so needy, she feared it would take control. She tensed, resisted. This was a mistake.

"Tell me your name." His voice was ardent, as hungry as her own desire. His breath was hot against her lips.

The question took her by surprise. She searched her reeling thoughts and came up empty. It was as though a shadow had slipped inside her, sealing her off from who she was, changing her character to a someone she didn't recognize; a sensual woman who fit inside her skin, saw through her eyes, and spoke to her in a language she'd never heard. *You got this, girl. You will be all right.*

The words flooded her with relief, bringing her back to herself.

"My name?" she said, stalling. She couldn't tell him her real name. It could get back to Haldor she had left the villa, and he would —

"It's not my usual practice to have consort with strangers," he encouraged. "What if I want to find you again?"

She hadn't thought about that either. Why would he want to find her if not to arrest her?

"Alba," she whispered, sending a secret thank you to the shadow woman inside her head. "My name is Alba."

"Albaaaaah," he moaned, drawing the word out in a sigh as he pressed himself against her.

He reached between them and ran his fingers over her straining flesh, sliding on the oils he'd poured over her.

God help her, she didn't want him to stop. She arched to him, meeting each caress of his fingers with a slow rolling movement that made her ache to have him inside. He pressed against her swollen sex and she cried out. By the gods, what was he waiting for?

He froze, his expression contorting in confusion, then pulled out and away from her like she had the plague, got up and crossed the room, the muscles of his buttocks clenching as he strode to the basin, his head thrown back.

"What is it? What did I do?"

He turned on her, wrapping his loin cloth about his hips. "You really don't know, do you?"

She shook her head. All she knew was that she wanted him back. She wanted that feeling again and again.

"Put on your clothes," he commanded.

Why was he angry? She had done, was going to do what he wanted. What he had paid for. Now he pushed her away? She should be relieved, instead she felt rejected.

She shook her head. He held his commanding gaze.

Half frightened, half humiliated, she drew on her linen tunic, and threw her palla over her shoulder, passion turning to shame. She wasn't good enough. That was it.

He dug in his pouch again, cupping coins in his fist, his eyes a lightening flash in the lamplight.

She stood in awe, afraid to move. He grabbed her hand, pressed two gold coins into it.

"You have my apologies, Alba. I truly thought you were lying to me about being unused. Forgive me."

Now she regretted lying to him about her name. She wanted him to remember. Remember her.

She stared into those eyes, dark russet shot with gold. In that moment she knew she would give up the coin if only he would come back and finish what he'd started. Their eyes caught and held for a few more heavy heart beats until she thought for a moment he would do exactly that. Then, he took a step back and her heart sank.

It wasn't right. This wasn't how it was supposed to be.

"Two coins? But you already gave me one, and we didn't--"

"It was my mistake, not yours. Take the gold. You won't have to subject yourself to another man this night," he said.

She stared at the coins in her hand and then back at him.

"Go," he said, running his hands through his hair. He folded her hand over the coins and moved further away. "Go, now, before I change my mind."

Kindra stared at him another moment while her heart pounded against her ribs, then as if waking from a dream, she scooped her sandals off the floor and fled the chamber, swallowing her tears as she ran.

Chapter Ten

Balboa Island, Republic of California, 2019 CE

"Tessa? You awake?"

Lexi's voice came to her from far away. She grappled to reach it, her response only half formed in her throat. She had awakened, sweaty and exhausted, covered in the fine sheen of a full-on orgasm. Confusion clouded her brain. Either she had just made love to a man with penetrating, rust-brown eyes or she'd had the most lucid dream of her life.

Maybe she should have asked Phillip to stay over last night after all.

But...no. Despite the rude awakening, she had the best night's sleep she'd had in a very long time and she felt better for it. She closed her eyes, willing herself to go back to sleep and pick up the dream where it had left off.

"Tess!"

Damn. "Coming."

She dragged herself out of bed, absently rubbing at her bicep. The skin felt like it had been burned. She padded barefoot to her dresser and looked in the mirror. A trail of tiny red blisters circled her arm like a brand. She traced her fingertips over the mark. The scent of lilies wafted through her mind along with a deep, mesmerizing longing.

Legs tingling like they would give out on her, she grabbed hold of the dresser and steadied herself, clinging firmly to her present reality. She held on tight, taking note of her surroundings. Her home. Her room. Her life.

The upstairs room was basically an open square with casement windows on two sides. Phillip had made her a place to hang her clothes, a rod hung from the ceiling on fishing line next to her dresser. Once the stairs were finished, this entire end of the room would become her *en suite* bath, complete with walk-in closet, vanity, and jetted tub. She drew in a deep breath, shaking off a chill, then stood on her own.

She clicked on her dresser light, found a linen tunic with embroidery around the sleeves and hem and pulled it over her head, then slipped into a pair of denim leggings. She lifted her brush, only then noticing the bracelet at her wrist. Surprised, she slipped it off and laid it on the dresser. It's ruby eyes glinted in the lamp light, and the scent of lilies returned, along with a sense she wasn't alone. She ran her fingers over the serpent's scales, eyes lifted to her reflection in the mirror, half expecting to see Marcus standing behind her. A frisson of alarm prickled her nape. The woman who stared back at her, wide eyed and olive skinned, had long dark hair and amber eyes.

She blinked several times at the reflection. The woman appeared to be as surprised as she for a moment before her surprise softened into a smile and the vision melted away. Tessa blinked again and once more saw her blond-haired, blue-eyed self in the mirror.

"Tessa? You all right?" Lexi called again from downstairs.

"I'm fine. I'm coming," Tessa called back, looping her hair into a messy bun. She scooped the bangle under a pile of folded panties in her lingerie drawer, picked up the bag of jewelry, and climbed down the ladder to the aroma of coffee.

When she sat at the table, Lexi handed her a steaming cup.

"Thanks." She dropped the jewelry bag on the table with a heavy thunk.

Lexi picked it up. She opened the drawstrings, peeked inside, and rooted around with her finger. "Are you sure you want to yard sale this stuff? I mean, look at it." She held a ring up to the light. "It could be worth something."

Tess gazed out at the little sport sailboat tied to their dock. It was pitched on its side in the sand because of the low tide. She felt a little off kilter herself after the last twenty-four hours.

"I just ... want to be sure, that's all. If Theo was stealing from the neighbors, don't you think I'm obligated to try to return what I found?"

Lexi pushed the ring onto her pointer finger. "I think if anyone had missed this stuff, they'd have reported it a long time ago. And that china? I'd have let somebody know for damn sure if I went to unpack it for Thanksgiving dinner and it was frickin' gone. Besides, wouldn't you love to see that china on *your* table?"

"I don't know. I guess I haven't ever thought about *my* table." She rolled her lips in a moment before she huffed out a sigh. There was a lot more to having a home than four walls, a roof and a good set of china. "I just feel funny about it. I won't feel like it's mine until I make sure it's not someone else's." Her biceps tingled suddenly. She scratched absently at the patch of irritation there. "Want me to make some eggs?"

"I was just waiting for you to come down and ask." Lexi slid a carton of eggs from the fridge. "What's going on with your arm?"

"What?" She glanced at her biceps; the mark was still there. She gave it a quick rub with her fingertips. "That funky bracelet, probably," she said, dismissively. "Apparently, I've inherited my mother's allergy to nickel alloy. Anything under 14K gives me a rash." It was an explanation she could live with. All the more reason to put the damn bracelet out at the garage sale with the rest of the junk. She would go up and get it later.

Lexi grinned at her. "Now that's my kind of allergy."

"Works for me," Tessa said. She worked at the stove with her usual flair, singing loud with the radio, and soon, the odd sensation she'd felt when she woke up drifted away on a chorus of a Rolling Stones song.

The yard show went as Audrey predicted: While there were a few regulars who made the promenade around the circumference of the island every weekend, most passersby were visitors or the next generation of family members, like Tess, who'd inherited the property and only recently started living there.

Lexi and Tess rolled out their story of found items dozens of times throughout the day as *looky-loos* handled pieces of glassware and bric-a-brack, riffled through unpacked boxes hauled out from the garage, and a few inquired about prices. As they'd agreed beforehand, the jewelry was not for sale at any price.

Only one person had shown any true interest in the junk. He was classic beach: sun streaked chestnut hair, baggy khaki pants, Hawaiian shirt, and well-worn sandals with no socks; deeply tanned and mildly aloof.

He browsed by early in the afternoon, an over-dressed woman on his arm. She'd appeared bored when he'd commented about Lexi's *"Klepto* Sale" sign.

The sign had been intended as a joke, but Tess posted it on the front gate anyway. She had explained apologetically about her uncle's apparent proclivity for *borrowing* from his neighbors, and how she came to own the house. "None of it's really ours," Tess went on as the man inspected one of the rings. "We found it sealed up in the wall when we did some remodeling."

"Anyone else interested in these pieces?"

He rubbed his thumb over the gold. Tess felt a protective urge to grab the ring away.

The woman — a near-anorexic, ash blonde wearing too much makeup for daytime — dug her bright orange manicure into the man's arm.

He patted her hand reassuringly. "So, this is all you found?"

Tessa pulled in a quick breath, her thoughts going to the bracelet in her drawer. "This represents the lot, yes."

The woman lifted her chin and the man turned his attention to a pair of earrings, chipping with a thumbnail at some encrusted areas Lexi's cleaning had left behind.

"Do you recognize them? We think they may have been ... borrowed ... sometime during the last twenty years."

He shook his head. "I don't know of anyone who wears a pair quite like these." He held them lightly in his fingertips, testing their weight. "I'd be very interested to know who claims them, though."

He offered his hand. "My name is Karl Johns. My shop's here on the island."

"Tess Madigan." *And the name of anyone who claimed them would be none of your business.* Her skin prickled. She wanted him to put down the pieces and leave. She folded her arms over her middle and nodded at Lexi. "This is my friend, Alexis Hill. She lives here, too."

After a long, uncomfortable moment, Lexi nodded with a reserved smile, and as if reading Tessa's mind, she held out her hand for the earrings.

Mr. Johns held Tessa's gaze a moment longer, then dropped the gold into Lexi's hand and stepped toward the arbor gate, where he shifted his gaze briefly to the front of the house. "Your Uncle was a bit of an eccentric, I take it?"

"You knew him?" Tess asked with renewed interest.

He laughed softly. "Not well. We seem to have something in common, though."

Now Lexi crossed her arms and stood shoulder-to-shoulder with Tess. "As in…?"

He pinched a tiny bud from one of Theo's miniature rose vines and threaded it through a buttonhole on his shirt pocket. "We're both … collectors, if you will." He gave them a broad smile. "I'll be back later this afternoon to see if there's anything left."

Tess watched them disappear down the sidewalk, anger bristling at the base of her neck.

Lexi laid the earrings on the table. "That was interesting. He was awfully good looking for being such a nerd."

"Psh-h-h." Tess sat back in her chair. "There was a woman on his arm, in case you didn't notice."

"Oh, I noticed. She was old enough to be his mother."

Tess laughed. "Come on. She wasn't that bad."

Lexi rolled her eyes. "I can't help being suspicious of a woman who doesn't say *a word.*"

"Really. That man is going to have nail marks on his arm when he gets home."

"You saw that, too?"

"Hard to miss when your nails are day-glow orange."

They laughed together and rearranged the items on the table; then relaxed against the rattan chairs. No one claimed a thing the rest of the day, and when one woman offered Tess five hundred dollars for the

Haviland China, Tess told her she couldn't sell it for that price.

Lexi eyed her, mouth agape, as the woman huffed out through the gate. "Why did you say that?"

She got up to call the woman back. Tess stopped her with a gentle touch on the arm.

"Five hundred dollars?" Lexi rasped in a loud whisper. "What's the matter with you? You could use a few unassigned bucks."

Tess grinned at her. "I wouldn't sell it for any price."

"What do you mean?"

"I mean, I'd really *like* to see that china on *your* table."

"No way."

"Yes way. While I enjoy your company, I don't figure we'll be living together forever." Tess leaned over and gave Lexi a hug. "It's the least I could offer my bestie for putting up with me for so long. Since nobody claimed it, I want you to have it."

Lexi tipped her head to Tess's shoulder. "You're the best. And, by the way, I did notice the snake bracelet wasn't out here today."

Tess smiled and stared out at the canal. High tide had re-floated the sailboat. The sight of it bobbing invitingly at the end of its rope lightened her spirit. She sat with her back to the gazing ball, her folding chair anchored in the center of the design she'd seen in the moonlight the night before. Deep in her consciousness she had concluded the mosaic had appeared to her in the same way dragons and elephants appear in the sky on a cloudy day, or the way people see patterns in seemingly random stimulus. She laughed to herself for knowing the name for it: pareidolia. A bit of trivia she would never have known except that her roomie and best friend was a psychologist. "Everybody gets it now and then," Lex had told her when she kept seeing a face on a billboard selling hamburgers. Like the dreams the jewelry had evoked, she'd let her imagination skew her perception.

Now, she played absently with the earring the stranger had held. It was a heavy gold-tone disc with a rolled edge. About halfway to the center a wire formed a circle concentric with the edge. The space between was filled in with tiny golden beads and a blood-red cabochon in the center. Tess had hand worked similar pieces in her jewelry class in college. On close examination, the earring appeared to be hand worked rather than cast.

She traced a finger over the design. *Déjà vu.* She'd seen those earrings before. *Chills.* She pushed it away. Too much touchy-feely could addle a person's brain.

She fished the matching earring from the pile and dropped them into Lexi's hand. "Yeah, you caught me. I'm keeping the snake bracelet, and I want you to have these, too."

Lexi shook her head. "No way. This stuff came from your uncle. The china and now these? I couldn't—"

"Come on. You'd pay thirty or forty bucks for a pair like that at Chico's or J. Jill, right? They'd look good on you."

Lexi weighed them in her hand. "And if they're real?"

Tess laughed. "I doubt they're real."

"But you said, Theo was a collector."

Tessa drew in a deep breath, rubbed the back of her neck, and suddenly remembered where she'd seen the design. "You're right. I used to pour through his books when I was a kid. I remember seeing pictures of ancient finds in them. They were fascinating."

"Do you still have them? The books?"

Tessa shrugged. "There are some boxes down in the garage apartment along with some old toys and games. I don't care to haul them up here tonight, but when I get home from work tomorrow, I'll check them out."

Lexi held the earrings up to her ears and wiggled them. "What do you think?"

"Definitely you." Her heart gave a little kick. These looked for all they were worth like cheap imitations, gold-filled if that. But, if they were fourteen-, or eighteen-carat gold, and if they were from the era Tess had read about in Theo's books, they would be worth a fortune.

"Well, it's four o'clock." Lexi stood and began to gather up the pieces. "Jewelry aside, I say we bag the rest of this stuff and I'll take it to Women's Shelter Thrift Shop tomorrow."

"I like that idea."

They lifted the loaded table and shuffled it into the garage. Lexi dusted her hands off on her jeans, as Tess snagged two of the crystal goblets and ceremoniously presented them to her.

"Let's keep all of these, too," she said, "To go with the china."

Lexi beamed. "I'm not going to argue with that."

They locked the garage door, climbed the stairs, and the rest of their usual Sunday night rituals began.

CHAPTER ELEVEN

Karl pressed his fingers into Valerie's back, hurrying her across the alley to his shop. Excitement prickled her spine. "Well? What did you think?"

"I don't believe you followed me over there," he groused.

She wanted to strangle him. They were that close to claiming those pieces and he just walked away. "It's a good thing I did. You were more interested in that girl's ass than the gold."

He closed his eyes a moment then huffed out a sigh. "You know better than that, Val. And, we don't know it's gold." He unlocked his back door and pushed it open. The glint in his eye said he knew damn well it was.

She stalked into his office, unzipped her knee-high boots, and pulled them off. There was a lot to love about living in the extravagance of Newport Beach. Money, fancy clothes, amazing food, luxury, technology, convenience. Sometimes she wondered why she'd even think of leaving. But the answer was clear. Here in this place, she was just another pretty face behind a mask of makeup and pretense. She had no real power or recognition. She'd married into money; the quickest way, she'd learned, to get by in this world when you had a beautiful face going for you. But what good was a pretty face, a marriage contract, and a pair of fancy boots when you had no power? She'd once been respected. Held the position she deserved. She wanted that back.

The jewelry piece she was looking for wasn't in the pile they'd seen at the yard sale; but, there could be more where that came from. She'd lived on the island years before marrying Karl's brother. She could easily have been a victim of the woman's Uncle *Klepto*.

It would explain a lot of things. And if Karl wasn't willing to push to find it, she could damn well do it herself. She stood in front of him, unbuttoned her blouse. She knew she looked great for her age, and Karl couldn't resist. Usually.

This time, however, he glanced up, sighed and went back to perusing the pages of the oversized volume opened on his lap. "I'm not in the mood for this, Val. You need to leave."

Valerie didn't like being dismissed. In fact, none of this would be happening if it wasn't for her. Men. They always put themselves at the center of their universe. How little they knew.

She clucked her tongue and sighed impatiently, then moved behind his chair and ran her hands down his chest until her dark, razor cut hair fell around his face. She pressed her cheek against his ear. "You're working much too hard, as usual, Karl," she crooned, worming her fingers inside his shirt. She needed to know what he was after.

He sighed deeply. "All right."

He captured one of her hands and threaded his fingers through hers. "I've been wanting to get inside Theo's garage for years. That Yard Sale was like a gift from the gods. And if my hunch is right, there's more where that came from. But I need some time to research. Indulge me in that, won't you?" He gave her hand a squeeze.

She'd waited a long time. She supposed she could give him a little more. "You said you thought Theo was a senile old man lost in his own fantasies. Now you think he was telling the truth?"

"Everything I'd learned backed that theory. I believed Theo's ravings about having a large cache of stolen antiquities were just that. An old man lost in his dreams."

"And now?"

"After what I saw today, I'm not so sure."

Karl continued to flip through the pages. "I know I've seen those earrings before. What were they? Etruscan? Roman? Was it this book? Or was it one of my journals?"

He was talking to himself now and she straightened, eying the book over his shoulder. "Wait. Go back."

"What?" He turned back one page.

"That!" Val pointed at one of the photos. "That pin. I think it was in the pile. In fact, I'm sure of it."

Karl stood, laid the book out on his counter, traced his finger over the photo of a simple yet elegant gold fibulae with a single black stone at its clasp. "Good eye," he crooned. "To think I've been so close all this time, then Theo dies, and his niece lays it in front of me like cookies at a bake sale."

Valerie studied the photo more closely. The timing was right, fourth century, and the style.

"This is cause for celebration." Karl reached for her hand again. "Why don't you stay after all, and we'll have some champagne."

Her smile stretched tight. It was the closest she'd come to finding the trail she had lost so many years ago. There had to be more, and if there was more, it could mean the piece she'd been looking for could be right across the alley. She needed to talk to the woman, without Karl running the show.

"Darling, I'm so excited for you, but Lars is home tonight and not feeling very well. I've got to be there for him, you understand?"

Karl smiled at her, and let his hand fall away.

"As you wish, my dear," he said, returning his attention to the book. "I've got plenty to keep me busy right now."

CHAPTER TWELVE

Tess had just finished ironing the collar of a silk blouse she planned to wear to work in the morning when there was a knock on the back door.

"I'm in a towel," Lexi called from her room downstairs.

Tess unplugged the iron. "I got it. It's Phil."

She felt the familiar tingle at the base of her spine whenever she was about to see him, and a little part of her settled. There'd been a thread of anxiety tugging at her all day, some of which she attributed to sending him home last night. *He must think I'm an absolute goof.* But here he was, doing exactly what he'd promised. Again. Score a few more points for Phillip. Not that he needed any. He was fast becoming a kind of book-boyfriend, un-put-downable, essential element in her life.

He'd joked about living on top of his parent's garage. In truth, he was there by choice. He'd been a late baby — his own words — and he stayed close helping his dad since his mother had been diagnosed with dementia.

"Come on in," Tess called on her way down the ladder, anxious to see his bright eyes. But whoever was out on the stoop knocked again.

Huh.

She had given Phil a key since he'd been working on the house, and he had no problem walking right in, even when he wasn't invited. It was kind of late for other visitors. But because they hadn't yet installed the peep hole in the door, she had to open it to see who was there. Half of her expected Phillip, of course, standing there, arms loaded with something that prevented him from opening the door. The other half felt uneasy, a low clench in her gut. It was a bit silly, but she'd learned in a self-defense class to pay attention to her gut. Right now, it said only open the door wide enough to see out.

A pair of stone gray, heavily mascaraed eyes blinked back at her. It took her a moment to recognize the woman who'd been with the man at the yard sale.

She thought, *I must look like an idiot with my mouth hanging open.* But it wasn't until Audrey's cat bounded past their visitor and into the kitchen, that she shut her mouth and cleared her throat.

"I'm sorry — Hello — you were here earlier today, right?" There was that, but there was something else familiar about her. Tess wasn't quite sure what it was.

The woman stood on the landing, her head cocked to one side as if to see around the half-opened door. She still wore the tailored jacket, rhinestone-studded jeans, and Michael Kors boots she'd been wearing that afternoon.

"Sorry I'm so late. I hope I'm not disturbing your evening." She extended a hand. "I'm Valerie Johns. Karl sent me?"

The moment Tessa touched the woman's hand she felt an overwhelming urge to pull away. Mrs. Burness's cat hissed and arched his back, echoing Tessa's reaction.

"Rags," Tessa scolded, and pushed him aside with her foot.

The woman smiled. "I can come back later if it's inconvenient."

Tessa shook her head. Gut aside, the woman wasn't the boogey man, after all. She felt silly. Again. "No, no. Please come in. I didn't mean to keep you standing out there." She opened the door wider and invited the woman into the dining room.

A moment later, Lexi joined them, a bath towel wrapped around her head, her expression as surprised as Tessa's had been the moment before.

The woman reintroduced herself, pulled a card out of her jacket pocket, and handed it to Tess. "Karl sent me over to see if anyone claimed the jewelry."

Tessa scanned the card.

TOUCHSTONE FINDINGS
Balboa Island, California
Karl Johns
(714) 555-1111
WWW.TOUCHSTONEFINDINGS.COM

"You work with Karl?"

"No. I ... he's my brother-in-law, actually."

Tessa turned over the card. Two gold-embossed letters stood out on a flat-black field:

AU

"Gold," Tessa said, passing the card to Lexi.

"You know your periodic table," Valerie Johns said.

"Well, I know gold at least; I work for Cauldron Industries."

Valerie raised a brow. "Is that right? What do you do there?"

Lexi bent the gold toned business card as if testing its authenticity.

Tess let go a low laugh. "I'm a Research Analyst. My specialty is precious metals. But I have to say, for now at least, I'm just a glorified technical writer. Are you any relation to Lars Johns?"

"My husband."

"Ah." Tess glanced at Lexi. "Lars Johns is president and CEO of Cauldron."

Now she knew why she recognized the woman. She had seen her at company events and in the social pages of the Orange County Register.

Lexi shrugged and handed the card to Tessa.

Valerie visibly recoiled when Rags jumped to the dining table, his back a ridge of ginger fur.

"Sorry." Valerie's expression was anything but. "I'm allergic to the creatures."

Lexi scooped up the cat, defensively. "He's not too fond of you either, apparently."

"I have to admit," Tess went on, hoping to dilute the tension in the room. "I noticed Karl's shop the other day when I was cutting through to the alley. He's got some interesting items displayed in the window."

Displayed wasn't exactly an accurate description. The floor between the window and an old wooden desk was littered with excavating tools; rolls of yellowed, dogeared drafting paper; and a few interesting artifacts that begged closer attention. Overall though, his space resembled someone's messy office, rather than a retail shop. But then it didn't front on Marine Avenue. Instead, it was tucked down a narrow courtyard and hadn't yet undergone a makeover to attract weekend tourists.

"I've never seen his shop open," Tess said, realizing the silence had stretched between them.

"Oh, he's not open to the public." Valerie waved Tess's comment away. It was clear she didn't want to discuss Karl's business. In fact, the way she craned her neck to see around the room, it appeared she was there on business of her own. Her gaze shifted to the living room, taking in the walls and mantle. "He's more of a collector, actually. A purveyor of antiquities, if you will. What he can't acquire, he often makes in replica. That's where I come in."

"You?"

"Well, I'm not an expert like Karl, but I am a good saleswoman. Even if your pieces aren't … authentic … I can get you a good price for them. You wouldn't happen to have more would you?"

Goosies prickled the back of Tessa's neck. She didn't like the direction this was going. Did this woman know something about the jewelry? Or was she just fishing? Whatever it was, Tess had had enough. Where was Phillip, now that she thought of it? She checked her watch.

"You know, I really don't have time for this right now. My contractor is on his way here."

"Really? Must be quite nice to get a contractor to work for you on a Sunday night."

"Well, yes. He's a friend. Actually. Helps out in his spare time." Why was she *'splaining* to this woman? This was her house. She sent Lexi a *rescue me* look.

Still holding the cat, Lexi did what Lexi was good at. She placed herself between the woman and the living room and closed in, holding Rags high on her shoulder.

Valerie retreated back to the dining room area, but instead of heading for the door, she turned her attention to the yard, stepping out the open door to the veranda.

"That is an interesting bit of work down there; I've often wondered, walking by this place, what is buried under all those tiles?"

"You've walked by here?" Lexi shot Tessa a *do-you-believe-this-chick* look.

"Oh, many times. Before I was married, I lived just a few houses down from here. I didn't know your uncle personally; I never saw anyone here at all."

"My uncle was kind of eccentric." Tess went to the back door, opened it. "If you don't mind, I do need to get ready for the contractor."

"Right. Forgive me." She gave Tess an unnerving smile that set her teeth on edge, then nodded and moved toward the door.

"Thanks for stopping by." Lexi smiled at her in a way any woman knows means the opposite.

Mrs. Johns stepped into the doorway, then hesitated again. "You know, Karl has something in his shop that may interest you. You should come by tomorrow and check it out."

The look on Lexi's face betrayed her thoughts. She was evaluating their guest. Psychopath? Serial Killer? Schizophrenic?

Tess squashed the images down. "I've got … plans tomorrow." She squeezed the doorknob. She was going to have Phillip install that peep hole tonight. And a chain lock. Maybe a whole stack of them.

"That's a pity." Valerie drew out the words. "Maybe later in the week?" Her lips curled into a tight smile, but the look in her eye was chilling. It sent a jolt somewhere deep in Tessa's brain. She needed the woman out of here. Now. But the woman held her ground. "We could have lunch."

Tess rolled her shoulders. Dammit. It appeared the only way to get rid of her was to agree. "I suppose I could come by on my lunch hour, tomorrow." Her shoulders tightened. *Shit, shit, shit.* "Is noon okay?"

"Right. I'll meet you at the Bistro for lunch and then we'll go over to the shop from there." She started down the back stairs. "Oh, and, bring those earrings with you, the big gaudy ones?"

Not on your life.

"Thank you for coming." Tessa leaned against the door until she no longer heard the woman's footsteps in the alley.

"Good work, Tess," Lexi crooned. "You not only caved in, but now you have a lunch date with her."

Tessa huffed out sigh. "I know. What was I supposed to do?"

"Gee, let me see?" Lexi said, scratching her chin. "Say no?"

Tess deflated. "She's the wife of my company's CEO."

"Yes. But this is your private residence. She has no right coming here and imposing herself into your life."

"Yeah. But we did advertise the yard sale."

"True enough."

They both turned to the door when footsteps pounded up the back stairs. Phillip burst through, without knocking. Before she could get her arms around him, he stomped past her to the living room. "Well, hello to you, too."

He turned on her, an uncharacteristic scowl on his face. "What the hell was Valerie Johns doing here?"

"I — What?" She followed him to the living room. "We met her at the Klepto Sale. She came to give me Karl's card. He — "

"Karl Johns? Oh my god." Phillip stomped back past her and into the kitchen, opened the refrigerator and took out a beer. "That guy is a total creep. And that woman is a scheming, manipulative bitch."

A sick feeling hit the back of Tessa's throat. She hadn't seen Phillip all day and now he burst in here yelling at her. Phillip, the easy-going guy who up until this moment, she was beginning to feel comfortable with.

She'd had a relationship with a hot-headed, jealous man, and she had the scars to prove it. No way would she tolerate another. After the incident with Valerie, she was in no mood to deal with a male temper tantrum. Neither did she want to let some asshole from her past trigger her into a tantrum of her own.

"So, you know her pretty well, I take it?"

He glared at her. The words were out of her mouth before she could stop them. Now she wished she could take them back.

She lifted her eyes to Lexi who'd been standing in the kitchen watching the exchange. She scratched her head. "I'll just take Rags into my room," she said, ducking around the corner.

Phil watched her go, then twisted the cap off the beer and let out a sigh. "She's a little old for my tastes, and she's the wife of our company's CEO, so there's that."

Great. Tess blew out a deep breath, then sank into a chair at the dining room table. "Look. I'm sorry. It's been a bad evening."

Phil leaned against the kitchen counter. "How on earth did you get mixed up with those two?"

Tess leaned her head back and moaned at the ceiling. "He showed up at the yard sale with her on his arm. He was interested in that jewelry." She gestured to the stuff on the table. "He sort of invited himself back to see if any of it was left. Then she showed up instead. I'm really glad you got here when you did. I was having trouble getting rid of her."

Philip tipped the long neck to his lips and drank.

"Not surprised." His voice was returning to normal, easy going Phil. "Karl's father's a criminal."

"A criminal. What makes you say that? He founded Cauldron Industries, didn't he?"

"Trust me," Phil said, then lifted his arm and invited her into his embrace.

She pressed into him, letting the lean warmth of him melt into her stressed-out soul. "She wants me to bring some of that jewelry to his shop tomorrow. I suppose he thinks they might be real."

Phillip stiffened against her. "I don't trust either one of them. I don't want you going there."

"What makes you think he's a bad guy? I'm not arguing, mind you. He seemed kind of creepy to us, too. I just want to know why *you* think so."

Phillip was rubbing her back now; slowly, soothingly, as if doing so calmed his nerves as well. "I've worked at Cauldron for a few years. I've heard some stories that'd curl your hair."

Lexi returned to the dining room, holding up her phone. "I tend to agree with Phillip. Those two are an interesting pair."

"What? You Googled them?"

"Don't have to. I don't actually know *that* much," she went on, " … and I can't tell you who or what — *so don't ask* — but one of my clients has mentioned him and it wasn't flattering. He seemed overly interested in her jewelry as well. That's why I went to my room, to listen to the recording. I thought I'd heard the name, but I wasn't sure."

"Well?" Tess fought for control. This conversation was heading into iffy territory.

Lexi nodded. "It was him."

"That's it?"

"You know I can't divulge anything I hear in my practice."

"But this is *me,* Lex; not the Code of Conduct police.*"*

"It was bad, Tessa, *muy malo,* poo poo, *bad mojo,* take my word for it."

"But…"

Lexi held up her hand. "I told you not to ask."

Phillip threw up his arms. "That settles it. I don't want you meeting either one of them."

"I'm going to go to lunch, in public, right down the street, then his shop afterward, for, maybe, fifteen minutes. It's practically right behind my own garage for heaven's sake."

Tess went to the kitchen and opened the refrigerator, then shamelessly swigged from the squeeze bottle of Hershey's Special Dark chocolate syrup. She turned, confronted with the astonished faces of her friends. "What?"

Lexi rolled her eyes. "What yourself?"

"What if the jewelry is ancient? Wouldn't that be fun? Wouldn't it be worth it to find out from an expert? I mean, the guy is an expert, right?" She scooped up his card and pointed it at Phillip. She already believed the serpent bracelet had special qualities, but she wasn't ready to share that bit of information with them yet. With anyone.

Lex and Phillip held their ground, in cahoots. She couldn't believe they were being so childish about this whole thing.

Lex grabbed the chocolate syrup out of her hand and put it back in the fridge door, clucking her tongue at Tess. "You could go to anybody, call the university, look it up on the Net."

Tessa picked up the gaudy earrings, jingled them in her hand. "He's right here on the island; why go anywhere else?"

Phillip finished his beer in three long glugs and reached in the fridge for another. He twisted off the cap. A faint wisp of cold escaped from the bottle as he pointed it at her.

"Look, Tess. I know I have no right to tell you what to do." His features softened into the Phil she knew. "You're a big girl and I know you can take care of yourself." He was gaining points again. "But don't say I didn't warn you."

"Why don't you come with me? Then I don't have to spend lunch alone with them."

He studied her for a long moment. "No. I think it would be best if you went alone. He may have sent his messenger girl, but Karl wants something. I doubt he'll show his cards if I'm there. He'll just postpone revealing himself and keep you on the hook."

His words made her shiver. He was probably right. "You make him sound so sinister."

Phil lifted a shoulder, his grey-blue eyes telling her how much he wanted her to listen. "People don't change, Tess. At least, that's been my experience." He swigged from his beer again. "How about I hang out here for lunch, and if you're not back across the alley by, say, one-thirty, I stroll on over to his shop."

She shifted her gaze between the two of them. "I feel like some kind of conspirator."

Lexi shrugged. "Better than feeling like a fool."

"I'll drink to that." Phillip tipped his bottle to her.

Tess let out a relieved sigh. She leaned through the kitchen archway, gave him her big sad eyes. "I missed you last night."

He shook his head, then circled his arm around her shoulder. "I missed you, too." He held her close. "Sorry I yelled, first thing." He kissed the top of her head. "But when I saw that woman come down the stairs, it just set me off. That whole family is really bad news."

She pulled back and gave him a questioning look.

"Really," he went on, eyes convincingly solemn. "Their father may have started a legit business here in the OC, but the story goes the grandfather spent time in prison in France, and his mother committed suicide. And his wife? She's like, from another world. Showed up out of nowhere. Then, they have this big family crypt up at Forest Lawn in LA, and they all go trailing up there like a ritual every month."

"Now that is creepy," Lexi said, "But it squares with what my client said.

"Well I've had enough of Karl Johns and his family for today." Tess let her hands skim down Phillip's arms, hooked his fingers with hers and led him to the ladder.

"You sure you want me up here before we're married," he teased, tickling the inside of her thigh. Lately, he'd managed to squeeze a reference to marriage into every conversation.

"Shut up," she countered.

"Is that a proposal?"

Tessa heard Lexi's laughter downstairs.

CHAPTER THIRTEEN

Tessa let Phillip nuzzle her neck and ear like a teenager until they heard Lexi leave for her shift at the suicide hotline. She would be back at midnight, but that left them the evening alone. After hot, stress-relieving make-up sex, Tessa talked Phillip into walking to the Mexican restaurant on the island, and over taco plates and hibiscus tea she talked him into hauling Theo's books up to her room before he left. They said their goodnights, agreeing to connect at least by phone the next day, before her meeting with Karl.

Once he was safely on his way, she poured herself a glass of red wine, ear-budded up into her iTunes, and cleaned all the jewelry again using mild soap and water and a soft toothbrush. Once the pieces were cleaned and polished dry, there was little doubt in her mind what she had before her was anything but high-quality gold studded with semi-precious stones. She held a fibulae to the light, feeling the heavy metal warm to her touch. She imagined tiny nanoparticles of gold migrating into her skin cells, feeding off her own heat on an elemental level. She closed her hands around two of the earrings and the same sensation permeated her skin. Of all the metals on earth, gold had a unique capability to captivate the human soul.

People liked to say diamonds were forever, but to her mind, diamonds would be nothing if not surrounded by gold. Whether melted with quartz and shot through cracks in the earth; washed from a canyon in an ancient tertiary streambed, or buried at the bottom of the ocean for two thousand years; you could dig it up, clean it off, and you still had gold, virtually unchanged from its creation in the universe. You could make diamonds in the laboratory and most people couldn't tell the difference between the counterfeits and the real thing; but as far as she knew all the gold on planet Earth was here when it was formed, and that's all there ever would be.

She squeezed her eyes shut against the mind-tilting concept, took a sip of wine, and got back to reality, kicking her linear brain into action.

There were ten pieces in all: three pair of earrings, two fibulae, two heavy gold rings, a simple, gold disk brooch, a pendant, and the snake bracelet, of course. She would photograph each piece and pull it into a reference document later, but for now she wanted — needed -- to feel the pieces in her hands. She masking-taped a piece of white shelf paper to the surface of the dining room table, then plotted a grid of squares, two rows of five, in orange marking pen. Next, she placed each piece in its own square, drawing a cartoon image of the snake bracelet on the last. She planned to identify each as she found it with the referenced source, page, and paragraph. The odds of finding the exact pieces in Theo's books were slim, that didn't blunt her excitement. She had the Internet and she could contact some of Theo's connections with museums in Europe as a last resort.

Using a magnifying glass, she studied each piece closely. While each was unique in and of itself, the method and designs were similar, and Tess surmised they were made at about the same era, most likely by the same hand. Along with a stylized H like a modern hashtag, each piece had a distinct delta mark somewhere on its interior surface.

She got a new set of chills each time she picked one up and inspected it. Did the snake have the mark? She went upstairs and fished it out of her drawer. She followed the double coil from the serpent's head to its tail and found no specific marks at all. Hum. She slipped the bracelet on her arm and went back down to her work.

She poured over the reference books, most of which cataloged ancient digs over the centuries. Various articles described well-known finds, their locations, the time periods thought to be relevant, detailed drawings of the pieces *in situ*, the entity responsible for the excavation, and the current location of the pieces. Some were in private collections, but most were housed in various museums across Europe and Asia.

While she'd found some interesting collections, some of which featured designs and methods represented by her pieces, there were none she could say exactly matched the group as a whole or any of the individual pieces. Still, she could barely contain her excitement. Whether they were true ancient works of art, or modern replicas, they were definitely magnificent and in her educated opinion, at least eighteen carat gold; though by the color, probably finer.

From what she could glean from all she'd seen, these pieces could comfortably fit in a time period from early Etruscan to the mid Roman empire, as much of the methods remained unchanged throughout those centuries.

With her laptop at one hand and Theo's books at the other, she hardly noticed the hours passing. The Internet sucked her down several fascinating rabbit holes, but none of the sites produced a direct hit, which sent her back to Theo's room down in the garage.

There had to be more.

What would be the point of sealing the pieces in the wall, unless there was something special about them? Something Theo wanted to protect.

Or hide.

She flipped on the lights in the little L-shaped room and proceeded to open every box in the place. She didn't know exactly what she was looking for, but her memory prodded her on. She had seen those earrings before, she was sure of it.

An hour later, she sat amid a mess of wadded up newspapers and foam peanuts, having gone through every container in the room, including a couple of plastic buckets and an old hat box. She had found enough odds and ends to start her own thrift store and a few gems, like the toy Magic 8-Ball Theo had given her as a child, and an antique stereopticon featuring pictures of Theda Bara's Cleopatra, which she'd learned had been filmed only a few miles up the coast.

Her eyes were drying out with fatigue when she noticed the corner of a box sticking out from under a twin bed shoved against the wall. She got down on her hands and knees and dragged it out.

The box was covered with a thick layer of dust. Not a cardboard box like the others. This one was leather; a suitcase, actually, with riveted corners and a notched belt around its middle; the kind of thing people bought at garage sales in hopes of finding something of historical significance. She remembered a box like this from one of her visits with Uncle Theo. She balanced it on her lap, pulled back the buckle, released the clasp, and opened the lid.

What she saw took her breath away.

Inside were two cloth-bound, three-ring binders of the type high-schoolers carried in the sixties. She lifted one out and opened it.

The binder was full of articles, each carefully excised from a magazine, and slipped into a plastic sleeve. On top, was the cover of *Aurum Journal - World Gold Council Magazine - International Review for Manufacturers, Designers and Retailers of Gold Jewelry.*

Oh my god, here were the pictures she remembered. She leafed through the pages, her fingers tingling with excitement.

She scooped the binders into her arms, carried them up the back stairs, and spread them out on the dining room table.

Ten minutes later she found what she was looking for.

✤

"Wow, what are you doin' up?" Lexi said when she arrived home. "You look like you just had three rounds of incredible sex."

Indeed, Tess's ears were burning with heat. She'd been holding the 8-Ball for the last fifteen minutes, alternately checking the clock and watching random answers to unasked questions, materialize on the bottom. The moment she heard Lexi's footsteps on the stairs, she straightened and stretched the stiffness out of her back.

"You are not going to believe this."

Lex dropped her backpack and purse on the kitchen counter. "Signs point to a tall, dark stranger who is going to sweep me off my feet and take me to Fiji?"

She poured herself a glass of milk, then looped a generous string of chocolate syrup over the top and stirred it in.

Tessa set the 8-ball on the table. "No, this." Tess gestured to the grid on the table.

Lexi's forehead crinkled. "What is it?"

Tess handed her a plastic sleeve with the article inside. "You were right about Uncle Theo."

Lexi's eyes skimmed the page. She read out loud. "... part of a collection of jewelry circa 325 CE made during the reign of —" she lifted her eyes to Tess. "Emperor Constantine?"

"The first." Tess rolled her hand to keep Lexi reading.

"Reported to have been recovered from a shipwreck in the Bosporus and later stolen from —" she broke off, her eyes flashing to Tess's. "Stolen."

Tess swiped the article out of her hands. "They were in a shipment of ancient jewelry being transferred across Europe by train, bound eventually to the British Museum after World War II. There

110

was a robbery, at least two of the thieves were caught. But not all the items were recovered." Tess swirled her hands over the table. "These ten pieces among them as a group."

She turned over the page and handed it back to Lexi with a wide grin.

Lexi stared at it, then at the pieces laid out the table. "Holy shit."

"Yeah. And, they all have the same makers mark."

"Maker's mark?"

"The personal stamp of the person who made the jewelry."

"You mean like, 'Please Return to Tiffany & Co.'?"

Tess grinned. "Yeah. Like Tiffany & Co. But in this case, it's much simpler."

Tess showed Lexi the tiny delta on the inside of one of the rings. "Some of them have an H, but they all have this delta." Except the snake, she thought, then quickly dismissed it as an oversight.

Lexi examined each piece and grinned when she found the mark. "Wow. They even have the same little nick."

"Good eye for an amateur." Indeed, the instrument that made the delta mark was like a damaged typewriter key that gave itself away with each impression. "The piece they used to make the mark, probably brass, had a little nick near the top right side of the delta."

Lex placed the pieces she'd removed back on Tess's grid. "But, if they caught the thieves, then how did Theo—"

"I know, right? And according to the article, there's more out there somewhere."

Lexi folded her arms over her chest. "So, we've got stolen jewelry."

Tess drew in a deep breath and exhaled. "Technically."

"What do you mean *technically*? We have it. We know what it is. We have to call the authorities and hand it over."

"Of course, we do. Eventually."

Lexi pointed an accusing finger at Tess. "That's not like you, Tessa Madigan. You're the girl who let shop-lifted ice cream bars melt up the sleeve of her sweater rather than eat them when we were kids."

"I know." Tess paced the room, thinking about the snake and her erotic dream. "But right now, nobody knows we have it, so—"

"Karl Johns knows we have it. And that *sister*-in-law." Lex said 'sister-in-law' as if she didn't believe it for a minute.

Tess slumped into her chair, bunching the front of her hair in her fist. "He must have known the moment he saw it."

"Yeah. And he didn't share that little piece of information with us, did he?"

"Maybe that's what they were planning to tell me tomorrow."

"Maybe. Or maybe he was going to report you to some authority."

"He said he was a collector. More likely he was going to give me a lowball offer to take them off my hands."

Tess went back to the article. "Ten items were never recovered." She quickly matched the photos on the page with the pieces on her grid — the earrings, the fibulae, the rings, a brooch. "We're missing this one," she said pointing out a colorful piece in the article. "It looks like cloisonné."

Lexi read the description: "Gold cells inlaid in a leaf pattern in red, white, green and blue glass and enamel. Four garnets, one at each termination of a stylized cross. It is said to have been made for Empress Helena as a gift from her son, Constantine I."

Tess turned over the sheet and read to herself a moment before she continued. "It says Helena spent years traveling the empire, tearing down pagan temples. She was supposed to have discovered pieces of the *true cross* at this Temple of Venus and later, her son had the Church of the Holy Sepulcher built over it."

Lexi rolled her eyes.

"Don't laugh," Tess went on. "Whether you believe it or not, this piece," she tapped the photo of the brooch in the clipping, "is probably the most valuable of them all because of the provenance, first because of the Helena connection, and second, because it was recovered from a shipwreck and then stolen. Interesting that it's the one missing."

Lex dropped heavily into a chair at the table. "Except that we've already got ten pieces." She eyed the little drawing of the snake.

Tessa's hand went to the bracelet which she'd absently pushed up her arm. She re-read the article, but she already knew what she'd see. "It's not reported in the theft?"

"Seems odd. An oversight, maybe?"

Tessa frowned. "I don't think so. These articles are scholarly and peer reviewed. Those academic types don't let you get away with shabby research." And, the snake didn't have the delta mark.

"Which begs the question…" Lexi prompted.

"Where did it come from?" Tess shrugged. "Just another piece of Theo's junk, I guess." But deep in her heart of hearts, she knew it wasn't true. Still, she was all too happy to scratch it from the list of items they would have to report to the authorities.

She grabbed her beloved Pink Pearl eraser from a box of pencils and colored pens, erased the snake drawing, and filled in a rough likeness of the cloisonné brooch.

Her hand went to the bracelet, its temperature matching her own. For a moment the light in the room dimmed and she had the sensation of the floor falling from under her feet like an old spinning carnival ride. She closed her eyes.

"Tess? Are you all right?"

Tessa drew in cool air through her nose, opened her eyes, and clasped her hands in front of her on the table. The room settled and she saw her friend's expression of concern.

"Yeah. I'm, just—" She dropped her forehead in her hand a moment. "I need to get some sleep. Let's put this stuff away and talk about it more tomorrow."

She scraped the jewelry off the table into the beaded bag, rolled up the shelf paper grid, then was stopped by Lexi's pensive expression. "You think we should call the authorities."

Lex lifted a shoulder and pursed her lips a moment. Then she picked up the 8-Ball, shook it, and turned it over.

"Well?" Tessa grinned and let go a little laugh.

"Reply hazy, try again later."

"Okay. Good answer. We'll talk in the morning." She gathered up her laptop and hobbled up the ladder to bed.

❧

"Would you like a refill?" The server's voice brought Tessa back from visions of Ancient Rome, steam-filled grottos, and lush hanging ferns. She slid the snake bracelet from her bicep to her wrist and glanced at her watch. Karl and his sister-in-law were a no show. Fine. After being up nearly all night, she was too tired to deal with them anyway.

The moment she'd slipped off the bracelet the night before, the sense of falling subsided, but she'd still spent the night thrashing in fitful sleep, waking several times with the image of the brooch tattooed to the inside of her eyelids. It seemed like she'd had only a moment of sleep before her alarm went off and she had to leave for work.

She'd spent the morning organizing her desk and beyond that, she'd accomplished nothing.

"No, thank you," she told the server, trying to break out of a fog. "Could you just bring me a French dip to go? It looks like my lunch appointment couldn't make it."

"Sure. No problem." The server picked up her glass and headed for the kitchen.

A wave of relief rolled through her, then left her unsettled. A part of her wanted to meet Karl and see what was so important he wanted to show her. Maybe it would help her get rid of the anxious feeling she'd had since they found the jewelry. Another part wanted to skip going back to work, crawl back into bed, and pull the covers over her head.

The server delivered her sandwich and she was about to pay at the counter when she sensed a presence at her back.

"Sorry I'm late," Karl said. The heat of his breath at her ear invaded her space. He scraped the bill away from the counter. "How about we talk over dessert. My treat."

CHAPTER FOURTEEN

Disappointment lodged in Tessa's stomach, leaving no appetite for dessert. Karl Johns. By himself. "I thought your sister-in-law was coming."

He leveled his gaze at her a moment before he put on a reserved smile. "Something came up."

Damn. She should have called Phillip the moment they were a no show. They'd agreed to meet when the lunch was over, but that was before something came up for Val Johns.

Karl gestured to a booth at the back of the restaurant. "Let's go where we can have a little more privacy."

Before Tess could object, the server wheeled up the dessert cart, innocently blocking any last-minute exit. "I'll follow you," she said cheerfully.

Tessa sighed. *Great. Thanks for the help.*

The moment they were settled, Tessa lifted a plate of Tiramisu from the tray. Best to get this over with as quickly as possible. She put on a polite smile. "And a coffee, please. Black."

Karl ignored the dessert cart. Instead, his eyes were riveted to the snake bracelet at Tessa's wrist. "That's an interesting piece."

Tessa's smile wavered. "A gift from my mother," she lied, giving it a twist.

Karl's eyes went wide. "Is that right?" He reached toward it; Tessa folded her hands in her lap, feeling violated. If the serpent really had some

117

magical power to whisk her away, now would be a good time for it to kick in.

"Well," he said, his expression pinched. "Your mother has an eye for antiquities like her brother."

"Hardly." Tessa licked her lips and pulled her sweater sleeve down to cover the snake. "Thrift store would be more her style."

"Come on." He gave her a cagey look. She guessed he didn't believe her. "Aren't you a little bit curious?"

Tessa straightened in her seat. "What I am is busy, Mr. Johns. If you have some information for me, I'd appreciate hearing it now. I need to get back to my office."

"All right." He rested his elbows on the table and threaded his fingers. "That pile of junk as you call it could be a pile of authentic artifacts worth – maybe," he rolled his hand as if calculating, "a million dollars, or more."

The number jarred her gut. "Worth a million dollars? To whom?" In the light of day, Karl appeared to be just another classic nerd, not the monster Phillip had made him out to be. "If the jewelry is authentic, then we'd need to see that it gets into a museum where it belongs."

The glimmer in his eye flared to a disturbing glare. "Museum, ha!" He ran his fingers through his hair, leaving a shock out of place over his forehead. "They have all the precious pieces locked up. You can't even touch them, feel them next to your skin--" Tiny beads of sweat had formed above his eyebrows. His cheeks turned ruddy.

Tessa's senses went back on alert. Maybe Phillip was right after all. She forked a tiny corner of the tiramisu into her mouth and slipped her hand in her purse with the other. She took out her cell phone and checked the time. "Oh. My goodness. I really do have to--"

"Wait," he said, reaching for her hand. His palms were sweaty and soft. She drew away.

"I'm sorry. It's just that, when it comes to antiquities, I — I get carried away." He blotted his lip on his napkin. "I'd really like to get a closer look at that collection, is all. Take that bracelet you're wearing, for example. I can use the same methods they used in the fourth century and be accurate as to its gold content within two percent."

Tessa twisted the bracelet on her wrist. What made him think the jewelry was part of some collection? A shiver tingled across her shoulders. "Like I said. This bracelet isn't part of any collection. I'm sure it's a costume piece."

He raised his brows. "Collection or not, it looks authentic. Could be Etruscan, even as old as Egyptian."

Tessa shook her head. She fingered her phone. "No. I don't think—"

"Five minutes in my shop. You'll have your answer." He slipped a twenty from his wallet and dropped it on the table.

Tessa blew out a breath. There were a half dozen jewelers in Corona Del Mar alone who could quickly test the bracelet. But Karl's shop was right down the street. Five minutes. As unsettling as it might be, it was the quickest way to verify the purity of the snake; plus, per their previous agreement, she had Phillip for back up.

"Okay. Sure." She slid her unfinished Tiramisu away, picked up her purse, and stood. "Let's go."

❧

Tessa stood at the counter of the tiny shop. There was barely enough room for a workbench, let alone a customer. Karl's tools were laid out as if he had planned this whole scenario in advance. *Fool.* Of course, he had.

"If you would give me the bracelet, I'll get started."

She hesitated a moment. What if it didn't come back to her? What if it slithered onto his wrist and became part of *him*? Her lips went cold at the thought. She clenched her hand around the bracelet. If it proved to be fine gold, a token of the ancient past, then maybe everything else could be real, too.

She dropped her hands and took a step back. Maybe it was better not to know.

"Miss Madigan?"

His voice jarred her. Of course, she wanted to know. It was a stupid piece of junk. The test would prove it, and then she could sleep at night. She cleared her throat, straightened her shoulders, and removed the bangle and held it in her palm. Her arm felt suddenly naked, exposed. But after a heartbeat, she let go a nervous laugh. "Okay. Let's get this over with."

He reached under the counter and brought out a black velvet-covered board like she'd seen in the local jewelry shops. He unfolded it and placed it atop the glass. "Just put it right there."

Tessa did as he suggested, and watched barely breathing as he laid a smooth, black stone next to the gold. He ran his fingers affectionately over its surface with a ritualistic flourish, then removed a collection of rods from the case below. He arranged them on the velvet, meticulously picked through the assortment, and finally held one up to the light.

"If my suspicions are correct, this one will do quite nicely." He rubbed the surface of the stone with the end of the rod, leaving a thick trace of gold color. "There. See that? That's about the closest thing to pure gold artists use these days."

He lifted the velvet board and carried it to the tiny sink at the back of the shop, took down a small apothecary jar from a shelf above the sink, and opened it.

"Come on, back here, you've got to see this." Cool beach guy had disappeared, replaced by the mad scientist hunching over the sink. Tessa hesitated, a prickling sense of dread flooded her veins. She was riveted to the spot. It was as though she straddled two worlds, one foot on Marine Avenue, Balboa Island; the other in a villa near Chalcedon.

Don't be ridiculous. You are firmly in the here and now.

She set her shoulders, knowing it was true. All she had to do was step outside and there would be automobiles, not oxcarts; there would be cheery shop windows, not stalls in the dirt; stereos would be blasting music from different stations, not hawkers yelling in unfamiliar dialects; and frozen bananas would be on sale right next door. *Are you going to stand here like a fool? Or get over there where you can get a better look?*

Curiosity won. She pulled in a sip of breath and moved to stand where she could see over Karl's shoulder.

He rubbed a mark on the stone using the tail end of her bracelet. Her stomach flip-flopped. She had seen this done before. *And now he's going to pour something over--*

"And now we pour this solution over the two tracings and see what we've got," he said as he did so. Tessa dared not move. Images floated through her consciousness. Through Kindra's eyes she had watched Haldor perform this process dozens of times, his eyes a twinkle with the same light that shone in Karl's this very moment. Her stomach clenched into a tight knot.

There was a movement at the corner of her eye. She glanced over her shoulder to the windows. Had she seen Phil out there?

"My God," Karl whispered, drawing her attention immediately back to the sink. "I didn't dare believe it was true until I did the test, but there it is and no room for doubt." Wiping his forehead in the crook of his arm, he left the touchstone in the sink and backed away.

Tessa searched his face for further explanation, but he only pointed at the sink, his eyes gleaming.

She stepped forward, retrieved the stone. The scratch Karl had made with the touch needle had diminished noticeably, but the scratch next to it, the one made by her bracelet, shone just as brightly as it had before he poured the solution over it. She looked back at Karl, still holding the stone in her hand.

"Does that mean what I think it does?"

"It means," he said, holding the bracelet up in the light, "that if there's any alloy in this thing at all it's going to take some pretty sophisticated equipment to detect it."

So much for the blisters on her arm being caused by an allergy to nickel alloy.

"So, it's fine gold?"

He nodded, the light in his eyes glittering. "I'm assuming, if this bracelet is solid gold, that the rest of the pieces you found are as well. You could leave it with me for further testing, if you like. I'll give you a receipt, of course."

That's not going to happen. She snapped the bracelet out of his hand, shoved it into her purse, and headed for the door.

He gawked at her with a startled expression. "What? You don't trust me?"

"No, I — I mean. No thank you. I'm out of time. I'll have to get back to you."

CHAPTER FIFTEEN

Phillip was indeed waiting in the alley when she burst out of Karl's shop. He matched his stride to hers and wrapped his arm across her shoulders. "Told you the guy was a creep."

"At a minimum." Tess let go a relieved sigh as she leaned into him. "I need a frozen banana."

"Now?"

"Yes. Right now."

Tessa savored the very here-and-now crunch of chocolate shell and peanuts, then creamy frozen banana as she filled him in on what she'd discovered the night before and the results of the ancient test.

"If Karl learned the same thing — and it was relatively easy to do — you uncovered something extremely valuable in the walls of my house and possibly exposed a violation of international law. You think Karl's the type to go to the authorities or try to get the pieces for himself?"

"I'd put my money on the latter. Seems like if he were going to the authorities, he'd have done it already. Instead, he's poking around, trying to pressure you to show him more."

She exhaled her frustration. "Right. You're probably right."

"So, back to work, or..." Phillip thumbed a piece of melted chocolate off the corner of her mouth. The bright look in his eye as he licked it off his finger said he was hoping for the *or*.

She gave his arm a friendly slug as they crossed the alley to her back steps. "The first thing I'm going to do is put that gold in my safe deposit box."

"Now?" His eyes glinted with that familiar spark that sent a sizzle straight through her.

"Um, maybe a little later. I'm definitely not going back to work. No way would I get anything done. The adrenaline rush I got in Karl's shop is wearing off." She circled her arms around his neck, pulled him close. "So, you can stay. I mean, will you? For a little while, at least?"

Phillip followed her up the back stairs. "For a while. I promised my dad I'd give him a little respite and stay with mom for a couple of nights. He's heading up to Bass Lake with his brothers for some fishing this weekend."

Tessa's heart sank a little. She'd miss him in her bed. But she loved that he helped his folks out as much as he did. His mom's Alzheimer's Disease had slipped to a new plateau and she was increasingly challenging to manage. Phillip was a good man and a good son. She wouldn't want him any other way.

With the jewelry nestled in her safe deposit box at the bank, Lexi working the late shift at the Women's Center, and Phillip taking care of his mother, Tessa let herself relax into the late evening alone. She stoked a small fire in the refurbished fireplace, feeling the walls of her home close comfortably around her. She thought of Phillip's mother and father, William and Greta Koenig, their forty-year commitment to one another, something her parents had never managed. She had sworn to herself she would never marry until she knew it would last.

She'd thought she'd made the right decision once. Her college boyfriend — handsome, accomplished, heading into law practice with his father — hadn't hesitated to promise marriage when they'd accidently conceived. Her future looked bright. But when she'd miscarried weeks before the wedding, handsome law boy skipped out and she learned a lesson. The only person you can depend on is yourself.

It was a lonely place to be. Truth be told, she had never felt so free and loved than when she was with Phillip Koenig. It would be easy to let herself slip fully under his spell. He certainly thought she was the one for him. She wanted — needed — to believe it was true. But what had he to compare marriage to? William and Greta. Mr. and Mrs. Perfect.

Tessa wasn't perfect. Not by a long shot. She wasn't raised by William and Greta. If it wasn't for Theo, she'd have had no family at all. What did she know of how to make a marriage work? And after waking up this morning barely able to function, haunted, afraid, she doubted she ever would.

Long after her good night phone call with Phillip, she lay awake on her bed, elbows propped on the windowsill, staring across the bay where Phillip kept watch over his mother until the fog crept in and erased the hillside from view. Thoughts of Kindra invaded her soul, her passion like a tsunami rushing the shore, seeping into every crevice of her being, lifting her up, sweeping her along the corridors of time, then taking her down, until she could no longer raise her head above the flood.

CHAPTER SIXTEEN
Village outside Chalcedon, circa 326 CE

Kindra arrived at the villa to find no light at the windows, no movement in the atrium. Everything was as she'd left it. Thank the gods Haldor had not returned early and discovered her missing. She hurried to the courtyard and let herself into the shop where she wasted no time transforming herself from *Kindra the courtesan* to *Kindra the goldsmith.*

She removed the snake bracelet from her arm and reached for the brooch at her shoulder, finding nothing. Alarm shot through her. The brooch! She ripped off her palla and shook it out. By the gods, what had she done? Panic raced through her veins. Where to start? Had she left it in the man's chamber? Had it been lost on the way back? She had no way of knowing. Haldor would kill her if he returned and found it missing. She had to go back.

She ran to her chamber, folded her green palla on her bed and wrapped herself in the woolen one that would conceal her head.

No sooner had she finished than she heard a commotion near the front entrance to the villa.

Curses. Threats. Loud voices, one of them unmistakably Haldor's.

She had made it back in time, but just barely. She braced a hand against her doorway and listened.

"I told you not to bring that here." Haldor shouted, his words slurred. He was drunk.

129

"You are out of time, old man. My family has grown hungry while you gambled away our profit. I'll have my share now."

"You'll get nothing if the palace guards followed you here. We'll both end up in the stocks."

"No one followed me."

"How can you be sure?"

There was a guttural snarl then a thud, as if a heavy weight had been dropped inside the entry. "My share now, or I'll go to the Prefect myself." The order echoed menacingly through the colonnade.

"If the guards show up at my door, I'll see to it your family never eats again," Haldor roared. Then the heavy door slammed, shaking the walls.

Kindra covered her mouth, listening while blood pounded in her ears. A drunken, exhausted Haldor would drag himself to his chamber and remain there until the sun was high in the sky. Add anger to the mix and Haldor, no matter how exhausted from his journey, could ride it through the night, eventually taking it out on her. And if he found the brooch missing…

She listened until all sounds in the front of the villa faded, then let out a purging breath. Whatever troubles Haldor had brought upon himself this night, he had taken them to his bed.

Despite the fact that he would likely sleep through, she couldn't take the chance of leaving now.

It wasn't until she'd undressed again and lay under the covers on her bed that she allowed herself to think about what she had done at the bath. What on earth had possessed her to do such a thing?

Never once in her life had she lusted after a boy or a man. It was like some hidden force deep inside her rose to the surface and possessed her soul. She pulled her green palla to her, inhaling the lingering scent of him.

In the beginning, all she wanted was the coin and the freedom it promised, but the moment she looked deep into his eyes, all she wanted was the man, and the promise of something she couldn't name. That longing eclipsed her poverty, her hatred of Haldor, her urgent need to flee.

She ran her hands over her stomach and down to her thighs, amazed at the way her body responded, even now. It was as though she could feel his presence, his heat, his sex. Never had she felt so strong a pull to another person in her life. If he were here right now, she would have tried to climb inside his skin.

A pity she didn't know his name. He wore the thick neck ring of the emperor, which meant he was from the palace. He would be leaving soon, if he wasn't gone already. Her heart sank at the thought she might have left the brooch in his chamber. How had she been so careless?

Her only respite from impending doom was to let herself dream about the way he felt in her arms, until Alba's words returned to her in admonition: *You are there for the coin, not to fall in love.* Was that the truth? Or had Kindra discovered something Alba never had? Her mind and body were tormented with doubts and fear until at last, exhaustion gave way to sleep.

The sun had barely touched the hills in the distance outside the windows when she heard sounds stirring in the hallway outside the workshop, and Haldor's labored breathing. It was early for him, especially after what she'd heard the night before. He was dragging something heavy, cursing as he went.

"Woman! Get yourself out of bed." His voice sounded ragged and dry.

She rose and swept the curtain aside at her door to see him glaring at her, his robe unfastened, revealing his gray-haired chest and stained loin cloth. The smell of rancid alcohol sweat nearly gagged her.

Fear and disgust stabbed cold through her heart. In all the time she'd labored under his orders, he'd been a ruthless taskmaster, working her long hours until her fingers were raw; but he'd never forced himself on her. She doubted in his diminished condition that he could.

No.

Something else was at him.

Something that had him pacing the room like a trapped animal. Something she feared could be worse than mere carnal advances. And then she came fully awake and remembered. The brooch. Had he discovered it missing?

She wrapped her palla around her, taking the warrior stance. It had worked before when she needed to stand her ground with him. "What is it old man?"

He blanched at her boldness. She no longer cared. Since she'd taken her future into her own hands, she'd stopped thinking of him as her master. There was nothing he could do about it. If she stopped making his jewelry, he would have no income. If he took her before the prefect for not performing her duty, her very existence would expose him as a fraud.

"Put on your sandals and go to the door." He wheezed out a cough. The effort of dragging the bundle into her shop had obviously winded him. What on earth was in it that could be so heavy?

"The door?" It was Haldor's habit to keep her out of sight. So, this wasn't about the brooch? What was going on?

"Two men are coming to the door. Tell them I'm not here." His voice came in a gruff whisper, his gaze darted to the bundle. It was covered in heavy linen cloth. Her thoughts went to the argument she had heard the night before. As much as she hated it, both their lives were in his hands.

"Haldor, what have you done?"

"Do not question me, woman. Just do as I say. Tell them I am in Macedonia and you don't know when I'm due back." He pulled his thick wool robe around his shoulders.

"Macedonia! That's two weeks travel from here. What if they don't believe me?"

His eyes went to the courtyard door. "You'll make them believe you if you want to preserve your life."

"But--"

"I'm going down to the vault by the stream. I'll stay there until you come and get me."

She studied him a last moment. His eyes glinted with desperation, then flew open at the sound of banging on the villa's entry doors.

"Stop balking and go before they break it down. Stall them as long as you can."

Kindra swallowed hard on her anger and hurried past Haldor out of the shop.

Three heavy knocks came at the door before she got to it, drew back the bolt, and opened it a crack.

There stood a young man, his thumbs hooked in a wide leather belt at his waist. He wore the same leather armor as the Praetorian guard Alba had met in the dark the night before. If there was another man, as Haldor had said, he stood out of view.

"We are here for Haldor The Goldsmith," the young man announced officiously, his reedy voice giving away his youth.

Kindra gripped the door tightly and repeated what Haldor had ordered her to say, then with eyes downcast, she pushed it closed until it stopped, a sandaled foot blocking the way.

Her heart leapt to her throat. This is what she had been afraid of. Her fingers tensed on the door as her eyes raised slowly, taking in a muscled calve, sinewy thighs, a bracketed chest plate, and a wide gold circlet around a thick neck.

Afraid to raise her eyes, she focused on the pulse bumping against that gold, powerful enough to move it with each beat.

He removed a scroll from his belt, and opened it, then announced. "We're here from the palace treasurer." His voice was heavy with authority, and to Kindra's shocked surprise, familiar. She lifted her gaze to his face, and nearly staggered back when she recognized him.

He glanced briefly at her, then went on, "By the authority of --" He stopped, refocused on her face and his brows drew sharply together.

Kindra covered her mouth with her hand. The man whose arms she had left only hours before stood like a massive wall in front of her, the shock of recognition in his eyes.

Her heart pounded against her ribs like a prisoner trying to escape. Tears welled in her eyes and she willed them not to fall. His dark eyes narrowed on hers, first in surprise, then in what? Shame? Regret? Or was she reading into them her own feelings?

After a few, terrifying heartbeats, he rolled the document back into a cylinder, his eyes blazing with intensity. Without taking them from hers, he slapped the cylinder into his assistant's chest.

"We have been given the wrong summons," he told him. "Return to the prefecture at once and inform them."

The younger man nodded, tucked the summons inside his belt, and trotted off without so much as a backward glance.

When he was completely out of hearing range, the man let go of the door. "Alba?"

Never in her short life had she wanted more to tell the truth. If Haldor was in trouble, and by association, herself; she didn't want Alba to be the one to take the blame.

She cast her gaze to her feet, calling on every ounce of her courage to find the words. "I … lied to you last night."

He moved in closer, tipped her chin up with a finger. She couldn't read his expression, except that there was no threat in it. "You are not a courtesan?"

She shook her head. "My name is Kindra." She lifted her chin defiantly away from his touch. "Alba is my friend. If Haldor is in trouble, I don't want her implicated. None of this was her fault."

His brows raised, his eyes intense on hers now in a way that made her hold her breath. "None of what, my lady?"

"None of, my … deception." The enormity of her admission bore down on her, filling her with doubt. Did Haldor deserve her loyalty? Or could this man be the key to her escape? Her hands were trembling.

She looked at her feet, stammered, hoping to right her mistake. "I asked Alba to show me how she earned her coin."

He looked confused. "So, you are here as courtesan to Haldor? At this hour?"

By the gods she was digging herself deeper. "No, I … work for Haldor … his household."

He folded his arms over his chest plate, the corners of his mouth twitching up in a way that made her heart stop. "In what capacity?"

"I am … a house servant. He bought me two years ago. He pays me well," she added, hoping to explain the jewelry she'd worn the night before.

"And yet you sell yourself at the bath." There was a hint of disbelief in his tone, but no judgment.

Her face heated. Lies didn't come easy to her. She needed to move the conversation away from herself before he pressed further. Had he found the brooch? Was that why he'd come?

The new thought sent a stab of cold to her already queasy stomach. "What do you want of Haldor?"

The man no longer looked amused. "It has been reported to the palace treasurer that a gold shipment bound for Constantinopolis was stolen and transported to a village near Chalcedon instead." He leveled his gaze at her. "This village. Haldor is the only one licensed to work the trade in this prefect. I want to question him. Perhaps he has seen or heard something to help us identify the thieves."

Her lips went cold at the memory of what she'd overheard on the doorstep the night before. He must have seen the color drain from her face, for his eyes narrowed on hers. *By the authority of* didn't sound like a question, it sounded like something more serious. Was he misleading her, or had he changed his mind?

"May I come in?" His strong hand applied pressure to the door.

Kindra's stomach knotted. She stepped out of his way to let him in, unsure how to proceed. She took a quick mental inventory of the gold and other raw materials Haldor had stored in the workshop. A workshop directly off her chambers, not his. The bulk of their stores were kept in the stone vault near the stream at the back of the property where Haldor now hid. But there was a good deal of copper and gold sheeting, small ingots, and precious stones on the shelves below her workbench to give her ready access to materials. Could any of that be ill gotten?

And then it hit her. She braced a hand against the door. The bundle Haldor had drug into her shop just now. Had he set her up to take the fall?

She backed against the wall and squeezed her eyes shut. Her chest heaved with anticipation of the worst. This man — the man whose hands she'd dreamed of having on her skin again — was going to find the stolen shipment in her possession and arrest *her*.

She heard his footsteps scrape on the floor. His scent filled her sharp intake of breath, sent a tingling through her body she could not deny. What a terrible betrayal that one who affected her so, would be the one sent to condemn her.

She bit her lip, squeezing her eyes tighter, waiting for him to make his move.

"Kindra." His voice was melodious, like he was trying out the sound of it on his tongue. "Look at me." She could feel the heat of his body close to hers. What was he doing?

She opened her eyes slowly to find the man who had curbed his response to her last night now pinned her with a look so heated, so sensual, it seared her soul.

He put his hands on her shoulders, his russet-brown eyes darkening to onyx. "I can't believe my fortune to find you here, of all places. I have thought of nothing but you since I allowed you to leave last night. There is no reason why this should be so, yet something about our ... encounter ... planted a seed of doubt."

"Doubt?" His words caused her to hold her breath.

"Something about you — your story — did not ring true. I get the sense you are not who you claim to be." He teased a stray tendril of her hair behind her ear. "You don't belong here in this place. Of that, I am sure."

Kindra swallowed hard, unable to take her eyes from the man's lips as he spoke. What was he saying? That he didn't believe she was a courtesan? Or that she was a servant? She shook her head, unsure how to respond. Yet from somewhere inside, she felt compelled to tell the truth: that she had thought of him, too. Wanted, with every breath she took to finish what they'd started.

What was wrong with her? Her life was in peril and all she could think of was to have his lips on hers once more? And then he was looking at her lips, like he would devour them with his eyes. All she had to do was reach out her hand. She realized in that moment it wasn't him she was afraid of.

"Haldor —"

"Isn't here."

His voice was a lusty breath against her ear.

She cast her eyes to the atrium. "He'll be back soon --"

He cupped her face tenderly in his huge hands, his thumb brushing her cheek. "You said he was in Macedonia. That's far away. How long ago did he leave?"

By the gods, she could hardly breathe! What if Haldor came back while he held her?

"I — I don't —" She flattened her hand against his chest, but it was like trying to hold back a raging current with a feather.

He swooped in and covered her mouth with his, his kiss an all-consuming fire that could not be put out. She melted in the heat of it.

"Take me to your chambers." His voice was low, husky with desire. It stroked a place deep inside her she hadn't known existed before last night. As if reading her response, his hand tightened at her back and pulled her against his thighs.

Oh my god, girl, this is it. Let yourself go, woman, you've got this. He won't arrest you if he wants you that badly.

A chill spread down her spine. It was as though some other woman, much braver than herself, pushed her forward. The same one who told her to stand tall when she was on the slave platform. Now, the voice spoke directly to her inside her mind, compelling her to open to this man. Was it the voice of lust? or reason? Or maybe it was simply her own inexorable will to survive. By the gods, she would.

She remembered what Haldor had said, with disgust. *Stall them as long as you can.* Why should she protect *him*? She had nothing to lose at this point. If she gave the man what he asked, he would help her retrieve the brooch. It was worth a try. Besides, his thighs pressed against hers were impossible to ignore. But could she trust him? She didn't even know his name.

She swallowed on a dry throat. This man could hold the key to her freedom, regardless of what Haldor had done.

"Who are you?" she asked.

He tilted her face to his, his fingertips at her chin, his lips pressed together a moment then spread into an easy smile.

"I am Marcus, Chief Aide of Emperor Constantine. Which means, I am sent to do his dirty work." He said it as though he were ashamed rather than proud.

"What?" She wasn't sure she had heard him right.

He slumped on the upholstered bench in the entry, bringing her down to sit next to him. "Indeed, I am no less a slave than you."

"But you wear the circlet of the Emperor." She lifted her fingers to the shining metal. She knew full well if a man were careful, he could live years on what it was worth in gold alone. She could have made this very one.

"The heavier the circlet, the graver the work one is expected to perform." His eyes bore into hers now, dark with desire.

"And you came here to arrest Haldor and his accomplice." There was no point in holding back. The chief aide to the emperor had the full authority to do whatever he wanted.

"I came to arrest a thief. Instead I find the woman I thought I'd never see again." He threaded a lock of her hair through his fingers. "I pray they are not one and the same."

A new heat wound through her. There was no point in dragging this on longer than necessary. It was as she'd dreamed the night before. She wanted to feel him inside her again, finish what they had started. If after that, if he took her into custody, to the stocks, to prison, or worse, at least she would have ended her life fulfilled.

She lifted her hand once more behind the strong trunk of his neck and dared to gaze into his eyes. "I cannot vouch for Haldor. I have no control or knowledge of what he does outside these walls. But whatever plot there might be to relieve the Emperor of his gold is not of my making, I can assure you."

"That is a relief to me." He took her into his arms again. His mouth claimed hers in a searing kiss that increased her desire beyond any resistance she might have.

She smoothed her hand over his shoulder and down his arm, the heat of his skin under her touch sealed a connection between them; and in that moment, nothing else mattered. Not the assistant, not Haldor's gold, not the place or the time. It was as though all her life — her trials, her sorrows, even her fears — were the logical steps to bring her to this moment. This union. This surrender.

"Marcus," she whispered, pulling his hand to her breast. "Fill me like you wanted to last night." There was an urgency now, borne of something inside her she had never experienced before, but knew, as surely as night comes at the end of day, she must complete or be left wanting the rest of her life.

A moment later his armor was off, as well as his sword and tunic. His sex was hard and heated against her skin, and she was wet with her own desire. There, on the padded benches in Haldor's entry way, she opened to him, drew him in, and silenced the voice in her head by succumbing to all that she was meant to be.

There was pain, but there was also scintillating pleasure beyond anything she could have imagined.

Afterward, she held her palla over her throbbing bosom and watched him dress and assemble his armor and weapons, wondering at the unseen force that had brought him to her, and the voice that had driven her to let him inside. Whatever it was, she was grateful for it, even if it meant she would be taken into custody.

When he was dressed and stood at the door, the look of longing in his eyes said he could be having the same thoughts.

"I will come back tomorrow to see if Haldor has returned. I beg, if you are able without putting yourself in danger, do not tell him of my visit."

She bowed her head, her entire body buzzing with the physical effects of what they had done. Twice. She gave him the slightest of nods, knowing full well her decision would make her complicit in Haldor's eventual arrest. Right or wrong, she had chosen sides. She could only hope it was the right one. It wasn't until he was out of sight she remembered the brooch.

CHAPTER SEVENTEEN

Kindra retied her purse around her waist and pulled her work tunic over her body, then wrapped her palla around her shoulders. Every inch of her skin radiated the essence of Marcus. She lifted the fabric to her face and breathed him in. As much as she wanted to savor the memory, she knew she needed to wash it away. Any man who had been with a woman would know that heady scent. With a last look around the entry to ensure there were no signs of Marcus left behind, she slipped on her sandals and headed for the stream. He would return tomorrow, and she would ask him about the brooch.

Hopefully she could distract Haldor until then. For now, she had done what he'd asked. How could he argue?

The moon rode high in the sky before she found the energy to rub life into her limbs and continue to the vault, only to find it bolted shut with no sign of Haldor.

Where had he gone? She made a circuit around the rock-lined enclosure, looking for any signs that he'd been there, and saw none. Had he lied to her? Had he suspected she would tell the men where he was? Or worse, had he never left and so had witnessed what transpired between she and Marcus?

Fear assailed her as the bitter truth surged up her throat. Would Haldor be waiting for her when she returned?

She had to return to the villa, she had nowhere else to go. Adrenaline spiking, she kept to the shadows on her approach. Moving as close as she dared, she learned her instincts were correct. Men's voices echoed through the atrium. As long as she had lived at the villa, Haldor had never let anyone pass through his doors. They must have forced their way in if they made it this far.

A chilling dread gripped her. She crouched behind the bushes at the back of the workshop, then pushed the branches aside just enough to see through.

Two men she didn't recognize stood facing Haldor. One had a large body with the stooped carriage of someone who had spent years at hard labor. The other was tall, sharp shoulders of a fine-boned frame jutted under a dark robe.

They had Haldor cornered, cowering; then the tall man's fist flashed out, catching Haldor across the mouth. Before he could catch his breath, Tall Man's other hand pinned his neck against the atrium wall.

Haldor's eyes bulged; his knees buckled. When the man released him, he groaned miserably, then slipped to the ground like a straw man.

Kindra gasped and clamped her hand over her mouth. The slender man glanced over his shoulder, but seeing nothing, he turned his attention back to his victim.

He hauled Haldor to his feet, and Thin Man ripped away his tunic. With a slash of a blade, he cut away Haldor's hidden purse. Satisfied the purse contents were what he wanted, he let Haldor's limp body slump back to the floor.

Kindra flattened herself against the wall, barely daring to breathe until the sounds of the men's retreat faded in the night. With a low moan and a curse, Haldor dragged himself up and staggered toward his private rooms off the atrium, supporting himself with a hand against the wall.

She waited to see if he would come out again, but all was quiet.

At last daring to take a full breath, she let herself into the workshop and turned up the flame on the lamp. Everything appeared as it should be; nothing disturbed. She slumped against the counter a moment, willing her heartbeat to settle and her hands to stop shaking. She had witnessed her master beaten twice in twenty-four hours. No doubt, he deserved it. With luck he would pass out in his chamber and leave her alone.

She was just beginning to remove her tunic when she heard leaden footsteps outside the shop. *Kindra, get up! Now!*

She dragged herself awake at the sound of the familiar voice whispering in her head. "Who are you?"

I'm Tessa. No time to explain. Just get up, get ready. He's coming.

"Kindra!" Haldor dragged in a ragged breath as he blundered into the workshop.

She swept the curtain from her alcove door to find him supporting himself against her workbench. The apple of his cheek bore a large purple bruise and the eye above it was swollen shut.

"How dare you betray me!" His bellowed words garbled in his ruined mouth. "You were supposed to send them away." His good eye was red with fury, his mouth bleeding where the man had struck him.

"I — " She *had* sent men away. Just not the ones he expected. These were the men he'd feared, not Marcus and his sergeant. Was it possible he didn't know about the Emperor's men? The idea put a new slant on her position.

She pulled herself up to her full height and jutted out her chin. "*You* are the one who lied, old man." She accused him, keeping her new-found discovery to herself. "I went to the vault. *You* weren't there."

He took a step closer, blocking her exit. "Lies! You set them upon me!"

"No Haldor! I sent them away, like you wanted." A partial truth.

He swayed on his feet. His body reeked of sweat, blood, and too much wine. Rage contorted his face. He drew back his arm. Seeing it coming, Kindra avoided the fist aimed at her face and pushed past him, then ducked as he swung at her again. This one missed her head but hit her midsection. She staggered back, the coins in her purse jangled as she hit the stone floor.

He rounded on her, eyes wide, then stunned her with a stinging blow to the jaw. He yanked up her tunic, shoved his hand between her thighs, and ripped her purse from her body. The coins and gold shards she collected over months of work spilled out onto the tiled floor. Splayed on her back, still holding her face, she scrambled out of his reach.

"You ungrateful little slut! You thieving filthy dog." Out of control, he threw his awkward bulk at her again. An animal snarl ripped from his throat.

She pulled herself up, her back against the wall. He rounded the workbench, sweeping tools and jewelry to the floor.

"Where is it?" he wailed. He cast his gaze wildly about the work shelves where the brooch should have been. "You witch! You sold it behind my back! You've cheated me after all I've done for you--" His bellow rattled her ribs.

"No, Haldor." She held out her hands and slid sideways along the bench. "You don't understand."

His eyes bulged with fury. "Lies!" he bellowed, then lunged at her, snarling like a crazed beast.

His stench filled her nostrils, his clawing hands grazing her skin. He would kill her if he got a hold of her.

She kicked her work stool into his shins, making him stumble, but he kept coming, crawling on the floor at her feet.

She stifled a scream with the back of one hand; her mouth dry and aching. Her other hand came to rest on the hilt of her wooden mallet.

Use it, Kindra. Do it now. He'll kill us if you don't.

Us? The voice again. Compelling her to act.

She froze, and time stretched, slow motion. Her fingers closed around the mallet's handle, her chest heaved with every burning breath. His hands clamped down on her ankles. He tried to pull her down.

"No!" She gasped and tightened her grip on the mallet. Could she do it? Did she have a choice? No.

She raised the mallet over her head and brought it crashing down with all her might. There was a sickening crunch as the first hit crashed into his skull, and then she was beating him down; beating him down, down. His hands came up to fend off the blows, and then fell to his sides.

She kept going.

Again and again the wooden hammer head slammed into his. With each blow, she thought of the wrongs she'd endured. What kind of man sells his daughter into slavery? What kind of monster holds a woman in contempt who makes it possible for him to live like a king? Threatens her life, beats her, holds her prisoner while he drinks and gambles and robs from the treasury then sets her up to take the fall?

Again and again, the hammer struck. Kindra's face was on fire; slick with tears and splattered blood. The hammer, now wielded in both hands, mashed deeper and deeper into the mass of blood and hair that had once been a man's head.

It's over, girl. Stop. You can stop now. Get yourself out of there.

But she could not stop.

Not even as her own gorge blocked her throat.

Not even when her arms ached.

Not until the fear was gone. The hate. The anger. The hopelessness.

Not until she had avenged every night of hunger, every strap mark on her back, every hour her young life had been robbed of freedom, of pleasure, of love.

Not until he stopped twitching, jerking. Not until he lay motionless at her feet, his face unrecognizable.

And then, as suddenly as it had begun, the mallet ceased possession of her, slid from her blood-slickened fingers, and thudded to the floor next to Haldor's lifeless body.

Chapter Eighteen
Balboa Island, Republic of California, 2019 CE

Tessa's eyes flew open, her heart pounding hard in her ears. "Holy Christ!" For the second time in as many nights, she awoke to find the serpent bracelet constricting her bicep. She didn't remember putting it on. She had *not* put it on, dammit. She had talked with Phil late into the night until she could barely hold her eyes open, turned off her light, and fallen asleep with thoughts of his warm body spooned against her back. No way had she gotten up and put on that bracelet. But there it was, clinched tight around her arm like it owned her. She ripped the damned thing off and threw it across the room.

Breathe. She rubbed her clenched fist against the adrenaline rush in her chest as bloody images flooded her mind. The memory was so visceral, so real, she could smell the alcohol on the old man's breath and the acrid salt in his sweat, taste the metallic tang of his blood. A dream? No. She had been there as surely as she was here now. She had held the wooden mallet in *her* hands, pounded it into her assailant's skull, over and over. She raised her hands, expecting to see blood, but they were clean.

The images burned into her soul. She had made love with one man and murdered another on the same night. Guilt bore down on her like a tombstone. The surety of her deed made her break out in a sweat. She threw back the covers and lay in nothing but her panties and camisole, heart racing, consumed by a sickening dread.

I killed a man. I. Killed. A. Man.

She covered her face with shaking hands, paralyzed by the images until a noise downstairs reminded her, she wasn't alone.

"Lexi?"

She sat up and dragged on a pair of sweats, grabbed her hoodie and shoes, and padded down her new stairs to the kitchen.

Alexis sat at the table reading the Sunday entertainment section, bed hair escaping a silver clip atop her head, a cup of coffee steaming at her elbow.

"Morning," she said brightly without looking up. "You won't believe this. *Florence and the Machine* is going to be at the Santa Barbara Bowl. We can take the train up and spend the night, and…"

Tess sat without saying a word. It had been a week since she'd met with Karl Johns. Working each evening with a local carpenter, Phillip had supervised completion of her stairway, finally fitting a piece of sturdy plywood over the hole in her bedroom floor. It was rough, but once all the construction was complete, slate floors would extend out onto the sundeck and rollaway doors would complete the indoor-outdoor feel. She had pictured it in her mind's eye for weeks.

Now, all those plans seemed frivolous and vain, replaced by an overwhelming cloud of dread. She could no longer hold it in. She had to tell someone.

"Lex?"

"The StubHub is closer, but who wants to see Florence in a giant stadium? Santa Barbara will be more expensive, but --"

"Lex," she said, a little louder. She had to push out the word, as if still restricted by the veil of time.

"Phillip can come, of course. I mean, if the tickets aren't already sold out," Lexi went on, excitedly, fingers already tapping out an address on her cell phone.

"Lex!" Tess slapped her hand on the table, making the coffee cup jump.

Lexi looked up in surprise, and her mouth dropped open. "Jesus, Tess. You look like you just climbed out of a dumpster."

Tessa rubbed her arms, suddenly cold. She squeezed her eyes shut and the back of her throat stung on a sob.

Lexi got up and knelt next to her chair. "Tess, honey, what the hell?"

Tess pulled in a couple of breaths. She had to say it out loud. Make it real. It was either confess or lose her mind. She rocked back and forth and forced out the words: "I ... I killed somebody."

"What?"

Tess propped her elbows on the table and supported her head with shaking fingers. "Not me, Kindra. I ... I made her do it though, so it might as well have been me."

"Who's Kindra?" Lexi shook her head.

Tess raised her eyes to her friend. "She ... made the brooch."

"Again, the brooch."

Tess nodded. She had to make her understand. "I know it sounds bat-shit crazy, but you've got to listen to me. This ..." she raised her hand waved it in the air next to her head, "It's really happening ... not here, but ... but somewhere. I—"

Lexi scooted a chair next to Tessa and put her arm around her shoulder. "Okay. I know you've been upset over the jewelry thing. And Karl Johns, he's spooky. No doubt about it. But you got that put away, right?"

"Lex, I'm out of control." Tess hated the way she sounded. Weak and weepy.

"No shit." Lexi's gaze locked on to Tessa's arm. She grabbed her elbow. "What's this?"

Tess glanced at her bicep, knowing what she'd see before her eyes landed on it. A blistered, red line spiraled around her arm like a brand.

She raked shaking fingers through her hair. "I ... we ... need to talk."

Thirty minutes later, they were slipping past the Newport Jetty in the sailboat, Tess on the rudder as Lexi hoisted the sail in a decent wind. They rocked along in silence except for the breeze whisking the sails and a gentle metallic ting as the rigging rhythmically caressed the mast. Once they cleared the jetty, they turned up the coast along the Newport Peninsula, the wind picked up, and the little boat heeled gently to starboard.

Lex had promised to listen, no judgment, until Tessa got it all out. There was no one she trusted more. Still it was difficult to start. Not just because what she was about to share was outrageous.

Impossible. Ridiculous. But because, telling Lex would take it out of the dream world and put it on the table in the light of day.

She began by telling her about Kindra being sold as a slave in a Roman auction.

Lexi tightened her grip on the line. "You dreamed you were a slave named Kindra?"

"I was inside her, Lex. Seeing through her eyes, feeling her fear. Some men in the crowd jeered. I wanted her to stand tall, stick out her tits, you know? If they were going to sell her then they'd damn well have to pay what she was worth."

"And did she? Stand tall?"

Tessa sniffed. "She's young. Inexperienced. And it seemed the deal was done before she ever got there. An old man stepped up and bought her without so much as a bid."

"So, a lucid dream."

"What's that?" Tessa eased to port on the rudder, heading more directly into the swell. Some of the anxiety she'd experienced on waking dissolved in the brisk feel of light spray on her face.

Lexi's gaze went to the sky and she huffed out a deep breath. "In a lucid dream, the dreamer knows it's a dream. Theoretically, she can make things happen. In the dream." The wind decreased, the sails catching a gentle tension. Lexi relaxed her grip. "Never to my knowledge has someone been physically affected by the dream."

"Physically affected?"

Lex rolled her eyes. "Your arm?"

Tess rubbed it absently. "Which takes me in another direction."

157

"How so?"

"The bracelet."

Lexi tightened her grip, turned the bow into the wind. "Go on."

"The first time I put on that bracelet, I was wide awake, but I immediately connected with it — or something connected to it."

"The night we found the plate in the chimney. You left us for a few minutes."

The vacant feeling drifted through her memory. "I saw the brooch."

"You put on the bracelet and saw the brooch?"

"Not the actual brooch. Just the design, superimposed over Theo's yard. A perfect match, now that I've seen a picture of it; but Lex, we didn't know about it then."

Lexi trimmed the sail to keep them on course. They were nearing Newport Pier, as far as they'd planned to go, and would need to come about soon. "And ..." She rolled her free hand in encouragement.

"And ... there was Marcus."

"Marcus?"

Tessa leaned on the tiller, cleared her throat, and told her the rest. All of it. How Kindra had responded to him. How Tess had encouraged her. "He was hot. That time, I woke up in the throes of a freaking orgasm."

Lex sent her a teasing smile. "Now, that's a lucid dream. You were wearing the bracelet that time, too?"

Tess nodded. "I vowed after that not to wear it to bed. I buried it in my lingerie drawer."

Lexi sent her a disbelieving look. "I don't know, girlfriend. I think I'd have kept it right there on the nightstand."

Tess let go a natural laugh, relieving another level of tension. An easy silence descended over them as they came about and let the boat seesaw gently over the water, heading south along the coastline.

Lexi broke the silence. "So, I take it, it happened again."

"The orgasm?"

Lexi snorted. "The bracelet. You wore it again."

Tess studied the face of her friend thankful for her clearheaded support. "I honestly don't remember putting it on. What I do remember is lying in bed, aching to see Marcus again. The next morning when I woke, it was there, on my arm." My god, did she just admit having a thing for a guy in a dream?

Lex stared at her a long moment, probably thinking the same thing.

Tess gazed off to a shoreline edged by multi-million-dollar estates as they rode the swell. Seventeen hundred years ago, in Constantine's Rome, Flavia talked lovingly of her son, Marcus; and the Emperor built his crowning achievement, the palace at Constantinople. At the same time, Newport Harbor — the heart of Orange County's extravagant wealth — was nothing but a swamp populated with hunter gatherers.

She laughed out loud. In a way, nothing had changed.

They sailed wing-and-wing back into the channel, putted to the Grand Canal and tied the sailer to their dock. Tessa scooped up a clay pot full of dead begonias, wondering how long it had sat there. She carried it back to the house, vowing to replace them with live ones.

Ten minutes later, and dressed in dry clothes, Tess felt somewhat better. After talking with Lex, the entire dream thing felt silly.

There was a bright side to every story, right? Some people actually worked hard to have lucid dreams, something that obviously came easy to Tessa.

Sitting at the small cocktail table on the veranda, she checked in with Phillip. The sound of his voice sent a familiar glow of warmth to her heart. She missed him. Wanted to feel his arms around her again soon. He invited her to dinner with his mother that evening, the last night until his father returned home.

She finished her conversation just as Lex emerged from the kitchen carrying a tray with a bowl of chips and salsa, a pitcher of lavender lemonade and two shots of tequila.

"Don't think I better." Tess sat back in the chair. "I'm going out with Phil and his mom for dinner tonight."

"After opening up like that? About the dream? You deserve the whole bottle."

Tess laughed, relief huffing out in a sigh. "Okay, just one shot. Got to be on my best behavior."

Lexi scooped up a chip full of salsa and munched it down. "My hotline shift starts at midnight, so as long as I eat dinner, I can spare a few brain cells for now. You look better than you did this morning, by the way."

Tess lifted the shot glass for a toast. "I feel better, thanks to you." They clinked, sipped, chased with lemonade. "Feel a little guilty cheating on Phil with a Praetorian soldier, but other than that…"

"Listen honey. I can verify you were snoring in bed when I got home last night. I could hear you all the way down in the garage."

Tess winged an elbow at her friend. "I do not snore."

"Believe me, sister. You do."

Tess shook her head. It was good to have a friend with her head on her shoulders. "One thing is bothering me, though. About the dream." It was easier calling it a dream than believing she had actually traveled back in time. "Kindra lost the brooch."

Lex sent her a scrunched-up look. "Lost it?"

"Yeah. When she, they … you know …" She rolled her hand. "It was important to her. A really big deal. I just get this feeling she's in trouble, you know?"

Lexi eyed her warily. "I … suppose you could put on the bracelet and help her find it. In the dream, that is."

Tess's stomach did a little flip at the thought. She knew Lex was half kidding, but the idea settled in her chest like a nesting bird. The raw patch on her arm tingled.

"Not sure I want to go back into that." Even as she said it, she felt the pull of the past, felt Marcus' breath on her neck, his hands grazing her hips. She tossed back the rest of the shot. "No." She sank into the chair. "No, I need to get past it. It's having too much of an effect on my real life."

❧

Dinner was at Phil's mother's favorite, the Five Crowns. Not a place for the millennials, but Phillip had promised, and his mother beamed from the moment they poured her glass of wine to the tiramisu dessert. Watching the two of them together set a warm glow in Tessa's heart. Her childhood had been anything but warm and it was pleasing to sit at a table where family love added sweetness to the meal.

They dropped his mom off at her home on the bluff, making sure she was settled for the night, then Phillip wound along the road to the park overlooking Corona del Mar beach.

He took Tessa's hand and led her to the bench on the cliff. She shivered the way she always did looking out over the edge of the continent at night, the vast Pacific spreading under a patchwork of clouds and stars.

"You cold? I can get the car blanket." Phil stretched his arm protectively across her shoulders.

She snuggled against his body, rested a hand on his chest. He felt solid, warm, real. "I'm good. I really loved dinner tonight. Your mom was bubbly."

He let go a breath so full of resignation, it broke her heart. "It's hard to see Mom losing herself bit-by-bit. She's holding her own right now. I see bits of her shining through. She still owns enough of herself to put up a good front."

Tessa could relate. Sometimes she felt she was only half in this world, a faded version of herself. "You're good to stay close to them."

Phil let out a low rumble of a laugh. "It has its benefits. I've been able to save most of my salary while I've been there. Rent's not cheap in this town, in case you haven't noticed. Doesn't hurt they live on the bluff. Not sure I'd be so keen if I had to commute to Cauldron Industries from Lancaster every day."

She squeezed his hand at her shoulder. "I hear that. Anyway, I love the way she looks at you." Her own mother, always miserable, had never looked at her that way. "She's amazing. I love listening to her stories. The youngest of twelve children raised on a North Carolina farm? And she ends up here."

"You never know what life's going to bring you."

"That's for sure." Images of Marcus reeled through her head. She pushed down a twinge of guilt. The best way to banish the dream was to focus on the here and now. On Phillip. Her hand went to the waistband of his slacks, slid across his stomach. "Take me home?"

"I thought you'd never ask."

❧

Lexi had left for her shift by the time they arrived at the house and it was a good thing. Phillip had Tessa in his arms before the back door was closed. He lit a fire in the hearth, and they made love on the floor in front of it. Tess abandoned herself to his touch, dissolving into the moment. Phil was better than any dream lover she could conjure, taking her to the point of orgasm a couple of times before they both lost control.

After a cup of chocolaty cocoa, they headed upstairs for round two, settling into each other's arms.

He nuzzled her ear. "Wish I didn't have to leave tonight."

She pulled away enough to see his eyes in the pale moonlight streaming in through her window. She feathered her fingers across his forehead. "Me, too. But your mom appreciates you being near, and I get it. I'm not going anywhere." *Even in my dreams.*

His amber eyes went dark. "We really should get married, you know."

She propped herself up on an elbow. "Phillip, we've talked about this. We've only known each other—"

"Relax." He let out a soft laugh, drew a finger down the line of her jaw. "Just thinking out loud."

"You're being serious, aren't you?"

He sent her a lazy blink and rolled his lips together a moment before he spoke. "I've been single a long time, Tess. Been with a few women, but none I wanted to be part of my family, to make a family with," he went on wistfully. "Watching my mom and dad, how they still dance together in the living room on Friday night, how they finish each other's sentences, how they look at each other when they think no one else sees, how my dad's fingers caress her shoulder as he gets up to refresh her coffee at breakfast. I want that, Tess. Honestly, I feel like we're already there."

"Me too," she said, smiling at him. "We're there without the ceremony, the paperwork." All the good it did her parents.

He twisted a length of her hair around his finger "You've been a bit ... distracted lately. I'm not sure what that's about, but if an anchor is what you need, or at least knowing it's there when you're ready ..."

He *was* serious. She snugged back into his arms, a warmth spreading through her entire body as he kissed the back of her neck, her ear, the corner of her eye, chasing away her doubts. They were there. Almost. Were it not for the turmoil going on in her sleep, she would take him up on it right now.

Like a couple who completed each other, she saw in his eyes the moment he recognized her hesitation. "No pressure, Tess. I just wanted you to know, I love you. I've known it since the moment you walked through that door at Cauldron."

She laughed at the memory. "Right; like that really happens."

His grin widened, that mischief she loved playing in the tiny lines at his eyes. "I saw it in your eyes when you dropped me off that day when I begged a ride."

"Yeah?" The memory made her heart squeeze a little. She had to admit he was right. She rolled up onto his chest and stretched out on top of him, settling her body into those planes and valleys of his that fit her like a well-worn glove. "Yeah. What did you see?"

"My future." His eyes narrowed on hers. He was dead serious. "You just say the word."

He kissed her softly and she believed him. "But I'll have to take a rain check on round three for one more night."

"Yup. You're right," she said on a sigh, then rolled off him and gave him a hand up.

"You'll lock the doors when I leave? Don't answer to anyone?"

"Babe, this is the island. There's no trolls hiding under canal bridge."

"I was thinking more about that creep across the alley."

She gave him a salute. "Done. History." In more ways than one.

She hated being there alone since the incident with Karl, too; but she didn't want to send Phil away with that fear on his mind. One more night, his father would be back in town, and he'd be back in her bed. They could pick up the thread of this conversation when she'd had a chance to sleep on it. She kissed him goodbye at the back door and watched him shuffle down the stairs, then locked the door, checked the veranda, and climbed her stairs to bed.

Clouds wheeled over the moon; the same moon that had watched over Kindra and Marcus nearly two thousand years before. Were they part of an elaborate, lucid dream? Or a lifetime lived before this one?

Despite her focus on Phillip, the thought of Marcus sent a shiver through her bones. In her mind's eye, he was standing before her, intense dark eyes and raven hair, so alive and real, he could walk through her door any moment. The two men were exact opposites. Marcus the warrior, bound to obey his emperor, willing to kill for him. Phil, the golden boy, free spirit who would rather be surfing than designing space-age switches, whose first loyalty was to his family.

Marcus had stolen into her dreams with a passion that couldn't be denied; but it was Phil who warmed her heart, was willing to promise her a future.

She should feel giddy with delight. Instead, she rubbed her fist against a cold regret settling low and sorrowful in the hollow of her chest.

Marcus' dark eyes scorched her from behind a shimmering veil of longing. Dark, possessive, hungry. A pulse of heat went straight to her sex. God. How could she promise Phil her future while she ached for a warrior from the past?

The moon cast its mocking glow over the canal, a grinning, hypnotic image distorted by the rising tide. *A dream, Tessa. Marcus is a dream.* But he was a dream with the power to make her question reality. The last time she'd been with Kindra they had beat a man to death. Did she really want to go back?

No.

Could she leave Kindra alone to face the consequences? She searched her conscience and saw the answer like it was carved on an ancient wall.

Never.

And she knew with all of her being, dream or not, she couldn't make a promise to Phil until she knew for sure Kindra was out of danger. Because, she couldn't shake the feeling — no, the conviction — that if Kindra didn't survive, Tess very well might not exist.

Like a sleepwalker stealing deep into a dark night, she rose from her bed, went to her dresser, dug out the serpent bracelet, and slipped it up her arm.

CHAPTER NINETEEN

A small village outside Chalcedon, circa 326 CE

Kindra floated in the nebulous realm between truth and fantasy, denial and acceptance of what she had done. Her conscious mind scoffed at the vague notion that this was only a dream. A nightmare brought on by fear and confusion. A false hope. But this was no dream. Her hands, icy cold, throbbed with pain; the sharp odor of blood filled her senses; pieces of flesh and hair clung to her fingers, her arms, her ankles.

He would have killed you. The words came in calming reassurance. *You did what you had to do. Now you've got to get out of here. Survive, Kindra. You must survive.*

She sank her teeth into her bottom lip until she tasted blood.

She swallowed hard one more time and stepped over the gore. She pulled down the muslin curtain from her doorway and draped it over Haldor's body.

At the stream, she tore off the ragged, bloody remains of her tunic, used a sharp-edged rock to dig a hole away from the stream, buried the rags in the hole, then added a pile of rocks. Then she washed blood and gore from her skin and hair. She worked and worked, rubbing her skin raw until the adrenaline surge from what she'd done left her system. At last, she sluiced her face, holding cool water to her cheek which she only now realized had begun to swell.

She was exhausted and she was cold, but nonetheless, a strange calm descended over her and her breath came easier.

Survive.

The voice. She would never have had the courage to strike Haldor were it not for that voice. And, if she were really honest, there was a time during her rage when the mallet took on a life of its own, as though the force driving it came from somewhere outside herself.

Haldor attacked her and she had killed him. That was the simple truth. But she was a slave. The voice in her head — her accomplice — was right. She had to leave. If she was discovered in the villa, there would be no questions asked. She'd be lucky if she made it to a magistrate. More likely, she would be dragged to the center of the village and stoned.

With a shiver, she wrapped herself in her palla and returned to the workshop. The smell of death invaded her senses, made her want to gag.

She skirted the room, avoiding the huge lump on the floor. Gray beams of light cast pale shadows across it. There were still a few hours before dawn. She longed for sleep, just a few moments to erase the horror from her mind; but sleep was out of the question. Light would bring knowledge of what she'd done.

She had Marcus's coins and the last shipment of the Emperor's gold, plus scraps enough to buy her way out of this place — anyplace — if she just kept her head.

Chalcedon, only a short walk away, was a major city on the trade route between Britannia and Asia. From there, she could travel almost anywhere and begin a new life.

It wouldn't be easy. A woman would have trouble traveling alone, but she had no choice at the moment.

She paced back and forth, shoving her hair out of her face, tugging at the threads of a plan. She had coin. She could buy herself out of trouble. But even as she thought it, she knew being a woman would be her biggest obstacle, not to mention having gold ingots and raw gold sheets in her possession. It was true. A woman would have a difficult time entering a new city without a man to speak for her.

But a man — a man?

A boy.

Kindra straightened as the suggestion took hold. Whether a slave or a servant, she would have much better chances of getting out of the city if she were male. A young male would be practically invisible.

Charged with a new surge of energy, she stepped to the hearth and pulled down a thin cord she used to tie bunches of herbs. Throwing her ragged tresses over her head, she tied them 'round with the cord so that she succeeded in piling the tangled mass of hair on top of her head.

No.

That wouldn't do. She would have to keep it covered and if the cover came off, she'd be discovered.

The hair had to go. A new wave of nausea threatened her resolve, but she shoved it deep inside.

171

She bit hard into her knuckle; the threads were weaving into a sturdy cloth. She closed her eyes and saw it as clearly as if it were written on the wall before her: She would pose as a young man: Haldor's apprentice, which although she'd never gotten credit for it, never even been seen by one of Haldor's clients, that's exactly what she had been.

She would go forward as a man, make the deliveries to Constantinopolis as Haldor would have done, receive the payment he would have received, and make her way as far west as her skill could take her.

As if shot from a catapult, the thoughts hurled her into a furious frenzy of activity. She filled the guttering oil lamp in the workshop, gathering tools from the floor until she found her sharpened blades.

She gathered her hair again, but her new determination hadn't stopped the blades from shaking in her hands.

"Coward," she said aloud. "What good has being a woman ever got you?" How could she lose something she'd never had? How could she give up someone she'd never been? The young woman inside her moaned softly in protest, remembering Marcus's touch. She had known the joy of being with a man. But, if losing that man was the price of her freedom, then she would pay it.

"Survive," she growled, "You — will — survive."

Without benefit of mirror or comb, she raked the sharpened blades through her thick tresses. The young girl within her retreated deeper and deeper inside watching through a veil of tears, as each uneven shock of hair fell to the stone floor. When she was done, a tiny door closed in her heart with a final, sorrowful *click*.

She could carry her meager belongings and tools in a mule basket, purchase bread and fruit along the way, and as a young man, she could sleep in the open without challenge. Once she was satisfied she could be ready to leave at first light, she lay down on the bench in the entry where she and Marcus had held each other only hours before, imagining his hands on her for the last time.

It had seemed that she'd only just closed her eyes when a knock at the door startled her awake. She froze. The events of the night before had left her mind drained and her body sore. She had intended to get an early start, and not have to face inquiries so soon; yet, on rubbing sleep from her eyes, she saw through the atrium arches that dawn had given way to a bright morning sky.

CHAPTER TWENTY

Marcus stood silently in the Prefect's vestibule, his impatience growing with every moment the ineffectual little man kept him waiting. Judging by the crowd of men waiting outside the gate, the Prefect took great pleasure in making his supplicants wait on his appearance, the Emperor's men notwithstanding.

Marcus supposed he should count his blessings. At least he had been allowed inside. And, a more officious prefect might have questioned his delay in bringing Haldor the Goldsmith to task. As it was, he'd had the distinct fortune to reconnect with Kindra, the woman who had not left his mind since their first meeting.

The quiet sanctuary of the prefect's entry afforded him a moment of reflection. In his entire experience of women, he had never felt hair so silken, skin so soft, or heard the sound of a voice so sweet. The memory of her fair, young face took his breath away.

Or, maybe she bewitched you in order to save her master.

Had she deceived him? Probably. There was no doubt Kindra had lied to him about something. Their spies had followed the men who stole the Emperor's gold shipment directly to Haldor's door only that night. No man involved in such an enterprise would allow a delivery of that value without being there to receive it in person.

Yet, the fact that Kindra was there didn't mean she was complicit in the theft. Judging by her nervous demeanor, he could imagine she had been threatened. But there was something else about her that gave him pause. For a woman who had obviously been unspoiled, she bore about her a sensuality that belied her complete innocence. This fact baffled him. His desire burned deep, bright, consuming. It was as though his will had been swept into another world where the two of them existed as one being, entwined for all time, inseparable.

He felt it still.

A sound at the vestibule pulled him from his thoughts. He looked up to see a gaunt guard, and the Prefect — a man who obviously liked his time at table — striding toward him. Marcus straightened to attention.

"I see you have come to me empty handed." The obese prefect's tone accused. "The Emperor would be displeased."

Marcus relaxed his stance and, hands on the hilt of his sword, smiled down at the shorter man. "I don't believe you would be stationed at this lowly outpost of a village if the Emperor believed you could read his mind or command the activities of his Chief Aide."

The prefect's eyes narrowed, the barb hitting home. "So, you have justification for your failure to bring Haldor to justice?"

Marcus tightened his grip on the sword, but reminded himself of his office. He knew where he stood with Constantine; whereas, he doubted *this* man had ever met the emperor in person. In other circumstances Marcus could take off the man's head with one swipe of his blade and his Emperor wouldn't question his reasons. It wasn't required that he meet with this fool at all, other than to secure the official arrest decree.

"The document provided me by your office yesterday was incorrect. If you seek to get credit for the apprehension of the thief, you'll need to provide one that will hold up at the tribunal."

"That's preposterous!" the man sputtered. "I drew up that document myself the moment your messenger arrived."

Marcus raised a brow and cocked his head. The document had indeed been drawn up correctly, naming Haldor in the theft of a shipment of gold. However, it took more than one person to accomplish the theft of an armed delivery, and Marcus used that to further his cause. If his suspicions were right, Haldor was not as far away from his villa as his servant would have had him believe. He planned to return under cover to catch the old man at his game. And, all right, he wanted to see Kindra again, perhaps to remove her from the scene and suspicion. "Nevertheless, the documentation was inadequate for my purpose."

The man's face went scarlet. "How dare you accuse me —"

"I accuse you of nothing, other than ignorance of the situation. I need more time to broaden my net. Once I have all the participants firmly in my sights, I will request the appropriate decree and I don't expect to be kept waiting at your door when I do."

"Now see here. You don't order my duties in this village --"

Marcus ignored his outburst. The man may be a glutton and a sloth, but he knew full well where he stood in the chain of command. Marcus strode to the door, opened it wide, and gestured for the men standing near the entrance to come in. "The Prefect is ready to see you all now, I believe."

It was well on toward noon when he reached the market square where he purchased a heavy robe of a plain design that would allow him to pass through the streets like any other middle-class citizen. He did not want word of his presence making it to Haldor's villa ahead of him.

His senses were on high alert as they always were when working under cover, but there was something else at work in his system and it made his fingertips tingle. He couldn't put the anticipation of seeing Kindra again out of his mind. As he made his transaction with the merchant, his gaze fell upon a bolt of azure blue silk, the edges embroidered with a fine golden filament and all he could think about was how that fabric would look draped over Kindra's shoulders. On an impulse he could not deny, he purchased the bolt of cloth as well, and tucked it under his arm.

Leaving his man behind, Marcus stabled his horse at a livery near the entrance to the road leading to Haldor's villa. Few men owned a horse the size and carriage of the Emperor's men. Indeed, there were many more mules than horses in this part of the country and a horse would call undue attention to his arrival. He wanted it nearby should he need to make haste in his retreat, yet far enough out of sight not to give himself away.

He pulled his robe close around his body to ensure his armor and sword were hidden, then draped a section over his head to conceal his features from all but someone looking at him straight on. Then he tucked the bolt of blue fabric under his arm, hoping to appear nothing more than a merchant delivering goods to a wealthy household.

He surveyed the villa from afar for a few moments before he committed to his approach. There was a mule tied near what could be a back entrance. He hadn't seen that the night before. He hoped that was an indication Haldor had indeed returned. As far as he could see, nothing else had changed. However, the villa was the last dwelling on the outskirts of the town, with free access to a robust stream, which, if followed, eventually flowed into the Bosphorus.

Armed with determination to see Haldor brought to heel, and the expectation he might see Kindra, he approached the portico. When his first knock on the heavy wooden door went unanswered, he pounded twice with his fist, his eyes flicking to the side of the dwelling to make himself aware of any witnesses or perhaps someone inside getting advance identification of who was at the door. He saw nothing, but at last heard footsteps approaching from inside.

There was a heavy scraping of iron against wood, and then he was met with the surprised expression of a young man. A boy, really, judging by his smooth cheeks and absence of facial hair. It was hard to tell because the moment their eyes met, the young one lowered his. Still, Marcus didn't miss the bruises on his cheek, and the very obvious swelling of the unfortunate one's nose, as though it had been smashed in a fight, possibly broken.

"What is it you want, sir?" The young man trained his gaze on his dusty feet.

Where had this boy been last night? Perhaps the mule belonged to him.

"I need to speak with Haldor the Goldsmith." Marcus kept his voice even so as not to scare the young man further, for he could not mistake the mark of fear on his countenance.

"He's not here, sir." The boy closed the door half the distance between them.

"When do you expect him to return?" He might as well see if the boy changed the story he'd learned from Kindra the night before.

The boy's shoulders pinched down tight as if a weight was about to fall on his head. "I—I don't know. He's far away." His voice quavered. He closed the door a little further. He was so distraught Marcus had the sense someone stood just out of sight ready to clobber the poor lad if he answered wrong.

What was going on here? Had Haldor come back with this boy? Beaten him, sent him to the door with a lie? Or was the child telling the truth? He had no way of knowing, but his gut told him something wasn't right. And if that were the case, what had happened to Kindra? Why hadn't she come to the door?

"What about Kindra? May I speak with her?"

The boy flinched and nearly closed the door in his face. Marcus blocked the closure with his foot. "Wait. I —" He pulled the bolt of silk from under his arm and held it in front of him. "I have something for her."

The boy's eyes lifted and widened a moment before he cut them away again.

"Please." Marcus shoved the fabric into his arms. "Give this to her. Tell her Marcus of Constantinopolis delivered it to her."

The young man stood stock still. Were his shoulders trembling under his tunic? Then with an arm nearly as bruised and battered as his face, the boy took the fabric carefully in his hands, nodded to Marcus without making eye contact, and Marcus allowed him to shut the door.

CHAPTER TWENTY-ONE

Kindra leaned against the barrier between them, gulping air into lungs deflated in shock. They'd stood face-to-face, Haldor's body not twenty paces away, her heart stuttering in her chest the whole time. Thanks to her bruised, swollen face and her cropped hair, he hadn't recognized her. Or if he had, he'd made no sign.

But he'd made his feelings plain, hadn't he? The bolt of silk she held in her arms was a soft, twilight blue, and shimmered as if touched by firelight. She edged to Haldor's chamber window and watched Marcus stride away, wanted with all her soul to open the door and run after him. Confess her crime. What kind of man could bring her such a gift and not have mercy on her? Surely, he would see Haldor's killing could only have been self defense and stand up for her.

Desperate little fool. Once Marcus reported the killing to the authorities, it would be out of his hands.

She pressed her back against the wall. She had only two choices and both meant she had to leave in secret. She could either take what was left of the jewelry she'd made for Haldor and deliver it to the palace treasurer as agreed, or sell it on her own for what she could, and risk being labeled a thief, or worse.

Regardless, if she stayed here another hour, she'd risk discovery, and that was not an option.

She lay the bolt of cloth on the table next to two loaves of stale, black bread she'd retrieved from the hearth. She needed to retrieve her tools from her workshop, as well. And — by the gods, she was letting her fear impede her good sense — she needed Haldor's signet ring. There would be no passing the palace gates without it. As much as she wanted never to return to the workshop where his body lay, she had no choice but to enter it once more.

She crept down the corridor, stopped in the doorway, her gorge returning to her throat at the sight of the lumpy mound on the floor. She swallowed it down, pushed herself forward, but hesitated before lifting the muslin curtain. She knew there was nothing but a twisted matting of bone and flesh where Haldor's face should be and she didn't want to see that again. Thank the gods, his right hand protruded from under the cloth. Still the odor of urine and feces was enough to make her want to run away as she lifted his hand. Body fluids had swelled around the ring. Her stomach lurched and she cried out.

Don't stop now, Kindra. We've got to get out of here. Your tools. Get your tools.

Kindra swallowed another wave of nausea, then opened the wide leather strip she kept on the workbench and removed a pair of snips from their pocket. With a corner of her palla clenched against her nose and mouth, she cut through the distended flesh, and pulled until it gave way. Gritting her teeth, she twisted the ring until she dislodged it. Oh, god, the odor nearly made her faint. Holding her breath she wiped the ring first on the muslin shroud, then cleaned it again with one of her polishing cloths, then wrapped the cloth, the ring, and the rest of her tools up in the leather case and tied it with a thong.

Stepping back, she nearly lost her balance when she stumbled against the heavy box Haldor had dragged into the workshop the night before. She had forgotten that, too.

She approached cautiously, slowed by an unreasonable fear the dead man might arise. The air in the room was stifling with an invisible thickness. It pulled at her limbs as if she were mired in quicksand. She stood a moment longer before she worked up the nerve to lift the lid from the box. The glinting contents took her breath away.

It was filled with gold jewelry — fine pieces, fit for an empress, and, what's this? She lifted a pair of earrings from the box. Hadn't she made a pair like this only last year for the daughter of Constantine himself? They had stuck in her mind, for Haldor had told her the shipment had been stolen before it reached the treasury, an event that happened often in the current environment, which was why, Haldor had entered an insurance contract with the treasury. She turned over one of the earrings. There was her delta mark on the back.

The current order had been to replace the pieces as on the original order, yet here they were.

So, Marcus was right. Haldor was robbing from the treasury by arranging to have his own shipments stolen, then returned to him. He profited twice, once by not having to purchase more gold, and once by claiming the treasury's insurance. Suddenly, his odd behavior became clear. Secret trips, hours spent at the smelter where she was not allowed. And some of the rough gold bricks she occasionally had to work from. All of it putting her at risk of collusion.

The thought sent a new wave of nausea to her stomach. But there was no time to worry about Haldor's indiscretions now. Maybe he planned to have the brooch stolen before it ever made it to the palace. It was no longer her concern. With the gold she had on her work bench, and the pieces she'd found in the box, she could deliver her new pieces to the treasury and sell the duplicates to start a new life.

"Or get yourself hanged," she said aloud. But it was too late to change her mind. The smell of Haldor's body would soon drift to the nearby village and bring citizens to his door.

She hauled the box to the atrium along with her tools, some bedding for the road, and some clothing suitable for her deception. A last frantic search of Haldor's chamber turned up a cache of coins and the key to the stone storage building by the stream. She could hide herself there until cover of dark, load Haldor's mule, and head, disguised as a young lad, toward Chalcedon and the Strait of Bosphorus.

Chapter Twenty-Two

Kindra stood inside an alcove at the back of the caldarium where she had spent the night. Her mule nudged her shoulder. She gave his trusty nose a rub. While a fine mist had owned the night, morning dawned dry and promising. Her spirits lifted by degrees as the streets and walls about her steamed in the brightening sunshine.

She tightened the straps around her midsection. Haldor's robe was too big for her woman's frame, but the extra wrapping helped to conceal her curves. His leather belt went two times around her middle adding to the bulky effect. She touched her fingertips to the tender spot on her cheek. If it looked anything like her arm, citizens would think she had been in a fight. She hoped letting her short-cropped hair fall forward would help conceal it. Traveling from Chalcedon to Constantinopolis would indeed have been impossible had she not been disguised as a young serf.

Crossing the Bosphorus had been her biggest worry. She knew she would have to persuade a boat owner to let her on board with the mule. With a flash of coin from her purse, she had merged with a small troupe of merchants who banded together to pay a ferry fee to travel across with their livestock. With her head down and her mule close, she was just another traveler, and no one had been the wiser.

Once outside the walls of the metropolis, she abandoned the group and made her way to a public bath to plan the next phase of her push to the palace. Even with Haldor's signet ring, she couldn't present herself looking like a stable boy who'd been in a fight.

A soak in the hot caldarium boosted her spirits and an alcove at the back of the structure provided shelter for the night.

Tightening the straps holding her belongings on the mule's back, she straightened her shoulders and stepped from behind the bath and onto a narrow side street where family laundry hung overhead from open windows.

Low, featureless buildings created a whitewashed maze around the outskirts of Constantine's great city, which would, by Imperial decree, be enclosed within a towering wall by the end of the summer. Few men were about the streets at this early hour, but several women dressed in gray wool or cotton robes and tunics hurried about, carrying baskets of bread fresh baked in the early morning hours.

Kindra's mouth watered at the aroma. She stopped one of the women who was likely heading for a lesser market to offer her loaves for sale. She was not disappointed. The bread tasted as good as its heady aroma promised. After a few voracious bites to satisfy her gnawing hunger, she nibbled at the crust as she followed the baker deeper into the city.

The streets broadened. Square, whitewashed houses of the poor gave way to more elaborate dwellings. Window boxes bloomed with color, trailing red geraniums and crocus. And where the real flowers left off, frescoed exterior walls bloomed with flower garlands — yellow, gold, and red, running around doors, archways, and window frames — so lifelike one could scarcely tell where the fresh flowers ended, and the painted ones began.

Such color! Haldor had told her of Constantine's love for the new Capital of his empire and had grumbled that the treasuries had been stretched thin to make Constantinopolis the most beautiful city on earth.

Kindra thought the money well spent, soon forgetting the base dwellings of the poor. Fatigue faded behind the rainbow of color and she envisioned, as she did in all things, the patterns and colors transformed into gold filigree and precious stones.

More people stirred in this part of the city. The baker led her to a square where many others sat around the foot of a frescoed fountain. The young woman held her earthen jar under silver sheets of water spilling from the fountain bowls. Another woman washed upturned faces of children clinging to her robes. The women's clothing reflected the color of the streets. A mother and daughter shared the same pattern on their pallas — strips of color embroidered around the hemlines and sleeves — some women had patchworked whole scenes into the skirts of their white cotton robes.

Kindra's heart swelled with the dream of one day creating and wearing such finery. The color and beauty of the square lifted her thoughts away from her plight, and for a few precious moments she felt as much a part of the morning ritual as the others.

But as she scooped another handful of water into her mouth, she raised her eyes to find that nearly every woman at the fountain was staring at her. Her face flushed. It must be as bright as the tile pattern around the base of the fountain.

She was a stranger after all — a young man who did not belong in this place of women at this time of day. She had let down her guard. Dreams of clean gowns, flowers, and children would have to wait. She had business to attend and it would do no good to be caught out this early in her quest.

With lowered eyes, she moved away quickly, drawing her mule down the flag-stoned way.

The street grew broader, and as the morning advanced, more and more citizens milled about, jostling her at times, drawing her into a flow of energy and excitement pushing ever closer to the heart of the city.

She forgot her hunger and her ill-fitting clothes. The splendor of Constantine's city broke over her like a consuming wave, depositing her at last upon a thoroughfare lined on either side with great, marbled statues. A single, wide passage shaded with olive trees led to the southern-most gates of the Emperor's palace.

The palace hunched like a gilded giant, ten times larger than Kindra had imagined. A square tower guarded each corner of the stone fortress and lesser towers flanked either side of reinforced gates in three of the four walls. The fourth wall faced the Sea of Marama near the Bosporus, connecting the watery passage to the Black Sea.

The crowd pulsed suddenly forward, surging this way and that as people jostled for a better look. What had caused the excitement? Kindra craned her neck to get a better look.

Two soldiers strode on foot through the spectators, pushing them back. "Watch it there! Ho there! Make way, I say you!"

Kindra set a foot on her mule's pack and raised up to see above the level of the crowd, but all she saw was chaos.

What is happening?

One of the soldiers shoved Kindra back, knocking a bundle from her mule. She fell against a woman who held one corner post of a merchant's canopy. The fall knocked the wind out of her.

The two women stared at each other in surprise. Kindra blinked, catching her breath. "I'm sorry. Are you all right?"

"Yes, yes. Here. Help me hold this." The woman thrust the pole into Kindra's hands as she pulled her out of the way.

"Wait, my things!" Kindra made a grab for a corner of her bundle which had been kicked out in the road when it fell off her mule.

"Get yourself out of the way, child," the woman insisted.

Kindra struggled to her feet. "What's happening? What is everyone waiting for?"

"The Emperor's family is visiting the palace. Their entourage is about to come into view." The woman pointed near the palace gates. "See the dust billowing just there?"

The Emperor's family? So, they had arrived in the city on the same day. There had to be something in that.

"Oh, see there?" The woman went on excitedly. "The horsemen are coming, and soon, the buglers."

"Buglers?" Kindra had heard of buglers, but never heard their sound.

She stood on tiptoe to see beyond bobbing heads. By the gods! Helmeted men on great steeds approached amid cheers from the crowd. Constantine had proved himself truly worthy of wearing the Purple. He had made their city strong — a jewel among all of Rome. They welcomed his family with all the honor and wonder their great collective heart could bestow.

The horns blared like a gaggle of flying geese, heralding the arrival of the Imperial party; and then, as if by royal decree, the bugling stopped.

Kindra turned at the sound of grating behind her. The massive palace doors swung wide. A new wave of excitement surged among those closest to the gate and spread through the crowd, pressing them ever tighter into one pulsing mass. She had no choice but to move with the crush. Holding tight to her mule's tether with one hand and the woman's pole in the other, she was pushed further away from her bundled belongings which still lay tumbled in the street.

The horsemen drew closer, towering above the people. The first horse deftly sidestepped the bundle; foaming sweat flew from its flanks and pelted her in the face. She tried desperately to make a grab for the package, but the crowd seemed always to push her away from her goal.

Her best palla and her beautiful blue silk, would be trampled in the street. She would never be able to replace them. She must break free. She must!

As the first horse and rider passed, she let go of the post and made a desperate dive, landing square atop her bundle, but before she could gain her feet and scramble to safety, the second horseman was on her. The rider guided the horse's hooves from the obstruction, but another wild surge ran through the unruly crowd. The beast shied and stamped, catching Kindra on the forehead with a sickening blow. She held tight to her precious bundle until her vision blurred and her knees buckled. The only thing keeping her upright was the suffocating press of the crowd.

The procession continued through the gate, more horsemen, and finally, covered litters carrying the Emperor's daughter and young son, and in her own litter, draped in silks tied back at the corners with gold braid, rode the Empress Fausta herself.

"Faus-ta, Faus-ta!" the crowd chanted. Her litter was flanked by twenty foot soldiers all bearing the seal of the Emperor on their shields and wearing gold neck circlets as a sign of their allegiance to Constantine.

Kindra stared at the spectacle as long as she could, but as the procession moved away, the sickening dizziness overtook her. She fell against the wall of a building and slid down. Her world narrowed to a tiny dot of light for one frightening moment, and then, all was dark.

CHAPTER TWENTY-THREE

"It's a nasty gash, but not one to put an end to your life, my child." The woman's voice was soft and gentle. Kindra opened her eyes. Faces swam into and out of focus. Try as she would, she could not shake the feeling she was under water.

Visions floated in her mind as she groped for the surface. Gold coins dropped into a woman's hand. Swirls of azure blue silk. Blood.

She tried to lever herself up on the cot. Dizziness overtook her. There was a firm pressure on her arm.

"You're safe," the gentle voice came again.

"Mama?" Kindra whispered. *Please, let me see her face just one more time.* Instead, memories of events marched forward. Not her mother's face, but the face of a handsome man with eyes on fire, and then … the face of another man beaten to a bloody pulp.

Her stomach lurched and she coughed. *Haldor. Oh! Yes.* She was alone and on the run. A murderess. A sinner against God. She prayed for the blackness again with eyes clenched tight.

The woman drew a cloth from a bowl of water on the table next to the cot where she lay and wiped her face in gently caring strokes. "You should be all right in a day or two — with some rest."

Kindra shook her head. "Please. Where am I? How did I come to be here?"

The woman released a melodious laugh. "Oh, my dear, you practically fell through my doorway. Cursed be the soldiers who give no thought to the citizens they trample in the street." She refreshed the cloth with cool water and pressed it against Kindra's forehead. "Though it is probably a blessing they paid you no heed. You are better served in our household, considering …"

Kindra closed her eyes, the cool water was soothing, but the bump on her forehead throbbed. Images flooded back: The gate. The crowd. The horses. Her bundle.

"My clothes." She moaned, raising to one elbow. Blinding pain stabbed beneath her brow, and the room slipped sideways. She clutched the woman's shoulders. "Please. Where is my mule? My package?"

The woman tipped a cup to her lips and bid her to drink, then pressed her gently, but firmly back onto the palette. "It would seem you have an interesting story to tell, my daughter, but now you must rest."

Daughter?

Kindra lay back on the cot. Realizing for the first time her garment had been changed to a light cotton tunic, similar to the ones she had seen the women wearing at the fountain. It was clean and sweetly scented, like in a dream she had once had. She cupped one breast in her hand and then realized to her dismay, the cloth wrap she had used to flatten her chest had been removed.

Daughter.

It had been long since she had heard the word, and an eternity since she had ever thought of herself as one. The woman seemed sincere in her ministrations, yet Kindra's heart raced with fear at the knowledge that this stranger knew she had been concealing at least her sex, and with that, probably a lot more.

All of her mind was bent on retrieving her belongings and getting on her way, but her body would not respond. Instead the sweet smell of herbs wafted through her being, crossing the threshold of pain, lulling her back into a peaceful oblivion.

Kindra rocked under sail on a quiet sea, a gentle wind at her back; effortless, euphoric, free. When she first became aware of the tinkling sound, she thought it was part of a dream. But as consciousness pulled her thread-by-thread from the tapestry of sleep, she surrendered to a confused wakefulness.

She was alone in a pleasant room. Warm daylight filtered in through an open window. She rose carefully from the cot, testing each new angle of her body for pain before making her move.

Thankfully, the only real sensation dominating her being was a gnawing emptiness in her stomach. She stepped gingerly to the window and looked out upon a sunny courtyard paved in colorful tiles and graced by a lovely three-tiered fountain whose dancing waters she now recognized as the source of the music that had teased her awake.

The walls had been frescoed with a hunt scene, alive with green vines, golden sun, and a brilliant blue sky. If she had not yet heard tales of even richer grandeur, she might have thought herself already in the palace of the Emperor.

"I see you are feeling much better today."

Startled by the intrusion of a voice when she had thought herself alone, Kindra turned to find her benefactor standing in the doorway.

She put her fingers to her forehead and traced over a sizable knot. "Yes. Much. How long have I--"

"Two days. The swelling of your brow has gone down a great deal."

Two days? How could that be? "I don't know how to thank you. All that I have belongs to the Emperor."

"In that you are no different than I. I would be living like the poor on the outskirts of the city were it not that my son is one of the Emperor's chosen men and my daughter, Anastasia, a part of the Imperial household."

"Where are my belongings?" Kindra looked around the room. "I can't trouble you further for I cannot repay --"

The woman only smiled. "Do not worry, daughter. You are not a burden to us here. You must be starving. Let me prepare you something to eat, then we will talk about your … situation."

Kindra's body, which had never known the luxury of fat, had lost much weight over the last few days. Except for a bit of bread before the Empresses' procession waylaid her plans, she couldn't remember the last time she had eaten. She felt like a sylph, barely there. Yes, food first. Then she would have to be on her way.

She knelt at the woman's feet, touching her bruised forehead on the floor tiles. "I am much indebted to you."

The woman offered her hand. "Arise, my child. You are no servant here; you are my guest." She opened the large basket at the end of the cot and produced Kindra's bundle, neither opened nor tampered with.

"I am Flavia," the woman said, and led her from the bedchamber to the adjoining dining room, talking as she went. "Do not let our rich surroundings fool you. You remind me of myself as a young girl. Were it not for the notice of a young soldier who fathered my son, I might still be of the servant class myself."

The woman told her she had little opportunity to speak to those who have traveled far, as surely she must have. Flavia eyed her worn, dusty sandals. Kindra watched her as she moved across the room, the sunlight streamed through the courtyard windows and glinted off golden threads woven into her linen robe; each step displayed panels of colored scenes and intricate embroideries about the hem.

Kindra lowered her eyes, reminded of the tattered condition in which she had arrived. Their two worlds, she realized, were separated by a gaping abyss, one she had been born never to bridge. But Flavia continued to speak as if entertaining a friend of her own class.

"My son ranges far in the service of the Emperor, and I see him little. I am happy to have a companion, if only for a short time."

Kindra seated herself at the side of a long table laden with fresh fruit and bread, a bounty not even Haldor had enjoyed. Indeed, this woman was well provided with the amenities of those privileged to work directly for the Emperor. Flavia lifted an ewer of copper with gold trim and poured a deep-red wine into two tall-stemmed goblets, then passed one to her.

Kindra selected a piece of bread from the platter before her and brought it to her nose. Her mouth watered at the aroma and visions of herself gorging on it and washing it down with wine, but she held herself in check.

In all her memory, she had never been treated in any manner near the charitable, loving way that Flavia had done. Perhaps she could trust this kindhearted woman. She had made a deal with herself, hadn't she? Freedom at any cost? She would have to trust someone. She returned the bread to the platter and fixed Flavia with a straightforward gaze.

"I am Kindra -- a craftswoman." She waited for the woman's reaction. For a slave to proclaim herself part of the craftsman class was near blasphemy.

Flavia laughed, goodheartedly. "You are in need of food, my dear. I do believe you are delirious."

"Perhaps I am," Kindra replied, and let her eyes wander over the high-ceilinged dining room decorated in the same frescoed murals as in the courtyard. Horses and hounds leapt among the tall grasses and here and there a fox's red coat glinted between graceful reeds. Then she returned her gaze to Flavia who smiled reassuringly.

"Go ahead then, Kindra the Craftswoman. Break your fast in peace. You are welcome to stay here until you have regained your strength and then — well, then, as I said, I am alone here — I can use the company." She smiled gently and began to eat.

200

Kindra, following her example, gave way to her hunger and ate without speaking further. After the meal, she returned to her room to rest. Sitting on the cot alone, she clutched her old life in her arms. What kind of life had it been anyway? Wasn't it worth taking some risks for a new one, even if her effort came to naught? She opened the bundle and pulled from it the blue silk. Perhaps she would have a little time to make herself a robe of it — she may never get a chance to wear it — for her freedom plan to work, she must be known as a man — but for a time, even if only a few days, she would feel its softness against her skin, remember a warm night in Haldor's anteroom where she had been treated like a woman. She was grateful for the brief moments she had shared with that man — Marcus — regardless of the outcome.

She would make from the silk a blue palla and whenever she wore it, she would remember the eyes of the one who gave it to her.

She unfurled the bolt and began to drape the fabric over herself, planning the shape the garment would take and how to best accomplish the task.

It was several days before the garment was finished and she was able to model it for Flavia.

"You look so lovely my child," she told her. "It is truly a shame that you feel you must disguise yourself so — few women are as beautiful as you. I wish you could just stay here with me. My son will soon be home from Thrace and wouldn't he be surprised to find someone like you at home when he arrived!" She took Kindra's hands in hers and smiled into her eyes.

"No one wishes my life could be different more than I." Kindra stretched out a leg to admire the fabric's drape. "I hope I will be able to earn enough on my delivery to the palace to start a jewelers craft shop of my own, and then — well …" She hesitated for she had no idea how to proceed at this point. "…it will take some time, I am sure."

She turned to the basket, masking a trembling sigh, and brought forth the remaining silk. "I want you to keep this in payment for all you have done; it is the only thing of value I own."

Flavia could likely have purchased ten bolts of silk that afternoon at the marketplace if she wanted, but the tender expression in her eyes said she recognized the sentiment that had spawned the gesture, and she accepted the gift without protest.

"Thank you, my daughter. It is truly an elegant gift and I consider the debt well paid. But you are incorrect in your assumption that it is the only thing of value that you own. You have an indomitable spirit. For that reason, it is a great sorrow to me that you won't be able to meet my son, for I would cherish a daughter-in-law who would serve him in such a fine spirit, and the grandchildren — Oh. Bless me, I'm getting a little carried away. Perhaps you may someday meet him. I hope you won't be dressed as a young lad when you do."

CHAPTER TWENTY-FOUR

***The messenger from the palace treasury arrived,
unannounced,*** on a sunny afternoon at the end of
the second month of Kindra's stay with Flavia and
her daughter. Fortunately for Kindra, who had been
passing her days without her male disguise, Flavia
had been the one who opened the door to the villa.

From her chamber, Kindra listened with mixed
emotions: excitement at the thought her plans were
about to move forward; sadness that her time with
Flavia would be coming to an end. She couldn't
remember a time when she'd been more content.
She had always known this day would come, but
now that it was here, she almost wished she'd given
up her quest.

It wasn't for lack of trying, after all. Once she had
recovered from her head injury, she had made
several attempts to approach the palace, each time
being turned away by an officious magistrate who,
even with her male disguise, refused to take her
claim seriously.

The last time, weeks ago now, had made her
wonder if she should simply accept her new life in
the city and forget the gold. She had stood at the
palace gates with likely the most valuable shipment
ever delivered at one time and a bloated man with
bulging eyes looked upon her as if she were the toad.

"Haldor the Goldsmith has no apprentice," the
magistrate had announced, as if she were a reptile he

could squash under his foot. "Go away and don't bother the Empress further."

She had half expected someone like the magistrate to see through her guise and arrest her for murder on the spot. At the least, they might seek to relieve her of her gold and send her away empty handed. As it turned out, they had no interest in her at all.

A wave of indignation ripped through her ego on that day. But as she returned to Flavia's down the now-familiar streets with their frescoed walls and musical fountains; mothers and children enjoying the sunshine in their respective sectors of the city; her indignation was replaced by a sense of relief.

She had been accepted as a member of Flavia's household and had all but forgotten dreams of creating jewelry for the rich. The women had become fast friends, and while Kindra did her share to keep the household going, she was never expected to do more than the others and she was treated as an equal.

She had indeed become like the women she had seen at the fountain when she first arrived in town. Their existence centered around home, food, and family. She had been lulled into an easy rhythm of peaceful life: soft voices, silky cloth, nimble needles. She relaxed into soothing elixirs of tea, fresh air, and peaceful sleep, uninterrupted by orders from a drunken taskmaster. Her commodious chamber, and the camaraderie of women and children suited her and fed new dreams of what her life could be.

She had hidden the box of gold under her cot and out of her mind, along with images of Haldor's body slumped on the floor.

It had been Anastasia's idea to apply directly to the palace treasurer, rather than try to gain entrance through the magistrate at the supplicant's gate.

"It is the treasurer who actually commissioned the work, Kindra. As a servant to the Empress, it occurs to me I can bypass that toad at the magistrate's office and take a letter directly to the treasury."

Now, as Kindra stood in the alcove outside her chamber and listened to the messenger's voice, Kindra wished she had told Anastasia not to bother.

"Kindard of Chalcedon," the messenger announced, "... is to be escorted to the Tribunal of the Palace Treasurer immediately."

Her heart slammed into her throat. *Tribunal? Immediately?* What did that mean? She fetched her basket from the corner of the room and spread the contents on her cot. She and Flavia had prepared an outfit suitable for going before the palace treasurer some time ago. But when the last chance proved unproductive, she had all but forgotten that, too.

"I'll go fetch the lad." Flavia's words, spoken louder than necessary, served as advance warning. "Please, wait in the garden."

When Kindra heard the sound of the front door scraping closed across the threshold, then Flavia's hurried footsteps rushing down the hall, she threw herself into action.

By the time Flavia joined her in her chamber, Kindra had already removed her embroidered-cotton tunic and begun to wrap a length of linen cloth tightly around her breasts. To her surprise, they had grown swollen and tender to the touch since she last wrapped them, a fact that caused her sudden alarm. Surely it was some effect of her injury, but as the truth dawned, she counted the time. Defeated, she recognized the signs. Her breasts hurt and she had not bled in these last two cycles of the moon — facts she had conveniently ignored. All the more reason to get her business over with and soon. She dragged her thoughts back to the task at hand, for it would do no good to dwell on the possibilities.

"This was my son's when he was fourteen years old," Flavia said as she helped her don the young man's clothing. Kindra saw in the mother's eyes the love she bore for her son and her hand went to her own belly at the thought.

"There, now," Flavia went on, dropping a leather corselet over Kindra's head, further hiding her breasts behind the carefully sculpted relief of a young man's muscular chest.

She nodded approvingly. "Speak as little as possible, keep those lovely eyes lowered, and you just might pass — her eyes went to Kindra's stomach — for a time."

Kindra's eyes met hers, then shifted away. Flavia turned her face back with a gentle touch. "I trust you were a willing participant in the making of this child? Because, if not, there are ways —

"No!" Kindra caught her breath at the thought. "No. If I never see the father again, at least I will see him in my babe's eyes."

Flavia gave her a knowing smile. "Bless you, my child. He would be a fortunate man indeed to find you again."

Kindra despaired of that happening but pushed her longing down deep inside where she could keep it safe.

❦

Kindra wished she had taken time to eat before she was whisked off to the palace. Her stomach complained bitterly as the afternoon dragged on. The guards bearing her to the palace bypassed a number of merchants gathered outside the gates. As they approached what she assumed was the Office of the Treasury, another group of citizens waited. Kindra's hopes of getting this over with quickly evaporated.

For a while, she entertained herself trying to guess what business the other citizens had. Taxes owed? Perhaps paying for a son's conscription into the guard? Or, as Marcus had lamented, receiving payment for some secret nefarious deed performed for the emperor?

But as the sun began to descend, casting long shadows through a window and across the chamber floor, she despaired of being seen by a palace rat, let alone the treasurer. Her shoulders drooped, and she leaned against a wall for support, eyes almost closed.

So it was that she let out an unmanly shriek when a tribune tapped her sharply on the shoulder.

"The Palace Treasurer will see you now. Follow me."

The tribune was off along the sides of the hall so quickly, Kindra had trouble keeping up. They passed out of the great hall and into a darker network of passages leading into the heart of the palace and away from the clamor of the main reception rooms.

The tribune stopped abruptly in front of a heavy door and knocked twice.

"Enter," came a booming voice from the other side.

The tribune ushered Kindra through the door and stood at attention by her side. The room felt more like the private quarters of a magistrate than the office of a palace treasurer. Along the walls, there were several couches covered in cushions and draped with animal fur. A low table in front of one of them was set with chargers of bread, cheeses and various cuts of dried meat. The scene presented a kind of relaxed atmosphere ill suited for conducting official business. Kindra had no real experience from which to draw comparison, but her instincts told her something was off. She was being isolated for a reason. She kept her eyes downcast, but otherwise remained on alert.

"Kindard of Chalcedon," the young tribune announced. She wasn't really from Chalcedon, but Anastasia thought it sounded better to connect herself directly with the trade hub than some insignificant village on its outskirts. Perhaps that was why her letter had gotten the attention of the treasurer. Perhaps not. Either way, now that she was here, the weight of what she was about to do bore down on her like milling stone.

"That will be all, Dracis," a man said, dismissing the lad. His voice was deep and resonant, but while it commanded authority, Kindra detected a hint of weariness. She could not help lifting her gaze from her feet to see the man who spoke.

He was tall; mature, with a full head of white hair expertly combed over his ears. His robes bespoke wealth and position as she might have expected, yet he wore the same type of touchstone on a leather thong about his waist as Haldor had done.

"I am Hector, Treasurer to Constantine and the Roman Empire," the man said, frankly.

Kindra's eyes shifted to her sandals once more.

"Hector," she repeated, keeping her voice in the lowest register possible.

Hector's pacing interrupted light streaming in through open windows and casting long shadows against the stone walls. His hands were clasped behind his back.

After two circuits of the room, he turned and addressed her. "It is not my custom to receive merchants in my private quarters, but I have made and exception for a reported delivery from Haldor the Goldsmith, a man whom I have heard only this morning to have been found murdered in his home some weeks ago."

Kindra could not mask a sharp intake of breath. So that was the urgency. "M-murdered, sir?" She swallowed hard.

"I assume, as his apprentice, you lived near his villa? Perhaps in his compound?"

"I — uh, yes. Sir. But —"

"And, I assume, that you have been making the rounds of his deliveries for him without knowledge of the situation?"

"N-no, sir. I mean, yes, sir. It is indeed a shock to hear this news."

Git a grip, girl. Straighten your spine and chill.

Chill? Of all times, the voice of her inner demon had returned?

Kindra clenched her fists and refused to be goaded into a weak position by the voice or Hector.

Stopping in front of one of the couches, Hector let himself drop heavily to sit. He exhaled deeply. "It is a shock to me as well, master Kindard." He looked her up and down. After a moment, his gaze went back to the window. "Haldor was a personal friend of mine. We served Diocletian together in the palace at Nicomedia. That was, until his ... retirement." He selected a small bread roll from the tray and took a delicate bite.

Kindra's stomach growled and she willed it to be quiet.

"He was once renowned in all of Rome, did you know that?"

Kindra shifted her stance, perceiving it was a rhetorical question. She'd been standing on her feet for several hours now and wanted more than ever to sit down. The aroma of the baked bread filled her senses and her mouth watered. She watched him covertly from the corner of her eye and held fast to her resolve.

"As a friend, I have to say it has been difficult to watch him decline from that lofty position to a slovenly man," he went on. "Crippled by disease and greed until his fingers were no longer pliant and his heart no longer trustworthy. At least not to honest men."

Kindra had nothing to say to that and kept quiet. She had no idea what was happening here, but since she could not contribute, she waited respectfully to let the man get to his point.

Hector laughed to himself. "But then, there are no truly honest men, am I right?" His tone made her glance up to meet his gaze. Perhaps the man was in his cups or playing with her. All she could do was nod her head.

"Oh, come on. Constantine himself could not have risen to supreme power without the sweat and deceit of men motivated by avarice and the possible attainment of positions of importance and power." He stuffed the rest of the bread in his mouth, then licked his fingers and chewed.

"Oh, please. Forgive me. I am a rude host." He swallowed the last of the roll, lifted the platter, and bid Kindra to come forward. "These are quite good, loaded with honey and cardamom."

Kindra nodded and, in the character of a young man rather than a girl, she snatched two rolls from the plate and sank her teeth into one of them. Indeed, the roll was sweet on her tongue.

Hector nodded and smiled, then indicated the other couch. "Sit, Kindard of Chalcedon."

Kindra welcomed the invitation for she wasn't sure whether she would faint from lack of food or retch in her next breath.

Hector watched her a moment longer, and then his brows hinged together at the center of his forehead.

"It was curious to me, Kindard, that even though you claim to have a delivery bound for the Empress, that no gold at all was found at Haldor's villa. Surely the Empress didn't order every last piece in Haldor's horde."

Bolstered with food and rest at last, Kindra found some courage. "You suspect a robbery, then Sir?"

The man studied her a moment longer before he spoke. "As I told you, Haldor was my friend. Meaning, I knew him better than most. I suspect Haldor was murdered because he was a gambler who let his hunger for winning get the better of him. Whatever twisted workings of fate had made it so are not my concern. Here in the treasury of the Emperor's greatest jewel, his beautiful Constantinopolis, riches can always be made in the gold trade, one way or another."

He stood once again and paced the room. "They said Haldor had been bludgeoned almost beyond identification." He let his words hang in the air between them a long moment before he went on. "He was an old man. Feeble and crippled. He could have been incapacitated with one blow to the head, don't you think? I mean, you knew him well, right? Worked with him. For him?"

She nodded. "He was weak and drank much, so, that would be an accurate statement." She fought to keep her voice steady.

"I'd say whoever killed him — murdered him — had a reason beyond robbery to take the beating so far."

"One would think," Kindra returned cautiously, the images of her arm swinging down, down, down, played in her memory. Her heart pounded hard against her ribs.

Don't let him see your fear.

Right. She willed the thumping in her chest to settle and lifted her chin, then she returned his gaze head on.

"But most curious was the fact that whoever did the deed cut off his left-hand ring finger. The finger lay by his body, but the signet ring identifying him as the master goldsmith of the emperor was missing. The signet ring you wear on your finger now, if I'm not mistaken."

His eyes took on the sickening glint of a snake ready to strike.

Holy shit. Oh my god.

Shhhhhh. Be quiet. Kindra had already thought of how she would address this issue should it arise. There was no point in hiding it. She removed the ring, rose, and strode the few steps to Hector, then placed it in his hand. "As you see, I do have a signet ring. If you look inside, it has Hector's mark — that *H* there —" she added with a lift of her chin. "If you know his work as you say, then you know his mark."

Hector raised a brow.

"As I often travel on his behalf at the same time as he, he stamped an identical ring for me, so that I could do business — no doubt, as we know — while he visited the ponies." She locked eyes with the old

213

man again. It was an outright lie. "But, we are wasting time, are we not?" The ruse was sapping her strength, but she had to hold on, take control.

She shrugged the satchel off her shoulder and lay it on the table. Digging out a small pouch, she lay a heavy cabochon ring and a gold circlet on the satchel. They had not found peace with gravity before Hector snatched one up and inspected it closely, a ring Kindra had made over the last weeks in Haldor's absence.

"Superior workmanship; it is beyond question," he said, turning it over in his hand. "No one in the empire knows this better than I. But I would be a fool if I did not check," he said, and brought forth the smooth, black stone from around his waist and rubbed the underside of his own signet ring against it, leaving a golden mark.

Kindra stood like a statue, watching as Hector used the cabochon ring to rub a wide mark on the stone next to the first one. Then he retrieved a small bottle from the table, removed the stopper, and poured the solution over the two scratches, catching the residual in a shallow plate.

Perspiration trickled between Kindra's breasts and thankfully soaked into the wrapping, so it did not betray her nerves.

Hector pinned her with a penetrating gaze. Kindra held her breath as the seconds ticked away.

At last, and to her great relief, he nodded, satisfied. "These pieces are magnificent. I trust the Empress will be pleased with the rest of the shipment."

"I'm pleased you believe so." Kindra steeled herself for the next step. "The remainder of the order is here in this pouch," she continued. "I've made a list of the pieces and the payment due."

"Payment? To whom? Haldor is dead."

She gathered her wits and steeled her jaw. "Why to me, of course. As we both know, with his ruined hands, Haldor could no more have made the pieces of jewelry before you than a dung beetle. These pieces — in fact, all the pieces you see here — were made by me."

"But they bear his mark."

"By his leave, naturally. How else could I sell them as his own?"

Hector's brows folded. "Are you saying you — his apprentice — made all these pieces?"

What difference did it make anymore, keeping Haldor's secret? In fact, revealing the secret could work in her favor. Give her credibility. "These past two years. Sir. Haldor has kept it secret so as not to soil his reputation, but I was hired by him for that very purpose. I have, in fact, made every piece you've received from Haldor for all this time, including that signet ring on your own finger. If you look closely, you see my mark on it as well." She pointed out the delta mark on her signet ring. "You'll find it on every piece made in the last two years."

It was a gamble, but the odds were in her favor. She had made several signet rings under Haldor's employ. There were only a few possibilities as to the officers privileged to wear them. Still, she held her breath as she watched Hector remove his ring. By the way he squinted as he compared it to hers, she doubted he could see anything but scratches, but his vanity wouldn't let him admit his fault. Before he commented further, she emptied the satchel and lay out all the pieces on the leather bag, confident the gleaming gold would capture his attention.

Hector arranged two earrings side-by-side on the table. "You have some high-minded ways about you, for one so young, master Kindard. If what you say is true, perhaps you might be persuaded to carry on in your dead master's footsteps."

Kindra let go a false laugh. "If it is not true, then you would have to believe that I murdered Haldor, stole his gold, and brought it directly to you."

He squinted at her. She imagined him mulling her words over in his mind. "Indeed," he said after a moment.

Kindra's heart raced. Working for the palace treasurery would work out well until her stomach bloated like a swine. "It is certainly something to think about, my lord, if what you say about Haldor is true. In the meantime, I require payment for this current delivery in order to arrange another place to live."

Hector nodded, approvingly. "You will be paid tomorrow when the Empress has passed her approval. In the meantime, you will be our guest." He bowed low, clapped his hands, and the tribune appeared in the doorway.

"Dracis will take you to your quarters." He slipped the earrings back into the pouch along with the other pieces and dropped the pouch onto the table, then turned his back on them.

Kindra relaxed a fraction. She had often dreamed of one day traveling to Constantinopolis to see the palace walls; never had she thought it would really happen, let alone actually be a guest within. The immense size and richness of the palace went far beyond her imaginings.

Dracis led her hurriedly down a passage that, if she had kept her bearings, ran the full length of the seawall, and then up several flights of stone stairs.

At a recess along a dark corridor, the young tribune unbolted a door and showed her into a small chamber. "I will call for you in the morning," he said before pulling the door closed behind him.

The space was considerably darker than Hector's had been; one narrow window, high in the chamber wall, let in a thin shaft of light. The room was meagerly furnished. There was a small table; a three-legged stool, and a narrow cot covered with a woolen blanket; no lamp and no food. Just an urn that Kindra hoped contained drinkable water.

Her shoulders drooped under the stiff leather chest shield. It seemed that no matter how grand and lofty a place, there was always an oppressive corner in which to humiliate the lowborn. Her initial rapture at being in the palace with its soaring, vaulted ceilings and gilded walls, diminished like the thin ray of sunshine struggling through the deep-set window. Even that was so high up she could not see out of it.

She sat on the cot, eyes closed, letting the conversation with Hector sink with a chill into her bones.

He had all but accused her of murder and were it not for his true appreciation for the work she delivered, she guessed he might have had her dragged away in chains. He might at this moment be discussing the facts with her guards, and soon they would come for her.

She jumped at every muted sound heard in the distant reaches of the palace. She cringed and covered her ears with her hands at a gull's scree near the window. Her courage flagged.

Bringing the jewelry here was a terrible mistake. She would never be free. She would never see Flavia again. Or Marcus. She would never again turn a lump of gold and colored glass into a work of art.

She let her head sink into her hands and stared at the chamber floor, fixed like a statue in her grief. Misery held her in its icy grip.

In all her memory she had never felt so warm and secure -- even loved — as she had during the time she had spent with Flavia. She could have stayed, given up her high ideas of becoming a member of the Guild, and been sitting in a sunny courtyard right this minute, wearing her blue gown, baking honey cakes with Flavia for the children, and one day her own child would come and it would have Marcus's eyes and that would be enough.

What a fool she had been. Of course, she wanted to work the gold when it was the only thing that brought her any pleasure. But at Flavia's, she'd had a glimpse of another kind of treasure. An actual life. Filled with toil? Maybe, but also filled with friends, children, and possibly someone to love.

She thought about the children now, playing by the fountain, begging at the arched doorway for honey cakes; memories of their bright smiles brought a hint of warmth to her heart.

She couldn't give up. She had come this far, and she wasn't dead yet. She sprang up, dragged the cot across the room, upended it, then leaned it against the wall. She climbed up the slats on the bottom until she could reach the window, then pushed aside a wooden shutter partially covering the opening. Below, the Bosporus glinted in the late afternoon slant of sun.

Great merchant ships and small fishing vessels crowded the harbor. Every dock and quay bustled with activity as men raced the sun to the end of day. Hardly had one great ship unloaded its cargo and pulled away from a dock before another landed, spurring another flurry of carts and oxen and men swinging webs of rope.

Kindra had been so absorbed in the beauty of the city, and then in her tangle with the horse, that this was the first time she had looked upon the sea since she had arrived. She watched at the window until the sun went down, staining the sea gray against a darkening sky, leaving her view featureless but for the occasional wink of a lamp on a boat as it bobbed on the tide.

With the cot back in place, she lay restless for many hours before she fell into an exhausted sleep, her hand resting on the hollow of her stomach, the slight bump there no bigger than a chicken's egg.

Through the night, her dreams rolled with unfamiliar sounds of a distant shore.

She stood on a bluff watching leviathan monsters belch white smoke into the air from tall black horns on their backs, driving foaming wedges through inky seas.

She sailed like a seabird over white-sand coastline where angular horse-like creatures rocked their heads endlessly, fixed cruelly to the ground by their noses like hideous, pathetic slaves.

The earth groaned as night turned to day; a ceaseless, churning like the grinding of grain under stone or river against rock.

She awoke suddenly, clammy and shaken, wiping at her nose. A sharp bang on the chamber door brought her up from the cot with a start.

Chapter Twenty-Five

Wrapping her arms over aching breasts she had released from the wrappings during the night, she held her breath as metal scraped against metal outside the door.

Dracis stepped in, bearing a bowl of chunky stew and a crust of dark bread on a wooden tray.

"The Empress has informed Hector she is well pleased but wishes to speak with you in the main hall herself."

The tribune, not much older than herself, bore the droop shoulders and broken spirit of a badly used servant.

"I thought you might be hungry." He set the bowl and bread on a low table at the end of the cot. He moved away without taking his eyes from it as if it were his own meal he had given.

"Thank you, Dracis, you are very thoughtful." All she had eaten in the last twenty-four hours were the small rolls she was offered in Hector's chamber, and her stomach complained bitterly.

Dracis waited in silence as Kindra broke off a piece of bread and soaked it in the broth, but the sight of his wide eyes and spindly arms would not let her eat. She broke off another piece.

"Come here." She patted the space next to her on the cot. "Sit down and help me eat this. I don't want to keep the Empress waiting."

The two young people slopped broth from the same bowl until it was clean and did not utter a word further.

❧

"Come," Fausta said to her as she nodded to Dracis to leave them alone. Hector's chamber had been impressive, but the Empress's antechamber was like being inside a dream. The floor was honeycombed in black and white marble and the walls covered in gilt and silken draperies. The ceiling vaulted nearly as high as that of the nave she had seen the day before, uninterrupted by columns.

Fausta reclined on a carved marble chaise, cushioned with silken pillows; and her mother, likewise. Several other women sat in chairs along the sidelines of the room or hovered about the Imperial women with trays of fruits, sweetmeats, and wine ready at their bidding.

One of them rose from her chair against the wall and eyed Kindra thoughtfully as she stepped forward and knelt on the furs at Fausta's feet. Kindra had no formal training in the etiquette to be shown to royalty and was unsure what behavior was expected.

"You may rise, son. This is not a formal hearing," Fausta said.

Kindra did so, remembering to keep her eyes lowered as Flavia had instructed.

"Your master is truly gifted, Kindard of Chalcedon." Had Hector not told her Haldor was dead? The Empress glided toward her until it was impossible not to look up. Her eyes — a gray, mossy green like fieldstone — gave nothing away. Kindra

222

gathered her quaking fingers into tight fists at her sides.

"All of the pieces are magnificent," Fausta continued, "However, I'm concerned about a piece my husband ordered specifically for his mother, Helena."

A chill jerked through Kindra's body. The broach! So, this would be her end. She dropped her gaze to her feet. A vision flashed, unbidden, before her mind: strong arms encircled her, and warm breath teased her breasts. Would happiness always elude her? Would she never know the warmth of passion again?

Fausta reached out and lifted her chin with her fingertips, forcing her to look at her once more. "This was a very special gift, Kindard. In gratitude for Helena's role in bringing down the pagan temple to erect a new church to honor the church of the true religion." She indicated a tray laid with the pieces Kindra had made. "That brooch doesn't seem to be here."

Kindra cursed the day she made the broach. There was nothing good in a world that put one man above another and make his brother a slave, and all the new churches would never change it. She fought for control, for some kind of response that wouldn't land her in a dark dungeon in the bowels of the palace for the rest of her days.

The Empress moved behind her, almost touching her body as she made the full circuit and then returned to her seat and rested her arms on her chair. "Perhaps you'd care to explain."

Kindra's pulse raced and her cheeks burned with the threat of discovery. Surely Fausta and everyone else in the room could see her great distress. Her spirit sank. The odds of her leaving here alive were shrinking by the second. She knew little of the royal family histories, but gossip of Constantine's first wife, Minerva, had reached even the slave ways. She had borne the Emperor's son, Crispus, but their alliance had not been one of dynastic power. To preserve his integrity, he divorced her. Banished was a better word for it, the way her name was stricken from the records and her son raised as if he had no mother.

Save yourself, Kindra. Stand up like you did with Hector. You've got nothing to lose.

True enough. She had an idea that might just save her skin. Kindra drew herself up, choosing her words carefully, so as to be frank, but not offend. "I assume you are aware of the situation regarding my master's demise?"

Fausta nodded. "I am."

"And that his villa had been ransacked and no gold was found?"

"Verily, I heard that as well."

Kindra took a deep breath, careful to keep her voice in the low register she had affected. It was difficult as she could scarcely breathe at this moment. "And, I assume, Hector told you that I am the one who had made all the jewelry delivered to the palace over the last two years?"

Fausta glanced to a woman on the sidelines, wide eyes asking the question. The woman nodded.

"I see," she said, her gaze sweeping over Kindra with new interest. "Do go on."

Kindra took a more powerful stance, her feet shoulder width apart, her thumbs cocked in the leather straps at her waist. "In truth, I am the one who made that brooch. I can't say what happened to it, but if the Emperor wishes to gift his mother with such a fine piece, I will be pleased to make another to replace it."

"Here? In the palace?" Fausta asked.

Kindra cleared her throat, her heartbeat racing at her temples. "Given the right tools and materials, I am indeed the only one who could, my Empress."

Fausta considered for a painfully long moment that had Kindra questioning her wisdom. She had overstepped the boundaries, and now she was going to pay. Her mouth went pasty, as the air seemed to leave the room.

At last the empress rose from her chair and motioned for the woman who had eyed Kindra from the sidelines to join her. It was all Kindra could do not to let out a gasp. The woman, whom she now saw wore leather armor like a praetorian guard, stood head and shoulders above the Empress and bore a riding crop with knotted strips of leather at the end. Kindra's knees felt suddenly weak and wobbly.

"This is Valeria. I put my trust in her," Fausta said. "She will direct you to a suitable workspace and provide you with what tools you require."

Kindra sucked in a breath. Her heart began to beat again, fluttery but enough to restore balance to her legs. Valeria moved closer, scrutinizing her from head to toe. She ran the smooth surface of her fingernail down the back of Kindra's bare arm, out of sight of the Empress.

Kindra grew tense, anger boiled within her; she sensed a threat in the woman's gesture; the nature of it escaped her, yet she dared not draw away. Danger or not, she had made up her mind to die, rather than to give up her goal. She stood rigid, pulled her resolve around her like a shield, and spoke, surprised at her own boldness.

"As I informed Hector yesterday, I am not merely a messenger, but a craftsman of the goldsmith trade. I require payment, for the pieces before any new commission, your grace."

Fausta stared at her, her eyes flashed wide a moment before she responded. "I do not concern myself with payment. You must take that up with Hector."

"What of the pieces already delivered. Were you not well pleased?"

Valeria clamped a hand on Kindra's shoulder. "Servant's do not address the Empress in such tone."

Fausta glared at Valeria from under drawn, angry brows. "Kindard is not to be considered a servant, Valeria, but a craftsman as he has stated."

Valeria retreated, raised her fist to her chest. "With your permission, my lady. Perhaps the young *man* is capable of what he claims. If so, we will have a master goldsmith at our disposal. The gods know Hector couldn't fashion a goat's eye out of soft clay."

Fausta raised her brow at her head servant. "Valeria, we no longer speak of 'gods' in this palace, nor soon, anywhere in the Empire."

"Your pardon, my lady. Old habits are hard lost." Valeria bowed low. Kindra slowly let out her breath.

The Empress brushed away the apology, gave Valeria a curt nod, turned, and marched out of the room, followed by the entire entourage of women, save Valeria herself.

The moment the room was quiet, Valeria ran her hand down Kindra's back and over her buttocks, then she turned her roughly by the shoulders to face her, using the riding crop to lift her chin. "You may be able to fool Hector and even the Empress, but you don't fool me." Her voice was low and menacing as she stalked another circle around her charge.

Kindra held her breath once more. She had thought she was out of danger, or at least would have a reprieve until she could make an escape. She forced herself to hold still, mustering all her strength not to run.

Valeria stood breathing hard behind Kindra's back a moment longer, then with forceful jerks, she unstrapped the leather vest from Kindra's shoulders, tore her tunic down to her waist, and stripped the breast wrapping away.

She spun her again roughly, a vicious glint in her eye. "So! You *are* a woman! I thought so when you first walked across the room, but you might have been a man, yet womanly inclined." Her eyes roamed over Kindra's quivering body. "And I dare say, a very beautiful one, with a little more meat on you."

Kindra straightened her shoulders and made no attempt to cover herself. It was clear this was a woman who fed on fear and she wasn't going to give her that advantage.

Valeria narrowed her eyes on her prisoner, for a prison master is exactly the impression she gave. "It is my belief you are the very one who killed your master and robbed him and tried to sell his gold to us. You are a clever girl to get this far in your charade."

Kindra lifted her chin in defiance. "I tell you I made every piece I delivered today, and I am no thief. But if you want to please the Emperor, I suggest you allow me to do as the Empress bids."

Valeria laughed with derision. "I doubt very seriously you can do any such thing; but if by some miracle you produce something of passable quality, your life may be spared. But know this, I say you are a lying thief and you will meet your death in this very chamber if you don't deliver.

CHAPTER TWENTY-SIX

Marcus traced his fingers over the cloisonné brooch, marveling at its precise design, perfectly balanced colors, and tactile perfection. Never had he seen a more artistic representation of a cross. Whoever made this piece was a master of the craft and far ahead of their peers in execution. All the more improbable that it should have come to him via a very young woman who claimed to be a house servant. To think he had very nearly crushed it under his foot. It would have been a tragedy.

He strode to the tall window in his room overlooking the Moselle, thinking of the woman who wore it and the ragged hole her deception had ripped in his heart. It was likely he would never see her again.

The days preceding his departure had truly been unsettling because of the events themselves and because of his reaction to them. He had met a woman he could scarcely drive from his thoughts; then discovered the very person he'd been sent to investigate — the woman's master — had been murdered.

She, and the young man he'd met on the morning of the murder, had vanished like spindrift, along with the shipment of gold reported to have been delivered only the night before. His mind reeled with possibilities, not the least of which was that the innocent, Kindra, had thoroughly deceived him, used sex to distract him from his duty, and accomplished a robbery few men of greater strength and experience could have done.

He rubbed his thumb over the red stone in the center of the brooch, his heart thudding against his chest. Forget her, he told himself and considered pitching the piece in the river the first chance he got. For now, he pinned it inside his tunic. He imagined he could feel a remnant of her body heat against his skin.

Though Trier thrived as the westernmost capital of the empire, the city was a lonely outpost for Marcus. It was a long journey from his family and each time the order came to meet the emperor there, he chaffed under the responsibility. Constantine often sent him there with the assignment to inspect the Imperial Baths and other construction projects near the river. Marcus suspected his true motive was to check up on his son, Crispus, as he had left him in charge of the prefecture once he moved his official palace to Constantinopolis.

This was the first time however the Emperor had sent Marcus on a mission without an escort of a praetorian guard.

But, when the Emperor commanded, Marcus obeyed without question. It was his duty and his great pride to be the Emperor's first man. Not his righthand man, for Constantine had his praetorian prefects, consuls, and magistrates to be his voice to the citizens and armies in Gaul and Africa and the other territories.

And not as a son, for any man in line for the throne, even a son or a brother, was, as history had shown, not a man the Emperor could turn his back upon for fear of losing his life before he finished his reign.

A wise Emperor — and Constantine was wise if ever a man was — needed a man to guard his back.

Marcus was that man.

So, upon receiving his orders, he dispatched his entourage back to Constantinopolis, and set out through the mountain passes to follow the Danube with only a pack pony and his own, giant roan.

As the travel days drew to a close, he avoided the inns as the Emperor had advised.

"It would be better," Constantine ordered, "if you are not seen upon the road."

To what great secret did he owe this clandestine visit to Moselle? Much as he honored his allegiance to the Emperor, Marcus had grown to fear more and more the appearance of the messenger with the sealed missives. More and more, his assignments pushed the boundaries of what Marcus considered honorable.

Supervising the progress of Helena's activities throughout the land in the name of the Son of God was one thing; but applying pressure to those as yet unwilling or uninterested in following Helena's example was something different entirely and didn't seem to come from the same laws of Christianity his own mother had taught. Yet he owed the Emperor the good life he had, and the good life he was able to provide for his mother and sister.

His Father had served well in Gaul and lost his life to the Barbarians who were constantly invading the borderlands. Having served in Diocletian's armies himself, and his father before him, Constantine knew the value of a loyal soldier and took great pains to preserve that loyalty in his men. Should they fall in battle, they could rest assured he would care for their families.

He agreed to take Marcus into personal service — anything but battle, as his mother had requested. There were ways more valuable than soldiering in which the right man could do himself and his mother proud. Marcus had been trained well, first by education in the finest schools while his mother and sister were housed in Constantinopolis; and privately, at the Emperor's back, with the knowledge of only Helena.

Marcus knew not in what capacity this private training would be availed, but by the time he was eighteen, he had spent several years in the Emperor's private service and had proved himself worthy.

Marcus' place had become, if not at the Emperor's immediate back, then wherever his most personal wishes were to be carried out, with or without the knowledge of his Praetorian Prefects and official tribunes.

Now, he lay on a sumptuous pallet, the quarter moon low enough on the horizon to show its silver face through the window. Little that cold orb cared whether men were Christian or Pagans, or who ruled Rome now or would rule a thousand years hence.

Marcus clasped his hands behind his head and waited for sleep to come. As the moon climbed high leaving him restless, his thoughts spiraled once more, some of his pride returning.

He had served the Emperor well. He had done nothing to be ashamed of; his father would have been proud. He had followed a shipment of gold from Africa when Constantine was informed of discrepancies in the logs of ships after crossing the Mediterranean. He had traveled to Thrace to report on the building of a new cathedral there and to supervise the installation of gold-clad crosses in the name of Helena.

The face of the moon had watched him at every point on his journey. Marcus often imagined as a boy that his father's soul had gone up to the moon and it was his face that beamed down upon him. How he wished he could spend just one night in counsel with his father again.

Wherever Marcus went, he was deported and housed as any ordinary loyal servant, even though he wore the golden collar of personal service.

At the gymnasiums of Thrace or at the Imperial bath in Trier, the churches and the quarries, those who were closest to Constantine — his sons, his mother, his stepmother, his wife — knew that Marcus could not be bought or manipulated. And this was also a thing of which his father could be proud.

Marcus pulled in a deep sigh. He had done all he could in the many weeks he'd been here in Trier and chaffed to return to his family. Tomorrow he would meet with the Emperor at last and hopefully be discharged for home. With a heavy heart, he covered his eyes against the bright moonlight, and welcomed sleep.

He rose early the next morning, his body refreshed, but his mind still in turmoil. A short ride from the local prefect's quarters brought him within sight of the emperor's villa above the Moselle River. He halted for a moment, looking down upon the peaceful valley where the river cut through fields and olive orchards and budding vineyards. The sight should have brought him some peace. Instead, dread crept into his bones.

He had been here many times before and never had such a foreboding overcome his being. He had the disquieting worry that the river, once crossed, would, like an invisible, impassable barrier, forever keep him from returning to the life he had known.

Sensing his master's turmoil, his horse stamped and shifted in place. Marcus shook himself to relieve his mind from these thoughts. They were ridiculous, of course. There was no call for anxiety. His meetings with Constantine nearly always took place in secret and most often, at Moselle.

What kind of a servant minces so about his duty?

"Nonsense!" he growled aloud, angry at his weakness, and he kicked the roan's flank, urging him down to the river's edge and across the stone bridge.

The villa was not of the grand dimensions of the one at Constantinopolis but equaled it in beauty. It sat atop the left bank of the river, cooled by afternoon breezes through arches leading to courtyards along the outer edges of the manse.

Mature groves of olive and poplar shaded its porticoes, and the rooms facing the common courtyard at the center of the grounds were filled with the music of its fountains. It was a cool refuge in summer, and a haven from the dreary rain-soaked winters of the Capital.

By virtue of his uniform and shield, and the undeniable verity of the golden circlet around his neck, Marcus passed the guards of the outer walls without interference, noting the number of guards had been increased about the gate, a further sign the Emperor and his Empress would soon be in residence.

He was given the usual greeting of the platoon leader at the North peristyle. Once inside, he was whisked quietly to the south wing, where, unknown to all but Helena and her private staff, he was provided a suite of rooms throughout the year along with a personal bath.

"I understand Lord Constantine arrives tomorrow," he said to the young servant woman who removed his hauberk and led him to the bath already prepared for his pleasure.

"Yes sir. Helena has been waiting quite anxiously to see him as well."

Although Constantine allowed himself no such service while at Moselle and spoke in public on the evils of fornication and concubines; Marcus was never surprised to find a beautiful woman in attendance at his private rooms. What the powerful said in public and what they did in private were often at opposite ends of the moral spectrum. It seemed to Marcus that it was the nature of power to feel oneself exempt from the laws of common folk.

The woman removed his sandals and unfastened the gold fibulae at the shoulder of his robe. He allowed this almost without thinking, as he would accept a hunk of bread or a draught of wine.

Not long ago he might have welcomed the woman's attention, as he had many times before. In fact, it wasn't often that the mere presence of a beautiful woman, as this one was, did not fill him with physical need, if not passion.

She was no doubt the daughter of a merchant or trader who would rather see her as a concubine in a wealthy house than a serf in the village. The cast system had become so hardened there was no chance at all for a young woman to make something of herself, or live better than her mother had done. And to be a concubine in the Emperor's house was more than could be hoped. Marcus thought of his sister in the palace on the Bosporus. Was this the life his service to the Emperor had bought for her?

He returned his attention to the girl. She was comely. Her tresses were gathered at her neck then twisted around the crown of her head, a curl rested tantalizingly at her nape, and her deep brown eyes sought his.

She bared her breasts, pressed forward. But in his mind, he saw only the raven hair of the girl he had met by the bath in Chalcedon. Why had he let her go? Of all the women he had taken, both willing and by the Emperor's leave, he longed for her alone. Why, with this beauty at hand?

Was it simply the very weak, human quality of wanting what one could not have? Would he be manipulated by the memory of one woman to the point of turning away all others from now on?

He took her by the shoulders. She waited, neither fearful nor willing, only stared into his eyes with stoic resolve. "Is there something wrong?"

"Do you not wish to receive as well as give, my lady?"

She cut her gaze away from his. "I am here for your pleasure sir, not mine."

Marcus held her a moment longer. Pleasure? There would be no pleasure in this, for either of them. "Then you are a fool," he scolded at last, and ordered her away. She would receive payment and lodging regardless of whether he made use of her. At least for one night, the girl could sleep in peace.

When she had gone, Marcus plunged into the marble bath, annoyed he had taken his anger and disgust out of the innocent woman. With any luck, he would meet with the Emperor early on the morrow and be on his way home to Constantinopolis before the noon meal.

❧

The call to meet the Emperor came early. Constantine was having his hair coiffed in his private antechamber when Marcus arrived.

"Well met, my lord," he began, down on one knee and affecting an attitude of respect. "The Imperial baths are faring well under Crispus' supervision, and the Basilica is also progressing on schedule as Thalius has reported. Helena's icons are not in place; however, they have arrived, and are currently under guard at the Prefect's vault--"

Constantine held up his hand. "I did not bring you here in secret to discuss my construction projects."

The servant slapped another daub of pomade into his hands and massaged it into what was left of the Emperor's hair. Constantine let his head roll limp, trusting in the man's hands.

Marcus eyed a long table laden with breakfast faire. He poured himself a goblet of wine from a gilt decanter, and slumped into a chair, hoping for early dismissal.

The Emperor groaned and sighed under the expert hands of his masseuse and Marcus heard him tell the man to prepare himself for the long journey to Constantinopolis for he could no longer bear the ministrations of his servant there.

Marcus nibbled at the food on his plate, his appetite not really all it could be, and cast his gaze about the room, if not to relieve the boredom, then to remove himself from the sounds of the Emperor enjoying his manservant's attention.

The cubicle was set in a row of similar rooms lined up on either side of the villa and refreshed by breezes off the river through arched porticoes along the outside wall. He went to the window, but all he could see were the eyes of the woman whose face had haunted him for weeks.

Those eyes and their expression of wonder and purity. Visions of her disturbed his sleep and interrupted even his waking thoughts. Her face appeared in his mind like a sea mist, sudden and penetrating.

It was in the midst of one of these intrusions that the Emperor spoke again. Marcus turned to find the servant gone and Constantine standing at his elbow. "I have a most delicate matter to discuss with you."

Marcus bowed low. "I am at your service, as always, my lord." He hoped his expression showed enough respect, for his mind was still full of the warmth of the dark-haired girl, his nostrils full of her scent, and his loins -- simply full. He hoped this "matter" would include a break in duty and a trip home.

"It has come to my attention, through trustworthy sources, of course," the Emperor began, moving to the arched portico, his back to Marcus, "that my son, Crispus, and my wife, Fausta are involved in — this is difficult for me — involved in a conspiracy against me."

Marcus' heart stopped a beat, his mind racing to conclusions almost as if he had heard this whole conversation before. This was the conversation he'd hoped never would come. The day the emperor would demand more than he could morally accept.

"If this is allowed to continue," the Emperor went on, pacing across the room. He gestured in the air as if he were giving a speech, "it could tarnish my efforts to unite Rome under one authority. You see that don't you Marcus?" The Emperor turned to face him.

"This is a serious charge, my lord. Are you certain? I mean … Crispus --"

Constantine's eyes narrowed on Marcus, his jaw hardening a moment before he relaxed.

"I appreciate your caution, Marcus. Your loyalty is unquestionable." He reached under his towel and scratched himself in an un-lordly fashion. "I have already given the order regarding Crispus, but Fausta requires a certain … finesse."

Marcus raised his gaze to meet Constantine's, and his meaning came clear. He already knew too much to decline without losing his head. Still, it was difficult to accept what he was being told. "You want me to—"

The emperor held up his hand. "This meeting never happened. Do you understand?"

He understood all right. He was ordering Marcus to carry out a murder in secret without any connection to him. He lowered his head and the weight of the order sank into his bones.

The Emperor clapped his arm about Marcus' shoulders in a hearty embrace and walked with him back to the portico. "Your loyalty to me gives me great confidence. Rest assured, you and your family will continue to flourish once this affair is put in order, as will the empire."

Marcus willed himself not to acknowledge the veiled threat, for surely that is what it was. "Yes, my lord," he said evenly as he felt his future slip away.

Constantine let him go and paced back to the table of food, selected a ripe fig and ate it heartily, then wiped his fingers on a cloth at the table.

"Plans have been set in motion that will put you in position to take care of this matter. For now, you will return home on leave and await orders, but keep yourself in readiness, man. When all preparations are in place, you will be informed and will have to move swiftly." He toyed with a dust mote on the marble floor with his bare foot. "No one must know of my connection with the plans, of course."

"Of course, my lord," replied Marcus, staring out into the courtyard. If there had been a sudden, cataclysmic shift in the earth's great bowels it could not have rent a more ragged gash than the wound that now tore Marcus' heart. Even if he could bring himself to obey the order, there was no possible way the Emperor would allow him to live in Rome with such knowledge, no matter what his assurances were today.

Marcus could never again bring himself to walk under a full moon.

Constantine stared out into the courtyard now as well. The two men faced their own invisible demons. Constantine's hand rested on the column at his left, his shoulders sagging under the weight of his order.

"My first born," he murmured, as if the deed had already been done. Then he continued in the same grave tone. "Get your personal business in order. After the deed is done, you will be escorted to the palace and safe passage across the Bosporus. It will be made to look like pursuit, you understand. But you will have nothing to fear, I assure you."

Nothing to fear, Marcus thought, from a man who would order his own son killed? A chilling terror sank into his bones. He was sure of one thing only: that he was a walking corpse. Whether the blow came from the Emperor, or from his own soul, his blood had already begun to run cold. There would be no safe passage.

Marcus raised his fist swiftly to his chest in formal salute. The Emperor remained at the portico neither acknowledging nor returning the salute. Marcus turned on his heel and took his leave.

Chapter Twenty-Seven

Marcus lowered himself to a chaise longue in his mother's private atrium at her villa entrance, exhausted from the trip home. He'd traveled non-stop since he'd left the Emperor in Moselle, the only thought on his mind to see her again. He retrieved the brooch from inside his tunic and passed it to her.

"This is magnificent," she said, breathlessly, lifting her eyes to his. "Wherever did you get such a thing?"

Her eyes were lit with excitement at seeing him at her door for the first time in many months. It had been a warm and long-awaited reunion. Since his father had died in service to the emperor, he had been the man of the family; his own service earning his mother high regard in the metropolis — this elegant villa, better than average provisions, and an annual payment of coin that more than adequately paid for anything they could want at market. His loyalty, Marcus now knew, was the price he paid to ensure their future.

"It's a long tale, mother. And I'm anxious to tell it to you, but I could use some refreshment first. He removed his hauberk and belted weapons and let them slip to the stones at his feet.

After he'd eaten everything his mother lay before him and drunk a flagon of wine, he leaned back on the longue and let out a deep sigh. "It's good to see you, Mother. You look well."

"You look like you could use a month's sleep."

"Indeed, I do. How is Anastasia keeping?"

His mother scooted a stool close to him, her eyes darkening with intensity. "She is well, and you are stalling."

"Stalling?"

"I want to hear about the brooch."

"Oh, is that what you want," he teased, knowing full well he had tantalized her by showing her the brooch first thing.

He drained the wine in his cup, set it down with a sigh, and told her about his assignment to arrest Haldor and meeting the girl who wore the brooch at the bath. He left out the part about their sexual encounter.

"Truly, mother; she was the most magnificent creature I have ever seen."

His mother was assessing him now in the same way she'd done when he was a lad and turned up home with a bushel of apples he couldn't explain. "She was a courtesan."

"No. She was just a young woman, mother. We only talked." A half-truth.

She sent him a slant-eyed grin that said she didn't believe him. "You think I don't know the kind of girls who wait outside the caldarium at the end of day?"

Marcus's face heated. "Will you permit me to finish my story before you have me down in the gutter?"

His mother sent him a loving grin. "You are a fine man, Marcus. I only love watching you squirm.

Do go on," she said good-heartedly, her eyes beaming with love for her son.

"Imagine my surprise when I arrived at the villa of the thief I was sent to arrest, to find the very woman I'd met at the bath!"

"Oh?" She sat forward now; her interest perked. "Was she part of the thievery?"

"No. At least I didn't think so." He was starting to, but that was another story. "Anyway, her master wasn't there, and she claimed not to know when he'd return so I decided to watch the house until he showed up." He ran his hands through his hair, remembering how he'd taken her there in her master's anteroom, how he'd agonized over leaving her. How he'd bought the silk cloth, thinking to make her a gift. Though he trusted his mother implicitly, he couldn't relate any of this to her. At least not yet. It was too painful, to raw. Too immoral.

"When I returned the next day, there was only a boy at the villa. He claimed neither the woman nor Haldor were there. Days later, I learned that Haldor had been murdered in his workshop and the two servants were nowhere to be found."

His mother's hand went to the base of her neck and her face grew serious. "A boy?"

Marcus got up and paced the room. "It is likely Haldor was dead when I arrived. The boy was definitely agitated, refused to look at me. His face was badly bruised." He turned to his mother. "I can't stop thinking the murderer was there, had threatened the boy to lie, and I missed it. When the magistrate called me back the next day to the murder scene, there was no evidence of any boy. It lies sorely on my soul mother." That and the emperor's command.

She went to him, put her arms around him as she had done in times of turmoil throughout his life. There was a sparkle in her eye he had rarely seen, especially after relating his tale.

"And the girl?"

"No one had seen her either."

"And, the brooch?"

"Ah. Yes. The brooch." He turned it over in his hand again. "When I vacated my room at the prefecture, I found it on the floor next to the bed."

Her brows went up and he realized his error. He dropped his head in his hands. "I wanted to return it to her until I realized, it was likely part of the missing jewelry." He lifted his gaze to his mother and let out a deep sigh. "She deceived me."

His mother stared at him a long moment before she spoke. "You are so much like your father, Marcus. You have his soul and his heart. Her deceit weighs heaviest on your soul, I see."

He considered her words. He could never fool the woman who stood erect and wise before him. "Perhaps."

She smiled as if she knew the greatest secret on earth and handed him the brooch. "Perhaps things are not as grim as they appear, my son."

If she only knew. But there was no way he could tell her what he'd been called upon to do. The horror of it would kill her. Instead, he pushed the brooch back into her hand and gently folded her fingers closed around it. "I want you to keep this for me — until I return." His hands remained clasped about his mother's and he gazed into her eyes, fixing her image in his mind. "I have to leave again soon — at a moment's notice. My days will be hard spent in preparation for my journey."

"Will it be long, Marcus?"

"Very long, I think." Maybe forever.

"But you can stay and take supper with me now?" His mother's eyes pleaded, and in their reflection, he saw himself a small child playing at her skirts by the fountain, tossed by his father into the air, standing by her side in the Catacombs at his father's burial. He squeezed his eyes shut. He must concentrate on the present. He forced himself to smile and show her a little of the Marcus she expected.

"Well, if you have any of your honey cakes, I'll stay."

CHAPTER TWENTY-EIGHT

"I always have honey cakes." Kindra had made them just that morning. Flavia had expected to hear from her by now. In fact, her first thought when she saw Marcus at the door was that her dreams had come true. Marcus and Kindra together. And if his revelation truly lined up to match Kindra's story as she believed, they were fated to meet again. If in fact she had been in his bed chamber — and she was in fact with child as she suspected — the possibilities made her heart race.

She helped Marcus bring his things into his chamber. Perhaps Kindra would return tonight. They would meet at her very own hearth. The idea made her chuckle inside with an anticipation she'd not enjoyed since her husband was alive.

But Kindra did not return that night, nor the next nor the day following. And soon, though he had not yet departed on his mysterious mission, Marcus spent most of his time away from her house.

Flavia went about her normal routine, embroidering the hem of a new tunic for her daughter and baking honey cakes for the village children who hung about her doors at all hours of the day, but pangs of worry were never far from her consciousness.

What if their disguise had failed and Kindra had been arrested? What if there were complications from her injury? Or worse yet, her pregnancy? Flavia agonized over each successive fear until, riddled with worry and haggard by yet another sleepless night, she paced across her darkened room, drawn with each pass closer to the wicker chest containing Kindra's things, as well as the most precious of her own.

Dare she open the young woman's belongings? What right had she to pry into another's life? But it was Marcus's life too, wasn't it? What if her suspicions were correct? Then she could allay his worries on one account, helping him find the woman he so wanted to see again, but she might add to them on the other, for had not Kindra as much as confessed to murder? It surely had been self-defense, as she had said, but a slave would hang from the gibbet, no matter what story she told.

Flavia paced across the room to the window overlooking the fountain, stared out for a moment, and then turned all at once, obsessed by a new thought. What action did an old woman have left in this world if not to do all she could for the ones she loved? If she let the moment pass, she might never have another chance.

Lord, let me do right by these children. She crossed the room again, knelt before the wicker basket, and lifted the lid.

Before she left, Kindra had neatly wrapped her bundle in coarse muslin, having removed the pouch containing the jewelry. She had carefully replaced her tools in a leather wrap, which Flavia now removed and unrolled before her on the top of the basket.

She lay several wood-handled implements out in a row, with little idea of their use. There was her sewing kit on top. Below that, a sharp-edged awl for cutting designs, she supposed; metal snips, two sizes of pliers, a tiny vice, and a small mallet of tightly coiled hide, pounded smooth on one side. Most interesting were three small earthen pots fitted with wooden stoppers, each with a different mark carved on the top. Flavia held one pot in her palm and twisted out the plug. She sniffed at the opening, and detecting no odor, poured a quantity of the contents into her palm and spread out a gritty substance with her thumb. It was a fine sand of a deep purple hue. Shrugging her shoulders without an idea of its identity, she scraped it back into the jar and refitted the stopper.

Another small glass vial contained a pumice-like substance she recognized as similar to what she used to polish her copper cooking pots.

Another box, hollowed out from a length of wood about the size her hand, contained two bronze rods, which she quickly found, by pressing a tip into the skin of her palm, left a precise mark -- one, an H, and the other, a tiny delta. This she pressed into her palm several times, watching the ridges of the mark turn white, refill with blood, and fade away. The delta! She stood up suddenly, scattering the tools all around the floor.

She retrieved the brooch from a fold in her palla and turned it over. There in the center of the gold backing was the triangular mark.

It was true! Excitement rose in her chest like a bubbling pudding. She could hardly wait for Kindra to return. *Please. Let Marcus still be here to meet her.*

To think she had daydreamed such a thing could happen and now it was coming true! Flavia was overcome with joy and laughed at herself for making such a mess.

How foolish she would feel if Kindra arrived just now to find her things scattered about so. She gathered the tools quickly, re-wrapped them in their leather binding, and returned them to the package next to the blue silk robe Kindra had made during her stay. She ran her hand over the lustrous fabric, most likely a gift to Kindra from her son; but as she folded it neatly back into the basket, her fears for Kindra were renewed.

She should really have returned by now. Maybe the two of them would be better served if she told Marcus all she knew.

A sharp rap in an unfamiliar pattern sounded at the front entrance. Startled, she dropped the robe hastily over the tools, closed the lid, and went to the door.

"I understand the tradesman, Kindard of Chalcedon, has left his belongings with you." A woman faced her in the doorway. She was vaguely familiar to Flavia, but she couldn't place her. She was tall, for a woman, and wore a short tunic of white linen, much in the style of a young tribune, crisscrossed with leather straps, and connected at the center of her chest by a gilded fibulae in the character of a ram's head. Her mount stood nearby, along with a pair of men in escort.

Flavia hesitated. There was something familiar in the woman's eyes, yet her harsh temperament, the slight forward cock of her head, and the sharp, jutting angle of her jaw did not engender in Flavia the desire to make small talk. The woman tapped a short crop impatiently in her palm, compelling Flavia to answer her without first presenting credentials.

"Yes. I do have some of his things." Flavia blurted it out, feeling the fool and stepping back to widen the space between herself and the visitor. She had cultivated, by the grace of the one God, a willingness to see good in all whom she encountered, but she was hard pressed to break the woman's threatening posture and had a sudden fear for her own safety. She must compose herself. Things were not right here, and if Kindra were in danger, perhaps she was the only one in a position to—

"I have come for the tools." The woman's impatient words knifed through Flavia's thoughts, biting and cold. "He will need them at the palace workshop for a time."

"Why hasn't he come for them himself then? Surely he is free to come and go as he wishes?"

The woman made no direct reply to the questions but pulled a royal signet medallion on a chain from under her tunic, identified herself as Valeria, a personal messenger of the Empress, and ordered Flavia to be quick.

"The tools, yes." Flavia hurried into the other room to the wicker basket. Better not do anything to arouse suspicion. Maybe they hadn't discovered Kindra's identity after all, and if she was cooperative...

Her hands shook as she lay the newly made gown aside and removed the packet of tools. She took a deep breath as she pulled herself up to her full, proud height and returned to the entrance.

Valeria removed the packet from Flavia's grasp quickly, as if she thought they might disappear. "If he has any additional clothing, I suggest you send that along as well." A sudden glint in the woman's eyes made Flavia's heart shrink, as the woman went on, "He may be...detained...for several days."

Detained? Now Flavia's heart froze. Something must have gone terribly wrong. Her shoulders fell in spite of her efforts to appear unruffled. She had fully expected Kindra to get into the palace, leave the jewelry, and return home in one day. Now, she feared the worst.

What if this were her only chance to help her get away? She had escaped danger once by pretending to be a boy, maybe that tactic would work in reverse. She returned to her son's room and opened Kindra's belongings again. There must be something here. Something that would help her if she got the chance. She lay aside the blue silk dress and felt something hard wrapped up inside. Moving swiftly, she worked her fingers through the fabric until she found the object. A pouch with a heavy lump inside, sewn into a fold in the cloth. She felt the shapes. Coins, a cuff bracelet most likely, and other loose chips she couldn't identify. Should she include them? Or keep them safe for the girl should she return?

She heard the sound of footsteps coming down the corridor. There was no time for indecision. She quickly wrapped the fabric, pouch and all inside a leather jerkin, then wrapped the jerkin inside two additional tunics that Marcus had worn as a teen. She wrapped them tightly with a leather thong and stood just as the woman appeared in the doorway.

She handed over the package, praying it would be delivered intact. "May I inquire as to the lad's welfare? He has become dear to me as a son —"

"A son?" The woman's glower send a chill through Flavia's heart. "How could such a whimpering puppy replace a son like Marcus?" She spat the word *son* as if saying it had spawned a bad taste in her mouth.

"You know Marcus?" Flavia's face went cold. She fought again to maintain a calm exterior. Valeria did not answer, only glared back at her with hatred in her eyes, turned, and summoned her escort.

Fear prickled at Flavia's neck. What was happening? She sensed a threat, but what form it was taking, she knew not. She only knew the sudden rush of anxiety a mother feels when her child is in danger.

∽

Valeria knew Marcus. Perhaps the old woman had forgotten, but she had not. They had been progeny of the same handout program -- their fathers, friends since boyhood, had died in battle and had been buried in the catacombs with great honor. The children were taken as Constantine's wards in recognition of their fathers' loyalty and educated and then trained in the Emperor's service rather than left to sure serfdom with no father to support them. Just another way to get slaves. Valeria let go a derisive sniff.

She crossed her arms over the bundle of clothing and tools and paced impatiently as she waited in the livery for her escort. Marcus was educated and trained as a tribune and sent around the empire on the business of state, while I am trained as a servant. Servant to the Emperor's wife and mother in the royal palace, but a servant still.

Given the same circumstances, the same opportunities, Valeria knew she could be better than Marcus could ever dream of being. As children, they had often played together and Valeria, though of smaller stature because of her gender, possessed a true aim and a warrior's spirit, often outwitting Marcus at warrior games where strength alone was not enough to win over ruthless cunning and agility. And, she knew, if it came to a showdown against her, Marcus would always back down.

Valeria mounted her horse and led her entourage under the eyes of curious citizens. She despised the prying eyes that mocked her while Marcus received open adoration at the gymnasiums and baths. They threw flowers at his feet, but only suspicious, judgmental glances at her.

Keeping her eyes straight ahead, she pushed through the crowds without a care for the safety of the citizens. They had eyes in their heads. They could get out of her way.

Marcus. Oh, he had shown her the difference between them when she was yet eleven years old and he twelve. That serpent between his legs that grew when she touched it. From that moment she had known her deficiency and the utter futility of trying to alter it.

How she despised him. And now, there seemed to be a connection between he and that smiling bitch who tried to pass herself off as a man. She may only be a servant, but she would show them what cunning was.

Valeria clutched the packet of tools in a vicious grip, as if she held his manhood in her grasp. How innocently she had touched him then, full of wonder and amazement. And how the memory burned into her soul; it was the very root of a power she would never possess. She had prayed fervently to the gods for many torturous nights to be changed into a man, to possess the serpent and the power within it. Her hatred for him and his God was fed each morning she awoke to find her prayers unanswered.

Oh, she had gained power all right. Power over a group of slave girls, but never over Marcus. Her mind seethed with anger as her escort brought her through the palace gates.

Valeria stormed through the halls, slamming portals behind her. She didn't bother to have Kindra called to her chamber but blew in upon her like a sharp wind through an unfastened shutter. "What are you to Marcus?"

KAT DRENNAN

CHAPTER TWENTY-NINE

Kindra turned, catching her breath. She had been standing on the rails of her upturned cot, passing her time watching activity in the harbor below.

"Marcus?" The look in the woman's eyes struck a physical blow to her gut. What was happening here?

"Don't play me for an idiot. You didn't fool me with your innocent lad charade in front of the Empress, and you're not fooling me now."

Valeria marched to the small night table next to the cot and slammed the packet of tools down, then kicked the cot out from under her, toppling her to the floor.

Kindra rose to her feet, her knees screaming from the blow.

Valeria ordered her back to her knees, but Kindra had had enough. She stood nose-to-nose with the woman's hardened mask of envy and hate. If this was to be her end, then so be it. She'd had all she could take of this woman's contempt.

Valeria grabbed her by the chin in a painful grip that ground the inside of her cheeks against her teeth. Kindra tasted blood, but she did not falter.

"You're lovers, then? I always suspected Marcus of being fond of boys."

Kindra was stunned. Marcus? What had he to do with Valeria?

"Don't play innocent with me!" cried Valeria, stridently. She jerked Kindra's head back in a violent snap as she released her chin. "The old woman tried to tell me you were like a son to her, as though you were an old friend of the family. But I know better than that! You didn't show up until Marcus returned from Thrace, did you? And all this business about being the goldsmith's apprentice. You'll never convince me you're anything but a thief."

Kindra pressed herself against the wall. She no longer wondered or cared what had brought on this storm, but she was determined to weather it.

"It's Fausta I've got to convince, not you. But since you took responsibility for it, I suppose you've got to hope I am what I claim."

Kindra felt the heat of malevolence upon her brow as Valeria's eyes burned into hers. If she had been made of wax, she would be melted into a pool on the stone floor; but she stood her ground. The same force that had driven her to smash the head of her former master rose within her now, and she took a step toward the glaring woman, trusting the power that burned behind her eyes.

Valeria's laugh was low and insidious. Nevertheless, she retreated toward the door, eyes fixed on Kindra's.

"You will go to Hector in the morning, and we shall see what we shall see. Sweet dreams, my pet. Dream of Marcus, because, by the gods, you will never see him in reality again." She slapped her fist to her chest in a mock salute then turned and stalked out of the room, carrying the rest of the package under her arm.

CHAPTER THIRTY

Kindra clipped a circle of gold sheet from the miserly scrap Hector had given her. She used the sharp-nosed pliers to bend the edge perpendicular to the baseplate to form the retaining wall that would hold the enameled colors of the new brooch in place. She took her time, for it was becoming very clear to her the longer it took to make the brooch, the longer she would stay alive. Alive to see Marcus again. Was it true he had returned to Constantinopolis? She could only hope.

Her back already ached from her cramped position at the workbench in the treasury. Constant fear and worry had assailed her for the last three days since Valeria had delivered her tools. The work at least occupied her mind.

Anxiety had haunted her dreams and tortured her waking hours since the encounter; the threat of her exposure a constant pressure on her heart. Was she any better off than when she worked under Haldor's roof? She wasn't sure.

The only thing she could be sure of was her ability to work the gold. She would show them. She had control over the outcome, confident, at least in this: she could make the brooch, even if Valeria doubted her. She would make a hundred brooches if it would secure her freedom.

To this thought she clung as her fingers worked and her eyes strained. She tried her best to ignore

Hector, who hovered about and questioned her every move. She only spoke to him once when he'd bent his face so near her work that he'd blocked out the light.

She labored into the noon hour; her hands steadier than they'd been for weeks despite the hunger gnawing her gut.

"They suspect a woman, you know," Hector needled, once more filling her mind with dread. Her jaw fell slack.

Had Valeria told Hector what she knew?

She nearly dropped the piece of gold. As hard as she'd fought to bury all memory of the night of the … incident, vivid images assaulted her: Haldor's florid, angry face and the bloodied mallet falling from her hand.

Damn him! Damn them all! Why couldn't a woman just live and make herself happy?

Hector could only be getting at one thing. He suspected her. She clenched her eyes tight. Her back to Hector, she forced herself to speak in a calm, even tone.

"Suspect a woman? Oh. You mean of killing Haldor?"

Hector slowly circled the room once more, his hands clasped behind his back, each step placed deliberately, as if stalking prey. She got the distinct feeling he knew nothing of her true identity, only delighted in torturing a defenseless soul.

Kindra bent her head back to her work, fingers cramped, white knuckles on the plier handles. The trembling returned, and she could scarcely grab hold of the edge of gold sheet.

"They say it was a serving girl in his household murdered him, stole his gold, and disappeared." His voice boomed from the far side of the chamber; hollow echoes magnified by stone walls.

Kindra hunched over the workbench. She could scarcely breathe.

"But then, we know this to be a falsehood; you have delivered the gold yourself!"

Don't Listen to him. He can't possibly know anything.

He came back across the room and stopped so close to her back she could feel the heat of his body through her robe.

"However, no one has said anything about Haldor having an apprentice." His lips brushed the corner of her ear, raising goose flesh on the back of her neck and arms. "No one," he whispered.

Kindra held back her emotions. Hector related all that he had heard of the murder and of the magistrates attempts to find evidence about the woman accused. She withdrew deeper into her work, let her fingers do what they'd been trained to do, and blocked out his threats as best she could.

Slowly, the fear that had penetrated every level of her consciousness gave way to concentration on the task at hand, and his words were replaced by a loud ringing, as sounds in the ears of a person suffering from a high fever.

Though no one had ever seen the completed broach accept herself, she did her best to reproduce it from memory exactly like the first one. If it ever turned up — and with her luck it would at the most inopportune moment — her veracity would be proved.

Hector continued to watch her closely, and asked questions as if he'd never seen the process before.

"The real work comes with the polishing." Her fingers worked the gold intuitively. She needed to slow down. But as long as he was in the room, she had to make some kind of progress or he'd guess her tactic.

"So. I assume that lets you off of suspicion, then, doesn't it?" he pressed.

"Sir?" She knew very well he was back on the subject of murder, but she wasn't going to give him an inch.

"That the authorities think the murderer was a woman."

"I suppose it does," she said, angry at herself for letting him draw her into conversation. Damn his soul. Why couldn't he leave her alone? She had already made enough mistakes to ruin the work she'd done.

"But at least one story has it a young man," he went on, making the hairs stand up on her arms. "A young man your age and description it would seem, was seen at the house of Haldor the morning of the discovery by a person whose word is highly regarded. It would seem this young man has not been heard from since."

Her heart sank at this news. "As I told you, sir," Kindra said, remembering to lower her eyes as Flavia had warned. "Haldor sent me with the shipment himself several days earlier, and did I not bring it directly to you?"

"Indeed, you did. All but the brooch," he crooned.

Kindra hoped to change the subject. "But I did not learn of his — death — until you informed me on my arrival at the palace."

"So, you have already told me. But I don't have to rely on the reports of a mere goldsmith's apprentice, you know." Had Marcus recognized her? Betrayed her? She had no way of knowing.

Her nerves had taken about all they could withstand. Between Hector's constant prodding and the heat of the kiln awaiting her work, she could scarcely breathe. Why didn't he just kill her and have done with it?

She fixed the unfired cloisonné into a brace on the surface of a long handled slate palette and turned, forcing Hector to move out of the way, as she transferred it to the waiting kiln.

She closed the door then turned to face the old man, arms crossed belligerently over her chest. "I had the greatest respect for Haldor." She fixed Hector with a straightforward glare. The threat of tears built behind her words, but she held her position. "Without his training, I could no more fashion that piece in there …" she threw her arm toward the heated kiln "…than make gold out of straw."

The words tumbled out of her mouth with conviction because they were absolutely true. How dare this mere bookkeeper challenge her skill?

Hector stared into her eyes for a long moment. She didn't see malice in his eyes the way she had with Valeria. But there was something. Something she might yet use to save her life.

She pitched her fists at her hips and stood, her feet planted shoulder width apart, and returned his scrutinizing stare.

"We shall see," he said at last. Without another word, he turned on his heel, and left the chamber.

The moment he was gone, she wrapped her hands in rags, grabbed her tongs, and pulled the brooch out of the fire. As she had suspected, the piece was a melted ruin. When it cooled, she cut it apart as best she could and tossed the pieces on the workbench. Heart aching, she sank onto the floor, pulled her knees up and wrapped her arms around them, then dropped her head in despair. They were going to drag her into the square and hang her.

Dracis returned at midnight, led her to her room, and sent her an apologetic glance before he closed the door behind her. She heard the bolt drop into place on the outside of the door as she fell, exhausted onto her cot.

Tired though she was, it was a long time before her mind quieted and she fell into an exhausted sleep.

CHAPTER THIRTY-ONE

Marcus returned to his mother's home on the eve of his departure to Trier. It was to be an occasion of both joy and sorrow. Joy because he was reunited with his sister, Anastasia, who had been given a surprise leave from the palace for a month. Sorrow because of the heavy weight carried in his heart. He could tell no one of his destination, not even those he loved. They would learn soon enough, and by then he would be gone from their lives forever.

Anastasia shared news that she was betrothed to a young man in the emperor's livery and Marcus was happy for her. She would become a mother and live in the village. Better than spending her life as a serving girl to the empress.

"My darling children, how I love you both." Flavia slid a tray of fresh-made honey cakes on a table near the hearth. "I'm so proud of you."

Marcus bit into one of the cakes, sensed sadness in her eyes as she spoke.

"My only regret is that your father did not live to see what beautiful children he begot, and that he would never see his grandchildren."

"Grandchildren?" Marcus laughed. "You get ahead of yourself Mother." He fought to keep his tone light so that he didn't himself break down. It had always been hard to leave home, knowing his mother missed his father so. This time, the separation hit him especially hard.

He took her in his arms. "It won't be long, Mother." It broke his heart to lie. "Anastasia will be here for a while, now; and that should help."

She raised her chin. "I know. Don't worry about me. About us. We've always done all right and we will get by." She smiled up at him through her tears. "I would like to show Anastasia the brooch," she said, her throat choked with emotion.

The brooch? He had put it out of his mind.

"Will you fetch it?" she asked. "It's in the wicker basket at the foot of your old bed."

He hesitated. What difference would it make? If he didn't return, they would have something of value. "You understand, Mother; you cannot show this to anyone else?"

She laughed. "Of course."

He hoped she took him seriously. "Very well, then."

His mother joined Anastasia in the anteroom, and he was cheered by overhearing the happy titterings of love in blossom as Anastasia told of her young man. He had put the spark back in Anastasia's eyes Marcus had not seen since his father's passing. Her betrothed was not a warrior as their father had been -- a respected soldier of high rank -- but perhaps a livery boy would live to see his grandchildren. As these thoughts gave him some relief, he lifted the basked lid, and gasped at what he saw there.

"Mother?" He straightened; the cloth clutched tight in his hands. He could not believe his eyes. In the time it took for his Mother to appear in the doorway, the heat had drained from his face.

"What is it my son?" Anastasia came to her side.

"Where did you get this cloth?"

She wrung her hands, her eyes darting between him and his sister.

"Oh, Marcus," she moaned, and the smile she'd put on for their benefit crumpled. "Let's go into the garden. I have a story to tell you."

CHAPTER THIRTY-TWO

A slight young man raced from the livery along the inside palace wall, holding a bundle tight against his chest. Predawn shadows loomed ahead of him, and he dodged them as if they were real, until Marcus grabbed him by the shoulders from behind and drew him into the space between two buildings. The boy's eyes flew wide in surprise and fear. He opened his mouth to squeal. Marcus clamped his hand over the entire lower half of the youth's face.

"Don't call out or I'll squeeze your eyes out of your head." The boy nodded vigorously. Marcus slowly withdrew his hand, and let the boy stand on his own.

"Wha—wha—what do you want with me? I have done nothing wrong." He shifted his weight from foot-to-foot, holding the package close.

Marcus grinned at him, dug a gold coin out of a pouch at his belt, and held it between his thumb and forefinger, watching the boy's eyes grow wider still.

"What is your name, son?" He needed the boy's trust, not his fear. "This coin is yours if you will help me."

The boy rolled his lips together a moment and looked around before his eyes snapped back to Marcus. He expected the boy had never even seen such a coin before, let alone been offered one. Still, his scrawny knees trembled.

"I —— I can't."

Marcus folded his arms over his chest and glared down at him. "You mean you won't."

The boy blanched. There was a battle going on behind those eyes, if Marcus was any judge. He'd been an errand boy in the palace when he was a youth and knew full well the demands that could be made. He was probably on some errand and he'd been threatened with a beating if he didn't hurry.

A flurry of activity near the livery caught their attention. Marcus moved them deeper into shadow. He was running out of time. "Do you know of a young man at the palace — Kindard?"

That got the boy's attention. He swallowed hard and drew himself up as tall as his small frame would allow. The name had hit a nerve. "And what if I do?"

"Don't be cocky with me, boy," Marcus growled. He hated using fear with a child, but the coin hadn't worked. He caught his face under the chin and tilted it up to meet his eyes. "I believe Kindard is in grave danger and I won't be put off by the likes of a scruffy miscreant like you."

The boy pulled away, stood erect on his own, and brushed dust off his tunic, his gaze flicking to the coin. "Yes, I — I know of him. He's in the tower along the seawall — I might be able to take you to him, but you'll have to—"

The sea tower? Not good news. It was cold and dank and definitely not appropriate lodging for guests. Now Marcus looked over his shoulders. "I want you to give him a message — can you do that? Bring me a token that you have done so and I will give you the gold."

"My name is Dracis." He pressed his lips tightly together and stood like a soldier. "I don't want your gold piece." He glanced toward the livery stable. "Valeria would just accuse me of stealing it anyway or question me where I got it."

"Valeria." Marcus let go a derisive snort. He should have known. The woman had forever been a pain in his side.

Dracis echoed the snort. "What is your message?"

"Tell her — ah — Kindard — that I know he is here, that I must leave tonight, but I will come back for him no matter what." Deciding he could trust the boy, he pulled a leather pouch from his belt and put in into Dracis's hand. Holding it by its leather thong, he closed the boy's fingers about it. "No one else must see this. His life may depend on it."

"What is it?" Dracis hefted its weight.

"I said no one must see it, and that includes *you*." With that he let go.

"Yes sir. Kindard has been kind to me. I will do this thing. You can be sure of it."

"You better be sure. If I find that you have done me wrong, I'll turn your scrawny hide into tallow." He gave the boy a last scathing glare, then drew back into the shadows.

Dracis stared into the darkness. "Don't you want me to give him your name?"

"He will know," Marcus rasped, keeping his voice low, and then he slipped away.

❧

Kindra woke to the familiar metal-on-metal bolt scraping at the door. She threw her bed wrapper around her shoulders and strained her eyes in the graying light to see who would enter.

"It's me, Dracis. Hurry. Valeria threatens to tether me with the dogs if I don't deliver you to her with the greatest haste." Dracis clamored across the room, arms flailing, nearly breathless, forgetting the package Valeria had given him until he saw it dangling at the end of his hand. "She sent this for you." He dropped the wrapped parcel onto the cot and waited. "You've got to change," he said between ragged breaths, "and come with me right now."

Kindra hesitated. The chamber was bone-chilling cold, and her hands trembled. If Valeria was involved, something dreadful was afoot, she was sure. She could still feel the woman's cloying fingers against her skin, and her mind reeled at the possibilities.

"Please, friend," Dracis pleaded. "I promised I'd bring you straightaway."

Kindra picked up the package and worried the strings loose, her fingers stiff with her night's work. Her eyes flew wide open as she unfurled from a coarse wrapper a robe of the finest blue silk. Kindra drew in her breath and shook her head in bewilderment.

Dracis's jaw fell, too, and he scratched his head. "Oh, Valeria will have my hide now; I've delivered the wrong package!" He began to pace back and forth, pulling at his greasy hair.

Kindra grabbed him by the shoulders. "No. Dracis. You've done nothing wrong. It's me that's wronged you. I should have told you the minute I knew I could trust you. I'm sorry you have to find out this way."

Dracis wagged his head, unable to think past his fate at the hands of the tyrannical head servant. "Told me what?"

Kindra stared up at the ceiling and asked aloud, "What now?" But of course, no answer came. As she had been since she was a child of no more than seven, she was now, and despairingly knew she would always be: alone and dependent on her own wits to survive. She saw that there was nothing to do but obey. Dracis had been her friend, shared his food with her, and, she suspected, given up his blanket for her. And she was about to repay him by revealing her treachery.

Her throat closed around words of explanation for what he was about to witness. The room was so small there wasn't a place in it completely hidden from the young servant's view. There was no point trying to deceive Valeria. She already knew her secret. Best to simply change into the garment and be done.

She stripped off the tunic in which she had slept, her neck growing hot with shame as she unwrapped the cloth binding around her chest and let her breasts fall free. Her nipples hardened in the morning chill.

Dracis's chin dropped open as he watched. Then his features relaxed into near comic relief.

Kindra held the blue silk against her chest. "You're not angry with me, then?"

Dracis ran a hand through is matted hair, cutting his eyes away. "Angry? No. Not angry," he said, blowing out a draught of air. "I'm saved."

"Saved?"

He nodded, and the first true smile she'd ever seen from him spread over his face. "Because I — well, I admit I had some feelings toward … Kindard. It was truly baffling. They make eunuchs out of boys who are that way, you know." His hand slipped to cover his manhood.

Kindra allowed herself a smile. She was obviously bound for much more dangerous things than the dog pen. The humor, however brief, relieved some of her anxiety. "Well, there's no need to worry about that now, thank the gods."

"Oh!" he barked suddenly, digging into the folds at his tunic. "I almost forgot this." He handed over a small leather pouch. "A man gave this to me for you."

Kindra took the little leather pouch in her hand. "What is it?" She pulled the drawstrings open. "Where did you--" Her words trailed off as she slipped the cloisonné broach onto her palm. A chill shivered over her shoulders. It was perfection in gold.

How could this come back to me here of all places?

She turned it over in her palm and rubbed across the shining surface of the baseplate with her thumb.

Indeed, the brooch bore her own delta mark and nothing else.

"Where did you say you got this?" She could barely push the words out through her astonishment.

"A man gave it to me just now, outside the livery. He said he knows where you are and to tell you he has to leave but he'll come back for you, no matter what." The boy blurted out the words as if a dam had broken, but stopped short, fingers to his chin and mouth agape.

"What was his name, Dracis?" There was no point in asking, there could only be one answer.

"He said you would know who he was. Said he would turn my hide to tallow if —" He looked up to see her tears. "Have I done wrong my lady?" Dracis moaned, his forehead folded into worried furrows.

Kindra stared at him in disbelief. "You have done well, my friend."

"Then you do know him."

"Not well, but yes. He means me no harm, I don't think, and … and I cannot imagine his turning your hide to tallow either. Besides, you have done as he requested, and I will tell him so. Did he say when he'd be back?"

"Nah. But you must hurry now. Valeria is waiting at the livery and the dogs are waiting in the kitchen." His eyes strayed away to what must have been a fearful vision, then back to Kindra's. "I'm sorry there isn't time for a bath and a proper grooming before you put on that silk." His face was heated red now, and she realized, he was indeed old enough to appreciate a woman's curves.

277

Kindra smiled, blushing. She had been sitting all this time with bared breasts. She covered herself. "Thank you Dracis, for all you have done. Now we had best go. I don't want to see you tied with the dogs today, or any other."

Kindra smoothed the gown over her body, remembering her days with Flavia fondly. "Valeria must have had her reasons for haste, or I'm sure she would have arranged some more amusing way to bestow this gift upon me." She ran her hands over the blue silk she had always dreamed she would wear, and her fingers came across the bulge in the hem. She threw back her head and laughed for the first time since she had been in the palace. Perhaps dreams came true, after all; even if this wasn't quite what she'd imagined. She had almost forgotten her hidden stash of gold and the serpent bracelet. What good fortune Valeria hadn't made a closer inspection of the package Flavia had obviously prepared for her.

A moment ago, she had nothing to look forward to but rotting in this little room, now she at least had hope that someone knew of her plight. And, most of all, if what Dracis said was true, she was going to see Marcus again. She didn't know when, but it didn't matter. The thought lifted her spirit in a way she hadn't felt since she'd escaped from Haldor's. She removed the pouch from the hem of her palla, added the one with the brooch and tied them both next to her skin. She may be able to make use of them yet. She hurried to follow Dracis down the damp corridor leading to the courtyard and the livery stable beyond.

CHAPTER THIRTY-THREE

Dracis led her to the livery and a small storeroom where servants scurried about loading wheeled carts with baskets of food, earthen pots of water and wine, and bundled parcels and boxes.

"They're preparing to take the Emperor's entourage to the mountains in Trier ahead of the anniversary."

Kindra stepped behind him as a worker wheeled a heavy cart nearly over her foot. "Anniversary?"

"Why yes. It's the annual celebration outside the palace commemorating Rome's unification under Constantine. It will be out of control for a few days. Fausta would rather not stay around for it."

"Won't the people expect to see her?"

"She will come back on the last day. By that time, they'll be too exhausted to make much of a fuss."

He led Kindra to the first litter in the lineup which had been covered in heavy muslin against the morning's chill. Dracis had turned to her and opened his mouth no doubt to continue his story when he suddenly clamped it shut again, silenced by something he saw behind her. His eyes met hers briefly, filled with regret; then he rounded the corner of the stable and was gone. Confused, Kindra turned to see that Valeria stood before her.

"You will accompany Fausta to Trier. You are to replace her personal maid. I will decide what to do with you when you return."

Kindra felt hesitant, but also relieved. Hector's insinuations hung in her memory like spider cobs, trapping every hopeful thought she had in a web of despair. The thought of leaving the palace had some promise — if not simply the release from her tiny prison of a room, then for the chance that an opportunity to escape might present itself. She masked the rising hope in her heart and replied evenly. "So, Fausta knows I'm a woman?"

"She knows Kindard, the apprentice; she has never met Niala, the servant, whom I have told her you are. No one knows of *Kindard's* departure except for me. I could have you thrown to the bottom of a well and no one would be the wiser."

Kindra thought immediately of Marcus' promise to return. How would he find her now? She swallowed hard on the sting that built in the back of her throat and behind her eyes.

"And what of the brooch? Will not Hector be expecting it?" She found the words difficult to say while the original brooch hung in a pouch under her robe.

"That is no longer your concern. She knows now only that you are a new servant. With your woman's clothing and the braiding you'll have woven into your hair, she won't be the wiser. Especially if I tell her that the one responsible to recreate Helena's brooch had been put to death for murder."

Kindra's hand went involuntarily to her throat. Valeria sent her a knowing grin. "Besides, she has had her mind on other things. Just be sure to do as she bids, and you'll suit her well enough. If you don't, you'll have me to answer to."

It had been true enough that Fausta had her mind on other things. She appeared to be a different woman from the one who had stalked Kindard in her chamber at the palace. Gone was the royal façade, and in its place was the soft, wistful expression of a woman bemused and content; happy to have a cool drink when offered and a warm bath along the road.

This, of course, had not been easy to arrange. Kindra had no knowledge or experience of the road to Trier. However, villagers were alerted to the Empress's passage. All Kindra had to do was express her needs to shopkeepers or tavern owners along the way, and they seemed to anticipate whatever Fausta wanted.

All-in-all, the duties of personal servant to Fausta had been the easiest in her life. Now that they were settled in their private suites at the baths, Kindra had her own room adjacent to Fausta's.

It was much smaller than the Empress's, of course, but was every bit as opulent. A row of windows faced out over a grove of cherry trees whose blossoms filled the air in her chamber with sweet fragrance. The floor was polished rose quartz inlaid with a geometric pattern in black and white granite, quite similar to the floor in Fausta's own chamber. It was a room of beauty beyond anything Kindra had ever imagined. It was clear now how Anastasia could be so happy working as Fausta's personal servant. She led a life of luxury nearly matching that of her empress.

Although the empress was accustomed to ordering servants, and maintained her air of superiority, she did not possess Valeria's vicious temperament.

In truth, Fausta had shown Kindra a share of kindness and camaraderie.

"People expect much of me," Fausta once complained while Kindra brushed her hair. She couldn't help but admire her fine red tresses and nearly parchment skin.

Kindra had never seen a woman of her coloring before. Fausta was as striking in contrast to her own olive complexion as were the ebony people of Africa.

Now, settled in their chambers, the empress poured out her heart in animated talk as Kindra applied scented oils to lengths of her hair.

"I am the Emperor's wife, but I am also a woman, like any other. I have no true friends here, only those who take my orders and smile because they think it pleases me."

She turned to look at Kindra, who noted now a hint of age hiding behind Fausta's delicate beauty. Kindra had never hated the rich, but neither had she held any pity for them. Power exacted its price, and Fausta was paying with early lines on her face.

"I have need of friendship and love as much as any woman. Do you understand me?"

Kindra nodded. Indeed, they had that point in common. The closest she had ever come to having a personal friend was Dracis. Until a few moments before she last saw him, she had deceived him, and her heart ached over it.

Flavia had been a friend, but more like the mother Kindra had lost. She missed her dearly. But to Fausta, she hardly knew what to reply, and only nodded and listened.

Fausta assumed a less vulnerable expression. "It's no good having a lover and not being able to tell a soul," she continued, jumping to another subject. "Half of loving is reveling in it, and shouting it to the gods — to God, I mean — But, my love is, is – She fidgeted on her divan as if she had made herself quite uncomfortable. Then she arose on an exhale.

"Niala, you have been good to me, and have listened through hours of my silly rambling. I must confess I was disappointed when I learned Anastasia was not to accompany me on this journey. She is quite dear to me. But you have been a good servant and companion, and your hands are gentle with the brush and massage. I am grateful. You will have the reward of freedom to roam and use the baths at will while we are here."

Kindra knelt and thanked her humbly. It had already been a great relief not to have to disguise her femininity, a chore that had become increasingly painful with her growing breasts. She kept her eyes lowered, however, still afraid she may betray a look or movement that would spark some recognition in Fausta's mind.

The empress stepped to the row of windows, propped her elbows in the deep-set opening, and rested her chin on her hands. "If Valeria were here, she would not allow it; but, thank the gods she was called back to the palace. The woman is more tedious than rain on a day of celebration." Fausta sighed and whirled back across the room, a much freer woman than Kindra had known at the palace.

"Use the baths, the oils, and perfumes as you please. Entertain yourself, Niala. You deserve it. If you will leave me alone now, I do not wish to be disturbed, nor will I require your services until the noon hour tomorrow. Then, the tepidarium will be reserved for my private use. At least there are some privileges to being an emperor's wife."

"Yes, Lady Fausta." Kindra wrung her hands. She felt almost a criminal. Her very presence here was a lie, and it took all her energy to maintain it. How she longed to let down her guard and simply be herself. Would Fausta understand? Or would she have her thrown out of the villa to manage for herself? More likely she'd have her arrested. Kindra blew out a breath.

"You are dismissed, Niala."

She touched a knee briefly to the floor, then bowed her head and rose. "As you wish," she said backing out of the chamber.

CHAPTER THIRTY FOUR

In the morning, Kindra arose early and made her way from their private suite of rooms at the west end of the Trier Baths down a high-vaulted colonnade spanned by lintels and hung with fragrant honeysuckle and climbing rose. She crossed into the main arena, silent at this early hour but for the calling of crows. They held their own games, swooping and soaring among the columns of the peristyle at the far end of the stadium. Others perched irreverently on the heads of marble statues that lined the arena.

Grateful for a few hours to herself, Kindra explored the complex alone. It was the first time she'd been alone since they'd left Constantinopolis. The sound of voices drifted up on the air from somewhere below. Kindra poked her head hesitantly into a dark corridor leading out of the peristyle. She tiptoed down a narrow flight of stairs, dimly lit by the orange, flickering glow of firelight. When the light grew bright, she squatted and leaned her head against a railing, from where she watched the scene below.

Twenty or more stokers, slow in their forced labor, added wood to fires that kept the caldarium hot. Their bodies shone slick with sweat in the firelight and their shadows loomed larger than life. Grotesque shapes slid against uneven walls in the cavernous room, lending a ritualistic quality to an otherwise ordinary task. Several cauldrons boiled at the center of the room, raising dense clouds of steam. A complicated maze of ceramic pipe channeled the steam to the caldarium above.

A wide tunnel ran out the back of the stoker's chamber toward the opening at the east end of the complex. The exit was between columns of an aqueduct that supplied fresh water to the baths day and night.

None of the men below had noticed her squatting there. In fact, it would be quite possible, if she were careful, to flatten herself against the shadowy wall at the back of the chamber and continue down the stairs without being seen. Once at ground level, a person might make her way through the chamber to the exit.

So why wasn't she running? Here was the opportunity she was looking for.

But she knew the answer before the word caught up in her throat.

Fear.

It gripped her heart in its cruel fist; a heated, sweaty vice that threatened to squeeze the life out of her. Was it possible she might never have the courage to run?

If she stayed with Fausta, she would eventually return to the palace and the threats of Valeria; or worse yet, be identified as Haldor's slayer. But, if she did not return, she may never see Marcus again. Was seeing him so important that she would risk discovery and torment?

Her hand slipped to cover what she now knew was a tiny life inside her. She had long passed the second moon since her cleansing time. There was little doubt her union with Marcus had been productive. Would he be pleased to get that news? Or would he abandon her as everyone else in her life had done?

She squashed the thought down and clamped her hands over her ears as if doing so would silence the doubts rising in her mind.

She would be foolish to flee now, with no food, and no better clothing than the thin gown she wore over her tunic. Her mule was likely still at the livery; another reason to return to the palace. But how could she wait until the end of summer? There would be no disguising her condition by then.

Her mind swung back to her only option. She would have to escape on her own from here; and the sooner the better. She would spend her free time in preparation and be ready when the chance presented itself. She might never see Marcus again, but her child would be born free.

She took another long look down the corridor. At least now, she knew the way.

She climbed back up the stairway to the main level, each step more resolute than the one before.

The caldarium was enclosed under a massive, vaulted rotunda. Kindra slipped her feet into a pair of wooden sandals left near the entrance to protect bather's feet from the heated floor, then ran her hand along the smooth, white marble surface of the interior wall as she made her way back.

The room was filled with steam as thick as the early morning fog over the harbor at Chalcedon. The hour was still early. She was alone in this smallest and hottest of the three bathing chambers.

The great baths and arenas of Rome were open to all citizens, from the wealthiest merchants to the most indigent. But this one was different. By the gods, Kindra had never set foot inside such an opulent place. Columns and arches soared high over pale green water that glowed in the filtered sunlight like a jeweled lake. A lowly servant did not belong here, but by Fausta's leave, here she stood.

She shook free of her mental bonds and stood firmly in the moment, a free woman, deserving of pleasure. She took one hesitant step, testing the waters, and then another, until the luxuriant warmth swirled around her calves and drew her all the way in. She propelled herself across the pool in one sliding motion and came to rest on the step at the opposite side.

Relaxing in the buoyancy of her body, she closed her eyes for a moment. Truly, it was a magical place that set her creative spirit free.

Rich green ferns swayed from baskets suspended overhead, thriving on the steam swirling from the bath. A tasseled cord hung from an aperture at the apex of the dome. Kindra reached for it, pulled, and watched amused as steam swirled among the ferns and exited the hole. A sense of calm seeped into her bones.

She traced her fingers around fanciful rows of lapis lazuli tile embedded in white marble, losing herself in the design. Partitions of gold separated the blue from the white, similar to the partitions she had used in the making of the brooch. It was almost as if she'd seen this design in her mind when she made it.

She slid further under the water until the top of her breasts and shoulders were caressed in silky heat. She closed her eyes and, feeling safe for the first time she could remember, she dared imagine Marcus at her elbow. The man who seared her soul forever with one touch of his lips.

This moment did feel like a dream, a fantasy she indulged until her blood raced and her breath came in short gasps. Her eyes flew open at the sensation. She sat, rigid with shock as the feeling melted away.

Tears welled, spilled over her cheeks. She pulled herself reluctantly from the water, scraped her skin with the strigil and poured a handful of oil from an urn near the steps. She smoothed it over her body, ending at the hollow of her stomach.

Reality asserted itself, took hold. Neither luxurious silks, nor perfumed oils, nor all the sumptuous marble baths in all the empire could replace the emptiness in Kindra's heart. She would one day bear this babe, and it would never know its father.

The rotunda had refilled with steam. She pulled the cord and light streamed in through billowy clouds. It must be nearing noon; she had better see to Fausta's needs.

She returned to her chamber briefly to change out of her wet tunic. Her blue robe, the only other thing she had to wear, hung over the back of a chair to relieve the wrinkles the journey had inflicted upon it. She smoothed it over her body and added a criss-cross of leather bindings from the tunic around the bodice. She rearranged her new braids, applied the pomade Fausta had given her, and let the shorter front of her hair curl softly about her face and neck.

The Empress's eyebrows arched high when Kindra entered the chamber behind a line of servants bearing the noon meal.

Fausta ordered them all to leave and bade Kindra to sit.

"That soft blue color becomes you, Niala. Where did you get such a lovely robe?"

Kindra blushed. "I made it, my Lady. The cloth was a gift from ... a friend."

"Indeed! I shall have you make a gown for me; you have done such beautiful work with the silk."

Kindra blushed again, her hands still folded in her lap.

"It is good to have you, Niala. I tire of eating alone."

The empress passed a plate of sweet meats to her. Kindra accepted the dish and tasted the pungently spiced cuts.

"So, you have a friend who brings you gifts. This wouldn't be a young man, now, would it?"

Kindra kept her eyes low as her friend Flavia had said. Even if she felt comfortable exchanging small talk with the Empress, she dared not reveal his name. He had told her, after all, he worked directly for the emperor and it was likely Fausta herself knew of him.

"It was a long time ago," she said low.

Her distress must have been apparent, for Fausta laughed brightly at her. "Oh. Calm yourself. You needn't answer. I can see it on your face. You have nothing to fear from me. I too have a young man."

Kindra couldn't stop her eyes flashing to Fausta's. "Oh! Don't look so surprised — we're two women here, am I correct? Not like that cold bitch, Valeria. She would like as not have every soldier's manhood lopped off and his head on a gibbet. I honestly don't' know why the emperor tolerates her. The woman make's my skin crawl."

Kindra could agree with that.

"Do you think I could survive on the scraps of attention the emperor pays me? If all I had to breathe was his passion, I'd have suffocated the first month we were wed."

"But you have four children." Kindra couldn't help herself, the words tumbled out.

Fausta sent her a disapproving frown. "A lot you know about love. There's more to it than planting a seed that is up to us to carry and then push out. I swear by the gods, if men were the ones to bear children, the population would shrink overnight. Take it from someone who knows, my pet. Making babes and making love are two entirely different things."

Kindra forced her gaze to the floor, her heart sinking with the words.

Fausta pushed herself away from the table and stretched luxuriously. "So, yes. I have a young man, and I shall see him today; and you, Niala, will stand guard outside the tepidarium while we are together. This will, of course, remain our secret."

Kindra nodded without looking up. "Of course."

The tepidarium was much larger than the hot bath Kindra had visited that morning. A dome of white marble arched high overhead, with two levels of colonnaded walkways around the perimeter. The covered hallway leading to the caldarium had been temporarily blocked to allow the empress her privacy. The peristyle at the opposite end had been cleared and the public confined to the arena and the larger cold pools.

Kindra and Fausta entered the tepidarium; their footsteps echoed sharply, amplified by the smooth marble interior walls. Gentle ripples spread across the water as Fausta stepped into the pool, their whispered voices joined musical notes of water falling from a fountain at the far end of the chamber.

A sudden noise outside the blocked entrance raised the hair on the back of Kindra's arms. The walls of the rotunda seemed to suddenly close in. They were safe, but as she took in her surroundings, she realized, they would also be trapped, with only one way out. The thought made her uneasy. She pushed down the urge to run.

"Will there be anything else, my lady?"

"No. Thank you, Niala. I will take a few moments here by myself, and then my love will join me. It is all arranged." She slipped out of her robe, passed it to Kindra, and stepped into the pool, her eyes alight with thoughts she didn't share.

Kindra was folding the robe over her arm when Fausta's gaze lifted over her shoulder and her smile broadened.

"Marcus," she said, a glint of pleasure in her jade green eyes.

Kindra froze. Marcus? Fausta's secret lover was Marcus? She turned, her gasp catching in her throat. Anguish gripped her heart. It was true. Marcus, clad in warrior's armor, sword at his hip, pushed past her as if she weren't there. He grabbed Fausta by her arms and dragged her out of the water. "Time to go, my lady." His words were urgent, forceful.

"Why? What's happened?" Water sluiced off Fausta's nude body, her breasts shaking as she resisted his grip.

He grabbed the robe out of Kindra's arms and wrapped it around her shoulders. "You must come with me, now."

There was shouting down the corridor. Many voices. Hurrying footsteps.

"No! Let me go, you fool," Fausta cried out. "Crispus is on his way here." The empress's voice was shrill; she pushed Marcus away.

"Shhhh," he urged, his hand covering her mouth. "You are in grave danger, my lady. Listen to me." He shook her shoulders until she closed her mouth, her eyes flashing anger. "I was sent to kill you. Do you understand? The Emperor has ordered it. It is only by the grace of God I disobey his command."

Her eyes flew wide. She opened her mouth to scream and Marcus clamped his hand over her lips. Her fingers clawed at his. When at last he lifted his gaze and met Kindra's, his eyes widened in surprise.

"By the gods, Kindra. What on earth are you doing here?"

The clamor outside the chamber grew louder. Fausta fought in his arms. Kindra shook her head, her throat closed crushing her words. His eyes held hers for a deep, soul-crushing moment before a man burst into the chamber, gasping for breath.

"The deed is done, Marcus," he said, his gravel voice magnified by its echo against cold marble. "Crispus is dead. The Centurions are on their way. Go now, or Fausta won't leave here alive."

Fausta's agonized scream escaped his grip, then she went limp. Lifting her in his arms, his eyes shot back to Kindra. "Stay here. Tell them you heard Fausta's cry, but when you got here, she was gone."

"Take me with you," she cried, and reaching out, she grabbed his arm.

"We don't have time for this nonsense," the other man snarled, and tore her away by the leather straps wrapped around her waist. She recognized shock in Marcus' eyes for an instant before a punishing blow to the back of her head sent Kindra staggering toward the pool. Her vision blurred an then went dark.

Kindra crawled over the shallow lapiz steps on hands and knees, fighting to recover her senses. She was alone. Blood swirled around her in the water. Pain seared the back of her head. She lifted her fingers, felt a gash. When she brought her hands in front of her, they were covered in blood.

Footsteps echoed in the caldarium, louder, louder.

Run! Came the voice inside her head. *Run for your life!*

She steadied herself with her hands, trying to get her feet under her.

Move. Move!

She willed her legs to respond. Shouts shattered off the walls.

Run! Go!

The voice was a relentless chant in her head pushing her forward, but as she dragged herself out of the shallow water, something bright and golden glinted in a beam of light coming down from the opening above. The brooch gleamed at the bottom of the pool. She patted her body in disbelief. But it was so. The straps of her leather girdle hung loose at her sides and her pouch was empty.

"No!" she cried, but by the sounds, the guards could only be steps from the entrance. They would be on her any moment. But she could not turn away. She stared at the golden treasure with longing for a fateful heartbeat too long. Valeria, flanked by a half-dozen guards, stepped through the arch into the chamber. She lowered her sword and her face twisted into a smirk.

Her eyes swept Kindra's bloodied hands and gown, then took in the swirling blood in the pool. "Well, well." She stalked to stand close enough for Kindra to see the flinty grey in her eyes. "What have you done with our Empress?"

CHAPTER THIRTY-FIVE
Balboa Island, Republic of California, 2019 CE

Karl pushed open the heavy mausoleum door, surprised to find it unlocked. He had always been the first to arrive at the family's monthly meeting at Forrest Lawn. His brother, Lars, never approved of his using the family crypt as a private bank vault, which was why he was here half an hour early. This time, evidently, he hadn't arrived early enough.

Lars had been campaigning to quit meeting here altogether since their father had died. "It's ghoulish and unnecessary," Lars had said during a particularly heated debate.

"Unnecessary? Can you think of a better place to keep our family secrets?" Karl wasn't budging.

"I don't believe our father's collection should be a secret."

"Really. And you're willing to go to prison for that belief? I don't think so."

Lars had been angered at that. "If we had turned the damned gold over to the authorities the day he died, we wouldn't need to keep it a secret."

"A secret worth millions," Karl had reminded him.

"Not if we can't sell it!"

And so, it went, year after year, Karl held the threat of arrest over his brother while he built his trade. He kept a low profile, of course. His client list was confidential. The *collection* had grown as Karl carried on in his father's tradition. The old man would be proud. What Lars Johns didn't know, wouldn't hurt him.

Karl pushed past the brass gate into the small, private rotunda prepared for a showdown with his brother. He was not prepared to find his sister-in-law, by herself, arms deep inside one of the empty roll-out tombs.

"Looking for something?" His voice echoed in the marble chamber. Valerie shrieked and whirled around. She would have to have gotten her husband's key to get through the gate.

"My god, Karl, you scared the devil out of me." She leaned against the tomb, rolling it back in place.

He closed the distance between them in two long strides, circled his arms around her waist, and pulled her against him. "Let's hope not."

He crushed his mouth over hers, then pushed back, taking in her obviously expensive outfit; a pale pink brocade suit with a short-cropped jacket and pencil-thin skirt. The kind of thing a married woman might wear to a wedding. It flattered her taller-than-average figure. She spent her husband's money well, and it might have been stimulating to Karl's libido, if he hadn't caught her snooping where she didn't belong.

No. That wasn't stimulating at all. He imagined pressing his thumbs into her neck until he crushed her windpipe but drew in a long breath through his nose instead. The only thing *that* would get him was life in prison, or worse. Instead, he pulled her harder against him. Better to be close to your enemies.

She grabbed his wrists, twisted away. "Karl. Lars wouldn't like this here in the family mausoleum."

"Like it matters." Lars was well aware of their intimate relationship. Welcomed it, in fact.

Valerie stopped smiling, straightened her jacket. Then she held up the key. "Would he give me a key if he didn't want me here?"

He would never give her the key. That Karl knew in his bones.

Her smile stretched over a set of expensive, perfectly crowned teeth. Her gaze swept the room and narrowed as it came back to him. He didn't like the expression in her eyes. Where there had once been lust, now there was something else. Challenge. She was daring him to call her a liar. He didn't like it. Didn't like it at all.

He'd never fully trusted this woman; not from the first time she'd strolled into the Johns' home on his brother's arm. Out of nowhere, it seemed, and just in time to rescue Lars from his father's edict: His eldest son would marry a *woman*, or there would be no inheritance. They all knew Lars had no inclination toward women; but suddenly, there she was. And what she wasn't able to get from Lars, she'd managed to get from Karl. For a while it had been exciting.

Lars and Karl made the pact. Lars got his inheritance and the CEO position of his father's corporation. Karl got his inheritance, the physical benefits of a willing woman when he wanted, without the incumbrance of having to take care of her or the business.

But recently, something had changed. Something he hadn't seen coming. Something that put him on alert. Whether by accident, or on purpose, Val had taken a sudden interest in Karl's private enterprise. Showing up at that yard sale had been completely unexpected. Now she'd invaded what he thought was sacred, family space.

He dropped his hands, stepped back. "What I want to know is what are you doing here on your own?" If Lars wasn't here, there was no reason to meet. He needed to get rid of her so he could make a *withdrawal.*

She hugged her waist. "I'm Lars' wife. I have every right to be here."

Karl stepped to the tomb he'd caught her looking in a moment before and rolled it open wide. "I'm sure that could be arranged."

She scrunched up her nose. "That's not funny."

He dusted off his hands. "Wasn't intended to be."

She shrugged it off, and Karl had to give her credit. She was no pushover. She crossed the room, and when she turned to face him, she had recovered her composure. "I think I'd rather be cremated than have my remains rot in this mausoleum." She trailed her fingers over the engraved inscription on his mother's rose-marble tomb.

His eyes narrowed in suspicion. How long had she been inside here alone? What had she seen?

"I agree with Lars, you know. I don't like meeting in here. It's just too ..." She shrugged and waved her palm, as if searching for the proper word "—

Gothic," she said, finally. "Like something out of a vampire movie."

"It was my father's idea. Different times, I suppose. Beats a bank vault all to hell for privacy, though."

She perched on the arm of a marble bench in the center of the room and brushed dust from her fingertips. "Hum."

"So, there's no reason to stay." Karl hadn't moved from his position before the crypt engraved with his own name and birth date followed by a dash.

"That's not entirely true. I actually came to see you -- I saw you drive away from the shop; I wanted to talk to you so I –"

"You want me to believe you followed me?" Karl glared at her as she rose and paced the room.

"You make it sound so sinister."

"You arrived here before me, Val." He scuffed his foot on the marble floor, fingered the coins in his pocket. "What did you want to talk to me about that was so important you had to lie about it?"

She stepped closer to the door and shot a hip in a stance one could only call provocative. He always thought his brother's wife looked more like a hooker than an OC wife, although of late, it was hard to tell the difference. Either way, he knew what she was after and he was tired of indulging her.

She wrapped her arms around on her middle and tapped her foot.

"Nervous?"

She stopped.

He sent her a menacing grin.

301

She picked at a crack alongside one of the tombs, shifted her eyes away from his. "Maybe it would be better another time. You seem … distracted."

"No more than usual, Val. I need you to tell me why you're here."

She turned back to him, pursing her lips as if deciding whether or not to be honest. Then she huffed, set her shoulders. "There was a bracelet. It went missing when I moved in with Lars." She raised a brow at him. "It was a … a gift, Karl. Something that meant a lot to me."

Karl folded his arms over his chest, crossed his legs at the ankles and leveled his gaze at her; Tessa's snake bracelet came to mind. "And you thought maybe I took it and hid it here?" He opened his arms to indicate the space.

She licked her lips; a woman about to lie. "Or found it, maybe? It's not that valuable, actually. I just … want it back."

He studied her. Not that valuable, he thought, yet valuable enough to steal the keys to the family vault, let herself in, and then lie about it. He narrowed his gaze on her. If it was the bracelet he'd tested in his shop, it was likely worth as much as his entire collection.

She started pacing again. "You met with Tessa Madigan after the sale. Perhaps she showed it to you?"

Karl decided to keep his information to himself. The fact that Val knew of the bracelet piqued his curiosity. There was obviously more to the little serpent than met the eye.

"Sorry, no," he said. "What makes you think she would have it?"

"She said her uncle was a Klepto. The timing would be right for when I lived there. Maybe he took it. Sealed it up in the wall with Helena's—" She stopped pacing, cleared her throat.

"Helena's …?" Karl rolled his hand to keep her talking.

Once again, she eyed him warily. He had the distinct impression he was being stalked. "I … Listen. You're right. I should have come to you first. I realize that now. I apologize." She tightened her grip on her purse and headed for the gate.

Karl grabbed her arm, spun her to against him. "Indeed, you should have." The fact that she hadn't made his gut clench.

She gave him a grin that set the hair up on the back of his neck. "No harm, no foul, right Karl?"

In her dreams. She'd come too close to his collection. He'd have to make sure it didn't happen again. He smiled at her, let her go. "Sure."

Like a chameleon, she morphed into the lusty broad he was used to. "Don't be angry with me Karl. Please. Why don't you come back to the house? Lars is in Cabo this weekend with his lover. Take a break from your shabby little storefront. We can have the place all to ourselves."

Karl never much liked his brother's sprawling estate in Cameo Shores. All pretense and glitz. He could give a shit about all that. What he did give a shit about was his enterprise. "All right. I've got some business to take care of first, then I'll be along." He held open the brass gate for her.

She gave him a peck on the cheek on her way out.

He watched her amble toward her car at the edge of the monument-scattered lawn, angry at himself. He'd ignored the red flags for too long. His brother's wife couldn't be trusted. The last thing he needed was someone else in the mix. Now he had no choice but to do something about that.

She turned and gave him a little wave before she slipped into her black Jaguar. He smiled and waved back. She was going to make it so easy.

CHAPTER THIRTY-SIX

Tessa sat at the head of her bed, her knees crossed under her, Lotus style. The pillows and blankets were limp with damp and cold. Moisture beaded on the windows. She rubbed a circle clear with the heel of her hand and peered out over the rooftops.

"Tess? You up?"

The voice drifted into her consciousness as if from far away. Tessa didn't move.

"Tess? It's 7:30, you're going to be late for — oh my god, it's freezing up here."

The bed jiggled under Tess. Someone was crawling toward her. She shrank from the movement.

"Tessa?"

Something icy gripped her arm. She clamped her hand over the spot. A double circle of metal cinched tight around her bicep. When she touched it, it loosened, slipped to her wrist.

A warm hand covered hers. "My God! You're cold as a corpse."

Someone pulled her frozen hands together to support a warm mug, then wrapped a blanket around her shoulders. She sniffed the hot liquid. Coffee.

She sipped carefully. After a moment, her teeth stopped chattering. She turned her head stiffly. A familiar face smiled back at her. "Lexi?"

Lex looped Tessa's hair behind her ears, held her face in her warm hands. "Talk to me, Tess."

Tessa exhaled. A tear seared down her frozen cheek. She sniffed, wiped her eye with the back of her hand. She was safe. In her room. Home.

"I went back." Her voice came out thready and faint.

Lexi took her hand. "Come on. You're going into the tub."

Tessa turned back to the window. "The soldiers, that woman, took her."

Lexi eased an arm around her and coaxed her off of the bed. "I know, honey. You dreamed again, but you're back here now and you're as cold as a fish." She teased Tess off the bed and guided her down the stairs.

Halfway down Tess grabbed the railing. "No. Not a dream. They took her; but there was blood. So much blood." She touched the back of her head. Nothing. "We ... we..." She buried her face in her hands, sobbing, as she slid into a heap and rested her head on the neatly-turned balusters of Phillip's new stairway. "Marcus took Fausta. They're going to kill him."

Lexi's arms came under her shoulders and lifted her up. "Okay. Wow. That's some pretty lucid dreaming, but we're still getting you into a hot bath."

❧

Tessa sank deep into her familiar pink porcelain tub. She ran her hands over the wide, flat edges and held on, allowing her present reality to sink in. She wasn't in Trier anymore. Or the royal palace. She was home, safe, in 2019. Her gaze followed the beltline of black and white tile around the circumference of the room before she took her first lungful of air.

Lexi's voice floated in from the kitchen. She was on the phone. "Hello? Mr. Hartman? Alexis Hill. Tessa's roommate?" A short pause. "Yeah. Listen. She won't be in today; she's got a bad case of the flu. Fever, chills, barf, probably contagious." Another pause, then, "You're right. We don't want anyone else sick. She'll call you tomorrow. Thanks; I'll tell her."

Bubbles mountained at the end of the tub as hot water gushed from the faucet. Life was returning to Tess's fingers and toes.

Lexi appeared in the doorway, the morning paper tucked under her arm. "He says don't you dare come in, and don't worry."

"You told him I had the flu."

"Would you rather I told him you were suffering from delusions, or how about time traveling?"

Steam clouds swirled around the old, high-ceilinged room, frosting the mirror and the tiny windows on either side of it. Delusional or traveling in time. Either way, she was out of control. She needed to get that back. "Not sure."

Lexi perched on the edge of the tub, sipped her coffee. "You wanna talk about it?"

Tessa nodded. "You must be getting tired of this." She sank deeper under the bubbles.

"Not tired. Concerned. Sane people don't sit naked in front of open windows in the fog. And, despite the hot bath, you're still white as cottage cheese." She propped the paper on the side of the tub. Read this. It will get your mind off the dreams for now. I'll get you some cocoa and toast."

"How 'bout you just bring me the chocolate syrup."

Lexi rolled her eyes and let out a low laugh. "Well, there's my girl again. But I'd say you need some actual nourishment with your chocolate."

"Lots of peanut butter then," Tess ordered as Lex stepped out of the room.

A vague feeling of dread lay low in her gut. Again.

She grabbed the newspaper and opened it. It took a moment to make sense of the headline, but once she did, her stomach did a flip flop.

"No. That can't be." She read it through again. "Lex?"

Lexi came running, saucepan in hand. "What is it?"

"Where was I last night?" Tears welled in her eyes.

"What?"

"Where. Was. I?"

"You were up there, catching pneumonia," Lexi said, gesturing at the ceiling with the pan.

"Are you sure?" Tessa groped in her mind for some clear recollection of the night before, but she could remember little other than vague horror and overwhelming grief. "Oh God, what have I done?"

It was happening again. A scene from a dream was bleeding through to her reality. "I'm warm enough," she said, stepping out the of the tub with a shudder. "I've got to get out!"

"Okay, okay. Take it easy. Here's a towel." Lexi put down the pan and wrapped a bath sheet around Tessa's body, then helped her twist another towel around her hair. She guided her to the dining room and sat her in a chair.

Tessa spread the bath-soaked newspaper out on the table and showed Lexi the story on the front page.

She poked her finger at the headline. "Brother of Cauldron Industries, owner, Karl Johns, found dead in the family's Cameo Shores hot tub."

Sherril Gregory, Staff Writer. Balboa Island Outlook — *Balboa Island resident, Karl Johns, was found dead in his brother's hot tub last evening by his sister-in-law, Valerie Johns. The coroner's initial report showed apparent excessive alcohol in Johns' system but made no further comment on whether the death was an accident. Karl Johns and his brother, Lars, are co-owners of Cauldron Industries, a local corporation specializing in aerospace-quality instruments and switches and other industrial uses of gold and precious metals. Lars Johns was not available for comment.*

"We've got to call the police," Tessa said. "I think, I…" She shook her head, trying to remember what had happened. A man knocked Kindra down in the bath. There was blood, but too much to have come from the cut on her own head. Blood, but, no body… "Lex, where was I last night?"

"Last night? What are you talking about?"

"Last night. Did you see me leave?"

"No."

Tessa pressed her lips together hard. "I tell you I was there. I must have done it."

Lex fisted her hands at her hips and scowled at her. "Done what? What the hell are you saying?"

"Killed Karl. That's the only explanation."

"Tess, that's crazy. Listen to me. You were here all night. Besides, what possible motive would you have to do such a thing?"

"Really? After what happened at the yard sale?"

"People don't kill people for being arrogant pricks."

Tessa bit her bottom lip. "No. But in the history of the world, how many people have been killed over gold?"

"Gold." Lexi rocked back on her heels. Tessa watched her expression segue from confusion to doubt. "Honey, you're letting this dream thing get an unhealthy hold on you. Even to the point of interfering with your job. You've got to—"

Valeria's face filled Tessa's mind, the similarity to Lars wife — her name, her build, her attitude. It sent a chill through her bones. She shook it off. "But what if it's not a dream?"

"Okay. I'll play. What if it's not?"

Tessa got up, raked tembling fingers through her hair, paced to the French doors. "What if I thought I was in the past, but I was really acting out in the present? I fought with a man in the baths in my dream, then Karl turns up dead in his hot tub, and —"

Lexi sent her a skeptical frown the way she'd done since they were kids. "I swear to God, Tess. I would have heard you if you'd gone out."

It was true. Lexi was a light sleeper, and the Volkswagen starting up in the garage rattled the house all the way to the rooftop. She didn't remember any of that. All she remembered was the blood in the water and Valeria's steel grey eyes drilling into hers. *What have you done with Fausta?*

Tessa sighed deeply and came back to sit, her legs suddenly liquid. Something had happened last night. And she knew in her bones it was somehow connected to her dreams. She wrapped her arms around her waist against a prickling chill. There wasn't a bath warm enough to take away the icy cold that knowledge had frozen into her soul.

An image of a cold, damp room took shape in her mind. She shook it away.

"What?" Lexi pressed, reacting to her shudder.

"Nothing. I don't know. I don't know what's happening any more than you do. I just have a feeling Karl's death has something to do with the jewelry. I need to talk this through before I do something I can't fix."

"Maybe you should start by telling me what happened at Karl's shop the other day."

Tessa peered at her friend, pulling her thoughts together. "Okay."

She stood again, her hand resting on the door frame, noting the height of the tide as she did often when she was at home. It was somehow calming, predictable, and no amount of human idiocy could change it.

Audrey's cat meowed on the landing and she let him in. With the cat weaving around her legs, his motor running loud, Tess told Lexi about Karl's test on the old touchstone and the way his eyes gleamed at the discovery.

"He wants — wanted — the jewelry, Lex. I think he was afraid I'd report it to customs, which would put it out of his reach." She slid back into her at the table and the cat leapt up and settled in her lap. "He actually wanted me to let him have those heavy earrings to do more tests."

"You didn't give them to him?"

"No. But I got the feeling he'd been looking for those pieces for a long time. Suspected Theo had them. That's why Theo hid it all away."

A fresh thought knotted up her stomach. Did Theo know about the bracelet's power? Or did that only work for her? She forced herself to breathe deep and slow as Lexi picked up the story line.

"And when Theo started to lose it, mentally, he must have let that fact slip."

"He was fond of telling stories of his adventures. Maybe he told the wrong person."

Lexi puckered her lips. "Holy crap. And we laid it all out there on the table for him."

Tessa stroked the cat's back. "Yup. But his test got me thinking. After I talked to Karl that day, I did a little research on my own."

"And…"

"And, if what I found is true, that jewelry is part of a larger collection stolen from a national treasury and transported to the US illegally."

Lexi dropped into a chair. "Get out of town."

Tessa told her about the articles she'd found in Theo's stash of goodies.

Lexi scanned the material, then fixed Tessa with her no-nonsense gaze. "In other words, we're in a world of shit."

"Not necessarily. Theo would have been in a world of shit if he in fact stole the jewelry and smuggled it here. But now he's dead, and all we did was find it in his house."

"And you think you can just call up customs and they'll be like, 'Oh, gee, that's nice. We'll just come right down and pick that up from you and thank you very much?"

"Why would I do that?"

"Why? Let me see." Lexi drummed her fingers on her chin. "International culture theft, smuggling, possible murder? I'd say we're talking about — um — life in prison. Granted, it would probably be white collar prison, but—"

Tessa sprang to her feet; the cat flew off her lap. "That jewelry belongs to Kindra!"

Lexi's mouth dropped open. "No, wait. Tell me you didn't just say what I thought you said."

"I know her mark as sure as I made it myself."

Lexi slowly shook her head.

Tessa sucked in her bottom lip. The light in the room began to shift. *Hold on. Hold. On.*

She slid her gaze across the bay to where Phillip's house hung off the cliffs, but all she could see was blood floating in an emerald pool and the brooch Kindra had made, the one she'd been accused of stealing, spinning and side-slipping its way to the bottom of the bath. Her ears filled with the sound of

313

footsteps rushing toward her. Valeria's face loomed in front of her, leering, menacing.

She dropped her face into her hands and sobbed. "Kindra needs me. I have to go back—"

"Tessa!" Lexi grabbed her shirt and forced her to sit. She pulled her chair close, their knees touching. "*I* need you! Right here, right now." She clapped her hands in Tessa's face. "Look at me!"

Tessa dragged her eyes away from the window, a crushing weight bearing down on her chest. Lexi's eyes burned into hers.

She sucked in a breath as if coming up for air for the first time since getting out of bed. "Oh my god, Lex. I'm … losing it, aren't I?"

Lexi pulled her into her arms and held her tight. "Not if I can help it."

CHAPTER THIRTY-SEVEN

Libra: What has been out of reach is now at hand.

"I remember seeing the Festival of Lights back when I was a young woman." Audrey sat on the edge of her chair; her body suddenly animated as the memory danced behind her eyes. Mid December and a late Santa Ana wind had brought with it the kind of mild heat wave characteristic of Southern California. Everywhere around the island and down the peninsula, people were out in shirtsleeves and shorts, preparing their boats for the traditional Christmas parade on the bay.

In the weeks since Karl's death, and at Lexi's urging, Tessa had worked hard to turn her thoughts to happier things, such as the approaching holiday and her relationship with Phillip. "Even if you don't feel okay," Lex had told her, working some of her shrinky-dink magic, "if you act as if you feel okay, it will have the same effect."

Surprisingly, the tactic had worked. With the stairway finished, she and Phillip had turned their attention to the kitchen. They'd torn out the wall with the man-sized patch and thankfully, there was nothing behind it but some dry-rotted studs that needed replacing.

Lexi and Tessa had spent this Saturday afternoon on the upstairs deck, soaking up what would surely be the last decent sun time before winter enveloped the island in her blanket of fog. Audrey had joined

315

them, and the young women listened as she related her tales of early island days, while Phillip and the carpenter he'd hired replaced the drywall over the studs.

"A man --" Audrey continued, full of excitement, "Heavens, I can't bring his name to my lips right now — I'll think of it in a minute — anyway, he had a string of Venice-style gondolas and he used to paddle lovers around in the evening and sing songs as he went."

She reached over and picked up Tessa's Mai Tai, sipped from it, set it back down on the arm of the old chaise longue, then continued: "Way back in 1908 — before I was born, by the way — he got some of his friends to join him and his gondolas in a parade with lanterns. It was a summertime thing that happened on and off, until after WWII, when it was started up again as a Christmas parade of lights. I wish I could remember his name," she said again, tapping the side of her cheek with a finger.

"Check it out." Lexi gripped Tessa by the shoulder. "Look at that!" She pointed excitedly to her drink sitting on a TV tray next to her chair. The ice cubes were tinkling and, yes, Tessa's were too.

"It's a quake--" She sat up on the edge of the chaise and looked from Lexi to Audrey and back. She had grown up with earthquakes and more or less took them for granted along with Southern California's crowds and occasional windstorms. A little sun, a little freeway congestion, a little earthquake now and then — she was grateful for the few would-be Californians each new report of earthquake scared away. It would stop in a second or two; just a small temblor, by the feel of it. Not nearly as bad as the start of the one she'd been in near the Borrego Desert, and not even near the strength of the one in Sylmar. But, were the vibrations coming harder? Should they go downstairs and get away from this rickety old house? Was this the one they had all been warned would dump half of California into the Pacific?

The shaking usually stopped before she got to the last question. And, true to form, as suddenly as it had begun, it ended.

Lexi relaxed into her rattan chair, Mai Tai raised to Tessa in a toast. "Cheap thrills," she said, tipping her glass.

Tess tinked her glass with Lexi's. "And, I've still got beach front property!"

Audrey slapped her knees. "John Scarpa!"

Tessa and Alex blinked at her.

"That was his name," she went on. "Guess that earthquake jarred my brain loose. Anyway, where were we? Oh yes. Nowadays, you see the tiniest sailboats and the biggest yachts all out there together; some of them have computers on board to control their lights."

Tessa settled back into the chaise, laughing to herself. She had forgotten the topic of conversation just before the quake, but Mrs. B'd hardly skipped a beat. Probably because Audrey had been a Californian twice as long as she and Lexi put together.

They had let themselves be lulled once again by her disjointed storytelling and dozed lazily, the tremor forgotten, until the influence of their Mai

Tai's and lengthening shadows drove them inside for supper.

It had been one of the most peaceful days Tessa had had in weeks, earthquake included. Tomorrow was Sunday, she could sleep in, supper could be late. Life seemed to be returning to normal since the night she had dreamed of the bath, an incident that paled in the face of what had happened in the real world. The death of Karl Johns had barely sent a ripple through Cauldron Industries, other than the business was officially closed for a couple of days after his death. He had been interred in the family mausoleum at Forest Lawn in a private service.

Things with Phillip had been a little rocky since she had so unfeelingly blown off another casual proposal. He hadn't stayed over as much, and she missed him in her bed. He was probably angry, and a little hurt, but she knew he couldn't stay away for long. He needed her the same way she needed him.

After watching him work shirtless in her kitchen most of the day, she *really* needed him. She had managed to coax him upstairs for a little romp in the sheets after Lexi went to work. But he begged off staying. He'd been called away on company business with an early departure the next morning and left without a second round; but not before eliciting sworn promises to keep her doors locked, including the new deadbolts he'd installed on both stairway doors.

She retired for the evening, hopeful of a good night's rest and for the first time in weeks, fell asleep without so much as a trip downstairs for milk and a shot of chocolate.

She slipped into a blissful, if not lonely sleep that lasted for about two hours, until a heavy bump from downstairs had her leaping out of bed. She checked the clock: three a.m. Lexi would have been home hours ago. Tess pulled on her robe and went to Lexi's room. "Lex? You hear that?"

Lexi roused herself to one elbow and flicked on her bedside lamp. She listened. "Probably the cat," she mumbled, sleepily, reaching for the lamp again.

"No. The cat is sleeping between your legs. I hear something — in the garage — listen."

Tessa pulled the covers off the half-asleep Lex and handed her a robe. "Come on. You don't want me to go down there alone, do you?"

"I don't hear anything! And what's to take in the garage, anyway? Whoever it is can have my car and good luck to them."

"All right then, I'm going myself." Tessa tied her robe and headed for the stairs.

"Okay, okay," Lexi moaned. She followed Tessa through the living room, grabbing the fire poker on her way. "At least get a frying pan or a broom or something," she ordered as she cautiously undid the dead bolts and opened the back door.

Tessa grabbed the wooden meat tenderizer off the butcher block in the kitchen, flinching at the draft of cold, damp air from the open door; it had reached near eighty degrees during the day, but the night had turned cold and damp as ever.

They crept down the back stairs; the cat, curious and under foot, as usual, slipped past them and led the way.

319

"Go on, get!" Lexi hissed, shooing him aside. They peered around the corner into the open garage.

At first, they could hear and see nothing; then Tessa noticed a man's head and shoulders silhouetted in the moonlight shining through the window of the small door from the garage to the front yard.

She pointed; her eyes wide. Lexi inched forward.

The man did not move, nor did he appear to be aware of their approach. Tessa's heart pounded. None of her frequent *bump-in-the-night* searches had ever yielded anything. Now that they had actually discovered someone there, she wished she'd listened to Lexi and left them to whatever they wanted. Maybe she should just let Lex go after him and she would call the police.

She shrank back, but Lexi turned and glared at her, motioning her on. Tessa raised her meat pounder a little higher and took a step forward onto the cat's tail, which sent him yowling and skittering across the garage floor right up to the man's feet.

Spinning around, he shined a flashlight into Tessa's face. "What the Hell?"

She couldn't see his face with the LED lights blazing into her eyes, but she knew that voice. "Phillip?"

He changed the angle of his light and glared at her. Tessa would have been relieved if his expression wasn't so angry. Without another word, he turned back to the window.

"Damn!" He pounded his fist on the door frame. "They're gone now, thanks to you ladies."

Tessa shuffled to the window and peered out into the moonlit yard. "Who's gone?"

"If I knew who it was, I wouldn't be standing here spying, would I? What are you doing down here anyway?" He fumbled with the flashlight.

Tess raised an eyebrow at him. "What are *you* doing here? You're supposed to be heading to San Francisco."

He stammered, and opened his mouth to answer, but Tessa cut him off.

She didn't suspect Phillip of any foul play, but he deserved a hard time at least for scaring the crap out of them like this and disturbing the first good night's sleep she'd had for weeks.

On the other hand, the way he looked right now, face flushed, hair falling over his eyes, she hoped he'd come upstairs and disturb it some more.

They had caught him off guard, but he finally recovered some of his momentum. "You think I'm down here because I like December beach air in the moonlight? Come out here and see for yourself."

He opened the door, swept the light beam from his flashlight across the walkway, then led them across the yard to the tile-covered mound near the front gate. "See this? They've dug up the end of the mound, and with your own shovel, no less. I knew I'd catch the bastard at something if I waited down here long enough."

He shined the light over the pile of dug up sand, catching some shiny objects in the glow. "What's are those?"

Lexi retrieved what turned out to be an ordinary kitchen fork. She held it under the light.

"Looks like restaurant-grade stainless steel. Jesus Christ on the dashboard," she said, flapping her arms against her sides. "I can't believe I'm out here in my pajamas in the middle of the night, picking junk out of the front yard." She glared at Phillip and Tessa in turns. "You two can stay out here in the sandbox if you want to, but I'm going back to bed."

She picked her way over the path.

Tessa watched Lexi's retreat a moment longer before she dragged her eyes back to Phillip. What she really wanted to do was hug him and take him upstairs, but her mind was reeling with the fact that her property had been invaded. She needed some answers.

"What do you mean, if you waited here long enough? How long have you been out here?"

"Three nights."

"Three — You mean while I was up in my room wondering where you were and what I had done to make you stay away, you were down here in the garage? And what bastard are we talking about?"

"Will you back off? I didn't let him get you, did I?"

"Who? The boogey man? Karl Johns is dead."

"His accomplice. Who else?"

"Accomplice? You mean, like, Lars?"

"Why not? Their father was a crook."

"Oh, honestly Phillip. I'm pretty sure the CEO of a major corporation would at least hire some thug to dig up my yard." Tessa knelt down and picked more pieces of silver out of the pile at her feet. She hadn't thought about the gold much since Karl's death and the renewed interest struck her not only as odd, but a little scary.

Phillip offered her a hand up, circled her back with his arms, kissed her gently. "Maybe. But I am glad of one thing." He pulled her tighter against him. "I was here when it happened."

He was right about that. Her light robe clung to her legs, already damp with fog. What if she and Lexi had surprised whoever it was, and they decided to come after them? She shivered at the thought.

"I told you that family was nuts."

"So, you really think it was Lars?"

"Couldn't tell; I got *interrupted.*"

"Well, I'm relieved all around." She lifted up on her toes and kissed him. "I thought you'd given up on *me.*"

"Never." He whispered into her neck. His eagerness pressed against her practically naked stomach. He ran his hands down over her thighs, but he was looking out over the canal. "Let's go inside, it's cold, and I have a feeling we're being watched."

Tessa craned her neck around, looking down the seawall walkway in both directions. "You don't think he's still out there, do you?"

A bright light shone in Tessa's eyes, momentarily blinding her.

"What's going on down here? You children all right?" Tess recognized her neighbor's voice, followed by the unmistakable meow of her cat.

"Audrey! It's three o'clock in the morning. You shouldn't be out here."

The old woman was shrugging into a heavy robe as she shambled down the walkway toward them. "I was out on my porch. We old folks don't sleep much at night. I heard noises, and I saw someone run by the seawall. What's going on?"

She craned her bent head around to shine her hurricane flashlight at the dug-up mound. "Why, someone's been looking for something." She bent down slowly and scooped up a handful of spoons and forks. "What's this, more junk? That Theo, he--" She swayed on her feet.

"Audrey?" Tessa stepped to her side. "Is everything all right?"

"Oh, it's nothing, I --" She took a couple of deep, shuddering breaths, "You children have a nice day." She turned to leave.

"Audrey? Wait a minute, we'll walk you back inside. Come on, Phillip." Tessa led the old woman gently by the elbow through the narrow walkway between their homes and then to her open front door. She seemed more frail than usual, and a little shaky. She dropped the spoons she'd carried from the yard on her way down the hall like she'd forgotten she had them in her hands. Tessa picked them up one-by-one behind her as they went.

She hesitated a moment, getting Phillip's attention. "I'm going to see that she gets into bed. She seems a little off to me, you know?"

Phillip nodded and sat down, then waved her on, distracted. She frowned at him. It wasn't like him to dismiss her like that. "Phil?"

"Huh, oh, sure. Yeah. Take care of Audrey. Whatever's necessary."

Tessa made sure Audrey was settled, filled a glass of water next to her bed, and turned off her bedside lamp. Phil had bolted the front door and was waiting in Audrey's kitchen when she came out. They turned out the lights and left by the back door. "I can't stay," he said as they climbed Tess's back stairs. "I'm supposed to be on mom duty tonight."

"Then we'd better get you home quickly." She threaded her fingers through his. "We've got make up sex to take care of first."

When they'd climbed the stairs to her bedroom, Phillip threw his sweatshirt over the back of her bedroom chair, sat in it, and untied one of his shoes, then slowly shook his head.

Tessa peeled her wet, soiled robe off and tossed it into her clothes hamper. The look in Phillip's eyes made her heart sink a little as she crossed the room to him. She lifted his chin in her hand. "What?"

"I was wrong about Karl." He dropped his shoe on the floor and rested his elbows on his knees. "I should have seen it sooner."

"Seen what?"

"I was all focused on him; he was such a weirdo. Keeping to himself, not involved in Cauldron, and that shop of his? What was he doing there? He didn't sell anything. But I didn't see." He untied his other shoe, his eyes unblinking.

Tessa sat in his lap, put her arms around his neck, the backs of her bare thighs against his. "Didn't see what?"

"There's got to be someone else in this. Someone who wanted him dead."

Tessa cringed. Saliva filled her mouth and she was afraid she was going to wretch. She popped out of his lap and paced across the room to her bed. She was just beginning to settle down over the dream business and his words brought it all back.

"But the police said he drowned in Lars' hot tub. Hit his head." They had written it off as an unfortunate accident. Lexi had read the story in the paper to her over and over until she'd believed it.

"I wouldn't be so sure." Phillip dropped his shoe, stripped off both his socks. "I did some digging after your encounter with him at the restaurant. I didn't think it mattered much anymore since he was dead …"

"But…"

"But, the records on his father's death five years ago were strangely similar and not as cut and dried."

"Phil, how do you get to just walk in and look at police records?"

"I have friends in low places."

"Come on, really?"

He came and sat down on the bed next to her, took her hands in his. "You're shaking."

She shrugged. "I'm cold. Let's get under the covers." She pulled back the sheets, let him in, let his body heat warm her. They lay facing each other; she focused on those amber eyes. "Tell me what you found out."

"Lars had just been married, the happy couple were getting ready to go on their honeymoon; they were only staying at the estate in Cameo Shores temporarily until they could buy something of their own. Anyway, they'd come home from a dinner before they flew out to, I don't know, wherever they were going … and…"

Tessa shivered again. "They found him in the hot tub."

Phillip frowned at her. "Valerie found him. Apparently, Lars was indisposed, and she was the one who went outside looking for him. He was dead in the pool."

Tess shuddered at the similarity between Karl's death, his father's, and her dream.

"And Caldron Industries financial record isn't all that clear either," Phillip went on. "They're first and foremost an R&D company and that takes money up front — money that isn't coming back in profit any time soon. They've invested heavily in research in the new, higher temperature superconductors; Tessa, even the big boys are having trouble keeping their people on that project. And where's Karl while all this is going on? In the laboratories where all good little PhDs should be? No. He's traveling around Europe, visiting friends on their super yachts."

He leaned up on one elbow. "And that cute little shop here on the island? Tax records show he didn't sell anything. He 'collected'."

Tessa was starting to relax. Just having Phillip near had a soothing effect on her. She propped up her pillow, winged her elbows behind her head and sighed deeply. "You know, Phillip; not to rain on your parade or anything, but you're an engineer, not a cop or an investigator. This all looks very creepy and wrong, but the police do know what they're doing." She really wanted to believe that.

"But what if they don't? Or what if Lars has friends on the force, too?"

"You read too many suspense novels."

He scowled at her. "Okay. Fine. Let's say you're right, and what we've got is just two similar, accidental deaths in the same family within five years of each other."

"Right."

"And, you find some gold jewelry in your house and Karl is just collector enough to show a more than passing interest, but that's all it is."

"Right." She needed this to be over. She needed him to take her in his arms and forget any of it ever happened.

"So, Karl's dead, you'll be calling the authorities about the jewelry, end of story."

"Right."

"So, tell me this: Why is someone still digging in your front yard?"

"Holy, shit, Phillip." The words came out on a helpless moan. She had only just begun to get her life back to normal. Now Phillip was digging it all up again. "I don't need you to be my savior here."

"But what if they come back?"

She groaned and pulled the covers over her head. "I'll call the police, okay?"

He tugged on the sheets. "I need to know you're safe, that's all."

She flopped the covers down, exasperated. The look in his eyes sent a surge of heat to her center. "Phillip Koenig, I need you to stop talking about Karl Johns and fuck me senseless, right now."

He stared at her a long moment before his wrinkled forehead relaxed, then rolled over on top of her and kissed her long and deep and sexy hot. "Karl who?"

CHAPTER THIRTY-EIGHT

Tessa awoke to the muted scree of distant gulls.
The familiar cries usually lulled her back to sleep on a Sunday morning. Today, they only added, in a minor key, to the worrisome refrain running through her mind. She ghosted downstairs and started a pot of coffee, careful not to wake Lexi in the process.

It had been an uneventful, but stressful week. It was good having Phil back in her bed most nights, but his presence hadn't chased away the concerns as much as she'd hoped. When she wasn't worrying about someone digging in her front yard, or Audrey wandering around in the middle of the night, her thoughts strayed to the young woman — Kindra, the slave girl, maker of jewelry — somehow bound up in her own destiny.

Every night she pieced together a little bit more of Kindra's life, and every day the sadness of it lay heavier on her heart. She'd tried to relegate thoughts of Kindra to a place in her heart that didn't interfere with her present. It was the only thing that made sense. She needed to move on and get her life back on track. And, for the most part, it was working. Phillip's return made her all the more anxious to get back to normal.

To hell with the brooch, right? Her sanity, and her relationship with Phillip in the here and now was more important. If they didn't have the damn brooch, they didn't have it. If Theo had ever had it, it wasn't here now. The smart thing would be to simply turn the whole mess over to the authorities. Let them deal with the missing brooch. Or not. It wasn't her concern.

As much sense as that all made, Tessa knew she was lying to herself. Most nights she tossed on a bed of confusion, images of the brooch and faraway places continued to dominate her dreams.

The last time she'd been with Kindra, she'd been in terrible trouble. What if there was something she could do to help? And if she did, would it change anything now? If she slipped the bracelet on her wrist, could she just see for a moment what had transpired? Or would it suck her down that rabbit hole again? Surely now that she knew how it worked, she could control how far, how deep, how long. Her fingertips tingled at the thought.

She poured herself a cup of brew and returned to her room, where she stopped in front of the dresser. She just wanted to look at it. See that it was only a piece of coiled metal. Okay. Gold. Very fine gold. But inanimate, right?

She slid open her lingerie drawer, moved her panties aside. The serpent's eyes gleamed ruby red in the lamplight. Inanimate, yet … mesmerizing.

She ran a finger over the scales, following the curving body from its head to its pointed tail. She drew in a deep breath, slipped on the bracelet, exhaled. Nothing happened. She was in her room, she could see the little island across the Grand Canal, the bay, and the cliffs beyond poking up through a thick blanket of fog.

Nothing creepy, nothing magic, no soldiers waiting to throw her into a dark dungeon. Just the soft light coming through her bedroom window and the memory of Phillip's arms around her before he left to spend the rest of the night at his parent's home. Relief swept over her, and, okay, she had to admit, a little disappointment. She sighed deeply and went downstairs again.

Misty dampness hung wet and still over the island, muting the traffic noise from the boulevard. She was surprised to hear footsteps coming up the back stairs, the slow but steady cadence of her elderly next-door neighbor. She wrapped up in her terry-cloth robe, scuffed on a pair of slippers, and went downstairs.

"Audrey? What are you doing out here in your nightie?" Again. Oh god.

The old woman was dressed in the same gown she'd been wearing the night they'd found her in the yard. It was dirty around the bottom from walking across wet sand.

"Oh, never mind that," she said, brushing her hands on her sides. Her voice sounded uncharacteristically sad. "I'm a tough old biddy. Is Lexi here? I have something to tell you both." She fingered the buttons of her nightgown.

"Tess? Someone's at the — Oh." Lexi wrapped her short robe over her and shoved bed hair behind her ears. "Well, *whadaya* know? Two fog-bound sleepwalkers in the same kitchen. And before seven a.m. How lucky can I get?" She sent Tessa a questioning look before she dragged a chair away from the table and plopped down.

Audrey waited for Lexi to settle, looking at her feet.

"Audrey wants to tell us something important," Tessa said.

Audrey crossed her arms over her breasts and quietly cleared her throat. She had the look of a bird about to take flight. Lexi touched her arm. "It's okay. I was up anyway. No worries."

Tessa got up. "I made some coffee." She headed to the cupboard for mugs. "Go ahead. Sit."

Audrey drew in a deep breath, then sat, smoothed her gown over her hips. "Actually, this is a confession. I haven't thought about this for a long time; guess I never thought it would matter to anyone but me. But it is important; I realize that now, and, well, you know. Life is short and all."

"What happened the other night?" Lexi asked. "There's nothing wrong, is there? You're all right?"

Audrey let go a soft laugh. "Of course, I'm all right. What I have to tell you is kind of romantic, actually; but, well, it's not me I'm worried about, it's Tessa."

Tessa brought mugs, cream, and sugar to the table. "I love romantic stories," she said, putting on a smile. She didn't like the tone in Audrey's voice. She wasn't ready for any more revelations.

If she could just have a few quiet days to reflect on her situation without being presented with yet another twist, maybe she could put things in perspective. The anticipation was frightening. She shivered and rubbed the goose bumps on her arms into submission as the coffee maker started to steam.

"You all right, Tess?" Lexi asked, "You look a little — iffy."

"Just cold is all." Lately it seemed she could never get warm. She was afraid. Didn't know what of, just generally fearful that some great cosmic shoe was about to drop and come crashing down on all the good things in her life. She grabbed the open package of Oreo's off the kitchen counter and brought them to the table.

Lexi pounced on the bag and helped herself. "Okay, Audrey. Tell us what this is all about."

Audrey's brows furrowed, and she lost her confident posture. "Maybe this isn't a good time after all. How rude of me to come over so early when you two aren't ready to have guests." She started to get up.

"Oh no you don't," Lexi said, covering her hand with her own. "No fair getting us all excited and then chickening out. Besides, you're still in your nightgown, too."

Audrey fiddled with the lace at her neck, then her cheeks pinked. "So, I am."

"Now go ahead. We're all in our nightgowns and we're all women here," Tessa said, "So, nothing to hide. Right Lexi?"

"Last time I checked."

Audrey looked suddenly strained and frail, her skin paler than usual; she had already shredded her napkin into little pieces and was picking them off the lap of her gown.

Tessa didn't want her to leave without saying what was on her mind, and now she looked to Lexi for support; she was the facilitator in the family.

"We women stick together. You can tell us anything you have on your mind and we'll love you just the same." Lexi brought the coffee pot to the table, filled their cups.

Audrey stirred sugar into her coffee, tasted it, and set it down. "Well, we were on our way to France from the West of Germany, on the train."

She certainly didn't waste any time getting into the story. "You and your husband?" Tessa asked, caught off guard.

"Noooo," Audrey began cautiously, licking her lips. "Theo and me."

Tessa's brows went up before she was able to stop herself. Audrey lowered her eyes for a moment as if unsure she should go on.

Lexi glanced at Tessa with a smile. "It's okay. No judgments here, right Tessa?"

Tessa coughed into her fist and sipped her coffee a little too loudly. That was a huge piece of information to throw out so matter of factly. "No. Of course not. Please, Audrey. Go on. We're listening."

"Well, for a while, before you came to live here, of course, Theo and I were — together — we were - -"

"Friends," Tessa said, trying to help out.

Audrey sighed. "No, lovers, actually."

Now it was Lexi's turn to cough.

Tessa got up and went to the windows. A light breeze rippled the water in the canal, the fog was beginning to move inland.

"Lovers," Tess repeated lightening her tone. It was a shock, but certainly not a negative one.

"Then you're not upset?" Audrey asked.

"Of course not," Tessa said. "In fact, I think it's kind of special. I always thought you were Theo's type, and I always wondered about his life and his travels. Please, go on and don't feel uncomfortable. Lexi here is experienced at this sort of thing, right Lex?"

Lexi pursed her lips and nodded in agreement, though Tess could see she was still in a bit of shock.

Theo and Audrey. Who'd have thought? But what she didn't know about her Uncle Theo was ... practically everything.

Audrey sighed deeply, as if a great burden had been lifted off her shoulders. "Things weren't so ... open ... when I was young."

She dipped a cookie into her coffee and sucked the juice noisily. "My husband and I traveled a great deal, too; but he was always busy with his movie people. Your aunt Lola was so young when she passed. After that, Theo, Henry and I were kind of a trio. Theo clung to us, and personally, I was grateful. Henry was always good to me, but Theo — he had a way about him. Even though he was older, he was so romantic. He seemed to sense there wasn't much romance in our lives, and would always show up bearing champagne and flowers, then remember some errand or commitment and leave Henry and me with the goodies.

Tessa's heart gave a little squeeze and she missed Theo a little more.

"Henry often invited Theo along on our European trips, to cheer him up, he would say; but I think it was to keep me company. It was almost as if

337

he wanted us to be together. Maybe he had someone else, and--" She stopped talking and rubbed her hands together a moment, then remembered the coffee and lifted the cup to her pursed lips.

Tessa sensed her embarrassment and sat down again. "Audrey, this isn't necessary, you know. What went on between you and Theo isn't any of our business."

"Now you see, that's the thing. You never know what life's going to bring you, or when it's going to bring it, so if I don't tell you now..." She glanced back and forth between them. "And, well, anyway, the jewelry. The jewelry is your business. And I'm too old to worry about such things any longer. I want to die with a clear conscience."

Tessa pressed her fingers to her temples. God. Here it was. The jewelry again.

"I hadn't thought about it for years," Audrey continued. "Even when you found the gold sealed up in the walls. I guess it's easy to forget things you're ashamed of. But the other night --"

Lexi warmed up Audrey's coffee and eyed Tessa carefully.

"Lexi, dear, could you pass me a few more of those cookies? These are the best I've had."

She twisted the ends off the cookie and nibbled at the frosting with her teeth, then washed it down with a sip of coffee. "Now let's see. Where was I?"

All signs of doubt had left her face and she seemed to pick up on the camaraderie. Tessa propped her chin in her hand. It was Sunday, they had all the time in the world, right?

"It was Spring, 1968, I believe. The three of us were in Paris. Henry needed to return to Hollywood. He was making money hand-over-fist off his actor/producer investors; but was always at their beck and call. It was so beautiful in Paris. I just didn't want to leave. Theo volunteered to stay with me, and Henry didn't seem to have any qualms about it. Theo had never given him a reason to wonder; and frankly, he had never given me a reason either. But I found out on *that* trip."

"What did you find out?" Tessa was almost afraid of the answer.

"Your uncle was a very passionate man," she cooed, and her cheeks pinked to match the rose pattern on the coffee cup. "And ten years younger than Henry. We were staying in the same room inside a week. I had been married so young to Henry, and it had indeed been a whirlwind romance, but once the honeymoon was over; well, you know all the clichés. Now don't take me wrong. Henry always took very good care of me. Loved me. But he wasn't much on romance."

"So, it was Theo who *really* showed you *Paris*," Lexi crooned in her best French accent.

"*Avec amour.*" Audrey raised her cup in a mock toast. "I didn't know what it was like to really make love with a man. Well," she blundered on, grasping for words in the air with her hands, "I knew what it was like to be — to get—"

"Laid?" Lexi asked, with a grin.

"Yes. Laid," Audrey said, slowly as if trying out the sound of the words in her mouth for the first time. She smiled brightly and let go a little giggle.

"With Theo, I learned it could be more of a *partie à deux*. We did have a glorious time; I don't regret a moment of it. It's wonderful to be able to share it with someone after all these years. To think that we lived right next door to each other the rest of our lives … Well." She waved the words away. "It's a shame Tess, how you keep that man of yours at arm's length. I see the way he looks at you."

Tessa rolled her lips together, then allowed a grin. "We do all right, Audrey. Really. Phillip knows I love him."

Audrey cocked her head. "Does he?"

She gazed out over the water and seemed to gather her thoughts. Something in that gaze sent a tingle to the base of Tessa's spine. She reached for the bracelet, found it resting loosely at her wrist. Still a feeling of foreboding tightened around her chest, allowing only the tiniest bit of oxygen to enter her lungs. "It's complicated."

Audrey shook her head, rested her hand on Tessa's forearm, and leaned in close to her cheek. "Life is shorter than we think, *mon cher ami*."

Tessa thought of Kindra, alone in a cell in the palace. Indeed.

Lexi caught her eye, brought her back to the moment. Audrey twisted apart another cookie. "Theo wanted to see Germany again; he had been there during the war, and despite the fighting, he had fallen in love with some of the country and wanted to show it to me. We got on the train in Paris headed for Trier."

"Trains are wonderful in Europe, rolling through countryside and towns you've only read about, and

Theo and I were so caught up in each other —
neither one of us really wanting to go back to real
life — so when the men came running through our
car, we barely looked up."

Trier? Tessa sat forward in her seat. "Men?"

"Yes. We had been seated in the second row
from one end of the car and the men came dashing
down the aisle, then stopped right next to us, just
long enough to look back at the police who were
chasing them." This she said aside to Lexi, "The
police burst through the door at the opposite end of
the car, and the man closest to me looked right at
me for a second. I will never forget those eyes —
desperate, like a war was going on in his mind. And
then, all of a sudden, he shrugged his shoulders at
me like he never believed they would get away with
whatever they'd done."

"The other man, never having lost his forward
momentum, jerked the man next to me by the arm
and out of the car exit. But just before the door
closed, he opened his coat let a package drop at my
feet. It all happened so fast! I started to call out to
the police, but Theo clamped his hand over my
mouth, and when the policeman turned to see what
it was I wanted, Theo nearly smothered my head
under his arm as he kicked the fallen package under
the seat in front of us with the toe of his shoe. He
told the officer it was all right, that his wife had just
been frightened, and then began rocking me and
soothing me like I was a little child. Thirty years old
and I was giggling under his arm like a schoolgirl."

The color was high in her cheeks as she related
what had probably been the most exciting time of

her life. Tessa forced a smile, but a sense of foreboding lurked just beneath.

"Theo didn't let me up until the officer had joined his partner in pursuit out the door and on to the next car. It was just like a movie! Women screaming, German police yelling *Polizei, Polizei! Stoppt den Dieb! Haltet den Dieb!*

"As soon as the police were in the next car, Theo retrieved the package and told me to put it into my bag. I told him he was crazy, that the men were obviously thieves and we could be implicated. But, as always, Theo maintained his calm. 'Their loss, our gain', he told me."

Audrey grinned. "That's where Theo showed his talent for thinking on his feet, or thinking on trains, if you will." She tittered again. "He said that whatever it was, it was stolen in the first place, so it was as good as ours! There was no way the thieves could ever find us, and no way they could claim the loss, so--" She snapped up another cookie and took it apart like a pro.

"So...," Lexi encouraged, rolling her hand to urge Audrey forward.

"I wanted to dump the package in the nearest trash can, but Theo wouldn't hear of it. I thought I was going to be sick going through the customs line, but the authorities were looking for two men. It wasn't like it is now to travel. No one so much as peeped inside my bag. We heard later that the men had been arrested, but there was no mention of what they had stolen."

Audrey's account of the incident was more than hilarious. And it gave a plausible explanation for the presence of the jewelry. It hadn't just materialized from a dream or her imagination or a past life, or any of the other fantasy scenarios that had been creeping through her nightmares. She drew in a deep breath and let it out slowly, feeling some sense of relief. "So, the jewelry was in the package?"

Audrey nodded. "We read in the paper on the plane home that a rather large cache of jewelry and other precious artifacts had been stolen from a shipment bound for the British Museum. So many precious items were stolen by the Nazis during the war, and there were organizations across Europe trying to return them to their rightful owners. At least some of that jewelry was in our package. I was really nervous about the whole thing."

"Theo was ecstatic. He acted like he'd pulled the caper himself! But I couldn't take it. I had been feeling guilty enough after our *rondes-vous d'amour*, and living next door was absolutely excruciating. Theo tried to give me a beautiful brooch from the package, but I just couldn't accept it. He was heartbroken. *What would it hurt?* he would ask me over and over. He wanted it to be a token of our time together — always the romantic — but as I said, I --"

"A brooch?" Tessa cringed, a wave of chills ran over her neck and arms. Her mouth went dry and she sipped her coffee. "But you never accepted it. You don't have it, right?"

"Well, no. I mean, I couldn't wear it in front of Henry. I convinced Theo to hide all of it away. That's when he added that awful dark paneling to his living room."

She sighed. "Theo was such a romantic. I wouldn't accept the brooch as a token, so he built that pedestal out there in his yard, right where I could see it from my balcony. You know that whole yard kind of looks like the brooch with that pretty red globe in the center."

Tessa's heart beat wildly. She stood; coffee sloshed from her mug. "So, there was a ruby in the center?" Tessa's lips went cold.

"Why, yes. Just like that globe on the pedestal dear, in the yard, you know--"

"I don't understand."

Audrey cocked her head. She picked up one of the cookies and held it up. "The brooch was a little bigger than this, but really colorful, like a rose window in a church, you know. Lots of color, gold, little pearls. It was breathtakingly beautiful, with a smooth ruby at the center of a cross in the middle."

CHAPTER THIRTY-NINE

Lexi and Audrey continued their conversation, but their voices faded away behind the thoughts reeling in Tessa's head. Theo had had the brooch at one point. But it wasn't with the other pieces. So where was it?

"Tess?" Lexi had touched her shoulder, bringing her back to the moment. "I'm taking Audrey home," she said, vowing in a quick whisper to Tess before she left, she would check things out at the older woman's house. "She seems…agitated."

Tess took more coffee out on the veranda, the criss-cross lines of a migraine aura blocking her vision. The chilly December breeze chased the fog away, jangling Lexi's chime, and blowing thoughts around Tessa's confused brain.

So, Theo and Audrey had an affair, brought stolen artifacts home from Europe, and then hid them in the house. What had it to do with her, other than that she now owned the house?

Nothing!

It was the only sane answer, and it came to her again and again like a nosy neighbor's unsolicited advice. It was her logical mind denying what her heart had already accepted at face value. And all the pacing and watching wouldn't make it go away.

But it wasn't just any jewelry, it was Kindra's jewelry. Hers. She could almost feel the weight of that brooch in her hands.

The image of it pulled at her like a magnet. Theo wouldn't have gotten rid of it just because Audrey didn't want it. It had to be here somewhere. They had removed all the paneling in the living room when they built the stairs. Phil had replaced the drywall in the dining room, nothing but jarred up clamshells hidden there. They had been through every crate in the garage. She had sorted every box in the downstairs apartment.

The thought she was missing something was making her crazy and she was getting really tired of crazy. Crazy was affecting her work, her friendship, her love life, and without sleep or relief, it was affecting her health. How could she face another day at work with this blasted headache? She needed to sort this out and had the rest of the afternoon to decide if she needed to take some serious time off work.

By the time she'd shrugged into her Levi's and sweatshirt, the headache helmet had eased back a bit. Perhaps a short walk in the briny sea air would clear her head and ease up the pain. She stood at the seawall deciding. Should she walk the promenade or take Beeks Ferry to the peninsula? The Santa Ana winds — a heated off-shore flow from the valleys typical of winter — whisked up sand and dry leaves along the wall. The island perimeter walk would probably be more comfortable, but the tide was as low as it gets, often revealing old cement blocks and moss dragged ropes; not her favorite time of day. Nope, it would have to be the surf and the big, horizon view. The ferry was only a few blocks away and a short ride across the bay to the Pavillion and the shore.

Zipping her hoodie against the wind, she walked briskly to the ferry and took a seat along the railing. The little barge carried her and three cars across the white-capped bay, holding its own among fishing boats heading out to the channel.

Seabirds screed overhead; gusty winds played havoc with their determined efforts to fly. The ferry's engines complained as the pilot threw them rumbling into reverse, spun the wheel to starboard, and deftly nosed the old barge up to the dock.

The wind whipped up the ocean's briny mist, adding a tang to the air. Leaning into it, she hurried across the avenue and down the sandy walk toward the shoreline. Sand stung her ankles as she trudged over the windswept dunes. She didn't love the beach in the wind, but she needed it today like some people need air. She raised her hood up over her ears and ran for cover to the nearest lifeguard tower.

The towers were empty this time of year, especially this far down the peninsula. Any remaining tourists would be closer to the pier or gathered at the infamous Wedge near the channel. Tucked into a corner of the tower, she was protected from the wind, and from there she commanded an unobstructed view toward the horizon.

There was something mournful about an ebbing tide, sucking back on itself in puny layers as if it had lost its power. Twelve hours made all the difference. Midnight's high tide had abandoned tangled clumps of seaweed high on the sand; the seabirds, tired of fighting the gusts, sat hunched amid the flotsam, their feathers ruffled.

As the wind disrupts the comfort of the seaside community, so Tessa's dreams had disrupted her life. She stared out at the horizon, aching. There was something familiar, at least. There had never been a time she could remember, looking out over the vastness of the ocean, when she did not have the feeling that something she had lost was out there, just over the curvature of the earth -- that if she waded out far enough, she would find it.

One thought played in her mind like the refrain of an annoying song stuck in her head. She could no longer push it away. Theo had possession of Kindra's brooch at one time. Audrey had described it perfectly. Somewhere among the many dreams she'd had, both waking and sleeping, she'd watched Kindra craft it, felt the weight of it in her palm, almost as if she'd made it with her own two hands.

Round and round the images spun: Kindra sold as a slave, Kindra making the brooch, losing it; Haldor's ruined face, Marcus's thick neck and powerful arms, blood floating in the caldarium's water; Kindra dragged into custody ... Audrey and Theo on a train, the stolen jewelry falling into their laps ...

A flurry of gulls swooped over the tower, stirring her out of her thoughts. She stood; her legs stiff from being tucked under her. She should probably head back; she hadn't told anyone where she was headed. And then like a video on rewind, something Audrey had said that morning put a vivid image in her mind. *Theo built the pedestal as a memento. She could see it from her balcony …*

Oh. My. Theo had put her hands on it that day in the garden all those years ago. With renewed energy, her headache forgotten, she scrambled down the lifeguard tower's ladder. A half hour later she was standing before the red gazing ball in the center of Theo's yard, his old wooden baseball bat clenched in her fists. The brooch was there. Inside the ball. She knew it. Knew it with all her being.

She had just drawn back to swing when a movement on the balcony caught her eye. Lexi was racing down the stairs. Her arms waved and her lips moved, but all Tess could hear was a high-pitched buzz inside her head. *It's in there. Swing. Swing!*

She cocked her arms, threw her weight into her hips and swung the bat as hard as she could.

The next moment shimmered in slow motion. The red glass ball shattered into a million pieces. An interior plaster ball split in two, shards breaking down further as they hit the tiled diaz.

It's there. It has to be. Tessa fell to her knees, scratched frantically through the shards of plaster.

Lexi knelt beside her. "Jesus, Tess. Your fingers are bleeding."

Tessa ignored her, clawing at the debris.

"Tessa, stop. Listen to me. Please."

Tess grabbed the last big chunk of plaster and glass, broke it against the pedestal, and there it was. A small leather bag, drawstrings cinched tight.

Lexi stared at it, eyes wide.

Tessa dropped the bag on the ground between them, perched on her toes, and rubbed her hands up and down her thighs. "The brooch," she said on a dry throat. "It's in there. I just know it." Her hands were shaking. "You open it."

Lexi shook her head. "Tess, we need to talk."

"Open it. I just can't."

Lex sent her a look she couldn't read, her shoulders drooping as if under a heavy weight. "Tessa listen…"

"Please. I can't breathe until I see it."

Lex stared at her a long moment before she huffed out a sigh and picked up the leather bag. "Tessa, I promise you, in a minute, none of this will matter."

Tessa bit the side of her cheek. "Just open it."

Lexi loosened the drawstring and turned the bag upside down. The brooch dropped out onto the palm of her hand. Even in the fading light, the gold shone bright yellow. The blood-red stone in the center, the cross, the flourishes, the pearls — all of it exactly like the picture they'd seen in the journal.

"Turn it over," Tessa whispered, barely able to speak. Lexi reached for her shoulder.

Tessa pulled away, rubbing her hands on her pants. "Tell me what's on the back. No, wait. I'll tell you." She closed her eyes. "A small triangle, a delta mark, behind the ruby." She opened her eyes again as Lexi turned the brooch over. She pressed her lips together and nodded.

"Then it's there?"

Lexi blinked once, blew out a breath. She held the brooch to Tessa. "See for yourself."

Tessa reached for it as if she expected it to burn her fingers. The stones were smooth, smoother than one could expect from something made seventeen hundred years ago; and so beautiful, the sight of it took her breath away. The delta was there, on the back just the way she'd seen it. Chills spread over her skin in waves that diminished as the gold quickly warmed to her body temperature. She weighed it in her hand.

Surprisingly, she was calmer than she'd been in days. Learning of the brooch from Audrey had shocked and alarmed her to her soul, but actually holding it in her hand had a settling effect. It was a tangible thing. There were explanations for tangible things. And if the brooch had made it back to the rest of the jewelry, didn't that mean Kindra was okay?

She closed her fist around it. From now on, she would deal with only the real and tangible. She would stop letting dreams rule her life. No more lost days. She had to hold on. She must.

She drew in a deep, ragged breath and raised her eyes to Lexi feeling fully present for the first time in weeks. "All right, news. I think I could handle just about anything right now." But the look on Lexi's eyes made her catch her breath. "What is it? What's happened?"

Lexi wrung her hands. "There's no easy way--"

"Phillip? Oh my god! Something's happened to Phillip?"

Lexi grabbed her arm. "No. Phil's okay. Listen." A tear welled in her eyes and spilled over her cheek. Tessa caught her breath. "Just say it, Lex."

"Audrey passed this morning. I guess, right after I took her home."

"What? How?"

Lex reached out a hand to her, helped her stand. "She apparently went back to bed. Died in her sleep. Rags was meowing at our door and I took him over to see if he was locked out again, and when she didn't answer, I went in." She took a gulp of air. "She was … gone."

The low keen started in Tessa's gut and welled up to a wail. "No. Oh, no, no, no."

"I tried to find you. To call you, then I realized you'd left your phone on your nightstand."

Tessa slapped her hand on her back pocket realizing for the first time she hadn't brought it with her. She had been so caught up in her own obsession, she had abandoned her connection with reality. Except … except she held the brooch in her hands.

Lexi's shoulders began to shake.

"I called 911, but I knew it was too late. She listed me, then you as contacts in her emergency paperwork," she said between gulps of air. "They want us to come down to the morgue. I was waiting for you, I couldn't…"

Tessa's heart fisted up in her chest. "Oh my god, Lexi. I'm so sorry."

She pulled Lexi into her arms. They swayed in their shared aching grief until at last Lexi lifted her head.

"We have to go."

CHAPTER FORTY

"I'm sorry to hurry you like this." Lexi's voice sounded wobbly through the bathroom door, like she was holding back a sob. "They transferred her from the morgue to the funeral home over half an hour ago. Apparently, she'd already made arrangements."

"I'm trying, really. I'm trying." Tessa stood under the shower and let the steaming water spray into her face. The weight of the truth made it hard to breathe. One day in your life you do something out of the ordinary, you break your routine, you deviate one tiny bit from what is expected of you and you lose someone you love. It wasn't fair.

"Tessa, we really can't delay any longer. I know this is hard for you, but think of poor old Audrey lying down there with all those dead people — wait. No. Don't think of that; I mean --"

Lexi nearly fell in through the threshold when Tessa pulled open the door. She stepped out, pulling her hastily dried hair into a slick ponytail, already dressed in an ivory wrap skirt and the baby blue angora sweater Audrey had always loved.

Using the porthole mirror in the hallway, she pinned the brooch to the collar. "Looks nice with the sweater, don't you think? Audrey would like that."

Lexi put her arms around Tessa's shoulders. "Yeah. I think she would."

Tessa wasn't sure. Audrey had refused to take the brooch from Theo and had buried the memory deep inside all these years. In fact, when Tessa thought of it, the brooch had been the source of pain to someone or other for centuries. Maybe it wasn't a good idea to wear it out in public. On the other hand, maybe, like all dark creatures, exposing it to the light of day would dispel its power.

Lexi handed her the keys to her old VW. "You drive. I'm too shaky."

Tess stared at her friend a moment. Lexi was always the strong one. The one who dragged her back from the abyss. The one who took control. But losing Audrey had pushed her past her power zone. It was time Tessa had her back.

She swiped the keys out of her hand. "Okay," she said on a sigh. "Let's do this."

She edged the car out onto Pacific Coast Highway toward Corona del Mar. The Santa Ana wind had blown itself out, leaving static electricity, dry lips, and crumpled fast food bags molded against fences and buildings, and homeless wrecks sleeping by the freeway. A large eucalyptus had blown down; city crews were in the process of sawing it up in the parking lot of Trader Joe's. It was somehow fitting for the kind of day this had been.

Tessa rolled down her window, letting the cold breeze sweep across her face, the gravity of their mission sinking in. "I still don't believe it. We had such a great morning with her. She seemed happy, right?"

Lexi drummed her fingers on her knees. "I think maybe she knew. She bared her soul to us. Confessed her sins."

The idea struck a somber note. Maybe Lexi was right. "Lex, I'm so sorry I wasn't here; I should have at least told you where I was going."

"I wish you had been here, too. It's not easy being the strong one who has to handle everything."

Tess shot her a sympathetic glance. "I expect a lot of you, I know. I don't know what I'd do if anything ever happened to you --"

"Where were you, anyway? I was afraid I was going to have to leave you the most awful note."

"I took the ferry over to the beach."

"For four hours? Without your phone? You never do that."

Tess had to agree. Like everyone else in the modern world, her phone was like an appendage. The fact that she had left without it spoke volumes about where her head had been.

"I was at the tenth street lifeguard tower." Tessa tried to concentrate on driving. "If I'd only known."

"Oh, Tess. Don't beat yourself up. How could you have known? She was almost eighty-one years old. She lived a full life."

Tessa fingered the brooch pinned at her throat. She knew things that happened nearly two thousand years ago on the other side of the planet, why couldn't she have known about something that was happening right next door?

At Lexi's gentle touch to her arm and a telling glance to the right, she pulled off the highway and into the mortuary parking lot. It was odd. She'd driven past the dun-colored stone building a thousand times on her way up or down the coast. This was the first time she had ever actually been there. Theo had been cremated and wanted his ashes spread at sea. His cremains had been delivered directly to the boat. She and her mother had lived in Lakewood when her father died and it had been so long ago, she didn't really remember anything except her mother complaining about how much it all cost.

Now, there was a shiny hearse in the breezeway parked like it was dropping someone off in a fancy hotel lobby. She let go a nervous laugh. "Where do we go?"

Lex pointed to the visitor's section of the parking lot. Tessa pulled into a space, shut down the engine, and rested her forehead on the steering wheel.

Lexi's hand came to rest on the back of her neck until Tessa raised her head.

Lexi's forehead rumpled.

"What"

Lexi looked away, tapped her long nails on the door panel. "There's … something else. Before we go in."

"Something else?" Tessa hadn't taken a full breath since they'd slid into the car. Now her chest deflated like a leaky bagpipe.

Lexi gave her neck a little squeeze, then she returned her hand to her lap. "The coroner said she probably had a stroke; that it was over quickly. She died in her sleep, probably not long after we talked with her."

Tessa nodded. Lexi had gone over all that before.

"There was no evidence of foul play, and she had been old," Lexi went on. "He was busy, the sheriffs were swamped, when the assistant reported the death; they transported her body straight to the morgue."

Tessa frowned. She could see by the droop in her shoulders Lexi wasn't finished. "Okay."

Lexi sent Tess a guilty look. She was wringing her hands. "She left a note."

Tess jerked upright. "A note?"

Lex nodded, tight lipped. "It was under her pillow. I didn't see it until after they took her. I didn't know what to do and I couldn't find you, and I just … I started tidying up; I was going to make the bed, you know, and …" She pulled a piece of baby blue stationary from her bag. "I guess she didn't want anybody to find it but one of us."

Tessa took the note slow and easy out of Lexi's trembling fingers and stared at her for a long moment.

Lex nodded. "Go ahead. Read it."

The folded, china blue stationary looked like it had been carried in someone's pocket for a year. There was a date scrawled across it.

"Last March? Her birthday."

Lexi nodded.

With a last curious glance at Lex for support, she quickly read the note once through.

> *Dear Tessa,*
>
> *Someone said, 'no one ever gets out of this life alive', so I figure I better write this now, because you never know when it will all be over. I'm one of the lucky ones who had a*

really fine ride. I didn't want to leave this world without telling you how lucky I've been to have you and Alexis in my life. What a gift to see Theo's eyes in yours every time you smiled.

My wish for you is that someday you'll see your true love's eyes in the smiles of your children. But to get there you have to let love in. You have nothing to lose but your empty heart.

Tell Lexi I left a package for her in the top drawer of my dresser.

If you're reading this, then I'm probably gone, either that or someone else is making my bed, which is tantamount to the same thing.

I will miss you. Think of me when the moon is full, and the tide is high.

Love, Audrey.

PS. Phillip is a keeper

Tessa willed the tears not to come, but they refused to obey. She looked back at Lexi through blurred vision. "Is this what I think it is?"

Lexi slowly lifted a shoulder. "Not if she really wrote it six months ago."

"Should we ... tell ... someone?"

"And have her cut up and poked and prodded to find out what we already know? She's gone. What difference does it make?"

Tess bit into her bottom lip; hot tears dripped off her chin. "No difference, I guess." She folded the note and stuck it in the side pocket of her bag. "Did you look? You know, in her drawer?"

Lexi sent her a sheepish grin, reminding Tess of why they were besties. "Not at first. It felt weird being in her house all alone."

"But…"

"But, when I couldn't find you, I started to get really worried. What if the package had to do with you being gone? I had just come from there when I saw you out in the yard banging on that damn pedestal." Her eyes went shiny with tears.

Tessa leaned in and shoulder bumped her. A little of the pressure squeezing her chest released. "Are you going to tell me or what?"

"What?"

"Duh."

Lexi gulped in air and handed her an envelope. "Apparently, she'd been working with Theo's lawyer, Phinney. Made him executor of her estate, named us as her only beneficiaries." She shook her head. "She had quite a bit of cash stashed away, apparently. I mean, the house is worth a lot, but her husband had been in the movie industry like, forever, and unlike a lot of the early actors, the producers were smarter about their investments. The document was pretty simple. We are to split that equally, but — She left me her house."

Tessa sucked in her breath. "Oh my god, that's amazing."

"Yeah. I know, right? She said she wanted us to be neighbors."

Tessa smiled out the car window, still fingering the brooch. "You just never know what's in store for you, do you?"

"Never entered my mind."

Tess pressed her lips together until they hurt. "I think we'd better go inside."

Lexi kept staring wide eyed out the window. "To think of all the nights I worked on that damned suicide hot line and then right next door —"

Now it was Tessa's turn to comfort a friend. "Not the same as a teenager making a bad decision, Lex. If she did take her life — and we don't know that — she knew damn well what she was doing, and at her age, I say she had a right."

Lexi shrugged. "Yeah. I guess so."

"Took some guts," Tess said, giving her a nod. "I hope I'm that strong down the road."

"Me, too."

"So, we're agreed? We keep it to ourselves?"

Lexi slipped her arm through Tessa's. "Don't see what it could hurt."

Tessa frowned. "I suppose someone could try to contest it."

"That's why she changed her trust. It's all spelled out. Phinney will be able to verify it. But if you'd feel better handing the note over to Phinney, I'm down with that."

Tessa shrugged, then smiled. "He's such a fuddy-dud. I can almost see him squirm."

"Yeah."

"Let's not worry about it now. Audrey's waiting."

Tessa's heart felt a little lighter as they headed arm-in-arm across the parking lot to the mortuary entrance.

❧

The funeral director showed them into a small reception room and asked them to wait for an assistant to show them into the viewing room. Lexi leaned into Tess's ear and whispered. "Are you sure you can handle this?"

"No. But we have to, right? It's what she wanted." She squeezed Lexi's hand; Lexi squeezed back. Tessa wasn't that excited about viewing the body. She wanted to hear Audrey laugh, just one more time; she wanted to see a smile crinkle the corners of her mouth. But when the assistant came to get them, she followed him, full of purpose and responsibility.

He led them down a hallway to one of several doors and into a room designed for the purpose of viewing. It was a little chilly, but other than that, comfortable, with upholstered chairs set invitingly in a small grouping. A curtained area cut the room in half.

The attendant asked if they were ready. When Tess nodded, he pressed a button near the door. There was a soft whirr as the curtain slowly drew back.

The attendant opened the door. "Take your time, ladies," he said. "Come on out this way whenever you're finished."

Audrey's body lay on a narrow table at the center of the room. She looked as if she were asleep, peaceful. Most of her body was covered in a soft, butter yellow blanket. Her silvered hair had been brushed back from her face. Her pale shoulders were bare, and a white sheet had been respectfully drawn up to meet the fragile bones of her clavicles.

Lexi took Tessa's hand. They stood still for a few painful heartbeats.

"I can't believe she left me her house," Lexi whispered.

"She's got nobody else, so why not you?"

"I don't know. After watching you for the last few months since Theo left his stuff to you, I'm not sure I need a rickety old house."

Tessa released Lexi's hand and stepped slowly to the table. She reached out and stroked the old woman's silky grey hair. "We don't always get to choose what happens to us. She gave you her home because she cared about you."

"Tessa--"

"No, listen — I know you don't believe things happen for a reason. Neither do I. I believe things happen because of our own choices; the things we set our minds to, the things we take responsibility for. If I take anything away from her passing it's that. She took responsibility and she made her choice. And, we should be happy for her."

Tessa pressed her hand to Audrey's forehead like a mother checking for fever. The older woman's skin felt cool and somehow comforting. "You know that past life regression we talked about?"

Following Tessa's lead, Lexi went to the other side of the table, smoothed the backs of her fingers over Audrey's cheek. "Yeah."

"I'm ready to do it."

CHAPTER FORTY-ONE

"I tell you, Chuck, Karl Johns' death was no accident." Phillip jabbed the last oyster, sluiced it through the extra order of horseradish, and let it dangle at the end of his fork while he talked. It had been a long time since he'd allowed himself to get this drunk. He'd probably regret it in the morning, but right now, he felt righteously entitled.

Charles Phinney's lips curled back in distaste as he eyed the slimy gray delicacy hanging in the air in front of him. A muscle twitched near his eyelid every time Phillip called him Chuck. Coral and green neon lights above the oyster bar reflected off his glasses and the top of his head. Phinney would have been more comfortable in the button-down conservative atmosphere of The Arches, but Maxi's West beat their oysters all to hell and Phillip needed oysters tonight. He'd spent the last hour regaling Phinney with his theories about Karl Johns.

"If we could get into the family crypt, you'd see."

"The family crypt? What are you talking about?"

"I've followed him there, twice, and I gotta say, he wasn't bringing flowers. There's something going on there and it's got nothing to do with paying respects to dead relatives. Somebody killed Karl. If we could get in there, I could give you a motive."

"We?"

"You're the only lawyer I know." On Tessa's suggestion, Phillip had used him to help update his parents' trust, adding provisions to ensure long-term care for his mother should his father predecease her, and some disturbing, but necessary advanced directives.

Phinney shook his head. "Crime isn't my thing. I'm a trust attorney. My advice is — free of charge, buy the way — if you really think there's something to this, notify the police and let them handle it."

Phillip gulped the oyster down and chased it with a shot of vodka spiked with cocktail sauce. It was difficult to tell whether the relief that now registered on Phinney's face lie in the fact that he wasn't into criminal law or that the last oyster was finally out of sight.

The bartender removed the empty tapas plate and wiped the counter. "That it tonight gentlemen?"

Phillip rolled up on one haunch and fished another twenty from his wallet. "Bring us another plate of oysters."

Phinney dabbed at his eyes with his handkerchief.

"And bring my friend here another Scotch."

Phillip chased his shot with a swig of Stella. "If you want to know the truth, Chuck, I'm more than a little worried about Tess. Karl was pressuring Tessa about that jewelry we found at the house. That's why I started checking him out. After he died, I was relieved; until I noticed someone had been digging in her front yard."

Phinney sent him a skeptical look. "What makes you think it wasn't a neighborhood dog?"

Phillip slipped his phone out of his jacket pocket and thumbed to a set of photos. "Dogs don't leave shoe prints in the dirt."

Phinney adjusted his glasses and took a closer look, then shot his gaze back to Phillip. "Like I said, I'm no expert, but those shoe prints look pretty small. Maybe even Tessa, or Alexis, or some curious kids. Wouldn't be the first time somebody dug up Theo's yard."

Phillip scooted forward in his chair. "It wouldn't? When?"

Phinney took a puckered sip of the scotch. "Four, maybe five years ago. Theo got all upset about it. Said the scoundrels had disturbed his design."

"Do me a favor and keep that to yourself. I don't want Tessa any more upset than she is. She nearly took off my head with a baseball bat the other night." He told Phinney about how he'd staked out the garage.

"And…"

"And the asshole actually used Tessa's own shovel and went at the site with a vengeance."

"So, you confronted him?"

"I would have, except that the girls heard the noise." He told Phinney what had happened. "Whoever it was ran off before I could get out the door. I know it sounds ridiculous, but I was suspicious, and it paid off. A person was after something in the front yard and I scared them away."

"The key word here, in my opinion, is ridiculous. You need to think about this when you're sober. You're blowing this all out of proportion."

"Out of proportion? If someone killed Karl, then Tessa could be in danger too. It's all about that stupid gold."

Phinney glowered at him for a long moment. "You would need a damn good reason to have a family crypt opened. The police report on Johns indicated no evidence of foul play. The man was a known lush. He polished off a quart of Chevas and cooked himself in his brother's hot tub. Happens every day. We'd need a lot more to go on."

"What about Lars' wife?"

"What about her?"

"I told you, she was there, at Forest Lawn with Karl, the afternoon of his death."

Phinney cast an annoyed glance over his shoulder at the dance floor as the band leader announced their return from break. The bartender brought the scotch and second plate of oysters, and Phil jabbed one.

The lawyer groaned. "Look. I know some people. I'll make some phone inquiries -- find out who's handling the Johns' estate at least." He downed the scotch and stood.

"Thanks, Chuck. I'll be at my folks the next couple of nights, and then I'm really am off to San Francisco. I'd feel a lot better if I knew something *before* I have to leave. Call me if you turn anything up."

Phillip watched the paunchy lawyer weave gingerly through the grinders on the dance floor and out the door, then he turned back to the bar, and poked around in his oysters with the tiny spiked fork. San Francisco. What a time to get called out of town for the company. He was an engineer not a marketing type. Clinton usually handled the sales pitches.

"Clinton's in over his head on this Mill Valley thing," his boss had insisted. "Lars wants a feasibility study done before we get in any deeper."

Phil had reluctantly consented to make the trip. As if he really had a choice. As far as he was concerned, the whole company was in over its head. Poor cash flow. Not exactly the best time to go expanding into new arenas.

He gulped another oyster and took a deep breath as the horseradish bit the back of his throat. He followed it with a big hunk of sourdough bread, the oyster shooters starting to take their toll in the form of a queasy stomach. It occurred to him that Lars may be the mastermind behind whatever was going on at the crypt, especially if the company was in trouble. With Karl gone, the only person standing between him and a possible company-saving fortune might be Tessa Madigan. Phillip knocked back another oyster shooter. Two more stared back at him from the glass plate. He drummed his fingers on the table. He had suddenly lost his appetite.

Chapter Forty-Two

"Now remember, what you will be doing here today is revisiting something that happened in the distant past, and at no time will you be in any danger from what you see. You will not be revivicating — reliving the experiences — only reminiscing about events that occurred."

"You will remain detached from those events so you can tell us about them later. If at any time you want to end the regression, all you need do is open your eyes and you will awake, feeling alert and refreshed."

It sounded like the disclaimer you hear repeated over and over before getting on a fast ride at Disneyland.

Please keep your hands and arms inside the gondola at all times.

It turned out Tessa had been nervous for nothing. The event wasn't in a clinic after all, but instead, in a quiet room in the therapist's private home.

Tessa glanced across the room to Lexi who smiled and nodded to her. Lexi had offered to do the regression herself but had admitted to being too emotionally attached to do the process justice. Bettina Roth was a respected hypno-therapist who regularly conducted regressions in the Newport area. They had agreed it was best to let Lexi supervise.

Tessa was relieved to have her friend there. She could step in if things went wonky. Now she gave Tessa an encouraging nod and settled back into her pillow by a set of double doors.

Tessa turned to Bettina. Maybe it was a little crazy to be here; but at least she was doing something — a wild ridiculous thing — Phil pretty much thought so — but it was better than spacing out in lifeguard towers, and it did fit the circumstances, after all, didn't it? She chewed on a hangnail as she refocused her attention on the rest of Bettina's preparation speech.

"Many people find they carry fears generated by events of a previous lifetime — fears and problems which have no logical basis in this life. Often, when those events are revealed through regression, the person is relieved of the fear and goes on to live a more useful, productive life in the present."

Realizing she had chewed her nail to the quick, Tessa clasped her hands together and held them tightly in her lap. Okay. So, she was reluctant to buy into the past life thing, but she needed answers. If her day-to-day life was going to have ancient scenes superimposed over it, she would at least like to know how and why, and knowing the how and why, she might be able to gain a little control over the when. That the dreams were some window into a past life memory was one of the saner explanations for all that had happened. Besides, Bettina was a *bona fide* psychologist with whom Lexi had studied and worked for several years, not a crank stage hypnotist like the one she'd seen in Maxi's West.

As usual with things she didn't understand, Tessa's preconceived ideas of what was about to happen were blown the minute they walked in the door. She expected a parlor with a round table in the center covered in a fringed paisley cloth and damask draperies darkening the room. *Too much TV, Tessa.*

Instead, they were in a cheery room; touchy feely, with maybe a few more Quan Yins and crystals than she was used to, but not in a creepy way. The only thing she'd been right about was the cold. She was glad she'd worn a long-sleeved sweater and now she pulled it down over her wrists and the snake bracelet she'd decided to wear at the last minute.

Bettina gave her a smooth, translucent stone to hold on to, which she explained was selenite, used for cleansing and protection. Then, she lowered the lights, pulled the drapes, and asked if everyone was ready.

Tessa held on to the stone, a surprising comfort, then answered "Yes."

"So now, pull up a pillow and lie back and relax, your hands at your side. Now clench them tight for a five count, then release." Bettina counted it out, then continued a series of relaxation exercises.

Tess could have done that at home, but she went along with the gag. Despite her skepticism, she sank deep into a heavy-lidded calm. After all the recent turmoil in her life, if she could just go to sleep now, she would have gotten her money's worth.

Bettina's voice floated into her consciousness. "Just breathe in slowly and let it out on a count of four."

Tessa did as she was told and when she had done it three times, she floated in a void. Not scary, just empty. No thoughts, no visions, just the gentle rise and fall of her breathing like the tide coming and going. Time stretched out and she found herself blissfully heavy, yet surprisingly alert.

Bettina's voice came slow and rhythmic. "Imagine you are holding the book of your life in your lap. Each time I ask you to remember a specific time, turn a page in your mind and go there. This will be effortless and peaceful, despite what you may see."

As Bettina guided her to think about events from last year, Tessa smiled remembering the day Phillip had lied about his car being in the shop to get her to drive him home.

"Now I want you to turn the page and see a day from your childhood. Tell me when you are there."

Tess breathed in slowly, turned the page in her mind and she was at Uncle Theo's house for her birthday. "There," she said, the word thick in her mouth. Mommy and daddy were angry. Theo gave her a bright plastic shovel and bucket and took her down the seawall steps. The tide had been out, gray sand pocked with little air holes. He showed her how to dig clams out of the sand. Tessa smiled at the memory.

"Now I want you to turn the page and remember a day in a lifetime lived *before* this one. This will only take a moment. When you get there, tell me what you see."

Right. Even in this blissful state, Tessa laughed to herself.

"Tell me when you are there," Bettina repeated, as if it were something they did every day. *How could she be so matter-of-fact? Surely there was more to it?*

Tessa turned her page. There was nothing but the afterimage of light floating through Bettina's windows on the insides of her eyelids.

"Tessa?" Bettina's voice was calm, but firm. "Tell me, what are you seeing?"

"Nothing," she replied, her tongue barely moving. There were shapes, vague colors, but no images she could recognize. *I knew I wouldn't be able to do this.*

"That's all right. Take your time. Be patient with yourself and the shapes will develop just like bringing binoculars into focus. Tell me when you begin to see something."

Tess tried to resist. This was a waste of time. But as her conscious mind argued against it, she began to perceive a scene — a place. A dark cave; no, it was a small room, dim and empty except for a low cot, a bench, and an earthen urn. Tessa's heart raced. She could see now that a girl lay on the cot, her knees drawn up, her hands tied behind her back with a leather thong. Tess was overcome with a feeling of dread.

It was Kindra. She was back in the chamber at the emperor's palace. A prisoner. *No. No! She had to get away.* She shook her head.

"Tessa, remember our talk before. You are only an observer, not reliving the events. Tell me what you are seeing."

Bettina's voice was gentle but carried a degree of authority.

"Room." She could barely push out the word. She rubbed her thumb over the smooth stone in her hand, her anchor to the present.

"You're just watching a scene now Tessa, you are not reliving it so there is no reason for you to be alarmed or afraid. Are you present in the room?"

Tessa hovered over the figure on the bed. "Yessssss."

"Tell me about yourself. How old are you? What are you wearing?"

"I'm Kindra." The words drifted from her lips like clouds, hers but not hers. "They're going to hang me."

"Alexis? Do you hear this?" Bettina's voice was a distant whisper.

Lexi's voice came to her as if from a dream, an echoing plea. "Bring her out."

Bettina went on, gently. "Tessa, do you wish to continue?"

"I —" Fear gripped the back of her neck, squeezed. It was like when she wore the bracelet, but not. She knew her friends were around her, but she felt solidly fixed in the past. "I —"

"Tessa, you must detach yourself from the events and tell me what is happening, or if you'd rather, we could end the session."

Footsteps were coming down the corridor outside the dark room. Someone was coming. Kindra needed her. "Keep … going," she said with some effort.

"All right. Take a few slow, deep breaths and let them out. You are only an observer, remember. Alert but detached."

Tessa was vaguely aware of Bettina's words. She drew in her breath, letting herself sink deeper into the past, into Kindra's mind. Tessa could no more detach from the scene than she could live without breath.

She was cold. So cold, her tunic sodden with damp, as was the blanket on the cot and everything else in the chamber. She had no idea how long she'd been there, but it felt like an eternity since she'd been in the bath with Fausta. Her lips were cracked and bleeding, and her stomach felt as empty as the room in which she lay. The cot smelled of urine and feces and sweat, and she was sure she'd heard the scurry of rats across the floor. She thought of the tiny babe growing in her belly and if it weren't for that, she'd have prayed to the gods to take her life.

Iron grated against iron. Her senses sprang to alert. The door opened. A tall figure lit from behind by someone carrying a lamp cast a menacing shadow against the wall.

"Ah, here you are *Kindard* the Goldsmith." The familiar voice oozed contempt. Kindra rolled to her side, her eyes squinting against the lamplight.

Valeria.

"You tried to protect Marcus and see what it earned you? He disobeyed the emperor and left you to take the blame." She strode to the cot and shoved Kindra back with her toe. "And all over a silly brooch."

Kindra's eyes went to a coil of bright gold around Valeria's arm — the serpent bracelet her mother had sewn into the hem of her tunic the day she was delivered for sale so long ago. Valeria must have taken it off her when she hit her at the baths. The injustice struck her in the gut.

"Marcus is coming for me," Kindra moaned, a pitiful sound that made her stomach clench.

Valeria struck out with her crop, caught Kindra across the shoulder. Her laugh echoed against the stone walls. "Silly fool. Why would Marcus bother with you? You're nothing but a liar and a thief."

Anger straightened Kindra's backbone. It was clear to her now why Valeria had sent Fausta's regular servant away. She was there as a backup plan should Marcus fail. Of course, it would take someone on the inside to see the plan through. Someone who knew the routine. "You used me."

"Ah, you're not as ignorant as I thought." Valeria sent her a malevolent grin. She reached into her tunic and pulled out a folded leather pouch. Inside were all the pieces Kindra had made for Fausta, and gleaming at the center of the cache was the cloisonné brooch.

"Those belong to the empress," Kindra accused.

"Belonged," Valeria corrected. "Just payment. Marcus failed his duty, and I am the one to clean up his mess. And now I am here, and Marcus and Fausta are on a doomed ship heading out to sea."

"And you call *me* a thief." The words were out of her mouth before she realized what she had done.

Valeria raised her crop to strike again, but at that moment, the hooded person holding the lantern stepped out from behind Valeria and swung it at her head. The woman went down hard, blood bloomed in a deep cut down the side of her face.

Kindra sprang to her feet. She was so weak from having nothing to eat for what had probably been days, she nearly passed out.

A familiar voice called to her. "Come on! Quick before her guards come looking for her."

"Dracis?"

He tore back his hood. "Yes, my lady. It's me." He pulled a blade from his tunic and slashed the ties around her hands and feet. "Now come. We don't have much time."

Kindra could not believe what had happened. Valeria lay splayed at her feet, unconscious, the jewelry spilled on the floor. "Is she dead?"

"Dracis knelt and pressed his fingers to Valeria's neck. "I don't think so."

Kindra scraped the jewelry into a pile and folded it into the leather wrap, tucked it into the waist of her tunic, swaying from the effort. "Let's go, then," she said, running on pure fear.

She stole through the door and heard the iron bar slide into place as Dracis locked Valeria in the chamber behind him. "That should keep her until someone discovers she's missing."

"If they're smart, they'll leave her in there till she starves."

Dracis sent her a grin and gently turned her into the corridor. Under a sky already lit with the first stars of night, she followed him down the stone wall leading to the water side of the palace where supplies were off loaded from merchant ships in the Bosphorus.

"She told Marcus you were dead, otherwise he would have waited. I couldn't say anything, or she'd have had me killed. If we hurry, we might catch up with his boat before it clears the dock."

Kindra did her best to keep up with him.

They saw the fire as they approached the quay. Valeria's words seared into her soul: *Marcus and Fausta are on doomed ship...*

A small merchant ship, its mast, square sail, and most of the deck engulfed in flames, was slipping out on the tide.

Dracis stopped, his hands went to his head. "By the gods, no!"

"Marcus," Kindra cried, knowing he couldn't hear her. Desperate, she broke into run. "Marcus!" Flames lit the night sky. "Marcus," she wailed and staggered into the water. It was cold and dark, but she didn't care.

Dracis waded after her, grabbed her arms, losing his balance as he tried to hold her back. "No, my lady. It's too late."

She fought out of his grasp and kept going, dragging one foot in front of the other until the chilling water reached her chin. She pushed off the bottom and flailed her arms to keep her head above the surface. The night sky was shrouded in smoke, the ship's hull silhouetted against bright orange flames.

"Kindra, no," Dracis' called. His voice grew fainter as she thrashed toward the burning wreck. She was out of breath, losing momentum; deep, cold water dragging her down. But there was no going back. The ship was in flames, but the father of her child might be alive. She couldn't give up.

She treaded water a moment, catching her breath, gulping as she struggled to keep her head above the brine. Smoke and steam billowed from the burning deck as the ship began to sink below the surface.

"No!" Kindra cried, anguish twisting her heart. She was almost there, close enough to see burned bodies on the deck. And then, as if rebelling against its fate, the ship rolled upright for a moment, blew apart with a defining explosion, sending splintered timbers into the night sky. Kindra threw her arms up uselessly to cover her face before the impact of the blast and the subsequent wave it produced, ripped the clothes from her back and forced her below the surface. The leather bag and all it contained fell away. She made one fruitless grab for it as she tumbled and fought to regain the surface, her lungs burning for air until she hadn't the strength left to kick.

Tessa gasped, "No!"

Bettina's voice broke through. "Tessa, what's happening? Can you tell us?"

"I ... can't breathe," Tessa wheezed. Her lungs felt crushed under a heavy weight. "I can't —"

"Bring her out!" It was Lexi, losing her mind. "Hurry." A warm hand gripped Tessa's forearm.

She shook her head. "No." She wrenched her arm away and squeezed her eyes closed. "I ... won't ... leave ... her." Her words came out heavy and slow, as if she were drunk, but her chest heaved.

"She's hyperventilating," Lexi cried, frantic.

"Alexis," Bettina cautioned, her voice calm, reassuring. "She's not in any real danger."

"But, she's —"

Tessa heard Lexi's muffled cry, the vision of the past fading. "Not … coming … back," she insisted, dragging the words from somewhere deep inside. She couldn't come back. Not now. Not yet. "Losing her. Take … me… back."

"Okay. Let's continue." Bettina's voice was hushed, in control. "I want you to breathe in slowly and exhale on the count of four, do you understand?"

Tessa nodded.

"Now, with me," Bettina prompted. "Breathe in, two, three, four; breathe out, two, three, four." Tessa relaxed her shoulders, breathed to the slow count until the sense of the room began to fade. "Now, as an observer, you are returning to the scene just visited. Tell me when you're there."

Tessa refocused her attention on the blank page in her mind. *Breathe in two, three, four; breathe out, two, three, four.* The smell of smoke filled her senses first, then suddenly, like diving into a breaking wave, she jerked as cold water hit her face. Salty brine stung her eyes. All was dark but for an orange glow overhead. Her lungs burned. She was sinking. Sinking into the dark.

No. Kick damn you, girl. You've got this.

Kindra opened her eyes, twisted around. She was alone under the water. Debris and mangled bodies floated overhead. Her heart contracted into a cold, tight fist. If Marcus was gone, what difference did it make if she lived or died?

Kindra! Listen to me! Save yourself. Save your baby. Kick. Kick!

Tessa's legs twitched. She dug her heels into the carpet.

"Tessa!" Lexi cried.

"Shhhh," Bettina ordered *sotto voce.*

Tessa drew her knees up and pushed hard against the floor, channeling all her strength. *Push, Kindra. Push through. You have nothing to lose.*

A sudden, electrifying power surged through Kindra's body from a well of energy she thought had run dry. A fierce blue light racketed around her like storm lightening, forced her to look up. She was deep, deep under the surface, but she could still see a faint glow above her. She began to kick, slowly at first, then lips pressed hard against the compulsion to haul in a breath, she stabbed her arms overhead, spread her hands wide and pulled down with all her might.

That's it. Again. Again.

With what felt like the last beats of her heart, Kindra kicked and stroked toward the light again and again until she thought her lungs would explode; and then, with one last stroke, her head breached the surface and she gasped in a life-saving breath.

Yes. Yes!

Coughing, gasping, treading water, she turned a half circle, orienting herself. The ship was gone. There was no sign of fire or smoke, no sounds but her own heaving breaths. Off in the distance, pinpoints of light glowed near the docks. A half-burned plank floated only a few strokes away. With precious breath feeding her resolve, she kicked to it, looped an arm over the top. The acrid odor of burned pitch assaulted her nostrils, but she held on. She splayed her hand over her belly. "Thank you," she said to the voice that had once again come to her rescue. Her teeth chattered and her arms ached, but she was alive. "Thank you. Thank you. Thank you."

She looped her other arm over the plank, turned toward the docks, and began a slow, steady kick.

Tessa breathed out a long, shuddering sigh. Her eyes fluttered open. She dragged in several ragged breaths, then sat up, gripped herself tightly around the ribs, fully expecting to be soaking wet. But she wasn't. She was safe and warm and dry.

Lexi was at her side, rubbing her back. "Tess, you okay?"

She blinked at her surroundings. Bettina gave her a knowing nod. Her breathing evened out, and an eerie calm descended over her. She scraped her fingers through her hair and exhaled long and slow.

"Yeah. I think I am."

CHAPTER FORTY-THREE

Lexi pulled onto Pacific Coast Highway and headed back to the island. She gave Tessa the fisheye. "You don't have to tell me if you don't want to."

Tessa took a long drink from the water bottle Bettina had given her, holding onto it with both hands. In her mind, she was under water, flames backlit the hull of a ship floating overhead. The experience was too real, too raw to put into words.

"I'll tell you. Eventually. I'm just not sure I believe any of it."

"Does it matter?"

Tessa glanced over at her friend. She had to admit, she felt more at peace than she had since the night they discovered the jewelry. She huffed out a laugh. "Maybe not."

"Well," Lexi said, sending her a smile. "You look better than you have in a long time. That wild stare is gone out of your eyes."

"Wild stare?"

"I'll know better when we get home and I don't have to keep you from sucking down a whole bottle of chocolate syrup."

Tessa laughed. "Do we have ice cream to go with?"

Lexi turned down Jamboree Road and headed for the bridge to the island. "That's my girl."

Tessa smiled out the window as they turned on Marine Avenue, almost home. "It's a bit hard to swallow."

"Ice cream?"

Tessa crunched the plastic bottle in her hands. "No. The past life concept. I'm having a hard time getting my head around it. I mean, if in fact I really slipped into a past life, that means I'm her, right? Kindra. Which would mean the jewelry found its way to *me*, not the other way around." The thought gave her a chill. "What do you think? I mean, really."

"My shrinky-dink brain tends to believe your mind filled in a story that makes sense to you. One you can live with because you are a naturally reasonable person and tired of all this shit."

Tessa shrugged. "Yeah. Right down to how the jewelry ended up on the bottom of the Bosphorus." She took another long pull of water. "At least your theory means I'm not going out of my *effin'* mind. Either way, I've got to figure out what authorities to call to start *that* ball rolling. The sooner I get rid of the jewelry, the better I'll feel."

Lexi pulled down the alley, stopped behind the house, and shifted the car into park. "I'm a step ahead of you there."

Tess opened the passenger door. "Yeah?"

"I spoke with a friend of mine at the Getty Research Library. You remember Alana Lin, from school? We used to tease her about wanting to be a librarian?"

Tessa pursed her lips, remembering. She, Lexi, and Alana had sat in the front row on graduation day with Uncle Theo the only 'parent' among them. "She works at the Getty?"

"Pretty cool, huh? Anyway, she says we could make an appointment to come down to the library and see what we can find. Ultimately, though, we'd be dealing with US Immigration and Customs."

"ICE?"

"I know, right? Sends a little shiver down your spine. But it's okay. Alana says they work with the Cultural Property, Art, and Antiquities section often and they would handle any inquiries."

Tessa looped her bag over her shoulder, warming to the prospect of finally being done with the ordeal. "Good to know."

"She said she could contact them for us, too. Knows someone in the LA office. It might make it a little less intimidating to have the Getty connection at the start."

Tessa let out a long sigh. "Okay. Sounds like a good next step."

Lexi grabbed her hand and gave it a squeeze. "Hold that thought, girlfriend. I promised Rags I'd get him a scratching pole and a new bed, and the pet store is open a while yet. I'll get some ice cream on the way home. You'll be all right?"

"Yeah. Sure. I'm good."

Tessa stood on the landing at the top of the stairs until Lexi disappeared around the corner, her mind still replaying images of the session. If someone had told her a couple of months ago she'd do a past life regression, she'd have laughed in their face. In her wildest dreams, she'd never expected any of it to make sense. The fact that it kind of did was still a bit hard to take.

She turned, put her hand on the doorknob, and to her surprise, it pushed open.

Hum. That's weird. She specifically remembered locking it because she'd thought of Audrey when she did. She slipped inside and shut the door behind her.

It was late afternoon, still light, but with Phillip on his way to San Francisco for real this time, and Lexi running an errand, the house felt dark and lonely.

She flicked on the dining room light, then quickly moved through the living room. When she twisted the switch on a table lamp, there was a thunk upstairs.

"Rags? Kitty, kitty?"

She rested her hand on the baluster and cocked her head to listen. Another thunk. "Rags, you little stinker, you better not have brought another pigeon in this house."

She mounted the stairs, more lighthearted than she had felt since they'd moved into the old place. With Karl Johns out of the picture, a path forward to doing the right thing with the jewelry, not to mention the reassurance this afternoon that maybe she wasn't losing her mind, she felt almost human again.

She flicked the light switch at the top of the landing, expecting to see feathers strewn across the floor. It took her a minute to make sense of what she saw instead. There was a mess, all right, but it wasn't anything the cat dragged in.

Every drawer had been pulled from the antique dresser and dumped out on the floor; the bedclothes were tangled in a heap in the far corner of the room, and her mattress lay slumped against the wall, victim of a slashing that left its guts strewn across the rug.

Phillip's new section of drywall had been hacked away, leaving the studs and insulation visible. A tire iron lay on top of the mess. Tessa's heart beat faster with every microsecond that passed.

A breeze billowed the curtains away from the sliding door. Tessa sucked in a breath. It had to be open; definitely not the way she had left it.

There was a scraping sound out on the deck. Tessa covered her mouth to keep from yelping. Whoever did this must still be here.

Adrenaline spiked, grabbed her by the back of the neck. She wanted to run down the stairs and call for help, but she forced herself to stay. She was done with running. Done with feeling helpless in her own house.

There was no way down from the third story deck. It would only take a moment for whoever it was to figure that out, and then, they'd be coming her way.

Tess slipped her cellphone from her purse, hit the photo icon, then bent to pick up the tire iron. She slid her back along the wall toward the door. She could hear the person breathing.

Stay calm. You've got this. She tightened her grip on the iron then took a quick peek around the doorframe. A woman stood at the edge of the deck, looking over the side. Not the scruffy-looking person you'd expect at a break in. This woman was dressed in a tailored gray jacket and a pair of pearl-colored, high-waisted silky trousers. Tessa leaned her head away from the door and back against the wall. Her heartbeat bubbled in her ears.

She blinked at the ceiling. Surprise was on her side. She would confront the woman on three. She nodded out the count, swallowed hard, then boldly stepped onto the deck, holding the phone out in front of her like a weapon. "What the hell do you think you're doing?"

At first Tess didn't recognize the woman who spun to look at her. She was tall and lean; her cheekbones pressed high through pale skin. And then, like some ghoul in a scary movie, her eyes glowed molten, like they could cut flesh.

Phone shaking in her hand, Tessa inched closer. She knew that face, those eyes.

Valeria. The woman who had carried out Constantine's orders. She licked her lips and thumbed the photo button. The phone bobbled in her shaking palm. Not good enough. She steadied herself and tried again. But when she saw the picture, the frightening image of Valeria was gone.

Her shoulders relaxed and her mouth curled into a nervous smile. It was Val Johns.

"Whoa!" Johns huffed with a sigh. "Am I glad you got here when you did — I was passing by, I saw — two men — run from the house and — naturally I — when there was no one home, I --"

Tessa wanted to believe her, wanted to believe that just when she was scared to death, someone was here to help; that she had let fear distort her vision.

But, all she could think of was Phillip's warning. With Karl dead, she was the only person standing between someone and a fortune in gold. That someone could very well be Valerie Johns.

Valerie took a step toward her. Tessa stood her ground. She had been careless, and Phillip had been right. "Stay where you are," she ordered.

Valerie laughed, light heartedly, still working her ruse. "I know it looks silly. But I swear to you, I was only trying to help."

Lexi would be home any minute. She had to keep her talking. "The hell you were. You were in here looking for the jewelry." Tess had caught her right in the middle of it.

"No. I realize now I should have stayed outside, called the police."

Tessa held up the phone, thumbed Phil's icon on her Favorites list, hoping he hadn't left for the airport. "I don't believe you." She edged backward. "You broke into my house and ransacked my bedroom." Tessa lifted the tire iron.

Valerie shook her head, held her hands out defensively. "No. No, I wouldn't — they —"

"There is no they, Valerie. We both know that."

Val shook her head. "No."

Backing toward the sliding doors, Tessa tripped over the threshold, the phone jittered out of her grasp.

The woman's evil laugh assaulted her. It wasn't Valerie anymore. Hair rose on the back of Tessa's arms, her skin crackled with static. She was standing face-to-face with Valeria from Constantine's guard.

This is not real.

Tessa clamped her jaw tight, gripping the tire iron with both hands.

She is not real.

Truth surged through her, adding to her resolve. When she spoke, her voice boomed with authority. "The jewelry is safe. You'll never get your hands on it."

Valeria's eyes flared molten once more. In a flash movement Tess didn't see coming, the woman pinned her throat against the window frame with one hand and ripped the tire iron out of her hands with the other. She pressed her lips close to Tessa's ear. "I don't care about that slave's jewelry. It's the snake I'm after. My ticket home. Do you understand?"

The snake? Home? Oh my god.

Under her sweater sleeve, the bracelet softened, warmed, and slid up to her bicep, a ring of heat tightening around her arm. Tessa gasped, shook her head. She could hardly breathe under the woman's grip.

Where was Lexi? Her eyes went to her phone. It had fallen face down. She had no idea whether Phillip had gotten her call. She fought, shook her head, clawed at Valeria's hand, trying to pull her fingers away from her throat. The window frame dug against the back of her skull.

"That uncle of yours took it and you know where it is."

Tessa squirmed, tried to kick at the woman's legs but she was losing consciousness. The coiled serpent was getting hotter by the second. If she didn't give in, the woman would choke her to death and get the bracelet anyway. It was too late. She was losing strength. She was slipping down.

Valeria squeezed harder, then let off a little.

Tessa gasped. Her chest burned and then she felt the power return, like a piston, driving up her throat, rising, rising to the surface. The bracelet's heat was unbearable, searing her arm, and then suddenly, lightening arced between their bodies in twisted ropes of blue fire.

Valeria's eyes flew open wide. Tessa raised an arm to screen her face from the flash. Valeria fell backward, stumbling against the low roof edge, her anguished cry pierced the night; and then, all was quiet.

Tessa gasped. The odor of singed hair burned the back of her throat. The force that had overtaken her body was gone. And so was the woman. Valerie, Valeria. It didn't' matter which. She was gone, and there was only one place she could be.

Tessa staggered to the low wall at the edge of the deck, took a deep, shuddering breath, and forced herself look over. A body lay crumpled in the yard below, its head twisted at an awkward angle, eyes staring sightless into the dusk.

Knees going liquid, Tessa sank into a heap against the wall.

A moment later, a vibration pulsed through the stucco wall at her back. A car pulling into the garage.

"Lexi."

She dragged herself down the stairs and met Lexi as she came inside. "I didn't do it! I never touched her! It was the light. It had to be that light."

Lexi spilled her shopping bags on the floor. "What on earth?"

Tessa collapsed into Lexi's arms. "She's dead. I know it. Go and see."

Lexi gripped Tessa's face in her hands and wiped tears off her cheeks with her thumbs. "Tessa. Look at me."

Tessa closed her eyes. Shame squeezed at the back of her throat.

"Tess. Look. At. Me."

Tessa gulped air, made herself look at her friend. "Valeria. Valerie. She's out there." She pointed to the yard. "We need to call the police."

"Okay, okay. Let's just...." Worry flashed in Lexi's eyes when she saw the marks on Tessa's neck. Tessa gingerly touched her skin. It hurt to swallow.

"Tessa, what happened? Take a breath and tell me."

"Val Johns. In the yard. I think she's dead."

"Okay. I hear you, Tess." The look in her eyes said she didn't really believe. "We'll go look together."

"No, I --"

"Okay, then you stay right here and I'll--"

"No!" Tessa grabbed her arms. "Don't leave me."

"Okay. I've got you. We'll call the police. Just let me get my phone."

Before Lexi could fish her phone from her purse, sirens blared nearby.

Tessa wrapped her arms around her middle and held on. "I tried to call Phillip, but I dropped my phone."

Their eyes caught and held as they heard cars screeching to a stop outside. Lexi went to the landing. "Looks like he got the message."

Tessa jumped to her side, relief flooding through her. Three Orange County Sheriff's cars blocked the alley, red and blue lights strobed across the backs of her neighbor's houses.

"In the backyard," Lexi said, and a pair of men shown their flashlights into the garage and headed through.

Phillip's silver Porsche skidded his to a stop behind the black and whites, and he sprang out at a run, taking the back stairs two at a time.

He clutched Tessa into his arms, held her in a vice grip. "Baby, you all right?"

She buried her face in his shirt, the adrenaline rush had gone, her legs nearly crumpled under her. She lifted her eyes to his. "You got my call."

"It took me a minute to realize what I was hearing, but yeah. Was that Valerie's voice I heard?"

Tessa nodded. "She was after the jewelry. Made a mess of things up in my room and I caught her in the act. She denied it, but we know that's what she was after. She ruined all your work."

Phillip grabbed her by the shoulders. "Don't worry about that now. I'm so glad you're okay. I was afraid I'd lost you."

Tessa shook her head, guilt bottoming out in her stomach. She clamped her eyes tight shut as if that would make the nauseous feeling go away.

"Tess? Just tell me, honey. Whatever it is, we'll deal with it."

If she said it out loud, it would make it all real. But she had no choice. The police would discover the truth any second anyway. He lifted her chin with his fingers, his eyes were filled with compassion and love.

"Valerie's dead," she said, her voice shaky. "I might have pushed her."

"Don't worry, Tess." Her ear pressed against his chest, his words were solid and real as his steady heartbeat. "Whatever happened, I've got your back. I love you and I won't leave. Ever. No matter what."

Audrey was right. Phillip was a keeper and it was time she let him all the way in. Trusted him with her deepest longings and fears. She dragged in a deep breath and blew it out hard. She could tell him the truth. He deserved that.

She dried her cheeks with her palms, gave him a shaky smile. "You know how you wanted to build a railing up on the roof deck?"

CHAPTER FORTY-FOUR

Lieutenant Garza of the Orange County Sheriff's department took Tessa's statement, then asked her to read it through to make sure it was accurate before signing it.

She had sat for nearly an hour after the paramedics checked her over. She'd refused to be taken to emergency, insisting she was all right. Now, she sat at her dining room table with her arms clenched around her waist, wondering if she'd made a mistake. Her body had been flushed with adrenaline throughout the ordeal; now it was gone, and she felt like she'd been drained of all energy. The whole incident had been a nightmare. It was bad enough that Valerie Johns had destroyed the room she and Phillip had worked so hard to create. Now, uniformed officers were crawling over her private space like cockroaches in a dirty kitchen.

She had been through her story three times already. She'd found the back door open, heard a sound upstairs, her room had been tossed, and then Valerie Johns attacked her on her balcony, almost choking her to death. The bruises on her neck attested to that. She'd nearly blacked out when she heard her attacker scream. What more could she say? That some supernatural power in the form of blue lightning intervened on her behalf and tossed the woman off the roof?

There was no point. Valerie was dead. The medical examiner said she'd broken her neck, among other things. Tessa had seen that for herself when she'd looked off the roof. It would be a long time before she got that image out of her head.

She lifted her eyes to Phillip, then Lexi. Phillip put the pen in her hand. "It'll be over soon, babe."

"Will it?" Tessa's hand went to the snake bracelet still at her wrist and she couldn't help wondering if it was Valerie down there in her yard, or a specter from the past.

"Ms. Madigan," Garza said. "Do you have any idea why the deceased was in your house?"

Tess did her best to recount Valerie's story about the two men. "But I didn't buy it. She was looking for the gold."

"Gold." Garza shifted in his seat, suddenly energized.

"Lieutenant Garza," Lex interrupted. "When Tess and Phillip remodeled the house, they found some artifacts. I'm pretty sure these were what she was after. Both Mrs. Johns and her brother-in-law, Karl, were aware the pieces were here and had shown more than a passing interest."

Garza sighed heavily. "Not the Karl Johns who was found dead in his brother's hot tub recently?"

Tessa nodded. "Um hum."

That revelation put a sparkle in his eye. He refocused on Tess. "What kind of artifacts?"

Tessa gripped her hands in front of her. "My Uncle was an archeologist, he—" She slumped in her chair. Where to start. She shot a glance to Lexi.

"Gold jewelry," Lexi said, cutting straight to the facts. "Tessa put it in her safe deposit box last week. We have an appointment at the Getty and Immigration and Customs coming up soon."

As far as Tessa knew, they hadn't actually made the appointment, but she was grateful for Lexi's quick thinking. She was running out of gas and her brain wasn't functioning at peak level.

"My engagement ring was still in its box on top of the dresser," she added, flashing Phillip a guilty glance. It should have been on her finger a long time ago. She realized that now. "I'm pretty sure some random robbers would have pocketed that. They'd have no way of knowing about the gold."

"Sounds like you made the right move," Garza said.

"Got that right." Phillip put his arm around Tessa's shoulders. "We about done here? My girl has had enough for one night." He was right about that. All she wanted right now was to sink into his body and curl her face into his chest.

Garza frowned. Tess could almost see cogs clanking in his head. He could see there was a lot more to this story and she could see that it intrigued him. Then his radio blared on.

"All clear, Lieutenant," a nasal voice said.

Garza pursed his lips a moment longer, then to Tessa's relief, he stood, hitched up his pants. "So, the body has been removed, Ms. Madigan. We'll be notifying the next of kin. I'll be in touch about … the rest of it soon." He slipped a card out of his shirt pocket. "Meantime, let me know if you think of anything else." He gave them a curt nod and headed down the stairs.

&

"Jesus am I glad that's over," Lexi said. Tessa's gaze shifted up to the ceiling a moment before she resignedly rested her elbow on the table, dropped her forehead into her palm. Phillip slipped out his cellphone and pressed the button for help. "The number for Pelican Hill Resort, Newport Beach."

Tessa listened without complaint as Phillip made reservations for two suites. He covered the phone with his hand. "No way are you ladies staying in this house until it's cleaned up and repaired."

Thirty minutes later, Tess was resting peacefully in the suite bedroom.

Lexi dug in the opened bar fridge and retrieved two cartons of chocolate milk, handed one to Phillip. "This was a good idea, Phil. I don't think I could have slept in the house after tonight either. But really, you should stay here, and I'll take the other suite. I think Tessa needs you tonight a lot more than she needs me."

"Right now, I think she needs her sleep. But," he said, grateful for his friendship with Lex, "I think I'll take you up on that. Tomorrow's going to be another awful day."

She sucked the last of her milk noisily through her straw and sat on the sofa next to him. "I know. If it was me, you'd be dumping ashes off a boat between here and Catalina. But Audrey wanted to be buried next to her husband. She'd arranged it all ahead of time."

"We'll get through it together," he said, his heart giving a little squeeze. His emotional response to Tessa's neighbor's passing surprised him. She was a sweet lady, of course, but he barely knew her. Hard part was, she was about the same age as his mother. He wasn't quite ready to think in terms of losing her. But there it was.

Lexi drew a throw pillow off the sofa and wrapped her arms around it. "I'll miss her. I'm afraid it was all that running up and down our back stairs in the middle of the night that finally did her in."

"You of all people should know better than to beat yourself up. The important thing was your door was always open. You and Tessa made the last few months of her life a lot brighter."

"Now don't go getting soft and understanding on me. I don't think I could take it." Lex pressed her face into the pillow. After a moment, her head popped up, her eyes red, but dry. "Welp, I guess I'll let you get to bed."

She went to the door to the adjoining suite. "Thank you, Phillip, for loving my girl."

Phillip stood, rubbed the back of his neck. "I have no choice in the matter."

She sent him a knowing smile. "Night."

"Night Lex."

Phillip leaned on the balcony railing, taking in the distant harbor lights, going over what he needed to pull off his plan, which now included restoring Tessa's room to the peaceful place they'd created. It was nearly two a.m. before he felt tired enough to actually sleep. He'd have to get up early to make it all happen in time.

CHAPTER FORTY-FIVE

Kindra floated motionless in midnight blue; *bright orange flames high above her head went suddenly dim. No bodies floated on the surface, no brave palace soldier swam to her rescue. She blinked her eyes and relaxed into a pleasant detachment. No longer able to hold lifegiving breath in her lungs, she let it seep slowly between her lips and began to sink. Just another lost soul destined to disintegrate on the bottom of the sea. This is how it ends. And why not? Marcus was gone, what possible reason had she to fight?*

Like a reminder from the gods, there was a gentle flutter deep inside, the butterfly kiss of life in her womb. She raised her gaze to the surface. So far away and nothing she could do about it.

No, Kindra. This is not how it ends. Kick, you little fool. Kick! Fight! Survive!

❧

Tessa woke with a start, gasping air. Words screamed in her mind. *Fight! Kick! Breathe!* But no sound came out of her mouth. She couldn't break through, couldn't breathe, struggled against a force pushing her down.

"Kick, damn you," she managed at last. A pair of strong arms came around her middle and pulled her against a hard, warm body.

"Easy Tess." Phillip's breath hissed softly against her ear. "Shhhhh. A dream, Tessa. Just a dream."

She opened her eyes. Where was she? Not in her room, not home, and not at the bottom of the sea. The snake bracelet lay curled on the nightstand; her clothes tossed haphazard on a chair next to the bed. Phillip rubbed a smooth pattern up and down her spine with the heel of his hand, and then it all came rushing back. The break in, the body, the investigation, Phillip packing she and Lexi off to the quiet suite at Pelican Hill.

Letting herself relax, she turned in his arms, curled into his embrace. Her heart broke for Kindra and her unborn child. Hopefully, she had been able to hold on to that old plank. What she knew for sure was that she was safe. Safe in Phillip's arms, and for that, she was grateful.

She leaned her head back and looked into dark eyes that seemed to see right into her. "I love you Phillip."

He kissed her forehead. "I know," he said with that half grin that made her crazy. She could already feel him getting hard against her belly. She socked him playfully, trusting with all her soul that he loved her to distraction. He'd said it nearly every day since they'd met, and she had no doubt it was true.

Except for the dream that woke her, she'd slept like a damned rock and she'd so needed it. But as reality rushed in, she knew today was Audrey's memorial and burial. It would be a small ceremony, including Rags as Audrey requested, and there was still a lot to do. What she needed most in this world right now was to feel Phillip inside her, confirmation of life.

She lifted her mouth and touched her lips to his, arching against him. "What time is it?"

He closed her in his embrace, kissed her ear, her cheek, and finally her mouth. "Time for us," he murmured, and kissed her again, this time searing her with pent up desire that matched her own.

She placed her hand on his chest and rolled up on top of him. "Did we bring protection?"

He kissed her again, deep and long. "Honey, we jammed out of that crime scene so fast last night, I didn't even bring a toothbrush."

Tess pulled him closer. "Might not matter anyway. I mean we've already had unprotected sex."

"Yeah. And it was really —" He kissed her. "Really —" He kissed her again. "Great. In fact, I think we should get married."

She let go a quiet laugh, smiled into his eyes, and brushed a shock of sandy blond off his forehead. "I've turned you down at least twenty-seven times. You sure you still want me?" She reached between his legs and took hold of him, running her thumb up to his tip.

His eyes rolled back in his head. "Honey, you had me at *no way.*"

She laughed and for the first time in weeks it felt real, free, and liberating. "Ask me again. Right now."

He opened his eyes. "Now? No, yeah. I can't."

Tessa threw back her head and laughed again. "*Whatdaya* mean, you can't?"

"It will spoil my surprise."

"Surprise?"

"Do you trust me, Tess?"

"You know I do."

He framed her face in his hands, kissed her with all the tenderness she loved, then the fierceness she craved. He rolled her onto her back and settled his heavy erection between her legs. "We need to get through today and get you back in your house. And then I promise, I'll make this all worth it."

She lifted herself up, crossed her legs behind his back, poised to take him deep inside. Uncle Theo used to always say "A bird in the hand is worth two in the bush". When she was little, she had no idea what that silly statement meant. Now, with her hard, lanky man in her arms, she finally knew. She still felt a hollow sadness for Kindra and how life had been so cruel to her. But she wasn't living Kindra's life. She was living her own — crazy, filled with challenges and disappointments, sure. But also full of love and trust and friendship. Things that mattered. Phillip had her back, and she'd have his, no matter what. "It's already worth it, Phillip."

❧

The December morning dawned foggy and wet, just like the newscast said it would. Tessa had been in no shape to plan a thing when they left her house the night before. Phillip may not have brought his own toothbrush, but he had thought of everything else. He'd taken the outfits they'd planned to wear for the ceremony and grabbed Tessa's make up bag at the last minute.

Lexi and Tess got ready together in Tessa's suite, doing their best to distract one another from what came next. They were in the hotel lobby breezeway waiting for Phillip to come back with his car when they were met instead, by a gold-flecked limousine.

Phillip got out of the rear passenger door and helped them inside. "It was in her arrangements. Limo pickup. I'll go by the house and get the cat." Also outlined in her instructions, Rags was to accompany them to the site.

Tessa missed Phillip already, but he'd been agitated since they'd gotten out of bed. Whatever he was up to, he was being very secretive about it.

She had to laugh when they settled into the posh seating in the limo. Opposite the spacious back seat was a champagne bar with two iced bottles at the ready, a pretty tin box of Oreo cookies, and a couple of tiny bottles of Hornitos, with a note that read, "Depending."

She looked over at Lex.

"No question." Lexi reached for the Hornitos and twisted off the two caps. They clinked little bottles, drank, and chased the hot liquid down with gulps of champagne.

Tessa rode along in silence, hardly noticing the traffic. A cold tightening had settled itself in a knot between her shoulder blades and stubbornly remained unresponsive to her kneading fingers. By the time they pulled into the mortuary behind the shiny black Cadillac hearse, she was starting to feel a little better. She'd been dreading the day, and Audrey had anticipated their distress, adding her own touch of care beyond her life in the form of tequila. A moment later, Phillip's car pulled up behind them and they headed for the cemetery. Audrey would be laid to rest next to her husband at the Pacific View Memorial Park.

They passed several other services, one with over a hundred mourners. Another had just ended and the last of the attendees were making their way slowly to their cars.

Some of them, it was obvious, had not seen one another for a long time, and Tessa shook her head. They hadn't bothered to come around when the deceased was alive, and now they would have to live with the guilt.

"I think this is it up here on the right." She pointed to the little map that had been waiting for them in the limo.

Up a small knoll to the right, a mound of dirt lay covered with a blanket of artificial grass and Tessa recognized the Rent-a-Chaplain from the mortuary. Mr. Burness's headstone was just a few feet away. Audrey had arranged to have a spray of flowers placed there as well.

Phillip got out carrying the cat inside Audrey's black and gold leopard carrier. Rags was uncharacteristically silent. Tessa didn't blame him.

The four of them made their way up the knoll and watched as the hearse parked at the curb. Two attendants loaded the coffin out the back and onto a special gurney used whenever there were no pall bearers. A lonely sight.

Until her husband's death, the couple had been prominent citizens of the community; but afterward, Audrey dropped out of social circles one-by-one, until Burness was nothing but a name skipped over in the phone book while looking for someone else. Except for Theo; Phillip, Tessa, and Lexi were her only remaining friends.

It was sad in a way, but Tessa was glad that none of the people who had ignored or forgotten her in life had showed up to make excuses at the funeral.

The ceremony was brief. Tessa barely listened. Audrey had not been a religious person in the way that most people understood. Any words said in that direction were better off falling on the mute blades of grass that grew without knowledge of some higher power and were green anyway.

Lexi stood and placed a small nosegay of miniature roses from the limo atop the casket before Tessa pulled herself away from her own thoughts and stood beside her. She twisted the bracelet on her arm. The damned thing had been more trouble than it was worth. All that really mattered to her in this life was standing on either side of her. Phillip, the man who wanted her the day they met, and Lexi who'd been her friend since she was fourteen years old. The rest was all a blur. Insignificant. History.

The thought came to her like a bubble bursting. She had a chance to free herself from whatever power had taken over her life since they found the jewelry. It occurred to her not for the first time that Theo had hidden the jewelry — especially the bracelet — for good reason. Had he known it was dangerous? Then why did he show her the gazing ball in the first place?

She would never know. One thing was sure. If she gave up the bracelet, she would never know for sure if Kindra survived. Maybe that was a good thing. None of what had pulled her life off track would have happened if they hadn't found the jewelry. Right now, in this moment, she had the power to make sure it never happened to anyone else.

The assistant funeral director had accompanied the casket to the graveside. She motioned him to come over.

"What are you doing?" Lexi whispered.

Tessa shook her head. The director was at her elbow. "Can you open this thing, you know, before you lower it down?"

"Well," he said crossing his arms over his chest, "I can, but people normally don't."

Phillip leaned to her. "Tess?"

"Open it," she told the attendant. Phillip stared at her for a moment, his mouth slightly agape. She stared right back. She wasn't sure how this would go, but she had to try.

She touched Phillip's shoulder, smiled at Lexi. "Could I ... have a moment?"

They gave her a matched set of furrowed brows that would be comical if she wasn't dead serious. She cocked her head and waited for them to return to their chairs.

The attendant stepped to the casket, flipped the latch, then lifted the lid.

Tessa moved closer, resting her forearms on the edge of the casket. She half expected the coffin to be empty – people weren't really buried in the ground — another childhood fantasy proved wrong. Indeed, Audrey's body still lay peacefully on white satin pillows. Her hair had been coiffed, her cheeks slightly blushed with makeup. She wore the pretty blue dress Lexi had picked out and an ivory sheet was pulled up to her waist. Her hands, only slightly deflated in death, lay peacefully across her chest.

Tessa twisted the snake bracelet at her wrist. Was it her imagination, or was it suddenly difficult to breathe? "I should have told you about this before," she said softly, words for Audrey alone. "I have a feeling you knew more about this jewelry than you let on. Pretty sure Theo hid this away for a reason, though, right? Anyway, I figure it will be safer here with you, than out in the open where it can cause more trouble."

Audrey lay silent. Of course. This was ridiculous. Maybe even a little morbid. But it was the right thing to do. Right? The only thing that made sense. Everyone would be better off with this damn snake out of business.

She dragged in a frustrated breath and grasped the bracelet to slide it off. To her surprise, it had sunk into comfortable grooves on her skin, like a reassuring hug. She pressed her fingers under the gold. It was almost as if it had melded with her skin. A feeling of peace washed over her. Everything around her grew silent. The grass under her feet and the hazy sky above seemed to disappear. She was floating, floating in an azure sea, rising to the surface . . .

"Tess!" Phillip was at her side now, pulling her away. "That's enough," he said, nodding to the attendant. She blinked at him, coming back to the present. She could feel the ground under her feet again and his hand warm at her back.

He nodded to the attendant who quickly reclosed the casket and held out his hand for them to return to their seats.

They watched as the casket was lowered into the earth and the fake grass was laid over the hole. Her fingers went to the bracelet, once again loose at her wrist.

"You ready?" Lexi asked, dabbing her eye with a tissue.

"Yeah. Let's go."

"I'll see you back at the house," Phillip said kissing her lightly on the cheek. "The limo will drop you off."

❦

"But where is he?" Tessa paced back and forth in front of the French doors in the living room. "He said he'd meet us back here. It's nearly six o'clock."

"Will you please just calm down? I'm sure he's stopped off at the market or something. Why don't you sit down and relax. Look at the beautiful job he did on the house. And did you see your bedroom? I bet you haven't even been up there yet."

Tessa hesitated at the bottom of the stairs fighting to keep the images from flooding her thoughts. "I'm not sure I want to go up there."

"Oh. I think you should."

Tessa sighed deeply. She did feel better. It was dark outside, the sun having set at 5:15 almost in unison with the high tide. It was true, the house was well lit and cheery and seemed more like home at that moment than it ever had. She mounted the stairs and took them one-by-one, then gasped in wonder when she got to the top. Her room had been put entirely back together. Even her wallpaper with the tiny rosebuds had been replaced. She ran and jumped onto her bed, obviously a new mattress.

"Oh Lexi, I never would have believed Phillip could be so wonderful; he can be such a pain sometimes." She scooted to her favorite place at the head of the bed and looked out at the neighbor's porch lights across the canal. "You know, I was really afraid I would never feel at home in this room again."

Audrey was gone and that was going to take a while to get used to. But Karl and that Valerie/Valeria was gone, too, and with them a huge lump of anxiety. "I feel like a veil has been lifted."

"Good to have you back," Lexi said, giving her a squeeze around the waist.

Her eye caught a movement at the seawall. She raised her finger to her lower lip and was about to mention it to Lex when the canal in front of the house sprang suddenly into a thousand points of color. Their little sailboat had been strung with colored Christmas lights from bow to stern and all the way round the triangle of her sail.

Phillip waived up at her from the dock. She opened the window and leaned out. "Phil. I love it!"

"Wait, wait!" he shouted, waiving his hands. Then he scrambled down into the boat again. The lights suddenly began chasing themselves like a Hollywood marquis. He jumped back up on the dock and took a deep bow. "Now get yourself down here, we have a parade to catch."

Tess turned to Lexi, the question in her eyes.

"Go ahead. I'll watch from the bay."

She gave Lexi a hug. "You know you are the best friend anyone could ever have?"

"Yes. I know. Now get going."

Tessa took one more look out the window and waved at Phillip standing expectantly out on the dock. His smile had never looked so appealing. She sensed the bracelet loose at her wrist, cold and detached. It was time to step back into her own world and forget the past. She slipped it off and put it in her lingerie drawer, shoving it to the back corner under a pair of long underwear she would most likely never have occasion to wear. Feeling more lighthearted than she had in weeks, she slid closed the drawer, grabbed her sweater from her closet, and hurried down the stairs to be with Phillip.

CHAPTER FORTY-SIX

***Tessa took Phillip's hand as he helped her onto
the boat.*** The entire railing had been hung with
juniper garlands, tiny lights twinkled among the waxy
greenery. The bow of the boat was filled with potted
poinsettias and white mums.

The tiny cockpit hosted a mini feast of oysters,
shrimp cocktails, and an array of cheese and
crackers, Oreo cookies, and a bottle of Dom
Perignon nesting in an ice bucket. Next to that was
Tessa's 8-Ball.

He picked it up, rolled it back and forth between
his hands.

Tessa laughed. "What's that for?"

"Verification."

"Verification?"

"Of our official engagement." He retrieved the
black velvet box from his pocket, opened it and set it
on top of the companionway. The beautiful diamond
ring he'd purchased months ago caught the light and
winked back at her.

Joy bubbled in her chest like champagne. The
light in his eyes told her everything she needed to
know. He'd loved her from the day they'd met, just
as he'd said.

She was finally ready, and he knew it. No doubts
or fears. "And you're pretty sure the 8-Ball has the
right answer?"

His eyes sparkled with that playful glint she loved. "Signs point to yes."

This man. This crazy, hopeful, capable, fascinating man. Life with him would be a wild ride, but one thing was certain, and she knew this to her soul. Phillip Koenig had her back and he always would.

He handed her the ball. She pursed her lips a moment. "How romantic," she drawled.

He lifted a shoulder. "Outlook is good."

"You'll go by however this turns out?"

"You may rely on it," he said, the corners of his mouth straining not to laugh.

Tessa giggled. No doubt he'd rigged the damned thing, but she didn't care. This was it. This was really it. There was no one else on earth, now or in the past she wanted to spend her life with. Somewhere out there, Audrey was smiling. "You're on, Lancelot. Go ahead. Ask the question."

His face grew suddenly serious, and he stared at her for a long moment. "I love you, Tess. I know you think love at first sight is just something people say, but I'm serious when I tell you that I knew there was something special about you on that very first day we met at Cauldron Industries. I've never stopped believing we belong together. Never stopped wanting you the way I did that day."

He got to one knee. Tessa covered her mouth with praying hands, barely containing her excitement. He was really going to do this. Now. Her heart swelled in her chest. Indeed, there was magic in the world and it had nothing to do with the bracelet. She could see it in his eyes.

"Marry me, Tess. I promise you will never feel lonely or unwanted again."

She blinked back tears. Happy tears a long time coming. She dropped to her knees beside him, wrapped her arms around his neck and drew him close. His heart thumped steady and strong against her breast, their bodies melding against each other in a perfect fit. She closed her eyes basking in the essence of their love. Timeless. Lasting. Real. The little boat rocked a bit under their shifting weight. She raised her face to his and kissed his lips, her eyes locked on his.

"So, that's a yes?"

She kissed him again. "So impatient."

He kissed her back, taking it deeper. "Been waiting since the day we met."

Tessa shook her head. "Of course, it's yes. How could it be otherwise?"

He nodded at the 8-Ball still in her hand. "Better check the Universe."

Tessa frowned. She didn't want a stupid toy to spoil the moment. "How about best two out of three?"

Phillip cocked his head and gave her a noble smile. "What? You don't trust the Universe?"

She grasped the ball in both hands. The Universe had thrown her some pretty crazy curves this year. If she were honest, she didn't trust it at all. But it had put Phillip Koenig in her life, and that had been the best thing that had ever happened to her. She loved him with all her heart. All she had to do was ask the question. "Not lately."

Phillip laughed. "Go ahead. Ask the question."

His expression made her laugh and cry at the same time, joy skipping through her veins. "Okay," she said, shaking the ball. "Am I going to marry Phillip Koenig?" She kept shaking long and hard while Phillips eyes gleamed.

When she turned it over, the inky black liquid gave way to the answer pressed against the glass:

YOU MAY RELY ON IT

Want more of the Serpent's Coil time-travel adventure? Follow Tessa's best friend, Lexi, as the golden serpent raises her head once more to link that past and present. Scan this QR code:

Fifteen years after Newport Beach psycho-therapist, Lexi Hill gave her child up for adoption, she discovers her mother's terrible secret. The young man her mother had convinced her had no interest in her or her child had indeed sent her a sign of his love.

Ethiopian born hospitality mogul and shipwreck diver, Zaire Negatu puts his life and fortune on hold to help his adopted son follow the trail to find his birth mother, only to find the path leads back to his own true love.

Awakened by Lesidi's Coin and Zaire's quest to uncover the truth about an ancient shipwreck, the Serpent's Coil channels Zaire and Lexi through ancient mariners, Lesidi and Keleb who are thrust into a deadly plot of revenge against the free citizens of Rome. Scan this QR Code to get Lesidi's Coin Now:

❖

AUTHOR'S HISTORICAL NOTES

The Dorestad Brooch

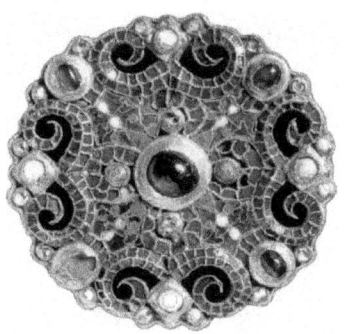

The Cloisonné Brooch fictionalized in my story was imagined after an actual brooch found while searching for the image I had in my head. My editor and I were combing through ancient finds online and on museum sites. When this image popped on screen, we both gasped. That's it!

It's not it, of course; my version is fiction. And, to be accurate, it's the wrong era (believed to be crafted around 800 CE). The actual piece is called the Dorestad Brooch and is located in a museum in the Netherlands, *Rijksmuseum van Oudheden*.

What's right about it is the methods and materials used in its creation are the same as those used by artisans who began working gold many centuries before the modern era.

The Dorestad Brooch has its own interesting story. Amazingly, it was discovered at the bottom of a well around 850, when the town was sacked during the Viking raids. It would be great fun to explore that fictionally, but that's another story.

Similar to my story, the Dorestad could very well have played an important role in the spread of Christianity and could have been part of a church treasury.

The image was used by permission of *Rijksmuseum van Oudheden*. For more information about the brooch and the museum, you can follow this link, but be warned: The link opens a very deep and wide rabbit hole.

Crispus and Fausta: A Mystery for the Ages

There is little doubt among historians that Emperor Constantine I ordered the death of his first-born son and his second wife, Fausta shortly after he gained control of the entire Roman world. Many stories abound; for example, that his son and his second wife planned his ouster, or that they were having an illicit affair. There is even speculation that Constantine's mother, Helena, a woman considered a saint by some, was involved in the plot. No one knows for sure as no bodies were ever found.

Acknowledgements

This book was a long time coming. From the first spark of the idea to completion, it took a lot of time, research, and education on my part. It was the first novel I ever tackled; and I have to say, by far, it has been the most challenging. I would be remiss, although this isn't a romance novel *per se*, if I did not give credit to a truly incredible organization, *Romance Writers of America*, for introducing me to the world of publishing; for providing limitless opportunities to learn and grow my craft, and for providing the first line connection to a wealth of support and camaraderie from fellow authors. I published five novels before finally completing this one and none of them would have come to fruition without the guidance and experience I gained through membership in RWA.

I am truly grateful to those friends and readers who insisted I keep going and held my feet to the fire to make The Cloisonné Brooch the best book it could be.

Many thanks to my Beta Team: Sally Crawford, Roslyn Hammer, Patty Latourell, Barbara Brown, Jayne Thoren, and Patti Van Dyke. Your input was invaluable, and I can't wait for you to read the final version. Also, hugs and thank you to my dear friend and developmental editor, Sharon Hall, for fighting through this project with me when you faced your own personal challenges this year.

I can't say enough for the dedication and thoroughness of historian, Dena Pollard, without whose meticulous scrutiny this manuscript would be sorely lacking. Any remaining historical discrepancies or technical errors found in this manuscript are entirely my responsibility.

Thank you to Hunky Boy (my husband) and my family for understanding my need to tell stories and giving me the support and space to see this project through.

Thanks for reading The Cloisonné Brooch. Authors survive by getting recognition and reviews. Please take a take a moment to pop back into Amazon, Goodreads, or BookBub and leave a short review. It will help ensure booksellers show my book to others who love to read this genre. Don't forget to check out other books by Kat Drennan.

A Classic Car Romance - Romantic Suspense
Book One - Mint Condition
Book Two - One of a Kind
Book Three – Hotrod Lincoln
Book Four – Five Window Pickup Coming Soon

Love on the Faultline Collection
Book 1 in Love on the Faultline Series: Borrego Moon
Love on the Faultline Historical:
Lies In White Satin
Love on the Faultline Standalone novel:
High Tide

Serpent's Coil Historical Time-Travel
The Cloisonné Brooch
Lesidi's Coin
The Serpent's Coil

Award-Winning Women's Fiction
The Goddess of Undo

About the Author

Kat Drennan writes sensual stories from the heart of the Golden State.

From the curling surf at the edge of the continent, to the granite sculptures of the Sierra Nevada; from San Francisco to Death Valley and all the way to the Mexican border and beyond, California's unique landscape and colorful, dramatic history step forward as characters in each of her novels.

She is an alumna of the Squaw Valley Community of Writers, as well as a member of Romance Writers of America, and past Secretary of the Contemporary Romance Writers Chapter of RWA.

Based in Ojai, California, Kat loves the beach, a challenging bike ride, cooking with a friend, and watching her two granddaughters grow.

She loves to hear from her readers. You can follow her at www.katdrennanbooks.com, sign up for her newsletter to find out about new releases, or follow her Facebook page to hear about new releases, freebies, and other promotions.

www.ingramcontent.com/pod-product-compliance
Lightning Source LLC
Chambersburg PA
CBHW050022030726
47506CB00001B/73